MANIPULATOR'S WAR

ELISE CARLSON

FARAWAY FICTION PRESS

Manipulator's War is a work of fiction. Names, characters, locales and events are either products of the author's imagination or used in a fictitious manner. Any resemblance to actual persons, living or dead, or actual events is purely coincidental.

Content Warning: miscarriage, suicide, grief and loss, moderate battle violence.

First published in Australia by Faraway Fiction Press
Text © Elise Carlson, 2022
Cover illustration and interior art © Elise Carlson, 2022
Moral rights of the illustrator Judah Lamey (glintofmischief@gmail.com) have been asserted.
Cover Design, map and illustrations by Judah Lamey

The font used for chapter headings is called Unzilash and was designed by Manfred Klein.

This book uses British English spelling conventions.

ISBN 978-0-6454633-0-9 Paperback
ISBN 978-0-6454633-2-3 Second Paperback
ISBN 978-0-6454633-1-6 Ebook

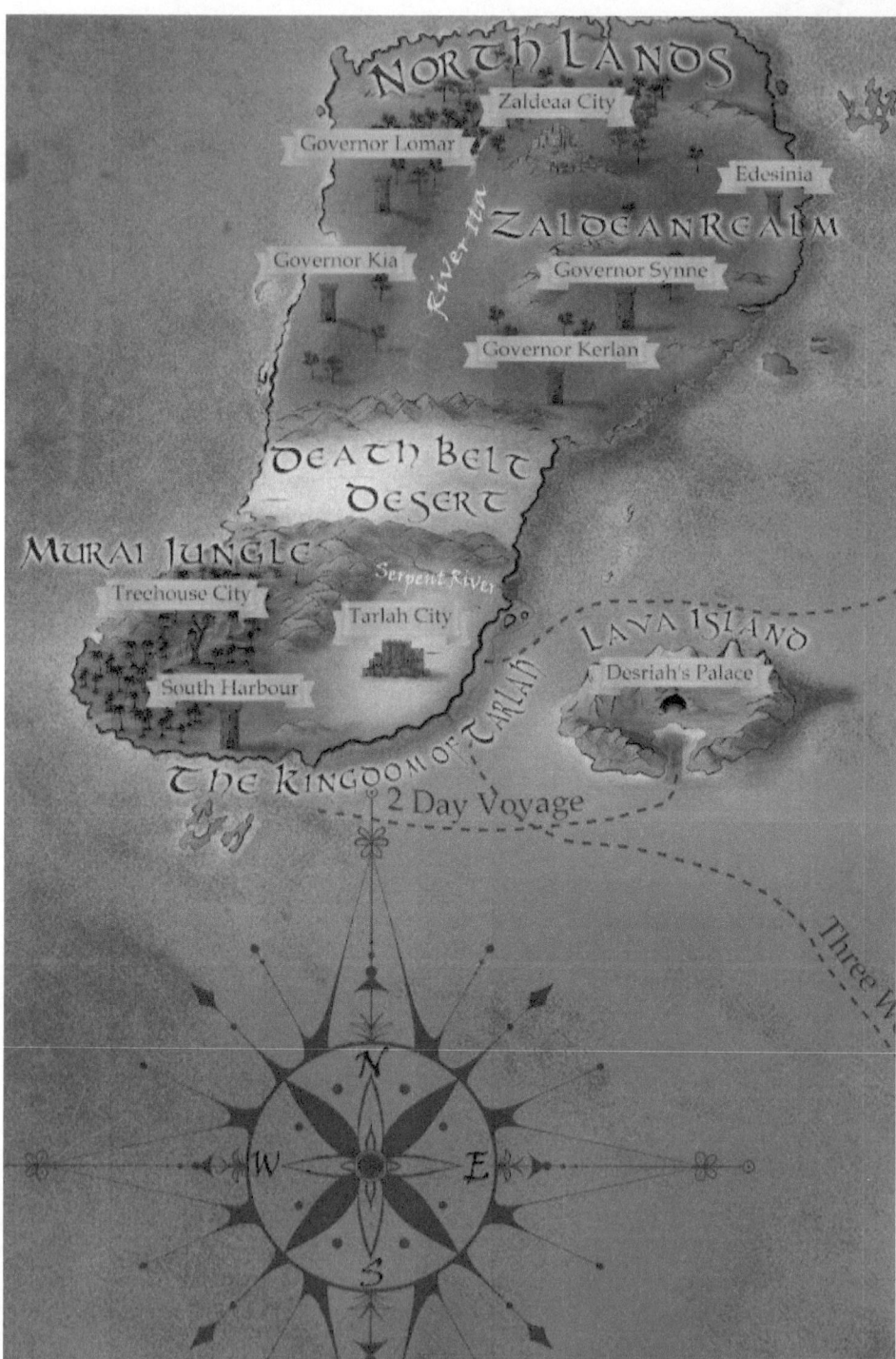

UMARINARIS

Five Weeks Voyage

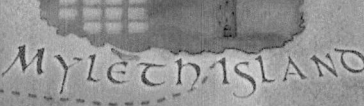

Myleth Island

Desriah's Castle

The Island of The Guardians

City of Peaks

Mijora's Dwelling

Dramatis Personae

Tarlahns

Heir Ruarnon (they/them)

King Urmillian (Ruarnon's father)

Queen Corina (Ruarnon's mother)

Prince Omah ((Ruarnon's uncle)

Princess Telena (Ruarnon's aunt)

Lenaris, Ruarnon's best friend (she/her)

Companion Pamoran (Lenaris' father)

Companion Tor, Ruarnon's tutor (he/him)

Advisor Monin (Pamoran's father)

Captain Arleath, of Ruarnon's bodyguard (he/him)

Ethlin, Lenaris' protégé (she/her)

Arlian, Ethlin's lover (he/him)

Aza, First General (he/him)

Takanis, Second General (she/her)

Zaldeaans

King Kyura (he/him)

King Kyomi the Peacemaker (Kyura's father, deceased)

Companion Karmarn, Kyura's half-uncle (he/him)

Companion Armar, Ambassador to Tarlah (he/him)

Companion Aoran, Kyura's friend (he/him)

Governor Syenne (Kyura's sister)

Governor Kia (Kyura's sister)

Governor Iomar, Kyura's cousin, Aoran's lover (he/him)

Governor Iagl, Kyura's cousin, Iomar's twin (he/him)

Governor Derlan, Kyura's uncle (Iomar's father)

AUSTRALIANS

Linh, Year 10 student, (she/her)

Fiona Linh's best friend, (she/her)

Troy, class clown and pain in backside, (he/him)

Michael, other science class, unknown quantity, (he/him)

TIMBALENS

Nuard, scholar (he/him)

Familon, archer and (Nuard's daughter)

Commander Imphin (he/him)

Captain Doorna (he/him)

Boormar, soldier, (he/him)

CREATOR GODS

(Absent since creation.)

Mijora (earth goddess)

Esla (sea goddess)

Esira (sun god)

Erhmun (wind god)

Chaos (god of sorcerers)

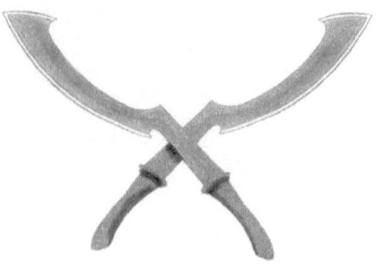

Prologue

Ruarnon: *the Zaldeaan Realm*

Heir Ruarnon fought the corners of their lips, which tried to twist in distaste. They succeeded only in forcing their mouth into a neutral line, probably a grimace, the best they could do. Before them, floor-to-ceiling frescoes of wanton slaughter dominated the corridor. Zaldeaan warriors in bronze armour impaled enemies on spears, every foot of both walls declaring: "We will cut down every man who dares oppose us." To Ruarnon it read more like, "We have big spears and big appendages and that puts us in charge."

Ruarnon suppressed a smirk. They doubted their body parts would count for much here. Zaldeaan servants scurrying past eyed them with open curiosity, the servant's gazes lingering on the kohl around Ruarnon's eyes and the spiral on either end, marking them as midlun. Bronze armoured guards stationed at an intersecting corridor stared at Ruarnon's trouser-covered legs, knowing both were clean-shaven beneath the silk. The Zaldeaan guards eyed Ruarnon insolently.

Ruarnon swallowed awkwardly. "Do you truly believe the body shapes the mind? That it determines gender?"

The largest, broadest man replied in Migryan, and one of Ruarnon's guards translated.

"How else could gender work?" There was a pause before he added "Benevolence," as his companion elbowed him.

Ruarnon slowed their pace. Companion Tor had warned them the Zaldeaans may be questioning, even disbelieving of their gender, but meeting a man who flat out denied the existence of midluns was still a shock.

A whisper from Ruarnon's bodyguards cut through their thoughts. "*His* mind must be thick, then."

Ruarnon glimpsed two men and two women smirking at the Zaldeaan guard before the captain's stern gaze swept around, and Ruarnon's entourage moved on straight-faced. Ruarnon breathed more easily knowing the men and women assigned to protect them had their back against more than just physical threats. The knowledge was a comfort while Ruarnon kept their chin up, striving to represent Tarlah well as its Heir, in their father, King Urmillian's greatest test of their readiness to become co-ruler when they came of age.

The corridor stretched on forever. An unusual number of Zaldeaan palace officials stood about, rubbing their oiled beards in twos and threes as they eyed Ruarnon appraisingly.

Ruarnon took a deep breath. Half the Zaldeaan court was here. And they were all men. Every man's gaze was fixed on Ruarnon, weighing and measuring Tarlah's youthful Heir. Ruarnon shivered, sensing an undercurrent of hostility that set their teeth on edge.

The soft pad of their bodyguard's sandals' on stone, trailing after them, no longer felt strange. Father and Companion Tor were right: Ruarnon's safety wasn't assured here.

At last, they turned into a quiet corridor. Ruarnon's shoulders relaxed as they stepped beyond judgemental gazes.

"Do we stare so rudely at visitors at home?" Ruarnon asked.

"They are curious about how Your Benevolence compares to their new king," Captain Arleath replied. "King Kyura is only a few years older than you."

Ruarnon's brow furrowed. "They don't think much of me. Kyura must come off well in that comparison."

Arleath's brows furrowed, and he eyed Ruarnon pointedly. Ruarnon almost stopped in their tracks. The walls here would have ears and probably eyes. Ruarnon couldn't say what they thought without it getting back to high-ranking Zaldeaans, or even King Kyura himself.

"Apologies, Your Benevolence," a servant called, his well-pronounced Timbalen catching Ruarnon by surprise. "The oil barrel lid came loose, and the corridor is a mess."

Ruarnon glanced at a stone floor so thickly coated in oil that it would ooze over their sandals and feet. "We will go another way," they said, and the servant bowed again.

Ruarnon doubled back, feeling the unfamiliar drag of their long, Zaldeaan style tunic sleeves and trousers resisting the air as they walked. The cooler Zaldeaan climate demanded warmer clothing, but they missed the ease with which bare limbs and a short Tarlahn tunic let them move swiftly.

"Servants have their own corridors," Captain Arleath told Ruarnon, his narrowed brown eyes scanning the corridor as he spoke. "And I wouldn't expect many of them to speak Timbalen. Most speak only Migryan. They may have been refilling oil lamps along the main corridor, but they may not."

Ruarnon tensed. What kind of trap was spilt oil? And would someone really teach a servant to pronounce two sentences perfectly in Timbalen just so they could tell Ruarnon to walk into a trap?

The corridor came to an end with a turning left and right. A folded wooden screen sectioned off the right, while daylight bathed the left. Ruarnon slowed as they turned left into a corridor that opened out to a terrace overlooking palace gardens. Ancient trees rose in all directions, creating a dark green canopy vaster than anything that could grow in Tarlah's dry climate. Dense bushes tangled with flowering vines rose to Ruarnon's height.

One of Ruarnon's guards shifted. The man's iron blade flashed as it hurtled towards the trees. Whom was he attacking? Another blade spun end over end towards Ruarnon. Ruarnon ducked instinctively. Iron rang against stone as the dagger struck the wall behind them. Battle alertness pulsed through Ruarnon's body as their training kicked in, and they drew their sword. But this wasn't training. It was attempted murder, and it set their heart thundering.

Sword in hand, Arleath stepped between Ruarnon and their attackers. Where had that dagger come from? Ruarnon scanned the trees.

"Archer!" their guards warned.

Arleath gestured. Ruarnon dived wide of a power-bow bolt that could have pierced the bronze disc tunic under their Zaldeaan linen.

"Keep moving, Benevolence! Guards! Follow!" Arleath commanded.

Ruarnon jerked their sword up. A second dagger clanged against their sword as they knocked it from the air. Then they ran, their heart pounding, eyes scanning the lawn on their left for more projectiles.

Leather slapped pavement ahead. Ruarnon raised their sword, anticipating an ambush. They and Arleath turned a corner. Before them, Ruarnon's uncle's eyes widened. Ruarnon gasped and lowered their blade.

Uncle Omah stepped aside. His blonde braid swished behind him. "Go to your aunt! Use the servant's corridors!"

"You can't stay here, Benevolence. We don't know how many there are and we've too few guards," Captain Arleath asserted.

Omah nodded, then ran alongside Ruarnon as they turned into a doorway and the dark, narrow corridor beyond. The flickering torches lining the walls were so spread out that Ruarnon could barely see the ground. They imagined someone following. What if someone had? What if they'd sent word to spill the oil and redirect Ruarnon to the terrace and the ambush? An ambush by who?

They hurried on in the cramped, confusing darkness, everyone's footsteps echoing off the walls until a door burst open, and the corridor ahead filled with daylight.

Ruarnon followed Uncle Omah through a doorway into the sitting room of their guest chambers. Aunt Telena and two guards approached.

"What happened?" Telena asked.

Ruarnon's gaze was drawn across the sitting room to green lawns stretching to more trees. They didn't seem beautiful now. Ruarnon half-expected the grounds to conceal more attackers. They gestured to a guard and exhaled with relief when the man bolted the doors shut.

"Assassins," Captain Arleath reported, his gaze sweeping the room, then fixing on Ruarnon's aunt and uncle. "Armed with throwing knives, easy enough to conceal inside Zaldeaan sleeves."

"I thought King Kyura supported his father's Peace?" Ruarnon asked, their mind scrambling to make sense of reality while their heart raced. "So, who just tried to kill me?"

"He appears to support it," Omah replied. "Your father isn't certain —that is why I am here— to find out and to persuade Kyura to uphold his father's Peace. But even if he supports peace, others of rank may not. Now we know one of them is well-resourced enough to attack you inside the Zaldeaan palace. We need to get you out of here. Now. Dangerous times call for decisive action."

"You intend to stay?" Ruarnon asked. If it was dangerous enough to send them back to Tarlah, why on Mijora's earth wouldn't their uncle accompany them?

Aunt Telena had opened Ruarnon's trunk on the bed in the room opposite and was pulling out clothing. The sandy fringe which usually framed her face was tucked behind her ears and her elegant, pale fingers packed nimbly, as if used to servant's work.

"You'll need your plainest arms-training tunic," she said. "Fetch yours, Arleath. And have a servant find our palace guide. I want Ruarnon out of the palace and halfway across Zaldeaa City before our supper with King Kyura is finished."

"Someone just tried to kill me," said Ruarnon. "We do not know who or why, yet you and Uncle Omah are staying for supper?"

"Kyura is only nineteen, and nine months into his reign. His wife is dead. His heir is dead. Do not forget that he is vulnerable. If he does approve of peace, now is the perfect time for those who favour war to twist his arm. I want to assure him he has our support, and to exert every influence I can in person."

Ruarnon felt a flash of resentment at their father for their favourite uncle having to put himself at risk for their father's plans. Then Ruarnon processed the rest. They were the child in the room sent to safety while adults did the work, at a time when they were supposed to step up and demonstrate that they could be Co-Regent.

"If the danger isn't too great for you, why is it too great for me?"

They didn't want to be skewered by a crossbow bolt, but they were tired of striving for their father's approval. It seemed within reach, yet now that they were in danger, it was being pushed away again. What would Urmillian think of Ruarnon running back to Tarlah the first time someone tried to kill them? Urmillian had faced multiple assassins when he came to the throne at fifteen because his reign began when Tarlah threw off Zaldeaan rule. Could Ruarnon ever measure up to him?

Omah stepped closer, his gaze piercing. "Whoever opposes the Peace sees you as a more valuable target than me. You are heir to the throne and last of our family's line. We cannot risk you by having you stay. Now that throwing knives in the garden have failed, perhaps it will be a crossbow in the theatre or a poisoned snack in the training grounds. Whoever tried to kill you, I expect them to try again soon. You must return to Tarlah. Once out of the palace, you will take a chariot to Edesinia and a private ship back to Tarlah City. When you return, your first task is to send your aunt and me word you are safe."

Ruarnon turned to Aunt Telena as she stepped back from laying out a plain white tunic and worn sandals on their four-poster bed. Captain Arleath was already pulling a tunic over his muscled frame and small clothes. In front of Aunt Telena. The breach of propriety impressed the need to hurry upon Ruarnon.

They entered their room, tore their red silk tunic off over their head, and pulled on a white linen one. They slipped out of their trousers, hastily removed the solid gold ornaments from their dark braid and seized a washcloth to wipe away the kohl around their eyes.

Then they returned to the sitting room, where Uncle Omah and Aunt Telena were giving hasty orders to Captain Arleath.

"Are you sure you will be safe?" Ruarnon asked.

Uncle Omah smiled. "When I was two years younger than you, I slew two Zaldeaan guards who attacked our home during the uprising which won our independence. I can protect myself."

Ruarnon couldn't help asking, "How many did Father kill?"

Omah's gaze darkened. "He wasn't there. He snuck out to join our father in assaulting the Zaldeaan Garrison and was proclaimed king of Tarlah when our father died of his wounds. Urmillian expects much of you, but I doubt he expects you to brave assassins yet. He will think no less of you for returning home, if that is what you fear."

Ruarnon's gaze fell. No matter how impossible Urmillian's expectations seemed at times, they found themself striving to meet them. But Omah was Tarlah's ambassador and Urmillian's brother, so if Omah thought their retreat was necessary, it should be all right. Omah smiled kindly, and Ruarnon knew their uncle had their back.

"Benevolences, we must hurry!" Captain Arleath urged. "If they intend another attack and predict our flight, it will come soon."

Ruarnon started to walk away, but their aunt snatched them into her arms. They smiled and hugged her back. Omah gave them a quick hug as well, then Captain Arleath was ushering them into another dimly lit servant's corridor and the door closed behind them. Arleath led the way through the quiet stone space, and Ruarnon wondered if, beyond the palace, they could step into the open and walk out of Zaldeaa City without being recognised, accosted, or attacked.

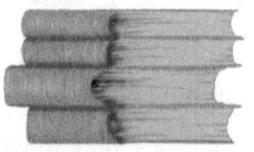

CHAPTER 1

AN UNANTICIPATED DESTINATION

LINH: Australia, Two Months Later

Refugee Crisis Continues; Climate Catastrophe Looms; Misinformation and the End of the Age of Reason. Linh ground her teeth as she scrolled through news headlines on her phone. Was it just her, or were adults taking the headfirst down the toilet? And she couldn't so much as cast her vote in protest for two more years. Her phone vibrated—a welcome distraction.

Have fun. Do not wander off!

Ba xx.

Her grandmother's profile photo showed aunts and uncles who had died in the Vietnam War. Ba had immigrated from Vietnam to Australia over fifty years ago, yet she still worried. What did she think could happen on a science excursion? Linh shook her head. And if the Australian Government had airlifted refugees to safety fifty years ago, why didn't they give a damn about refugees now?

Linh threw her phone into her backpack and buried herself behind the pages of *Origins of Modern Democracy*, retreating into the past to evade spending the bus trip in a bad mood.

"Ba worrying again?" Fiona asked on the seat beside her.

Linh rolled her eyes.

Fiona's pale, freckled face split into a smile. Her lank brown hair slipped over her faded blue school uniform dress as boutique shops, cafes, and smartly dressed adults sipping coffee flashed past their window. Linh turned across the aisle and gazed over green slopes extending to a sea punctuated by windsurfers and a container ship sailing a distant channel across Port Phillip Bay.

Fiona slid *Atlas of the Ancient* into her bag as the bus turned into a car park, and Linh zipped her book into the front pocket of her backpack. The rumble of the bus quieted as it pulled to a stop, and Mr Gentile stood. "The ferry to Noriyong Island is for the public, and your behaviour on board will reflect on Kinnara High. We expect you to act as ambassadors for our school."

"He says as if it's a revelation," Troy said, shaking his wild brown curls on the far side of the aisle on Linh's left.

"From the way *you* behave, it is," Linh asserted.

Troy's broad, bronze face split into a grin. His friends glanced meaningfully from him to her as they stepped into the aisle, where Troy towered over Linh and his chubby form dwarfed her petite one. She glared at his friends, suspecting they were mocking her.

A short walk brought both science classes to the end of the pier, where pedestrians disembarked from a white, double-decker passenger ferry. A cool sea breeze played about Linh's face and ruffled her black ponytail, as a crew member in a fluro yellow vest waved everyone on board. Troy and his friends rushed upstairs, and Fiona and Linh followed them into warm sunlight. They leant on the metal railing lining the deck, gazing across the deep blue water, inhaling the salty tang of the sea breeze.

The ferry's engines rumbled. Small children waved enthusiastically from the lower decks to bystanders on the pier. The ferry left the whine of speedboats and jet skis behind, generating splashing waves as it sailed towards the open sea. Linh's shoulders loosened as the crowded coastal street fell behind, and she turned to the vast blue horizon, enjoying the personal space of the upper deck. It was nice to get away from a that seemed increasingly troubled and too complicated to do anything about, even just for a day.

She sighed when Mr Gentile called them to the lower deck, and reluctantly followed Fiona down to the crowd of uniform pale blue dresses, navy shorts and pale blue t-shirts.

"We will reach Noriyong Island in five minutes. Please keep any valuables on you, get your observation sheets, clipboards, and pens ready, and get into your groups."

Linh's shoulders tightened again as people moved across the deck into the groups Mr Gentile had assigned. Working with Fiona and Troy might be all right, but Mr Popularity's best friend from the other science class might spend the day mocking her for taking pride in her work.

Troy eyed her hunched posture, then said, "Mic's all right. He won't talk much."

Students regrouped, and lanky, dark-featured Michael emerged from the crowd.

"Hey Mic," said Troy.

Fiona smiled in welcome, and Michael nodded. From his dark brows, brown eyes, and broad nose, Linh assumed he was Aboriginal, but his serious expression gave away little about his personality.

"Can we trust you to be the brains of the operation?" Troy asked.

Michael's lips twitched.

"Get ready to depart!" Mr Gentile called.

Linh gazed ahead. Noriyong Island was hilly and covered in short trees whose tangled branches cast strange shadows. The ferry slowed and manoeuvred against the island's pier. Mr Gentile made both science classes wait while a crew member waved off families. "You have an hour to make your ecosystem observations," he announced. "Collect your map from a teacher, carry your water bottles, and leave your bags with me. We will meet here at eleven for an early lunch. Don't be late!"

Linh's classmates spilt down the boarding ramp and pier, a sea of light blue shirts and school dresses, buzzing with conversation. Fiona collected a map from a teacher as they disembarked, and everyone dumped their bags with Mr Gentile, keeping hold of their water bottles.

"Which way do we want to go?" Troy asked as they stepped onto the sand.

Linh crossed her arms. "Not bush-bashing," she replied, gazing sternly at classmates wandering into the trees. "I don't fancy getting lost."

"Where's the fun in life if you don't take risks?" Troy asked.

"What's fun about exposing yourself to danger?" Linh snapped.

Troy's smile faded.

Fiona stepped between them. "How about we walk along the beach?" she suggested, her blue eyes twinkling as always. Linh never understood how she did that.

They turned left over sandhills, and Fiona carried their equipment towards a rock pool in the shallows, opposite a shore lined with banksia trees. As they walked, a shadow loomed at the corner of Linh's eye. She turned and glimpsed tree trunks towering above banksia trees on her right. Trunks that cut off slightly higher from right to left, peaking then cutting off lower on her left, in a vertical half-oval. It vanished. Linh stared, blinking at the clear blue sky. Her eyes must be playing tricks. This island was too small for trees like that.

Troy gazed at the trees too. Linh tensed and increased her pace along the sandy shore.

"Are you all right, Troy?" Fiona called from the rock pool.

"Fine," Troy replied tightly, as he crossed the sand.

Linh tried to shake the image of vanishing greenery as her group noted the rock pool's inhabitants. Her gaze fixed on a blue starfish distorted by the gently shifting tide, until Fiona turned to her and said, "I know you're not keen on wandering through trees, but there isn't much else to observe here."

Linh blinked at the filled-in top section of Fiona's observation notes on her clipboard.

"I can see a trail," Michael added, nodding at the banksias.

Linh sighed, and her shoulders tensed. It *would* be faster than doubling back along the beach. "All right."

Michael led them on a narrow dirt path winding between knee-length grass under a low canopy of white-backed leaves.

"So, you trust *Michael* to lead us into the wilderness," Troy said, eyeing Linh pointedly but ruining the effect by smiling. "Because his grades are as good as yours?"

Linh glared. How could he be annoying yet make her want to smile?

Fiona stopped suddenly, and Linh eyed her in surprise.

Troy's brows creased. "Do this hill and those trees seem bigger than they did a moment ago?" he asked.

"The wildflowers are gone," said Fiona, looking around.

Goosebumps rose up Linh's arms. She couldn't see banksias ahead, just dark-barked tree trunks. When did the trees get so tall? Like the ones she thought she saw above the banksias earlier... And why was there an ancient-looking stone pillar on her left? Linh shivered.

She took a deep breath and looked up. High in the canopies above, pale branches extended from stringy barked trunks. Impossible. These trees were triple the height of anything on Noriyong Island! The smell of salt was gone, and the air was cool and fresh on her skin. She looked down at bracken mixed with grass, and panic bubbled within her at the complete absence of the path they had been walking on a moment ago.

"How come there's blue between the trees ahead?" Troy asked. "The sea's *behind* us..." He broke off, his face pale.

Linh blinked, but the bracken at her feet remained.

Troy pushed ahead, and Fiona and Michael followed him around tree trunks wider than themselves. Linh didn't move. They had been walking on a small hill on Noriyong Island. Now they stood on a vast ridge carpeted with fallen gum leaves and ferns interspersed with mountain ash trees. How could an inland rainforest surround them?

She turned to go back and froze. There was no strip of sand or glimpse of the sea behind her. A stone column rose among tree trunks on her right, then across to the ridge's end, at sharp cliffs. Beyond, the blue haze of a eucalypt gum tree-covered mountain range curved unnaturally towards her.

Linh blinked and opened her eyes to the same impossible scenery. They *couldn't* be somewhere else. She turned and her feet crunched through leaf litter to the others, who stood on the far side of the ridge, peering through a downhill clearing created by a fallen forest giant. Beyond the thinning canopy, grassy plains extended to more hazy blue mountains curving unnaturally towards them. She blinked again, hoping against hope the impossibly shaped range would be gone when she opened her eyes. It wasn't.

"Can you *all* see it this time?" Troy asked weakly, the knuckles gripping his water bottle turning white.

"Yes," Fiona whispered, repeatedly blinking at the surreal landscape, seemingly unaware of shuffling back from it. Linh didn't have the heart to tell her it wouldn't do any good.

"I'm not sure that's reassuring," Troy said, his face going slack as he shook his head.

Beside him, Michael stared at the symmetrical mountain ranges with a dull gaze and his mouth open. "Impossible," was all he had to say.

Linh flinched, as Troy seized a fern and tore it up by the roots. He ripped it in half, frowned, then dropped it and shoved a tree trunk, which didn't budge.

"It's real..." he murmured. His features scrunched in bewilderment.

Fiona still stared at the clearing. Linh followed her gaze and spotted something she'd missed, a blocky stone castle on the grassy plains, ringed by mountains on three sides.

"We're somewhere else," Fiona whispered.

Linh's heart thundered against her chest. Ba had told her not to wander off...

"We *can't* be," Troy objected. "The beach is just—"

"It's not," Linh cut him off, hugging herself to suppress the dizziness rising within her. "It's gone."

Troy gaped. "You mean the universe just folded up on itself and let us walk to God knows where?"

"We *can't step* from one location to another... but I don't think we're on Noriyong Island anymore," Linh replied, her knees becoming weak. She sat in the bracken, as dizziness washed over her. Fiona gripped her shoulder with a trembling hand, gasping for breath.

Troy stomped away, and Fiona cried, "Be careful!"

Linh pressed her hands firmly against the ground, taking deep breaths and trying not to exhale too quickly. She looked up when the worst of her dizziness cleared and Troy's footsteps approached.

"We're surrounded by mountains," he said softly, his features wide with surprise. "This *is* somewhere completely different."

"It's like this place was sitting behind Noriyong Island. I saw the small hill we were walking up vanish, and this ridge was beyond it." Michael eyed Troy and Linh sharply. "Did you see something strange on Noriyong Island?"

"I glimpsed these trees," Troy replied.

"Rising semi-circle shaped above the banksias," Linh added. She turned back, searching between the trees for the stone column she'd seen earlier. It wasn't a column. She traced the round pillar up into the trees, until it curved overhead and down again, in a giant, familiar shaped arch.

"We walked through *that*?" Troy asked, crunching through the undergrowth behind her.

Linh rushed under the archway. The landscape didn't change. She still stood on dried leaves, ferns brushing her legs.

"It was here!" she insisted, wringing her hands as the others caught up. "The space between wherever the hell this is and Noriyong Island, the connection, or wormhole, or whatever the hell we just came through, was somewhere here!"

Fiona stopped beside Linh and traced a strange script spiralling up the arch in rounded letters ending in a spiral or two with a shaking hand. Her features narrowed with uncertainty as she said, "This script isn't in my *Atlas of the Ancient* . The letters are nothing like cuneiform or hieroglyphs, and they orient differently to English and don't look like any modern language descended from the scripts in my book."

Troy moved closer and probed bits of the pillar with his fingers.

"I can't see any buttons or levers," Michael told him.

"Then how does it work?" Troy asked, his voice rising. "How the hell did a stone archway get us here?"

Linh turned, scanning the forest for signs of technology, people, anything that could answer Troy's question. But there were just leaves, ferns, and forest giants. "There's nothing here."

"So it's self-operating?" Troy asked sceptically. "How are we supposed to get back?" he added, his voice rising.

"I doubt that," Michael replied, scratching his bristled chin. "My mob have been visiting Noriyong Island for thousands of years. If people have been disappearing from it now and then, there'd be stories, and I'd know them. Someone must have done something to bring us here. I don't think the universe has glitches like this."

Troy cracked a nervous smile, but Linh heard nothing reassuring in Michael's words.

"There's someone down there!" Fiona called from the far side of the ridge, pointing beyond the clearing to golden grassy plains. "A man in a red cloak walking towards the castle."

Linh tensed.

"I'm asking him what's going on," Troy said, and he walked to the edge of the ridge.

Linh blinked. They potentially stood in another , and he wanted to approach the first stranger they saw? She ran after him. "You can't just walk up to him! He could be dangerous!"

"Then I'll take a good look before I say hi," said Troy.

Linh gazed through the clearing. A long, thin object hung from the red-cloaked man's hip. "He's carrying a sword!" she objected. "What if he attacks you?"

Troy tripped on a tree root protruding from the leaf litter and fell. He cried out as he hit the ground. The man in the red cloak turned to face them, and Linh's entire torso tensed. The man raised an arm in greeting, then turned and kept walking towards the castle.

Troy stood and called out, "Hello down there!"

The man kept walking.

"Hey! Can you hear me?"

Anyone without a hearing impairment should have heard him, but the man in the red cloak didn't acknowledge a word.

"I wonder if he's reporting to someone at the castle," Michael said as he stepped beside Linh. "He may've been close enough to see us arrive, if he left this hilltop as soon as we got here."

Linh ground her teeth. "With what intention?"

"We won't know unless we go down there," Troy said, gazing after the man.

"And risk walking into an ambush!" Linh objected.

"Or we could watch what he does next and stay close enough to go back, in case the archway turns on again," Fiona suggested.

Linh sighed and tried to rein in her anxiety. She had no idea how Fiona was always so calm, always offering solutions. But Fiona was good at both, and when her best friend offered solutions, Linh listened.

Eventually, they all agreed to wait. Troy stood with both fists stuffed into his pockets. Linh divided her attention between the archway and the plains, while Fiona and Michael watched the man and the castle. As the shadows grew shorter and the sun moved directly overhead, the man continued walking. Then he disappeared inside the castle. After that, there was neither sight nor sound of people, just the damp forest, leaves rustling in the wind, and stomachs rumbling.

"I'm going down there," Troy said finally. "Waiting isn't getting us anywhere."

"What if the archway *does* activate when we're not here?" Fiona asked.

"I wonder if someone activated it to test if they could bring us through," Michael replied. "If that man told someone at the castle that it worked, and they used us as guinea pigs. It's the only logical explanation I can think of."

Troy shook his head but didn't seem phased by Michael producing a theory so quickly. Linh wished it wasn't a chilling one.

"We can't wait forever and we should stick together," Fiona said, stepping beside Linh.

Fiona's logic did nothing to counter Linh's powerful urge to wait, just in case. But their lunch boxes were in their backpacks with Mr Gentile. And it was warm, and they had all started drinking from their water bottles. Dehydration would set in soon, and they had no reason to expect the archway to activate.

"Are you coming?" Michael asked Linh and Fiona.

Linh nodded, and she and Fiona reluctantly followed the boys, as they snaked around tree trunks and bush-bashed downhill. The smell of grass, the sound of leaves rustling in the wind, and soft ferns and grasses brushing against her legs all seemed real. Time passed, and they remained dwarfed by mountain ash trees, crunching through dried gum leaves with each step. Linh's heart rate gradually slowed, but her senses remained alert to any sign of danger.

They left the forest giants behind, passing smaller gum trees and yellow grass. The trees gradually thinned, and Linh gazed across rolling hills sprinkled with wildflowers. She glanced reluctantly back at the ridge, but the slope obscured the archway.

Troy ploughed through grass up to his chubby thighs, and everyone followed him uphill towards the grey stone castle. Linh shivered. "We should cross these plains slowly," she cautioned. "We've no idea who's in that castle or what's in the grass."

Michael nodded and slowed. But Troy maintained a restless pace that made Linh nervous. Her clothes stuck to her sweaty skin under the hot sun, and she took small sips from her water bottle, emptying it by the time they neared the castle. She scanned the battlements carefully, but Troy's long legs carried him to the front door before she spotted anyone.

Troy paused, gazing up at doors rising twice his considerable height, and Linh wondered why they were so large. Then Troy knocked on the double doors, and Linh and Fiona hurried to catch him and Michael up.

Troy shifted restlessly as they waited for someone to answer.

"Is Red Cloak ignoring us?" Fiona asked.

"I'm not giving him a choice," Troy replied.

Linh shuddered as he pushed the door open. Late afternoon sunlight shone through an archway with golden luminescence spiralling up it, in the far wall of a large, empty room.

"Hello?" Troy called, his voice echoing through a vast marble chamber.

Linh peered in at empty corridors running left and right. Before her, a white marble floor spread towards a balcony lined with stone arches, including the sunlit arch. The room was the size of a cathedral, with unadorned walls and a high ceiling, consisting only of bare marble. There was no sign of Red Cloak.

"Where is everyone?" Troy asked, looking around.

Linh hesitated as Fiona entered the room, until she saw the inscription Fiona was approaching on the wall on their left. It was the same round script carved into the archway on the ridge, with many letters ending in spirals of different sizes. As Linh moved closer, Fiona gasped. Most of the spirals vanished. The words became: *Welcome, visitors from afar.*

There was no room for us in your world, but with our retreat to Umarinaris' warmest locations, Umarinaris has room for you. It lacks the wars you fled around the inland sea, and it shall be what you make of it. Use your chariots for transportation, knives for food preparation, bows and spears for hunting, and axes for chopping firewood. Umarinaris can be the refuge you seek, if you make it so.

Fiona gaped.

"No one's used that combination of weapons in our world for centuries," Linh said, bracing herself for more impossible revelations as the history-loving part of her mind engaged.

"The Near East?" Fiona suggested.

"It can't be," said Linh.

"The 'inland sea' could be the Mediterranean," Fiona added. "We've read about centuries of war around that area, and the Hittites and Egyptians both used chariots in battle."

"What's up?" Troy asked as he approached.

"We're wondering if people from our world settled here a few thousand years ago," Linh replied.

"No way!" Troy objected. "Who wrote that?"

"Giants, by the look of it," Michael called across the room. "Have you seen how high the stairs are? Each step's twice the height of ours, and the railing's almost up to my elbows. Maybe humans settled this place too. And learnt how to activate the archways and bring us here. What I don't understand is why, if someone brought us here, they're avoiding us."

Linh shivered at the suggestion of giants, but she couldn't hear any movement beyond the hall-like room, and when she turned back, there was no sign of anyone.

"That archway is glowing," Fiona whispered, pointing with a shaky hand to the day-lit archway in the back wall. "Maybe Red Cloak's still here."

Troy rushed up the balcony stairs to investigate, followed by Michael, but with their short legs, Linh struggled and Fiona fell further behind. The archway was triple the height of an average human. Linh squinted against the glaring sunlight shining through it. This archway was also made of circular, mortared stone blocks, encircled with a yellow glow. As her eyes adjusted, Linh gazed through it over rocks, a thin strip of sand, and open water, to an island across a channel fenced with stone. Further right, open water stretched to the horizon.

"Where'd the mountains go?" Troy asked, looking around. "And the giant trees?"

"I think that's somewhere else," Michael replied. "Another island."

Hope flared inside Linh, then swiftly dissipated. There wasn't enough sand for it to be Noriyong Island, and there was no sign of the mainland, or her classmates or teachers.

"I wonder if this is where Red Cloak went," said Michael.

"Well, I'm not following him," Linh insisted. "Does he think he can lead us down a rabbit hole and we'll just follow?"

She heard footsteps as Fiona caught up. Linh turned back. Fiona stumbled. Linh reached for her too slowly. Fiona fell, and her forearms hit a sandhill on the far side of the archway, sending her skidding down the slope, her clipboard and notes flying, her empty drink bottle rolling ahead.

"Fi! Can you stand?" Linh called. She hesitated, not wanting to step through the arch. But when Fiona didn't answer, she bit her lip and ran after her.

"I feel dizzy," Fiona croaked as Linh knelt in dry sand beside her.

"She's dehydrated," Michael said, leaning over her. "We should get her out of the sun."

"Is she ok?" Troy asked.

Linh turned back as Troy approached the arch, his wide-eyed gaze on Fiona. "*Don't!*"

She was too late. He stepped through onto the sandy beach, and the yellow glow spiralling around the arch vanished, as did Linh's view of the balcony and the castle's interior. She stared through the arch across a few sandhills and rocks, then at the sea. The new island was small, consisting only of sandhills and stunted trees, the waves lapping its low-lying shore in every direction. Across the channel, on her right, lay a larger island fenced with stone. But there was no Red Cloak, and they were cut off from the archway which had apparently transported them out of their world.

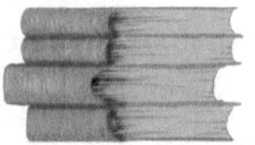

Chapter 2

The Guardians

Linh: *Unknown Island Far From Earth*

A re you all right, Fi?" Linh asked.

"I need to sit," Fiona replied, leaning against a sandhill.

Linh took deep, calming breaths, letting them out slowly and trying to ignore how being cut off from home made her stomach churn.

"How did that arch turn off?" Troy asked, eyeing it suspiciously.

"Maybe someone did something at the other end," Michael replied.

"But we didn't see anyone in that hall," Troy objected. "They'd have to be invisible!"

"I doubt both archways switched off the moment after we stepped through by coincidence," Michael added.

"It's not... magic?" Fiona suggested.

Linh turned to her friend with concern. She and Fiona loved history. They'd read enough to know that magic served as a logical explanation for natural occurrences in the absence of scientific knowledge. But instantaneous travel was impossible. As were mountain ranges forming a perfect oval. What *was* possible here? She shivered.

"Hello!" a male voice called.

"Who the hell was that?" Troy asked, his fists clenching as he turned around.

Linh looked up across the sea.

"Is anyone out there?" the voice added.

A small sailing ship with a single mast glided towards a channel between the island they stood on and the larger, stone walled island opposite. The people on board were tiny, distant figures, but Linh made out arms waving and muffled calls.

"Could they be talking to *us*?" Troy asked.

"How could anyone know we're here?" Linh objected.

"They're looking for someone," said Michael. "They might be able to tell us what's going on."

"Do you think it's safe to ask them?" Linh couldn't see any weapons, but that didn't mean the people on board weren't dangerous.

"We're stranded, dehydrated, hungry, and we've no way home," Michael asserted. "Sometimes, you need to trust strangers."

Linh disliked knowing nothing about the people on board, but if they were going to get home, they needed help. Besides,

Fiona was faint, and Michael had given her the last of anyone's water, but she still wasn't steady on her feet. She needed water and food as soon as possible. They all would soon, and there was none on this island.

Linh and Troy helped Fiona stand, then followed Michael to the small waves lapping at the shore.

"Hello!" Troy called as the ship came closer, cupping one hand around his mouth.

The ship turned, but stayed on course to sail past. Troy waved his arms. The figures on deck showed no awareness of him.

"Anyone got a mirror?" Michael asked.

Linh remembered the old-fashioned cosmetic mirror Ba had given her, oblivious to selfie-mode on modern phones. Linh took the mirror she always carried — to avoid hurting Ba's feelings — from her pocket and handed it to Michael. He tilted it, sending flashes of sunlight across the water. The ship didn't alter its course.

Troy reached for the mirror, saying, "I'll see if getting closer helps."

"Watch out for strange currents," Linh cautioned. She wasn't exactly fond of Troy, but she didn't fancy him drowning.

Troy nodded, taking the mirror and tossing his empty bottle in the sand. He kicked off his runners, stripped off his polo shirt and waded into the waves, where he swam with steady freestyle strokes. Then he treaded water, raised the mirror, and sunlight flashed again.

"Man overboard!" a voice cried from the ship's deck.

The man spoke English. Did that mean they weren't too far from home? Hope flared inside Linh.

The ship changed course towards Troy.

"Is anyone with you?" a man's voice called.

"They're on the beach," Troy replied, treading water.

"What beach?"

"On the island behind me."

"Ghost Island!" another voice cried.

"Don't worry, lad. We'll bring you aboard," the first voice assured.

"What about my friends?"

"They'd best swim to you, lad. Ghost Island is cursed. I'll come no closer."

"That sailor wants us to swim multiple Olympic swimming pools' length because he's superstitious?" Linh asked incredulously.

"If he thinks this island is cursed," Michael replied, "we're lucky he's willing to take us on board after visiting this place."

Linh's hands balled into fists.

"We're coming, Troy!" Michael called.

Linh threw down her bottle, then wrenched her shoes off. This world didn't make any sense, but Michael was swimming to Troy, and she would have to help Fiona swim if they didn't want to be left behind. She helped Fiona take her runners off, then kept a careful eye on her as they waded into cold water. Fiona floated on her back, sitting her runners on her chest, and did lifesaving backstroke slowly but well enough.

Linh dragged her runners across the surface with one hand, paddling with the other, and turned back to the shore. Open water lay behind her. Michael appeared in it suddenly, swimming with his head above water. Linh trembled. There was no sign of the archway island, just green waves to the horizon. The island *was* invisible from the channel. What was wrong with this place?

"What in the name of Chaos?" a voice said from on deck.

"Myths of Strangers indeed!" another exclaimed as Fiona and Linh swam after Troy.

The ship reached Troy. "Climb the ladder!" a sailor called, and others waved him to a rope ladder hanging down the starboard side.

Sailors passed their shoes up to the deck, turning them over and eyeing the coloured rubber soles with bemused looks. It was a short climb, as the ship sat only a couple of metres above the waterline, but Linh's muscles ached as she heaved herself up the ladder. Calloused hands helped her onto a small, crowded deck, where a sailor draped a blanket over her shoulders. "There you are," he said with a smile.

"Thanks," she said.

A single sail flapped from the mast overhead, which had no rigging or crow's nest. Sailors crowded around the edges of the deck while a wooden bench occupied its middle, a white-haired man seated on it. What kind of ship was this?

She stumbled towards Troy and the older man, whose pale blue linen toga and white hair ruffled in the wind. He smiled in welcome, creasing many wrinkles around his face. He seemed kind, but Linh wasn't sure how to interpret the enthusiasm sparkling in his eyes. Why was he wearing a toga? The crewmen weren't wearing clothing she recognised either, just pants of earthy colours and leather sandals.

"Welcome, children," the old man said warmly as Fiona and Michael dripped across the deck and sat down.

"How come you speak English?" Troy asked.

The man's eyebrows climbed towards his flyaway hair, then he smiled. "I speak Timbalen. Welcome to the south-eastern border of the Timbalen Empire!"

Linh's eyes widened. The castle inscription mentioned only one migration from Earth, centuries before English –let alone modern English– came into existence. Timbalen and English *couldn't* be the same. How on Earth could they understand the man? Or he them?

"I am Nuard," the man continued eagerly, utterly unphased. "I am delighted to meet you. It has been nearly two hundred years since our Umarinaris Book reported the arrival of Strangers to anywhere on Umarinaris."

"People have come here before?" Troy asked.

"Does that mean you know how to activate the archways?" Linh added.

"I only know what the Umarinaris Book and our myths tell us," Nuard replied.

Linh slumped. All myths were likely to give them was vague clues, probably dependent on people, places, creatures, or artefacts that never existed, if Umarinaris' myths were anything like hers.

"A *book* told you we were here?" Troy asked, his mouth hanging open.

"How can a book tell you anything about *us*?" Linh asked.

"It was created and written by the Guardians," Nuard replied reverently.

Linh shook her head, sagging against the bench. Instantaneous travel across time and space. Invisible islands. Gods spying on them. It was all too much, on top of hunger and dehydration, and it made her head spin.

Nuard studied her and the lines between his brows deepened. "Perhaps I should explain what I know at dinner. His Greatness maintains the former watch castle on Myleth Island as a second home for scholars like myself. You are welcome to join us there. We have already crossed the channel and shall reach the village soon."

Linh turned. Myleth Island's stone wall ran alongside golden grain fields, with an orchard and forest beyond, until the wall branched off, framing a sandy coastline and running inland before wooden houses. A small pier extended opposite double gates in the village wall.

They handed their blankets to a crewman as they neared the pier and Linh made a face as she pulled her soaking wet runners back onto her feet. The mainsail was reefed, rowers manoeuvred the ship, and men leapt the railing to secure it to its berth. Others positioned a gangplank. Linh helped Fiona to her feet and supported her as they squelched after Nuard to the pier, leaving a trail of wet footprints. Then their feet sank into dry sand before the village wall, beyond which a hilltop and castle rose.

"Welcome to Myleth Island," Nuard said proudly.

Linh admired the castle's grey stone walls and four narrow towers rising from a hilltop.

"Anyone else worried what the toilet's going to look like?" Troy asked quietly.

Linh shook her head. Of all the things they had to worry about, how could he worry about *that*?

"We should be," said Michael. "I'm pretty sure the shower is a bucket of cold water." He spoke seriously, but Troy grinned.

"Ah, well, we won't have to wait all day for the girls to finish with the bathroom."

"You'll be showering fully clothed if you don't watch it!" Linh retorted.

Troy smiled, and Linh shook her head, refusing to admit that his teasing made her feel more at home.

"Does he *ever* worry about important things?" she asked Fiona as they fell behind and she linked her arm in Fiona's.

"He likes a laugh," Fiona replied quietly. "And he's right. We can wash here. And we won't need to dig our own loos."

Linh froze. Dig their own toilets? Fiona smiled weakly, and Linh caught her gaze and smiled back, trying to push down the worry about whether Nuard could help them get home.

They followed Nuard through timber gates down a dirt road, weaving haphazardly between log cabins with thatched roofs and front verandas, under which fair-haired men and women sat mending fishing nets. A group of children took turns aiming stones between houses at a distant white rock, while wizened women gossiped as they scrubbed washing in a bronze tub beside a cottage. Smoke and the smell of fried fish drifted through holes in several roofs. It was primitive, yet somehow *normal*. Children laughed, adults talked, and the smell of cooking hung in the air, like evening anywhere.

They climbed steps up a creeper covered hillside beyond the village. The guard at the castle entrance inclined his head to Nuard, opening the double doors as they approached. His armour and bell-shaped helmet shone golden. Was that how bronze looked when it wasn't tarnished and centuries old? Judging by the colour, the sword belted at his hip was iron.

Nuard gestured them to a room with a washbasin. Servants brought water, rough sheets of fabric which appeared to pass for towels, and dry, pale blue robes for them all. Linh and Fiona changed in an adjoining room. Then Nuard led them down a corridor and into a dining hall with a long table at its centre. The pottery was glazed clay ceramics, the cutlery bronze spoons, the serving utensils wooden, and the glassware looked fragile and pre-industrial, like museum pieces in Fiona's *Atlas of the Ancient World*. Linh stared. Hadn't civilisation changed here since humans arrived during the Late Bronze or Early Iron Age?

Nuard motioned them to sit, and Linh helped Fiona into her chair. They didn't have to wait long before servants entered, carrying platters wafting the enticing aroma of meats and pastries across the hall. Linh's mouth watered.

"Take what you wish," Nuard said, serving himself pastries and vegetables.

Linh pursed her lips at the sight of foreign food, but she was too hungry to be fussy. Troy didn't hold back on his servings, and Linh copied. Nuard blinked politely; Linh waited for him to start eating first, and everyone tucked in. Troy grimaced at the discoloured water in one of two delicate glass jugs, and everyone helped themselves to the pink juice in the other.

"What do you know about our arrival?" Fiona asked Nuard.

"Beyond the Umarinaris Book reporting it a few hours ago, I have a theory as to who brought you here and how. When the Creator Gods made Umarinaris, they granted humanity the potential to become worthy of learning their ways. Humanity became numerous, so a fifth god was created to preside over us, but he misunderstood our potential and tested us by bestowing divine powers upon some humans. In so doing, he created power-hungry sorcerers who plunged the Far West into the Sorcery War.

"Chaos' sorcerers overran an entire continent, and many refugees fled east, here, until the Gods sent their servants, the Guardians, to restore order. I presume the Guardians enchanted and utilised the archways and Oval Island to deploy their forces. After the war, I believe they watched over the Far Western Land, using the archways to send strangers to aid it in times of calamity. In those times, the Myths of the Strangers refer to vanishing islands, archways, and strangers appearing."

But the inscriptions at the castle on Oval Island said nothing about the *Sorcery War*. They made it sound like the castle was built by climate refugees seeking a new homeland. Was Nuard mistaken?

"Can we speak to Guardians?" Michael asked.

"Alas, like sorcerers, the Guardians vanished within a generation of the war. Guardian-human children remained here in the east, serving the Timbalen emperor after the Wars of Unity, but no pure Guardian has been seen for centuries. But I can write to Imperial City to see if the Guardian's descendants, the Elite Guard, can help you."

Fiona thanked him but Linh worried that if the Elite Guard didn't operate the archway to bring her and her classmates, they might not know anything about the archways, or how to use them to send anyone home.

"Nuard," Fiona said, "when we arrived on Oval Island, there was a man in a red cloak. He was the only person we saw, and he entered the castle we travelled to this island through before us. Do you know who he might be or how we can contact him?"

Nuard froze. "Knowing what I do of the archways, I can only explain that man's actions if he is a Guardian."

"Get out!" Troy said. "Mythical dudes lured us from our science excursion to save the world? Are they insane?"

"Can you tell us more about the Myths of the Strangers?" Fiona asked.

"One myth tells of strangers arriving when a Far Western king bred a dragon army. The strangers attacked dragons with bows of metal, firing metal arrow balls with a bang and a flash like Chaos himself. They eradicated the dragons, and such was their deed that traders carried word of it across an ocean to our colony, Tarlah, from which it made its way across a second ocean to our empire."

Linh shivered. "That sounds like early guns. But the only weapons we've seen so far are swords."

"No weaponry this side of Umarinaris resembles the weaponry of that myth," Nuard told her.

Linh blinked. "Does the Western Land have bows and arrows like that?"

"Not to my knowledge," said Nuard, his eyes bright.

"What does it matter?" Troy asked.

"It matters because the cutlery we're eating with is bronze or wood, the guard we passed coming in had bronze armour and an iron sword, and if there's no steel or guns in Umarinaris, then the people in that myth might have come from our world. And if they got home, we can too."

A description of possible guns and bullets from perhaps nineteenth-century Earth was little to go on. But as Linh and her classmates had come here, and the inscription in the castle on Oval Island mentioned migration from the Mediterranean world, perhaps the slayer myth contained some truth. It might have clues as to how they could get home. If it was all Nuard could offer them, it damn well better do that much.

"The Slayers set sail for the invisible island they arrived on," Nuard continued, "and their ship vanished. Witnesses said the forecastle disappeared first. Then the main and rear decks moved into nothing. The ship was found weeks later, tossed by a violent storm. Its sails were bound, and it was empty."

In Linh's mind, Michael appeared suddenly, swimming into view. "They might have gone back home through an archway," she suggested. "But who brought the slayers? Who returned them?"

Nuard eyed them intently. "Whoever sent you, someone wrote in the Umarinaris Book: *They have arrived. Four youths of another world. The gateways are open once more.* I have studied the Umarinaris Book and the history and mythology of my people for over forty years. No new entry has appeared in my lifetime. One of my colleagues leaves the book open to the blank pages after its last entry just to tease me, but today, they were not blank."

Michael turned to Linh. "If you saw the rainforest from the beach, then it opened twice, the second time close enough for us to walk through. And the archway that led us to Nuard was open. And both archways closed the moment we passed through them. Maybe someone brought us here. But why lead us by the nose to you, Nuard, and tell us nothing? Why avoid us?"

Nuard sighed.

"You theorise that the Guardians brought us?" Michael asked.

"It is a good hypothesis," Nuard replied. "But as a scholar, I must admit there is too little evidence for it to be more than that."

"So someone might have brought us, but our only lead is that it *might* be servants of gods from a creation myth?" Troy stood abruptly and paced across the hall.

Linh wondered if Michael was right and a mad scientist had brought them to test the gateways.

"Is there any sign of calamity around this part of Umarinaris?" Fiona asked.

"None that I know of," Nuard replied. He turned, surveying them. "It is nearly time for me to retire for the night. I can have a servant show you to our guest chambers when you are ready to go up. We can talk again in the morning if you like."

Fiona thanked him and Nuard bid them good night and left.

"What do we think?" Troy asked, as soon the sound of Nuard's footsteps faded.

"After studying the Myths of the Strangers all his life," said Michael, "I think he's thrilled we might be evidence that the myths are true."

Linh shivered. "You think he's seeing what he wants to see?"

Michael nodded and rested his head on his hands.

"We don't know what's normal or what we can expect here," Fiona replied, with her usual optimism, but she also fidgeted with her spoon.

Troy shook his head. "The whole theory's crazy, and we didn't get to talk to Red Cloak, so we can't 'know' anything, assuming he even knows what's going on."

"We can ask Nuard who else can help, in and beyond the empire," Fiona suggested.

Linh hugged herself, trying to still the way her insides quivered at the uncertainty of their situation. She dearly wanted to believe there was a logical explanation for their departure from Noriyong Island and arrival in wherever this was, a person they could seek out and ask to send them home. But what if there wasn't?

Chapter 3

Loss

Kyura: the Zaldeaan Realm, Eight Weeks Earlier

King Kyura's beringed hand ran across a finely carved wooden cradle. His glistening eyes swept across the soft toys lined up inside it and the blankets spread before them. His gaze came to rest on newly woven swaddling, which ought to be warming his son, and the embroidery on it, a dragon sewn by his wife's hand. It was time to face this room and the future that could have been.

Footsteps approached. Only one person in the palace had permission to enter a room Kyura occupied during the Month of Mourning: his eldest sister, Governor Syenne.

"The court was very generous," he told her, his voice trembling slightly. He turned from the distressing sight of the empty cot to the painted wooden toys lining the walls of the empty nursery. "Such a nice welcome, he would have had."

The toys were an insufficient distraction. Kyura swept up the swaddling, eager to touch her handiwork, hesitant lest his rough fingers damage the delicate embroidery, the final work of her hands.

Syenne halted beside him.

"Lenine will look after him," Kyura told Syenne. "She was clever, sure of herself, and strong. That's why I married her. I don't know how I'll manage without her."

Tears spilled down his face. He could still picture the way the sun made her golden hair shine and the light of intelligence in those kind blue eyes, the first time she advised him, in a chance meeting in the palace gardens. It was a week since he had last slept beside her and sometimes he still tried to fight the idea she was gone.

"You do not rule alone, little brother," Syenne said curtly.

Sometimes he found his older sister forbidding, but tonight it was a comfort to feel the firm grip of her hands around his upper arms and to see the normally fixed lines on her face curve in concern. At thirty-nine, she was twenty years older than he, and he could see all of those years in her expression.

"I will stay in court for three more weeks. Cousin Iomar can visit the month after. I know you would prefer to have us both, but you must present a strong face to the people."

"Lest the war-hungry, brawny fools think their sensitive king ripe to depose?" Kyura said bitterly.

He drew a steadying breath, nervous of meeting her gaze because Syenne never flinched from the truth. Lenine had been right; Syenne would support him. Her loyalty to family was as strong as her military skill, which had enabled her to kill three assassins to date.

He braced himself and met Syenne's gaze. Had those care lines creased her mouth and eyes before Lenine's death? Syenne's pale face was more angular than Kyura's round one; her nose was pointed and the gaze of her pale blue eyes, as they rested upon him, was softer and warmer than he recalled.

She smiled. Then she swept him into her arms and he hugged her back, letting the tears fall. "You don't need to put on a king's hard face with me," she whispered. "I have many enemies, and while the list of your enemies may be growing, for politics, we are allies. Always. I was Father's right-hand man, and while my reputation would lead the court to think you are my puppet if I appear too close to you, that does not mean you cannot write for advice or that we cannot visit each other. Politics aside, you are my only brother to survive the Sea Plague, and I will support you through whatever the Gods neglect to defend you against."

"I keep forgetting what Mother said: the position isn't the person." Kyura stepped away. He exhaled deeply, blinking tears down his cheeks, until his vision cleared. He met his sister's eyes as she smiled.

"I know you don't remember her very well," said Syenne, "but when Father appointed me governor, she impressed that upon me. And Lenine loved you for more than your position, as does your friend Aoran. Keep him close, but privately. We don't want the court misinterpreting your relationship."

Kyura slumped. Aoran was the only friend he trusted as much as Lenine, but the court wasn't to know Aoran was Kyura's cousin's lover, not Kyura's. The consequences of the court drawing false conclusions about their relationship didn't bear thinking about.

Kyura turned back to the cot and swaddling he still clutched in both hands, caressing it without realising it.

"Father will find them," Syenne said gently. "He should be familiar enough with navigating the next life to do so by now."

Kyura took another deep breath and exhaled slowly. Losing his father, then wife and first-born child, only nine months apart, weighed on him so heavily that he felt thrice his years.

"I am sure he will. And he would want me to go on. I will attend the unveiling of his statue after the Month of Mourning, as planned. Let the people see that their king's capacity to cry does not make him broken."

When the Month of Mourning ended, King Kyura prepared for a public appearance. His servants fitted the diamond-studded helmet, which served as the Zaldeaan crown on formal occasions, on his head, and fastened the royal fur cloak over his silken tunic and black wolf fur trousers. They wiped his face with a cool cloth and brushed his golden hair so it sat straight across the line of his narrow, clean-shaven jaw.

He slid off his chair, ignoring how his bodyguards stood head and shoulders above their king, ignoring that his physique and temperament flew in the face of all his people valued in their men, and strode out of his chambers. Syenne met him in the hallway. Her hair was down in mourning, combed to golden silk. Her skin was porcelain from many hours indoors politicking, and her regal silk dress matched the colour of the sky Lenine and his son's spirits were traversing.

The frescoed corridors before them mirrored the emptiness of his heart but also gave him peace in which to rally himself, to show the influential members of his court that neither his age nor his youth meant they could take advantage of his grief. The King's Hall, separating the royal chambers from the rest of the palace, was anything but quiet. High officials stood golden cloaked in a cluster to his right, his generals and captains bowed in silver cloaks in the middle. Nearest stood his Uncle Derlan, a grave, silver-haired version of Kyura's late father. The court waited as his uncle approached.

"My brother would approve of you re-entering public so soon," said Derlan. "Do as you usually would, nephew, and show the unruly mob who their king is. But that is what your sister told you, isn't it?"

"Of course, uncle," Syenne replied, stately as ever.

"Are you coming to Father's statue's unveiling, uncle?" Kyura asked.

"I shall follow where you lead," Derlan replied, his head at its usually stately tilt, his gaze meeting Kyura's, yet somehow unreadable.

Kyura paused. Uncle Derlan had led soldiers in the Sea Wars and had never made much show of supporting his brother, Kyura's father's Peace, but they were in public, so Kyura forced a smile, then turned to face his court.

"Highest of Kings, our deepest condolences to you."

Kyura turned to the most eloquent and lowest of his High Officials, recognising the subtle insult in them nominating that man to speak on their behalf. The man had even found time to oil his fashionable beard before offering condolences. But this was the Zaldeaan court, and those who stood within it wore the masks tradition required as they clawed their way to power. No less was required of Kyura.

"You have our thanks," he said formally, a player on stage, reciting assigned lines with little genuine feeling.

"Buffoon," Derlan put in quietly, and Kyura almost smirked.

Kyura moved on. The silver-cloaked generals and captains had the decency to look grave rather than falsely upset, but was it his imagination, or was there an almost predatory look in some eyes?

"Our condolences on your loss, Highest of Kings. May Fahria and Jormaan make your next son a great warrior."

The First General looked sincere, though that was of little comfort. Kyura suspected the army primarily wanted a strong heir, to replace his weak father.

"I would have thought tactics would make generals more tactful," Derlan quipped, and this time Kyura's lips raised slightly at the uncle he had always thought of as a military man playing court jester.

At the back of the hall, Kyura's official companions waited in the position tradition relegated common-born men: last. Companion Armar bowed, his features solemn. When he straightened, his posture was still slumped, his gaze downcast. Armar tended to be sombre, but Lenine knew how to make him smile, and Kyura suspected he would miss her dearly.

His brooding half uncle Karmarn did not behave in the solemn, barely emotional manner Zaldeaan etiquette favoured. Acting perhaps as his Tarlahn wife would, were she present, Karmarn stepped forwards and embraced Kyura. Kyura hugged him back gladly, but heard a snicker as they stepped apart. He straightened, flushing, and stared down the offending low official, who swiftly smoothed his expression to the neutrality of the officials surrounding him.

Kyura walked on, bodyguards falling into step beside his Companions as he departed the hall, exchanging the alert and piercing eyes of a court he had not yet won over for a quiet corridor alongside offices of state. Syenne had been right to advise him not to invite Aoran today. He would have to fulfil his duties with family and companions of official rank.

Servants rushed to open the doors ahead, and guards bowed Kyura and his companions out of the palace's confines. As they descended the palace steps, the cool breeze brushing his face and broad skies in which a bright, warmth-less Planting Season sun shone were a welcome change. Crowds in the street, shoppers with money pouches at their waists, servants in black linens, the wealthy in fur cloaks, and the poor in homespun woollens, parted before Kyura with heads bowed. In the distance, he heard hawkers crying wares and trundling carts, but before him was a vast sea of silence. A woman suckling a child gave him a pained, sympathetic smile, and Kyura halted in his tracks at a sight he should see in his chambers every day but would not.

"Go on," Syenne whispered.

Kyura made himself walk, but he couldn't banish the grimace from his face. Elders signed blessings and women and children lined his path with flowers. Every day, scraggly things, not as perfect as those which would wreath the King's Hall for the Month of Memory, but here, among the people, Kyura felt acceptance. His bodyguards surveyed the crowds, their postures relaxing as they sensed the mood of the often-frowned-upon-in-court masses. No one noticed a child clutching a hand sewn toy slip through the crowd. Kyura stared in surprise, as the small boy said to him, "Mummy said you lost your baby. Would you like Tassy? He always looks after me when I'm sad."

The procession halted. A woman gasped, raising both hands to her mouth. The boy hadn't even addressed Kyura with a title. He looked about four years old.

Kyura smiled. "I thank you for this generous offering, boy. But you may yet need Tassy, so you may keep him."

The boy beamed, then ran back into the crowd at a summons from an older woman, who embraced him while his mother rushed forwards, wrapping him up in her arms. A small smile crept across Kyura's lips as he walked on.

Ahead, Kyura's late father's statue stood at an intersection, the bronze figure glistening in the sun as it towered above the crowd. King Kyomi was cast in Zaldeaan plate armour, but instead of brandishing a sword or spear like most great men, Kyomi the Peacemaker released a murin bird, the symbol of peace. As Kyura drew nearer, he noted that the birds' feet were bent, just about to leave his hands, and its wings were outstretched and spread mid-flap.

"It is ornate," Kyura said, acknowledging the silver-haired bronzesmith and his leather aproned assistants standing to one side. "Your craftsmanship is unrivalled," he added, taking time to appreciate the artistry of the bird, so heavy against such delicate feet that he was surprised it remained upright.

But his father's face had to be acknowledged. Kyomi's features were robust, his stature short and stocky. His determination to end decades of stalemate against the Timbalen Empire to claim the last independent kingdom on the continent — Tarlah — had sealed the first official Peace.

Kyura had been four years old. But the Timbalen Empire had been absent for years. Calls to retake Tarlah had grown louder since his father's death. Kyomi had surrendered to illness, leaving Kyura both his Peace to maintain and a growing number of opponents.

"I didn't always get on with him," Uncle Derlan said, "but he knew how to get the people on his side. I have always admired how well he did that."

"The Tarlahns are coming," Companion Karmarn whispered.

Kyura straightened, turning to face them.

"He looks marvellous," said Prince Omah in Timbalen.

Kyura's brain clunkily translated the language his late father had insisted all his family learn, so they could speak to the Tarlahns in their own language. Father was right. It could help diplomacy. If Omah's words didn't leave Kyura turning, blinking back tears.

Princess Telena smiled sympathetically. Kyura's guards shifted.

Omah raised both hands in a placating gesture as he stepped close. "I apologise for my timing," he said quietly, "but I would ask you, is it your wish to continue his work?"

Kyura sniffed at the Tarlahns taking advantage of his leaving the palace and its eyes and ears behind. Even so, not a single Zaldeaan would speak to him so bluntly, forcing the issue without preamble.

Kyura felt the emptiness his father, wife, and unborn child had left him. It wearied, pained, and upset him. But his faithful Companions, uncle, and sister stood behind him. He could still counter any officials who dared call for war. With support to counterbalance grief, he could resist an army of warmongers, as his father had.

He wracked his brain for appropriate Timbalen words, then replied, "It will not be easy, but I would rule as my father did."

"If there is anything Tarlah can do to make that easier," Omah said, leaning in, "let Karmarn know, and we will see it done."

Kyura managed a weak smile. So many coveted power in the Zaldeaan court that it was easy to forget that every Tarlahn approved of peace and wished him well in preserving it. But Omah wasn't finished. "Your Greatness should know that some of your subjects do not. They have already committed an act of rebellion. There was an attempt on our Heir's life this afternoon."

Kyura's chest tightened and his breathing turned shallow.

"Ruarnon is fine," Omah assured his brother-by-law, Companion Karmarn, whose Timbalen was flawless. Then he turned to Kyura. "Whatever internal challenges you face, your Greatness has Tarlah's support." He bowed and took a step back.

Syenne stepped beside Kyura and led the way silently back to the palace.

"Someone tried to kill the Tarlahn heir?" he whispered in her ear.

A void opened inside him. He hadn't even met the heir to the Tarlahn throne yet. They were supposed to take supper together tonight.

"There is opposition to Father's Peace in court," Syenne replied, her jaw set. "I am investigating it and I have people who can continue to do so after I return to my city."

"What if they try to kill Prince Omah?"

Syenne met his gaze, her posture rigid. "It is possible, Brother. These may be dangerous times."

Kyura kept silent until he bid the others goodbye and he and Syenne reached his chambers.

"How do I deal with the fact someone just tried to kill the Tarlahn heir?" he asked her, as they reclined on silk cushioned seats in his sitting room.

Syenne's gaze sharpened. "I will hunt them," she replied without hesitation.

Kyura sighed.

"Take each day as it comes," she advised.

"Is that how you managed opposition when you became governor?"

She nodded. "Some small battles can be won in a day, but grief is like a war, and trying to plan too much will exhaust you. Just do what needs to be done each day and let me keep watch over dissent."

Kyura nodded, feeling so weary he could happily lie down and sleep. But he had voices of doubt and criticism to silence and traitors to weed out, and proving the strength of his rule was integral to both. He would focus on that and trust Syenne's help.

CHAPTER 4

TROUBLE IN TARLAH

RUARNON: *Tarlah City*

When Heir Ruarnon reached Tarlah City, home
no longer felt so safe. The familiar sight of
braided heads in the streets, Death Belt
Desert's dry heat blowing in from the north, and sweat
trickling down their back were welcome. But as their carriage
sped past scurrying servants, merchants in silks going to
market, and labourers buying lunch at public dining rooms, it
struck Ruarnon how small Tarlah City was compared to
Zaldeaa City. It held so few people, yielding few defenders,
impressing upon Ruarnon how vulnerable their home was.

A night and a day's chariot journey to the nearest
Zaldeaan port city and three days at sea made Ruarnon
increasingly uneasy about the attempt on their life being an act
of war. Uncle Omah assured them King Kyura wanted peace,

but someone in Kyura's court wanted war badly enough to provoke it themselves. How safe was Tarlah?

When Ruarnon's carriage entered the open gates of Tarlah Castle, halting in the courtyard, Ruarnon was surprised to see their father had set aside his work to greet them. King Urmillian stood tall and straight on the castle steps, fighting fit and as immovable as the stone he stood upon. His colouring was typical of Timbalens, like Omah's, blond hair in a Timbalen braid, calculating blue eyes, and fair skin tanned by military training beneath a hot sun. They turned to their mother Corina, whose hair was darker, her skin tawny, her eyes a warm brown, indicating her Urai heritage, features she had passed on to Ruarnon.

Their mother smiled and embraced them. Ruarnon hugged her back. Urmillian was reserved, merely clapping them on the back, as though conscious of Captain Arleath and the guards flanking the entrance to the castle doors looking on.

"I am glad you are safe," said Urmillian. "My Council has been discussing the attack and is in frequent communication by bird with Omah. It is unclear who tried to kill you, though we believe you are safe enough here."

"Unless war breaks out?" Ruarnon asked.

Corina's mouth fell open and the premature lines across Urmillian's brow creased.

"I know the attack was an act of war," said Ruarnon. "If Kyura failed to prevent it and he wasn't behind it, then how much power does he have over his subjects?"

Urmillian blinked, then bowed his head in acknowledgement. "That is precisely the question my Council seeks to answer. Your mother and I had not expected you to pose it so soon."

Of course Urmillian hadn't. Ruarnon hadn't rushed to fight in a rebellion against Zaldeaan rule at fifteen, as their father had. Or defended Tarlah in the Sea Wars at twenty. Ruarnon was born of the Generation of Peace, and they were only sixteen.

"Only my Council knows of the attack," Urmillian added. "So far as anyone in Tarlah knows, you returned a day ahead of my brother because you were taken ill."

Ruarnon sighed. Urmillian didn't want people to panic. Not until he knew the exact threat to Tarlah, who posed it, and had positioned himself to respond. The conversation Ruarnon had waited four days to have with their best friend Lenaris couldn't be had. She would know something was wrong. But she wouldn't press if Ruarnon didn't speak of it. And they would worry and ponder in silence, unless they cared to bring it up with their father, which they didn't.

"It has been fifteen years since our allies were present in these waters in force," said Urmillian. "Whoever tried to kill you may think them truly gone."

Ruarnon blanched. Timbalen absence had resulted in the conquest Ruarnon's grandfather had overthrown with rebellion. The Timbalen return had allowed King Kyomi the Peacemaker to proclaim war was futile, costing the people a high toll in blood and the crown great expense, and that war's prizes were temporary. But if Tarlah's allies were truly gone...

"Omah is convinced Kyura's closest advisors support peace and will argue its case and support Kyura against opposition," Urmillian added.

Would that safeguard Tarlah against invasion? It must. Kyomi had been dead for nine months and all that had happened in that time was an attempt on Ruarnon's life, and only because Ruarnon had ventured to Zaldeaa City. If they and their family stayed away, and Kyura continued as he had, everything could be fine. Unless Zaldeaan warmongers used the Tarlahn absence to argue in favour of invading Tarlah, when Omah wasn't there to counter them. Ruarnon shoved both thoughts down.

"Omah and my Council will deal with it," said Urmillian. "For now, you are to return to your studies. Focus on what you can do, Ruarnon. Dwelling on what you cannot never brought anyone peace."

"Yes, father," said Ruarnon. *I will not warn my closest friend that there is opposition to the Peace. I won't tell her what is bothering me. I will pretend to Companion Tor that everything is fine, and dutifully return to my studies. Because you won't take kindly to me behaving in a way which suggests to the whole castle that something is wrong.*

"Companion Tor tells me you need a challenge with a blade. I suggest you ask Lenaris for a duel."

Ruarnon blinked. Their father was immovable in the face of an approaching storm. But Lenaris was the most skilled person with a sword of their generation. Companion Tor had paid Ruarnon a great compliment in suggesting that. Was that a hint of pride in their father's eyes?

Despite everything, that glimmer lifted Ruarnon's spirit.

"I will, Father," Ruarnon replied.

Their father smiled and bowed his head in acknowledgement. Then Ruarnon's parents led them to the dining hall. But their mind wouldn't stay quiet. Questions kept swirling through. They couldn't drink in the soft yellow stone walls of Tarlah Castle or the airy frescoes of colourful crystalline buildings in the Timbalen Empire's capital. Not when someone had tried to kill them and they didn't know who or why, exactly. Uncertainty kept their heart rate elevated, their eyes sweeping the room and ears pricked for sounds of danger.

The Dining Hall glowed golden from silver candles suspended around its walls and candelabra on its tables. Its walls were brightly painted with the bounty of the Earth Goddess Mijora, and talk and laughter drifted towards Ruarnon from officials and their families seated in rows beside the high table. It was a vast space in which potential assassins could lurk. Ruarnon tried to shake the thought and followed their parents to the head of the high table.

They greeted their father's Companions, Tor and Pamoran, and the Companions' families courteously, then

Ruarnon sat beside their mother. Laughter filled the room as the Companions and their families selected cuts of roast meats off silver platters with silver skewers and sipped wine from gold goblets. Ruarnon picked at the fruit on another platter, until their father eyed them sternly, then forced themself to eat as though nothing was wrong.

A flute's notes cut through Ruarnon's thoughts and conversations broke off, as their mother stood and played. Her lively Urai tune turned Ruarnon's mind to flights of fancy, monkeys swinging between ancient trees in the southern jungle and their wish that the Urai Tribes would emerge from their fabled treetop homes once more.

When Queen Corina finished playing, Ruarnon clapped with the others. Their mother took her seat beside Ruarnon, laying her flute on the table.

"Mother, do you think the Urai will contact us again?" Ruarnon asked.

"It is unlikely," Corina replied. "With the passing of each generation, more Tarlahns think the tribes and their jungle will become a mere myth, but I hope it is not so."

"Are you corrupting our future ruler with idle daydreams?" King Urmillian asked playfully from her other side.

"If they cannot conceive of daydreams, how can they conceive their vision of Tarlah and lead the people towards it in their reign?" Corina asked.

"I knew my parents had reasons when they insisted I marry you," Urmillian replied with a spark in his eyes that made Ruarnon turn away in embarrassment.

"It must be pleasant to know those reasons." Corina laughed. "I have always taken it on faith that *my* parents had reasons for demanding *I* marry *you*."

Ruarnon shook their head. Uncle Omah insisted their parents had bickered incessantly for half a year after marrying and took months to admit being in love, but Ruarnon found it difficult to believe.

People rose along the table, and their mother said, "Goodnight, Ruarnon," with a twinkle in her eyes. They bid their parents goodnight, but Lenaris approached before they could follow their parents out.

"Come with me," she said.

Her sleeveless pink silk tunic fluttered in the breeze as she strode across the hall wearing a silver chain for a belt and her golden hair braided into a bun, both touches fancier than what the Companions' families usually wore to dinner. Curious, Ruarnon followed their older friend through stone corridors and up spiralling stone steps, down which voices echoed from above. Had Lenaris' father, Companion Pamoran, told her about the attack? Could they discuss it? But Lenaris seemed happy. It must be something else.

At the top of the steps, Lenaris opened the door to a lamp-lit rooftop beneath a vast sky of twinkling stars and full twin moons. Tables lined the battlements with supper, silver goblets and glass jugs of drinks spread across them. The rooftop was crowded with talkative young people and musicians playing lutes.

Faces turned towards them, and Ruarnon nodded vaguely at the crowd, then edged instinctively around it, their heart rate speeding up as they stepped towards an empty space beside the crenelations.

They sighed with relief as people turned back to dance partners or conversation. Normally Ruarnon had a chance to brace themself before the stares of expectant subjects, or even the presence of crowds. Suddenly stumbling into one made them clamp down on spiralling nerves and seek space to compose themself in.

They took a few deep breaths through their nose, then surveyed the rooftop.

Lenaris eyed them uncertainly. "I hoped it would be a good surprise," she said.

"It might be," they said. "I just didn't expect... what is this? Why is everyone celebrating?"

"Welcome to the Festival of Life," Lenaris replied with a smile.

Ruarnon recognised the name. "But I'm underage!"

"That means you're a guest of honour," Lenaris said with a smile. "During the Wars, anyone could be called to battle the day after they came of age, so the Festival of Life grants everyone more opportunity to experience life before battle."

Ruarnon raised an eyebrow. "But the Wars ended fifteen years ago!"

"Do you think that is sufficient reason to tell everyone to stop celebrating?" she asked, her blue eyes shining with mirth.

"You want to learn how many drinks you can hold, Benevolence," Arlian, the Censar's son, called across the crowd. "When you first consume drink on your seventeenth birthday, everyone will be watching!"

"Surely my servants can tell me how much drink I can consume before becoming drunk?"

"Ah, but it's never the same from one person to another," Arlian objected with a wink.

"Here," said Lenaris, offering Ruarnon a goblet of wine.

Ruarnon held down the eyebrow threatening to raise again and smiled as they accepted the goblet. They took their first sip of sweetly fragrant, intense white wine. Others around them drank thirstily, and they suspected standard social protocols wouldn't apply tonight.

Harps were strummed and drums beat. Lenaris pulled Ruarnon towards a dance. The pair joined a human chain bowing left and right, and laughter rose as two people got it wrong and banged heads. Then the music slowed and softened.

"Would Your Benevolence care to dance?" Lenaris asked, her smile slightly mocking.

Ruarnon grinned and took her hands, deciding to set their worries aside for the night. They raised conjoined hands in a series of graceful motions, shuffling sideways periodically. Other couples shuffled around them, some women dancing with women, some men dancing with men, midluns dancing with any of the three genders. The merriment, public displays of affection, and some gender pairings would have been a scandal to the rigid conventions of the Zaldeaan Realm, but not here. This was home, where every Tarlahn generation save Ruarnon's had fought for its freedom, and in return, everyone let everyone be as they were.

Beside the dancers, Arlian kissed a serving girl passionately, and smiles around Ruarnon became infectious.

Later, a circle dance ended with half the dancers falling to the floor and the rest laughing hard. The musicians stopped playing, one shouting, "My friends! You have all had enough of Life tonight! Goodnight! And to those who continue celebrating: happy celebrations!"

Ruarnon blushed, as Arlian's serving girl laughed and tugged Arlian's arm towards the stairs opposite the dancers. Arlian smiled, gently tucking a loose hair behind her ear. She beamed back at him. Then they ran off hand in hand. Other couples hurried off together too.

Lenaris smiled mischievously. "They aren't the only ones. The festival also attracts captains and officials from South Harbour. And when his skill with a blade is near as accomplished as mine, and his intelligence, if not quite education, is a match, well..."

Ruarnon should have known. She *was* twenty.

"You had best go to bed, Ruarnon," Lenaris added. "You will be expected at your history lesson tomorrow. Older people say part of living is responsibility, not that lack of it has ever been a fault of yours."

Horses' hooves striking pavement hit Ruarnon's ears. A carriage travelled down a lane away from the castle, back-lit by lamps burning around the rooftop. Ruarnon stilled, noting that every window in the mud-brick apartments lining the street was dark, and the night had otherwise fallen silent.

"Lenaris, what hour is it?" they asked.

"Near midnight. Why?"

"There is a carriage moving away from the castle."

A woman's face appeared in the carriage window. There was just enough light to make out her tousled long dark hair. A hand raised before her mouth, fingers moving strangely.

"Is she miming a flute?" Ruarnon asked, feeling hollow.

"It cannot be," Lenaris whispered, leaning over the battlements.

The woman's head jerked from sight, a curtain was pulled across the open window, and the carriage moved on, fading in the semi-darkness of the two moons.

Ruarnon's heart raced. They shook their head. Enemies couldn't have their mother. It was impossible. But if a woman was being taken from the palace against her will, no one seemed to be doing anything about it. And there was only one way to be sure it wasn't Corina.

Ruarnon ran, hurtling downstairs. They skipped two steps at once and landed painfully on their right foot, Lenaris' footsteps echoing after them. They raced down a short stone corridor, their footsteps echoing through eerrie quiet, until they stopped suddenly. The night guards outside their parents' chambers lay slumped on the floor, snoring. Further down, their guards were positioned as though they had fallen and slept where they lay. Ruarnon gaped, and their heart began to pound against their chest.

Lenaris pointed silently. A broken pottery cup lay beside one of Ruarnon's parents guards. The guard next to her held a cup in his hand. Ruarnon shivered. The Night Guard were usually given kaf to aid their alertness. Someone had drugged it.

Lenaris snatched a torch from its wall bracket. Ruarnon was unarmed and intruders could lurk in rooms off the corridor. Their body tensed. "We need more guards."

She blinked. "You want me to fetch them and leave you here alone?"

"I should raise the alarm."

"But you intend to check on your father," she guessed, reading the longing in Ruarnon's gaze.

Duty to secure the area warred with Ruarnon's urgency to find out if their father was safe. They seized a torch off the opposite wall and their legs resumed running almost of their own accord, Lenaris hard on their heels. They pushed open Ruarnon's parents' door and ran around sleeping servants seated at a table in the antechamber. Beyond, Ruarnon's parents' bed was empty; its covers tossed on the floor. Dread shot through them.

"Raise the alarm."

Lenaris raised her eyebrows at their tone. She met their worried gaze, bowed her head, and departed.

Footsteps echoed in her wake. Ruarnon raised their burning torch before them as the footsteps grew louder. Six guards approached, presumably sent by Lenaris. Ruarnon sighed with relief and returned the torch to its wall bracket. The guards needed orders. A void of uncertainty opened before Ruarnon. Thoughts tumbled over themselves. Then years of listening to their father give orders returned, as did Uncle Omah's words, "Dangerous times call for decisive action."

Ruarnon straightened. They smoothed their face into the calm mask they had worn in the Zaldeaan palace and ordered, "Two of you, wake Companion Pamoran. Tell him the king and queen have been abducted."

The guard's eyes widened and several mouths dropped open. The man in the middle recovered first and asked, "Is Companion Pamoran to lead the pursuit?"

Companion Pamoran was a former chariot captain. He could lead the pursuit, but it would set out more swiftly if Ruarnon simply ordered everyone to get moving. Time was of the essence. They calculated ratios, then replied, "Yes. Two of you, wake a dozen archers. One of you, wake six charioteers.

One of you, go to the stables and tell the grooms to ready six chariots. I want the sixth man to keep an eye on the corridors and the rest of you to return to your posts as soon as your messages are delivered."

Five guards bowed, then dashed away. The sixth man also bowed. "The gates, Benevolence," he reminded them.

Ruarnon blinked at the hole in their defence orders. "Tell the castle wall guards to signal that we have intruders."

The last guard bowed and jogged away. Ruarnon stood in a silent corridor, their heart racing. Their parents were getting further away, and the further they got, the less Tarlah could do to protect them. It would take multiple chariots to overpower the soldiers in the carriage. But a lone rider with a bow could wound a horse pulling a carriage. And Ruarnon was an excellent shot. They could help recover their parents before the chariot escaped the city.

They ran to their chambers. Night Guards still slept on the corridor floor. They tried shoving the guards awake, but the men and women didn't stir. At the small round table in Ruarnon's anteroom, their servants slept hard. They paused. Inserting the pins which bound their cuirass would be time consuming, but they felt naked without armour. Instead, they flung on a boiled leather vest, belting their iron sword over it. Then they strapped on a bronze helmet, secured a quiver of arrows to the side of their belt, seized their spear and bow, and sprinted down the corridor.

Every dark section between torches felt unfriendly, but having a spear in hand was reassuring, and it was a relief to pass undrugged guards on duty. Ruarnon paused when they reached the head of the steps to the castle courtyard. Above it, blue flames rose from the castle gate towers, warning of intruders.

"Benevolence! Companion Pamoran asked me to watch over you."

Ruarnon turned. Captain Arleath was running towards them. Their heart skipped a beat. They should have sent for the man, not rushed to join the chariots without a bodyguard.

"I mean to ride out," said Ruarnon.

Arleath bowed his helmeted head. He wore bronze armour and carried a spear in his right hand. He kept up as Ruarnon rushed down the castle steps and across the paved stone courtyard towards Companion Pamoran, who was yelling orders to grooms and charioteers in the stables. Ruarnon nodded to a groom. They and Arleath were mounted on saddle blankets within moments, the horses' hooves clacking as they crossed the courtyard. Chains clanked as the outer gates opened. Ruarnon heeled their horse through and Captain Arleath followed.

The horses tilted down the steep hill Tarlah Castle lay atop, then trotted between dark, multi-storey mud-brick apartments. Ruarnon gripped their horse's flanks with their knees as they bounced on their saddle blanket. The clack of hooves echoed loudly off walls and down empty streets.

Ruarnon worried the carriage's occupants would hear them, but there was nothing to be done about it.

The silver glow of the twin moons dimly lit North Road, the swiftest and most likely path for the carriage to take to North Gate. Ruarnon's best chance of stopping it was shooting the horses before the carriage lost them among the hills of River Road. Buildings flashed past, and Ruarnon's heart hammered against their chest. Wielding weapons to attack enemies felt like playing at being their war-hero father, but recovering their parents inside Tarlah City was the surest way to get them back.

"Take care," a man shouted from behind. The first chariot sped into the city, driven by Companion Pamoran, who was warning Ruarnon and leaving off their title to conceal their identity. Their parents' abductors may be ignorant of the Festival of Life. The abductors may have expected to find Ruarnon in their chambers too. Maybe Ruarnon shouldn't have risked themself, but it was too late for that now.

The carriage careened around the corner of Centre and North Roads, charging down North Road ahead. If they could gain twenty feet on it, it would come within arrow range. Ruarnon leaned forwards on their mount, nudging it with their heels, urging it to move faster. North Gate loomed. Ruarnon tugged their reigns left, seeking an angle to target the horses. But the carriage shielded the horses. They would have to aim over it. Over the roof and driver, whose bare neck was exposed. They could kill the driver, but Ruarnon had never so much as wounded a man. But they couldn't let enemies escape with their parents.

Ruarnon seized their bow from its saddle holder with trembling hands. They fumbled it, then exhaled slowly. Gripping their horse's sides with their knees, they stood in the stirrups, drew three arrows from their quiver, and took aim at the back of the drivers' neck. Ruarnon hesitated, wanting to look away from the man whose life they were about to claim. But looking away meant they could miss, abandoning their parents to who knew what fate.

Ruarnon counted five beats of their heart, then drew and released all three arrows in swift succession. The arrows arced across the road. Over the carriage. A guttural cry from the driver cut short as he slumped below sight, two arrows sticking up from his neck. Ruarnon shivered.

Men shouted, and the carriage maintained its pace. Ruarnon couldn't see who was driving it now. The new driver must be crouched low in the seat. Should Ruarnon attack the horses instead?

North Gate swung open. The carriage raced through. The gates began to close.

"Aim for the middle," Captain Arleath instructed.

Ruarnon turned their horse till their leg brushed Arleath's. Something solid knocked the air from Ruarnon's lungs. They fell, cool night air rushing up to greet them. Their arm struck something solid. Then they were tumbling, stopping abruptly, and everything went dark.

When they came to, Ruarnon's head and limbs ached. Their arm was wrapped in a sticky bandage and they were lying on stone. They sat gingerly, trying not to put weight on aching limbs. Captain Arleath helped them.

"What happened?" Ruarnon asked, dabbing at something wet on the side of their head. Blood?

"Two men tried to steal our horses," Arleath replied, surveying the road ahead. "One knocked you off your horse. I managed to fight mine off, but he fled into the night."

Vague images of a race down North Road flashed through Ruarnon's mind. They rubbed their head with one hand, trying to ease its ache, and asked, "Does Companion Pamoran pursue the carriage?"

"Yes, but two chariots remained to guard you."

Ruarnon's head swam. Companion Pamoran's curses cut through the night. Ruarnon turned, but the timber sides of the chariot Captain Arleath had leant them against walled off their view.

Arleath remained silent. There was shouting, then the thump of hooves as a chariot approached. Ruarnon sat up as Companion Pamoran drove towards them, alone. The man's silver hairs atop his mostly dark head shone in the moonlight, but the arms holding the reins and legs keeping balance on a swaying chariot were hardened muscle.

"They lost us in the hills, reached the eastern shore, and boarded a ship which is sailing north," Pamoran reported with

78

a grimace. "Take Their Benevolence back to the castle. I've sent word that the pursuit must continue by ship."

Captain Arleath stepped onto the chariot and took up the reins. He checked Ruarnon held the handrail securely, then turned the chariot around and urged the horses after Companion Pamoran.

"You did well, Benevolence," Pamoran called over his shoulder. "Neither of us were fast enough."

Ruarnon heard the anger in his tone. Pamoran was the fastest driver in Tarlah. He also hated to lose. But not as much as Ruarnon dreaded it. It would take time for word to reach the castle and more for a ship to be readied. The abductors would have a long head start when Tarlahn ships were put to sea. Only three destinations lay north of where the chariot had boarded a ship, the no-man's-land of Death Belt Desert, the Zaldeaan Realm, and the reclusive North Lands. After the attempt on their life, Ruarnon worried their parents were in Zaldeaan hands and feared they were beyond Tarlah's reach.

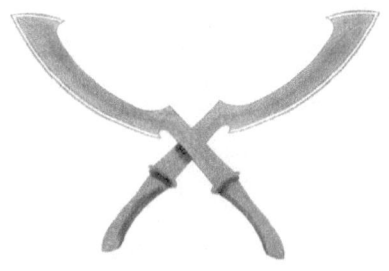

CHAPTER 5

SHADOW ON THE HORIZON

RUARNON: *Tarlah City*

Memories flooded back when Ruarnon woke the following day. The spark in their father's eyes as he and mother jested at dinner, and in their mother's as she told them to sleep well, knowing Lenaris was taking Ruarnon to the Festival of Life. They shifted in bed, triggering sharp pains on grazes from their fall on the road and the duller aches of their bruises from colliding with the gate. Getting up was not a good idea.

They lay back. If their parents had been recovered, Companion Pamoran would have sent word. A Tarlahn ship must be pursuing them at sea, with slim chances of catching up, let alone overpowering the Zaldeaan vessel. They were relieved when a knock on the door interrupted dark thoughts and Uncle Omah entered and sat by their bed.

"When did you get back?" Ruarnon asked.

"This morning," Omah replied, his eyes downcast. "Assassins attacked our First Trade Official not long after you left. It appears King Kyura feared he could not ensure our safety in his palace, so he sent every Tarlahn resident home, while he cleans out his house."

Omah met Ruarnon's gaze. "The ship pursuing your parents sails several leagues behind the vessel they are captive aboard, which is of Zaldeaan design."

Ruarnon's brows furrowed. "Whoever took my parents could have killed them in their beds, like someone tried to kill me in the Realm, but they didn't. Do you think my parents' abductors are different people to the ones who sent assassins after me?"

Omah's deep blue gaze studied Ruarnon. "The Royal Council suspects so. There may be more individuals or factions at work."

"But why take my parents alive?" Ruarnon wondered. "Unless... I read in the Zaldeaan Archives how their kings expanded the Realm by taking other kings' heirs hostage and raising them in Zaldeaa. Could someone have taken my parent's hostage? If Kyura is committed to peace, does he hope we will pay him tribute and acknowledge him as Prime Ruler in exchange for my parents' safety?"

If that were so, Ruarnon's parents might not be treated too badly...

Omah smiled. "Urmillian underestimated you. You lack war experience, but education has made your mind as sharp as any blade. Do you remember Kyomi the Peacemaker's second reason, other than our allies, for war being futile?"

Ruarnon considered it. "The revolt your father led. But if they don't provoke us with military occupation and executions this time, if all Kyura wants is tribute, does he hope that abducting my parents will appease whoever wants to rule us, without violating his father's Peace?"

Omah sighed. "Given that he too was raised during the Peace, that is the most likely explanation. But I suspect Kyura is fragile, and I doubt he has been in a fit state to conceive of such a plan in recent weeks. The timing suggests it may have been someone else."

"Either way," Ruarnon asked, "would our payment of tribute and acceptance of Kyura as Prime Ruler satisfy Zaldeaans who oppose the Peace?"

Omah turned away. "That would deprive the army of glory, its leaders of positions of power, and its soldiers of their best retirement plan. It could also undermine power plays within the Zaldeaan court. Whatever the Zaldeaans intend, we will make our own plans to recover your parents." He paused, then eyed Ruarnon. "Your servants believe your parents contracted the illness which sent you home early from the Zaldeaan Realm. Guards involved in the pursuit and our servants have been sworn to secrecy. I have informed the

Royal Council, but common knowledge that our Rulers were abducted will only rouse reckless anger and fear."

Ruarnon slumped at the authority in their uncle's tone. Omah had taken up the regency.

Ruarnon had grappled with the fact that someone had tried to kill them in the Zaldeaan palace. It made them nervous about being followed through corridors and of entering large rooms like the dining hall. At other times, it didn't seem real. It had happened so quickly, in a place they had never been before. They had rushed home like waking from a bad dream. The political implications of the assassination attempt were like one of Companion Tor's exercises in logic. Ruarnon could accept it on that level. But Omah's tone and regency made Urmillian and Corina's absence real. It made the threat of war more than mere speculation. It set Ruarnon's head spinning.

One clear thought rose from the chaos of Ruarnon's mind: dangerous times call for decisive action. They had an option. They just hoped it was more successful than their botched attempt to delay the carriage. "Uncle. I wish to take up a seat on the Royal Council. I want to know what is going on and to have the chance to help my parents."

Omah bowed his head in acceptance.

Within a few days, Ruarnon's grazes had healed enough for them to attend lessons, but their history lesson with

Companion Tor was interrupted by a summons to their first Royal Council meeting. Three days was the fastest time ships could sail between Zaldeaa City and Tarlah City. Ruarnon's heart drumrolled in their chest as they wondered what news that ship brought of their parents' fate.

"I suggest you say little in the meeting," Companion Tor advised, standing tall and broad as the pair strode down the corridor, silver shining amid the sandy hair stretching back into his braid, his expression thoughtful and distant as always.

"Former General Monin served under the king before the Bloody Occupation. He has advised your father since he became Co-Regent at fifteen. In his eyes, you are a child. Pamoran may be more open-minded than his father, but I suspect he will also see you as little more than a child at lessons, until you prove yourself. Learn what you can, but give them no excuse to doubt your ability. The Royal Council exists to advise you, but you will lead us as Co-Regent. When you lead, the Council's job is to temper the regent's and co-regent's decisions. You do not want to give them reasons to doubt your ability to make those decisions."

Ruarnon swallowed awkwardly. Their only thoughts about the Royal Council had been nervous ones of what they'd learn of their parents. But Tor was right: with their co-regency only months away, they needed to gain the council's respect. And as Tarlah's first midlun Heir, that might require more of Ruarnon than it had of male Heirs.

"Thank you," Ruarnon said, feeling strange speaking to their father's First Companion as an equal.

The Golden Meeting Hall was imposing. Silver busts of former Companions gazed expectantly across the room from niches lining the left wall. A table dominated the centre, with Ruarnon's aunt and uncle seated at its head. Silver-haired, scarred Advisor Monin sat on the left side and rugged Companion Pamoran on the right. From a dais behind the table, gold busts of former rulers gazed down on the proceedings. Each was believed to house the spirit of the person it represented, so the Ancestors could offer up their wisdom. As Ruarnon stepped into the Ancestor's gazes, they felt the weight of past and present Royal Council members judging them settle on their shoulders.

Uncle Omah motioned to the co-regent's seat on the right. Ruarnon kept their posture upright as Monin's stern gaze fixed on them. If anyone needed convincing that a midlun could rule as well as a man or woman, it would be the council's oldest and most conservative advisor, Monin.

Ruarnon sat alertly, marking a young messenger standing beside the table and a taller, grey-haired man, the Spymaster.

"Welcome to the second council of Regent Omah," Omah said regally once Ruarnon and Tor were seated. "Make your report," he instructed the Spymaster, who bowed.

"Earlier today, a spy at the Zaldeaan Palace overheard a conversation between nervous soldiers. One insisted that everything would be fine if they never mentioned leaving Zaldeaa City and forgot about 'that Tarlahn couple.'"

Ruarnon's body tensed. They had hoped their parents would be hidden in a Zaldeaan country villa. The Zaldeaan palace, in the centre of Zaldeaa City, would be far harder to free the royal couple from. Negotiation might be the only option, and Ruarnon didn't like to consider what the Zaldeaans may ask for in exchange.

Omah gestured to the messenger, who read from a scroll.

To His Benevolence Omah, Regent of Tarlah,

Our ship reached the seas near Edesinia this afternoon. We were prevented from making port. Two ships barred our way, threatening us with power bows and claiming Zaldeaan ports are closed to Tarlahn ships. They fly no flags. What are Your Benevolence's orders?

Signed,

Captain Noma, Tarlahn Navy

Ruarnon's face fell. If Kyura wanted to make demands, he needed to speak to Omah. So why hadn't he sent his ambassador to Tarlah? Was it Kyura who had Ruarnon's parents?

"Could warmongers be commanding those ships?" asked Companion Pamoran. "Hiding their identity from their king as well as us?"

"Declaring their ports closed amounts to usurping the king's power," Monin replied. "That suggests some Zaldeaans are on the brink of open rebellion."

"But if they are warmongers, oughtn't they to hold to the Warrior's Creed, or at least pretend to?" Ruarnon objected.

They braced themself as every face around the table turned critically towards them.

"Abducting my parents from their beds is an act of cowardice, but if they think we will declare war in retaliation, they are out of their minds."

"Indeed," said Omah. "If King Kyura did not abduct our Rulers, then who?"

"Sending home our officials while he hunts the attempted killer in his court shows Kyura's commitment to peace," Companion Tor replied. "Yet we have heard reports of some Zaldeaans clamouring for war. If he were usurped like his grandfather, who would be king?"

"Syenne has the ability, but many enemies," Monin replied. "Her cousin Iagl would be more popular and just as likely to want it. His father Derlan, who fought in the Piracy War, may never have taken his eyes off Tarlah. But deposing Kyura would mean a succession war, and in-fighting would weaken Zaldeaan might. Any traitor's best option is to retain Kyura as king and bully or steer him to invade us."

Ruarnon struggled to keep up. With advisors making such leaps of logic, it was no wonder their father had seemed all-knowing.

Across Zaldeaan history, ambition had led to all manner of scheming, but now, it might prevent Ruarnon's uncle from speaking to Kyura. Worse, it might be a warmonger who had abducted Ruarnon's parents.

It couldn't come to war. With Tarlah's allies absent, the only question was how long Tarlah could hold against its vastly more powerful enemies before it surrendered to a brutal occupation. Ruarnon wouldn't need to worry about the future then; they'd be executed. The idea made them cold inside.

"I will write to King Kyura by messenger bird," Omah told the Council. "Tell our spies I want to know who is blocking our attempts to speak to him," he added to the Spymaster, who bowed and left.

Omah dismissed the Council. Grave faces surveyed Ruarnon as they departed. Monin and Pamoran probably thought the news was too much for the kid at the table, and Monin likely doubted a midlun could handle it. Now wasn't the time to prove them wrong. Ruarnon was too overwhelmed by the stakes of Zaldeaan politics.

"Come with me, Ruarnon," said Omah.

Ruarnon paid little attention to where they were going, until they entered a room on the castle's southern side, where late afternoon sunlight streamed through the window. A map was strewn across the room's central wooden desk, with a pursuit at sea, alongside Death Belt Desert's coast, marked on it. A shelf filled with scrolls stood to one side, and tables topped with scribes' papyrus and stylus stood empty—the Royal Writing Room.

"Do not give up hope," Omah whispered, leaning towards them. "There may be much we are ignorant of."

"Including the extent to which Kyura is losing control of his court?" Ruarnon asked, slumping where they stood.

Omah looked down at them intently, then replied, "Yes. Urmillian has worried about that since Kyura came to the throne. The attempt on your life indicated we were right to worry. Your parents' abduction, if it were not by Kyura, is far worse."

Ruarnon turned away. Their uncle's confirmation that war was possible made their insides lurch with fear of the unknown.

"Kyura's grip on power isn't the only determinant of peace," Omah added. "I sent a ship to the Timbalen Empire asking for aid. At this time of year, it must use lateen sails angled to catch the wind, which may delay it a week or two, but if our allies send ships, it will prove that war now is as futile as ever, and they may aid us in recovering your parents."

Ruarnon nodded, but said nothing.

"Take time to consider everything. Discuss it with Lenaris if you need to."

Ruarnon's shoulders relaxed slightly and a small smile parted their lips. Their uncle returned the smile. If Omah didn't expect them to be stone, like King Urmillian did, perhaps Ruarnon could get through this.

They said goodbye to Omah, found Lenaris, and led her to a place they were sure they wouldn't be overheard, the battlements atop the front castle walls. Commands of captains drilling soldiers rang out behind them, while the usual hum of Tarlah City rose before them. Ruarnon gazed across flat mud brick rooftops, the wealthiest adorned with pot plant gardens, wondering how to tell Lenaris the truth after four days of silence.

Below, a boy carried a satchel of messages down a narrow side road, past a girl throwing a stone. The girl's friends cringed as a woman scolded them for throwing stones, pointing at the shining substance in her window, glass, a new and expensive invention. Double doors burst open ahead, and older children poured out, grateful that another morning of learning was over. How nice it would be, growing up like them, without knowledge or fear of the kingdom's future.

The thought tempted Ruarnon to soak up the city, delaying the inevitable. Further away, the hum of conversation, bartering, and animal noises rose from the marketplace, a confusing mass of stalls down North Road. Bare-chested farmers pulled wooden handcarts. Travelling merchants in colourfully dyed tunics strutted with armed guards. Servants of city families scurried about on errands in white linens. The adults of Tarlah also went about their business, their days unshadowed by signs only a few Tarlahns saw: that war with the Zaldeaan Realm might be likely once more.

"I don't know how long this will last," Ruarnon said, gazing across the city.

Lenaris eyed them sharply. "Your parents?"

Omah had kept it as secret as Urmillian wanted the attempt on Ruarnon's life to remain, but Ruarnon was sure she had guessed their father was also missing.

"Father was abducted too."

Lenaris' face fell. "I'm sorry."

Ruarnon grimaced. "Uncle Omah mentioned how long the Timbalens have been absent. I thought the attempt on my life was the Zaldeaan reaction to that. I worried about them attacking Tarlah City, but I never imagined this."

"Have they located your parents?"

Ruarnon shook their head and gripped the battlements.

"They're too valuable not to look after for negotiations," Lenaris assured Ruarnon.

Ruarnon sighed. That was true, but it didn't calm the accelerated beat of their heart. The question they barely dared think of in the quiet of their mind wasn't calming either. "How would the people respond if they had to fight?"

"The commoners have a saying," Lenaris replied, her posture straightening. "'If he cuts you down, stab him as you fall.' Companion Gathron put it more eloquently: 'If you are going to die, let it be with sword, spear, or bow in hand, for the sake of your people.'"

Ruarnon leant heavily on the crenellated wall. "I only thought of it as death, loss, and horror. Not a service to our people."

They clenched their fists, but their mask of Urmillian's thoughtful heir remained in place. They kept their voice steady, emulating their older friend's acceptance of frightening circumstances beyond their control. Still, they couldn't suppress a shudder as they admitted, "It may come down to our allies. On whether they answer Uncle Omah's call for aid fast enough to prevent war, or not at all."

Chapter 6

Training in Tarlah

Ethlin: *Tarlah City*

Four days after King Urmillian and Queen Corina took ill, Ethlin sneaked a glance over her shoulder at the Head Cook, who was bellowing at a servant who had left the kitchen door open and admitted a cat into her domain. Ethlin took advantage of the distraction and slipped out the back door, then down the servants' corridor, towards Tarlah Castle's main training courtyard. She paused at the corridor exit to hang her apron from a peg she had appropriated from the castle kitchens and checked that her flyaway brown hair was at least partially braided, then slipped outside.

The clanging of iron on iron rang in her ears, as did muffled thuds suggesting leather armoured soldiers were smacking into each other. Ethlin breathed in the scent of leather and slipped along the walls of the main training courtyard, a place her rank as kitchen servant would deny her access to, until war broke out and levied soldiers were needed, which, given Tarlah's history, was likely at some point. Then she crept past stone columns extending up towards a hot sun, alongside the Royal Courtyard. In her favourite shaded corner, she peered around a column, down to where her mentor Lenaris, the most skilled female fighter in Tarlah, trained with her father.

Lenaris was a flurry of blue tunic, her iron blade flashing in the sun as she slashed at her father, Companion Pamoran. Her lithe form danced aside from his heavy-handed strokes and she kept her distance from his solid figure. Companion Pamoran's face was care-lined, but he moved with the energy and enthusiasm of a younger man. Pamoran defended a flurry of strokes with his shield, his teeth flashing a grin.

Training in the Royal Courtyard was a privilege the Companions of Tarlah received as Kings' Companions, despite the Companions being common-born and many having attained their positions by rising through the army's ranks. Seeing Companion Pamoran and Lenaris train here always encouraged Ethlin's hopes of serving in the army to raise her status.

"Hasn't anyone told you it's rude to stare?" Arlian flashed his usual white-toothed grin, approaching so stealthily Ethlin hadn't noticed him.

"Didn't those etiquette lessons you and important people's children attend mention it's rude to sneak up on unsuspecting young women?" she countered.

Arlian's grin broadened, as he leant casually against a stone pillar. She suspected the officials' children he spent most of his time with were too well-bred for banter. But she and Arlian exchanged as much banter as they could during the training sessions they snuck away from other duties to attend.

"I wish you could come sometimes," Arlian replied, and Ethlin detected regret in his lowered gaze. "They're so sensible. Aspiring to rank and work like their parents. None of them has your sense of adventure."

Ethlin eyed him pointedly.

"Well, of course Lenaris, but no man can match her."

"So, you sought the only spirited woman in the castle who would have you?" Ethlin asked with her hands on hips, her face a picture of mock seriousness.

Arlian paused, eyeing her nervously.

"That's all right. If Heir Ruarnon were lively in private, I might have pursued them."

Arlian coughed. Ethlin winked, and his cough changed to laughter.

"You will not become the best fighting pair of soldiers Tarlah has yet to see if you stand about laughing," Lenaris asserted.

Companion Pamoran was gone, and Lenaris stood facing them, holding two blunted iron-tipped practice spears. Ethlin giggled as they leapt down the steps to claim the spears. Lenaris turned to Ethlin. She always duelled Ethlin first. Kitchen servants didn't have hours a day to train with expert weapon masters, and for all that she made do with broomsticks in spare moments, it showed.

Strike first this time. Try to take control before she gains the upper hand, Ethlin told herself sternly. Lenaris closed the distance between them in a single step. With the grace of a fighter in her prime, she moved lightly, aided by long, slender limbs. Ethlin was shorter but stockier and determined to find an advantage in it.

Ethlin attacked. Lenaris blocked her shoulder blow, and Ethlin leapt over Lenaris' leg blow. She countered Lenaris' spear butt with her own. She wondered where to strike next. Lenaris' spear point flashed. Ethlin ducked and sidestepped.

"Stand your ground!" Lenaris instructed. "Allow a mistake to flow into a counter move."

Ethlin struggled to keep up, relying on instinct instead of reflexes honed by extensive practice. But instincts were crucial too, when hesitating for a fraction of a moment could get anyone killed in battle.

Ethlin ducked a stab at her head, countered a leg stroke with the butt of her spear, and rammed Lenaris' shoulder with her own, making Lenaris smile. Lenaris' spear butt struck her calf painfully, as she turned. Ethlin winced and attacked again, doing her best to stand her ground. Sweat trickled down her sides, back, and limbs, as she parried high and low, pivoting on either foot to counter Lenaris' spearhead at ideal angles.

When they were finished, she wiped the sweat off her chin with her fingers and Lenaris gave her a few minutes to catch her breath before attacking Arlian and Ethlin simultaneously. Ethlin attacked, and Arlian beat back Lenaris' counterstroke. Ethlin leapt Lenaris' spear and Arlian attacked from the side, Lenaris' spear butt deflecting him.

This was the fight Ethlin was most comfortable with. She and Arlian watched each other at the corner of their eyes, complementing each other's moves. Arlian couldn't hold out long against Lenaris on his own, but together they could withstand her, as Lenaris pushed, probed, and pushed them again. Ethlin kept it up until weariness from being on her feet since dawn made her stumble. Lenaris retreated with a smile.

"Do not worry," Lenaris said. "If there were a war, you would be released from the kitchens to rest when you are not fighting. And the fact you can withstand me for so long after a day in the kitchens bodes well for your stamina in a real battle."

Ethlin bowed, and Arlian thanked Lenaris. Lenaris departed, but Arlian and Ethlin lingered behind the columns. Companion Pamoran and Companion Tor wouldn't arrive for their evening duel for another hour, and the royal family only trained by day. This was the one hour they could be together when Ethlin was free from the kitchens and Arlian's family thought he was studying.

Panting heavily, Ethlin sat and leant her weary body against a column, wincing at the red patch on her calf, which she suspected would bruise. Arlian caressed it and she smiled. No one would believe a high official's son could adore her so much, unless they were seen like this, which was why the rarely used Royal Training Courtyard was the perfect meeting place. It was more spacious and far nicer than the servants' corridor, where he had first met her training with a broom, while he was sneaking a late-night snack from the kitchens. How had that been over a year ago? A year since her dream of becoming a soldier began to seem achievable and a man she never expected to meet had walked into her life, claimed his place, and stayed.

"She is pushing us harder," Arlian commented, his usually playful face serious.

Ethlin sighed. "You don't think it's because she wants my rank to be high enough for us to marry before I fall pregnant?"

Arlian flashed a nervous grin, and Ethlin smiled wickedly. Kitchen servants under twenty weren't supposed to marry without the approval of their legal guardian, the Head Cook, and having unauthorised children could see her sacked.

"She's quieter lately too," Arlian added. "And Ruarnon keeps to themself more than usual in our lessons."

Ethlin shivered. "You don't think there's a chance of war? That she's pushing us harder so I have a chance of defending myself when the time comes?"

Arlian squeezed her hand. "No one expects peace to last forever. It never does with the Zaldeaans. I think she might. We'd better keep giving our training everything we have, just in case."

Ethlin nodded, then rested her weary head on his shoulder. He wrapped his tanned arms around her waist, and she felt the strength of them. If her chance to gain rank in the army, to become eligible to marry him, came more swiftly and brutally than they had hoped, at least they would face war together.

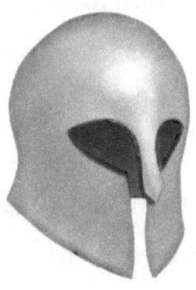

CHAPTER 7

TREACHERY IN THE ZALDEAAN REALM

10 MAR: *the Zaldeaan Realm*

That night, Governor Iomar leant on the cold stone battlements of his castle's keep. Lamps in his seaside stone city had long since gone out, leaving a dim world beneath twin moons, punctuated by the occasional hooting of owls and bats flapping through Wilder's Forest further north. Iomar missed Aoran. His cousin and king needed Aoran's support in Zaldeaa City, but Aoran and Iomar hadn't spent much time apart since they began courting.

Time alone meant time for Iomar to brood on his suspicions that his people accepted him as governor only because of his father and twin brother's power and reputations. Iomar lacked Iagl's military prowess and his bold leadership style. Zaldeaans weren't inclined to embrace quiet, introspective leaders like Iomar. He longed to be obeyed out of respect for his leadership instead of fear of his family, but it was late to be thinking of such things.

Iomar sighed as he turned towards the torch-lit spiral stone steps that led to his chambers' privacy. A gust of wind blowing a trouser leg out of the shadows was his only warning. He slid the blades concealed up his sleeves into trembling hands. "Don't give him a chance," Iagl had said during training. Iomar's breaths came raggedly as the man raised his arm. A blade flashed in the moonlight, spinning end over end. Iomar deflected it.

His attacker charged and Iomar kicked out, knocking the man's legs from under him. The man sprawled, cracking his cloaked head on the stone roof. Were those muffled footsteps? Another blade flashed towards Iomar. He ducked, throwing his first knife at a cloaked man emerging from the stairs. The second attacker clutched at his neck as Iomar's blade lodged in it. He fell.

Iomar gasped for breath, sweat streaking his brow as he turned to two guards thumping up the stairs. The guards his attackers must have walked right past...

A blade flashed near the ground. His first attacker was still conscious. Iomar leapt the slash and stabbed the man in the neck with his belt knife. He switched the blade to his right hand and drew a second knife from his boot.

The first guard's eyes widened at the sight of the fallen assassins. He reached for a weapon, and Iomar knew him for a traitor. Iomar threw his knife. It lodged in the man's throat before he could draw his short sword. The second guard opened his mouth to protest, but Iomar silenced him by throwing his boot knife into the man's chest.

Both men collapsed. Iomar gasped for air in the eerrie silence. Dark pools of blood expanded around all four men. Dazed, Iomar retrieved his boot knife, wiping it on his would-be attacker's clothes. Derlan had spent Iomar's entire childhood looking down on him for being quiet and reserved, for not showing the aggression that came naturally to Iagl in sparring. If Derlan had seen him tonight...

Iomar returned the clean dagger to his boot. He withdrew and cleaned his belt knife, breath coming too quickly, insufficient air reaching his lungs. He stowed the knife in its sheath and stood, leaning on the crenellations behind him.

More footsteps thudded up the stairs. Iomar's muscles went rigid with tension. The captain of his guards rushed out of the stairwell, sword in hand. His gaze swept Iomar, then scanned the tower. His eyes widened at the bodies.

"I am sorry, Excellency. I have failed you. I was suspicious of those two. One of my spies saw them receiving secret messages, but a search of their chambers turned up nothing." He shook his head. "Men are rarely so careful in concealing love letters from married mistresses. I should have realised it was this serious."

Iomar's brows furrowed.

His captain sighed. "I suspect the papers they received were orders to let these two assassins slip past."

"You think they were in someone else's pay?" Iomar asked.

"They have only served you for two months and they seemed better trained by their previous employer than most guards are when we first employ them. I wonder if that training included keeping their cool while committing high treason. My spy saw nothing suspicious or guilty in their behaviour as they waited for the assassins they admitted tonight."

Iomar shivered. Two months was a long time for another employer to pay people only actively working for Iomar. That and the fact his captain's spy hadn't noticed anything suspicious about their behaviour suggested the treacherous guards were employed by someone very wealthy.

The captain's brows furrowed as he studied the guard's bodies. Iomar's stomach roiled and he turned away.

"From the fact they came up here," said the captain, "instead of fleeing when they suspected the assassins had failed, I suspect they were ordered to finish the job should the assassins fail. That whoever ordered this attack thought they had taken every precaution to succeed and underestimated your skills in defending yourself."

He nodded at Iomar's first and second throwing knives, still lodged in throats. "They don't know your preferred means either. If I may, I suggest that when you report this attack, you mention that I helped defend you."

Iomar nodded slowly. Very few people knew he had trained with assassins' throwing knives. Iagl had suggested it and found his tutor, quietly. It was a secret he intended to keep as it gave him a greater chance of survival than anyone who wanted him dead would anticipate, as would people's belief he depended on his captain's assistance to defend himself. It was a bitter thought, but the memory of how blood pooled around the bodies still had his stomach roiling. He could never share his culture's pride in killing, not even to win his people's respect. He was determined to achieve that by better means.

"I will have the rest of your bodyguards moved to a secure room for the night and interrogate them in the morning. Regular castle guards can replace them. I will also change the roster so that only those who have served your excellence for a year or more are on guard duty while we investigate."

Iomar nodded, hearing the words but not seeing anything around him, the world spinning, as he tried to register that two of his bodyguards had just tried to kill him.

"I suggest heading back to your chambers and pouring yourself a large glass of whatever you drink in place of alcohol," the captain added. "I can accompany you and we can fetch more fitting guards for your door along the way."

Iomar smiled nervously. "I might like some wine after this."

He didn't usually drink. He preferred to remain sober and keep his knives sharp, especially now that King Kyomi, the man who had appointed him without widespread approval, was dead.

"I will have the servants send up a jug," said his captain. "And my men clear this mess," he added gravely. "A pity you couldn't leave one alive for questioning, but I assume you weren't sure how many there were."

Iomar nodded. "At this hour, I don't take anything for granted."

The captain bowed his head. "It appears neither of us can afford to."

The captain and his most trusted men guarded Iomar's door that night, and Iomar drank until the relaxing effect of alcohol made him admit he was tired, then went to bed.

The following day, while Iomar dressed and broke his fast, his gaze kept straying to his door and his thoughts to the men who guarded it. Only long-serving guards he trusted were on duty, but once he rose and left his chambers, his gaze was drawn to guards at every intersection of corridors inside the castle. When he entered the library, he was aware of how many librarians and scribes were present, where they were stationed, and of the soft shuffling each time one rose to move among the shelves.

While Iomar sat pouring over records, his legs tensed, his fingers tingled, and his heart raced to pump blood around his body to prepare it to fight. He put down the records and took a deep breath. The warriors called this 'survival sickness'— when the threat is gone but the body and mind malfunction, staying alert and prepared to fight, regardless of the danger having passed. With his trust in the people who were supposed to protect him broken, Iomar's home did not feel safe anymore.

He stood, deciding to visit Kyura and Aoran earlier than planned. He still felt tense when he climbed into his carriage, knowing guards rode with the driver ahead, and the journey would take a couple of days.

By the time they neared the palace, he felt calmer. Calm enough to consider who may want him dead and why. Some saw warriors taking each other as lovers as manly. Many weren't sure what to make of the quieter, more scholarly Iomar taking Aoran as his lover, but they were discreet, and his warriors accepted their relationship. He doubted hatred was behind this. With the money and organisation involved, the motivation was likely political. But trying to kill Iomar would only put Iagl on the warpath, and it wasn't a reliable way to seize his position as governor.

When Iomar reached the king's private gardens, he asked his guards to remain in the corridor. After all, only the king, his direct blood relatives, and their chosen attendants were permitted by law to wander these gardens. The voice of reason told him someone powerful enough to hire two well trained, traitorous bodyguards and assassins could be family, but his mind fled from the thought, as he entered the gates.

The gardens were no longer the place he usually admired. Flowers and leaves drooped, wilted, and the hedges protruded out over the gravel path, overgrown. As if Kyura hadn't let the gardeners in to do their job... Heir Ruarnon's would-be assassins had attacked from a concealed position in the palace gardens. Did Kyura feel untrusting of late?

Iomar halted before the trees concealing Kyura's balcony. If someone was bold enough to try to kill the Heir of Tarlah in the palace and Iomar in his provincial castle, would they dare to kill the king? Kings of old claimed that the royal line was descended from the War God Jormaan and the Mother Goddess Fahria. Kings were sacred. Only Iomar's grandfather had dared move against a Zaldeaan king, deposing his own father for hesitating to reconquer Tarlah after it revolted. But Iomar's great-grandfather had been confined to the palace, allowed to live out his last two years. Would anyone dare try to kill a king outright?

"There is a rumour in the streets that Jormaan turns to us favourably once more." Iomar's father, Derlan's voice drifted from the nearby balcony. "That with the Timbalen Empire absent, the wealth of Tarlah and its gold mines are ours for the taking. And that Jormaan will aid our warriors to glory and the conquest of the final province of our empire at last."

Iomar clenched his jaw. Kyura may not notice Derlan's tone, but Iomar suspected Derlan sympathised with the rumour he was reporting. It was a line from the Warriors Creed, which Derlan had always admired, despite it losing public favour when war with the Timbalens for control of Tarlah had dragged on too long. The rumour sounded designed to persuade the people to *want* war.

"With the Timbalen Empire's absence, I suspect this view will grow in popularity," Derlan continued.

"You would have us declare war?" Kyura and Iomar's half-uncle Karmarn countered.

Iomar's hands balled into fists. Was that the real reason Derlan had come to court? To whisper in Kyura's ear in the hope of persuading him to invade Tarlah? That instead of being governor of just the far south of the Zaldeaan Realm, Derlan may find himself governor of Tarlah too?

"If you would protect your wife's people from invasion, I suggest negotiations with Tarlah," Derlan countered. "They cannot hope to stand against us alone."

Iomar frowned. Was that how Derlan would counter Kyura's unwillingness to go to war? Pressure the Tarlahns to cede, because they didn't stand a chance against a Zaldeaan invasion without their allies?

"Please excuse me," said Karmarn.

Iomar heard retreating footsteps, then his father spoke again. "You know that Karmarn is very much in love with his wife? The man tries to be loyal to her, Tarlah, and the Realm. I would not rely too heavily on him if I were you. I would question his ability to read the mood of our people, as he does not want to recognise it because it does not align with all he holds dear."

Iomar's body went rigid. So Derlan wanted to discourage Kyura from listening to the uncle who approved of peace with Tarlah. Derlan was here out of self-interest, and if he spoke so openly, Aoran must be absent. It would be unwise to let Derlan continue thinking he was alone with Kyura.

Iomar strode forwards quietly so it wasn't obvious he'd been listening in. As he walked beneath the balcony, he called out and heard his father excusing himself. Iomar climbed the garden steps to his cousin and Kyura's face split in a smile as Iomar rushed forwards to embrace him.

"It is wonderful to see you," Kyura said as they stepped apart, gesturing Iomar into a chair. "Aoran has been good company. He's rarely left my side, but Uncle Derlan wanted a word in private."

"Be wary of my father," said Iomar. "I doubt compassion or goodwill for you brings him here. I suspect he has his own reasons."

Kyura raised his wine goblet, emptying it, despite it being only early afternoon. Iomar bit his lip. Their grandfather's reign had been significantly shortened by the man drinking himself to death.

Kyura's brows furrowed, and when Iomar looked closely, he saw dark circles ringing his cousin's eyes. "What troubles you?" Iomar asked.

Kyura grimaced. "My Spymaster and the captain of my guards cannot identify the Tarlahn Heir's would-be assassin, nor the origin of rumours that the time is ripe for conquering

Tarlah. Someone is promoting war against my will, and no one can identify who."

Iomar shivered. Talk of war in the streets and the attempt on the Tarlahn Heir's life suggested the attack on Iomar's life was to do with war. Uncle Kyomi had appointed Iomar, Iagl, and Kia as governors because they swore, as Kyura had, never to declare war. Was the attempt on Iomar's life an attempt to remove one of Kyura's allies from the cause of peace?

"I suspect members of my Council," Kyura continued. "I am unsure if my Spymaster is inept, assisting them, or a warmonger himself."

Iomar's grip on the goblet Kyura had offered him tightened. So Kyura was also facing treachery? He seemed highly functional, given how hard Lenine's death must have hit him. Did Iomar risk jeopardising that by telling his cousin someone had tried to kill him too?

"I am not certain father's illness was indeed illness," Kyura continued quietly. "All this talk of: 'Isn't it a great time to conquer Tarlah? And look, the Peacemaker has conveniently become ill and died, and our king is so sensitive that if we just twist his arm, he'll give in.'"

Iomar took a deep breath and exhaled slowly. Kyomi's death being murder by poisoning was possible and terrible indeed. And Iomar had overheard talk on his way to the palace which suggested it may be part of a conspiracy.

"Kyura, on our way here my guards overheard soldiers chatting eagerly about how the prize money for the upcoming

Military Games has been doubled. The Games will have every able-bodied man training in combat. Coupled with talk of war and a highly organised attempt on the Tarlahn Heir's life,"— *And on mine*, he thought—"it seems multiple ranking Zaldeaans may be conspiring to return our Realm to war. You may be right about Kyomi too: that may have been the beginning of a conspiracy."

Kyura shuddered. "I wish I had Lenine's head for politics! I miss her terribly."

His gaze fell, and he drank deeply from a second goblet of wine. Iomar's mind wandered to another Zaldeaan woman highly accomplished at politics, his cousin Syenne. On his way through the palace, Iomar and his entourage had passed a meeting in the Treasury. Every man present had been attended by a female scribe. He'd heard rumours it was becoming a trend in Zaldeaa City. There was talk of "how neatly women write" and how "good housewives keep orderly papers." And "women are so flighty it was not as if they would retain what men were dictating to them." If Syenne had started those rumours and put those women in place, then she was infiltrating Kyura's court with her spies at *every* level. It would be just like her to use Zaldeaan men's most ridiculous beliefs against them.

"What has Syenne been doing?" Iomar asked hesitantly.

"Keeping an eye on dissent," Kyura replied.

Fear clouded Iomar's thoughts. "Kyura, I suspect she has convinced half your court to take on women secretaries, and those secretaries are spies reporting directly to her. That would give her access to a lot of information."

The rumours that put those spies in place were similar to those encouraging war among the people. Surely Kyomi had made Syenne swear to uphold the Peace when he swore her in as governor? But if Kyura was right, and Kyomi's devotion to peace had got him killed, what if Syenne no longer supported peace?

"I know," Kyura said with a sigh. "I should take more control, as Karmarn and Derlan keep telling me. I wish Kia were here. She's the only one who doesn't always talk business."

"Why isn't she here?" Iomar asked.

"She wrote to say she was 'indisposed,'" Kyura replied. "Uncle Derlan fears she is pregnant out of wedlock and concealing it."

Iomar shivered at the timing. He could shield his cousin from his secret no longer. "Kyura, I was attacked a week ago. By a pair of assassins atop the highest tower in my castle. The captain of my guards and I are convinced two of my bodyguards were traitors from the moment I hired them, ordered to turn a blind eye and let assassins throw me down the stairs. What if Kia has been attacked too?"

CHAPTER 8

DESCENT OF DARKNESS

KYURA: *the Zaldeaan Realm*

Kyura's head swam, and he doubted it was because of the wine he'd been drinking so freely. He seized a glass of water and tried drinking that instead. It didn't distract him from the knowledge that his younger sister and Iomar were both pledged to uphold the Peace, and his most vulnerable supporters. Both might have been targeted by assassins, which made him wonder if Uncle Karmarn would be next. Was someone trying to bully him into declaring war by killing off his supporters? Or did they think he would stop insisting on peace if his supporters were all dead?

He shivered. To his knowledge, Syenne hadn't experienced an attempt on her life recently. But would she burden him with the news if she had? He was losing count of how many assassinations attempts she had dodged since becoming governor.

"Where does Iagl stand in this Chaos-ridden mess?" Kyura asked Iomar.

Iomar's shoulders slumped. "He was raised by soldiers as much as by my father after Mother died. He thinks war is inevitable, sooner or later, and that we are idealists who will be brought harshly back to reality. I doubt anyone would bother trying to kill him. They probably hope he will lead an invasion of Tarlah."

Kyura slammed his goblet down on the side table. It was almost as if Iagl made a point of being blunt, as if he chose to be the opposite of his reserved twin. But Iagl could be as pragmatic as Syenne, and Kyura suspected that despite all he hoped for, Iagl might be right.

A knock on the door in the wall behind him interrupted their conversation. The door opened before Kyura gave permission for anyone to step onto his balcony. He frowned as Companion Karmarn strode in, and reached for his water glass, suspecting he'd had too much wine to deal with Karmarn's news.

"What is it?"

"A thousand of our men are marching to war against Tarlah."

Kyura blinked, then swayed in his seat. That *couldn't* be true. But Karmarn's ever-serious face left no room for doubt. Kyura's head began to spin.

"Word is spreading on the border of Governor Iomar's province that we are marching to war. Governor Kia has halted farmers marching towards her capital, who assumed the call for soldiers to levy has yet to reach them. In Governor Iomar's absence, his levied soldiers have begun to march. Professional soldiers are marching with them."

Kyura dropped the water glass. It smashed, spilling across the floor. With Kia rounding up stray soldiers, Iagl was his only family member still at home. Surely Iagl hadn't done this while Kyura was distracted, giving in to what he saw as inevitable in his brother's province? Surely Syenne wasn't abusing her use of spies? Or had the First General taken matters into his own hands? How did Kyura counter treachery when he didn't know who the traitors were or how they would strike next?

Kyura turned at soft footsteps and saw Syenne entering the room. She pointedly eyed servants cleaning the floor, and the servants stood and hurried out. "I came to report that my spies have uncovered secret communication between the Second General and the Treasurer. The General sent orders to the countryside. Are soldiers moving without your permission, brother?"

"They're marching to war," Kyura replied. How dare they! They knew their king approved of peace. This was treason of the bloodiest kind! He leaned forward, hunching against the pain that they would dare take up arms without him. Did they not even acknowledge him as their king?

"I have ordered the Second General's arrest on your behalf," Syenne added, "but the movement of soldiers will make others think they too should march. This situation must be dealt with swiftly."

He felt his cousin's gaze.

"Do not give up hope, cousin! Those are your men marching, believing themselves to do so on your orders. Tell them there was a misunderstanding. Order them home."

Kyura blanched. It wouldn't be that simple. "What will people in the streets say when I tell them the war is off and they should go back to their lives, now that their heads are filled with dreams of glory, wealth, rank, and positions of comfort? What will they think of me telling them a thousand of my men marched to war by mistake? That I refuse to claim the last province of our empire, despite our greatest opponents, the Timbalens, appearing gone for good?"

They would think him a coward. Weak. Inept. How long would it take them to challenge his rule then?

"Kyura, you are their king!" said Iomar. "Every soldier is sworn to serve you! Make your will clear, and they will serve it!"

But would they? Kyura had tried so hard since Lenine died just over six weeks ago, but now people were conspiring against him and his army was mutinying. He could give the regency to Derlan and take a break from the pressure of swimming against the tide of war. But Derlan may prefer war to peace. Syenne was wise, calm, and stable, but Iomar was right. She was gaining too much power. And as much as he trusted Uncle Karmarn, his subjects would not accept the peace-approving bastard son of a late king, much less one who had married a Tarlahn. Kyura was too weary to see how to deal with the mutiny, nor could he think whom to appoint to deal with it before he lost control of his levied soldiers.

"Kyura," said Syenne, "deal with the situation at hand as best you can. Ask for help if you need it. And if you cannot manage at this time, appoint a regent."

Kyura shivered. He was too tired to deal with grief, treachery, and mutiny all at once. But if he didn't take the situation in hand, his reign and order in the Zaldeaan Realm could collapse. And whoever had tried to kill his cousin may keep trying to kill his relatives. He must do something, and he must do it now.

He strode out of the room towards the meeting hall, ordering a servant to summon the Council. He saw Iomar hesitate and motioned him forward. Syenne followed. Karmarn trailed after them.

The meeting hall's tall columns were plated with silver, the long central table inlaid with ivory figures of soldiers marching to war. Silver platters and crystal goblets adorned the table, the platters rimmed with crossed miniature sword blades. They made Kyura nauseous.

His advisors and generals entered, bowing their heads just enough to evade accusations of rudeness. His officials sat upright in feigned readiness to serve. All eyes focused on Kyura.

"Highest, it appears a fever for war has gripped the countryside. The commoners are quite losing their heads over it," the Rural Overseer reported.

"Apologies on my delayed report, Highest," said the Spymaster. "The rumours spread so fast that my spies have been tracing them in circles."

"This march of soldiers is an embarrassment to our office and yours, Highest. We must move to claim this movement immediately," said the Vizier.

They all wanted war. Were they working together? The Rural Overseer, had he spread talk of war to the provinces? The Spymaster—who better to spread secret messages the Realm over? The Vizier, was he running this show?

"Claim it?" Second Companion Armar challenged. "Highest does not approve of war. Do you propose he change his mind to suit the masses?"

"The alternative is for the crown to lose prestige by admitting that the masses are acting without consideration of Highest's will," the cunning Vizier objected.

Whether they wore masks of feigned concern or genuine nerves, all faces turned to Kyura. He was weak. They knew it. If he ordered those soldiers to ride home, everyone would know. His own Council had lost respect for him—if they ever had it. They were all going to suggest he order an official levying of soldiers to save face. What other choice did he have?

"Highest," said the battle-scarred First General. Kyura's body tensed as figures around the table leaned in. This was the argument they anticipated him giving in to. "With the Timbalen Empire gone, Tarlah will fall. I know you do not desire bloodshed, but the goal of our empire is near at hand. Our people long for it. Our greatest opponents over the sea can no longer keep it from us. Leading an invasion now and conquering Tarlah would make you the greatest of Zaldeaan kings."

"Is this the will of this Council?" Karmarn asked with such authority that he raised eyebrows.

Others spoke in protest, and Kyura saw Iomar noting men likely to support him rather than pursuing whatever offices they aspired to if Tarlah fell. But many agreed. How did one man resist the will of most of his kingdom and most of the people who were supposed to help him run it? Kyura had no answers. Trying to think of them felt like trying to drink from an empty cup.

"Kyura?"

Kyura hadn't noticed the Council leave. He vaguely remembered Iomar dismissing them. When had the people turned against him? When had his court begun thinking exclusively of themselves? It didn't matter now. Did he leave the warmongering fools to their fate and choose exile in

Tarlah? Did he wait for the next assassination attempt to kill someone he loved?

"I have two choices," he replied to Karmarn. "I admit I am losing control of my court, provinces, and army. I insist on peace and sit here doing nothing while my spies fail to identify traitors. I let people defect to whoever boldly leads them on the invasion they are clamouring for. I give whoever is plotting against me from on high the opportunity to usurp me like Grandfather usurped Great-Grandfather when he refused to invade Tarlah after its revolt."

He gripped his armrest and struggled to ignore the pressure and pain building in his head, but managed to keep his voice steady. "I try to weed traitors out of my court from a position of growing weakness."

Kyura's posture straightened. "Or I take command. I win the respect of my army before my lack of control causes them to view me with contempt. I act as they believe a king should, taking Tarlah and establishing my rule beyond the power of any to seize it from me."

He raised a hand to rub his aching head. He wanted to fight those ideas. It hurt just to say them. But ignoring that last option now meant accepting the failure of his rule.

"Then our enemies have won," Karmarn said softly.

"Don't let them," Iomar objected.

"What power is left to me if I do not?" Kyura asked as despair lapped at him.

"Interrogate the Second General Syenne arrested," Karmarn replied. "Have spies you trust note who is unnerved by his arrest and identify his allies. Beyond that, your people are being duped. Call out the liars. Publicly execute the general for treason, as a warning to the rest. Stand up and tell the people your will. Do not rely on second-hand reports, which may originate from traitors. Let your people show you their loyalty. They loved your father, and I do not believe they would forget his legacy so swiftly if they saw that his son has not. Many might change their tune, if your position was publicly announced."

"I made my position clear the day I was crowned king!" Kyura retorted, his eyes burning with tears. He had tried so hard to hold everything together, but it was all coming undone.

"A lot has happened since," Karmarn said sympathetically.

"They think that has changed me? I lost my father, wife, and son, so now I must wish to lead theirs and the Tarlahns to their deaths by declaring war?"

Derlan turned to him. "There is talk that having lost so much, you doubt yourself. You wonder if acting in line with Jormaan would restore your family to prosperity, as well as the kingdom."

"I lose those dearest to me, and my people believe *I* need to redeem myself? How faithless are they? What is the point of winning back such people?" He paused. "But there is no other way to win their respect."

"Kyura, if you declare war, I fear those who serve you for self-gain will only seek to manipulate you further to their benefit," Iomar warned softly.

"But if I win the army's respect, if I secure their loyalty through the conquest of Tarlah, I can execute the traitors with the army's backing. I can finally assert myself."

The idea that commitment to his father's ideals and his abhorrence of war was becoming his single greatest obstacle to maintaining his grip on power tore at Kyura. He seized a goblet and squeezed it, knowing commitment to his father's ideals now might see him deposed. It might even get him killed. And refusing to declare war would likely see more attempts on his family's lives.

He raised the goblet and hurled it, dashing it loudly against the wall. It rebounded, spraying the whitewashed stone with red wine, which dripped down like blood.

"I cannot save my subjects from their foolish beliefs about war. I am sorry, Uncle Karmarn, but that means I cannot protect Tarlah. I would save what I have left of my family, and my only hope of ruling this kingdom without following my father into an early grave."

Derlan blanched and Karmarn's eyes widened. "You do not think my brother was..."

"I do. Dead men can't maintain peace. But a king facing revolt can't achieve anything. I am not my father. As much as I want to be him, I cannot!"

"I would not have you invade my wife's country to protect me," Karmarn said quietly. "Nor would I see my nephews, nieces, my wife and son deposed and murdered. I would say kill the traitors. But I fear they are not all unmasked yet."

There was an awkward silence in which Karmarn sighed and Aoran's gaze darted fearfully around the room, but Syenne, Uncle Karmarn, and Uncle Derlan's faces were unreadable. The tiny part of Kyura's mind which still had the energy to analyse the situation wondered if it was wise to tell everyone in this room how he honestly felt. But it was too late now. Everything was too late. Perhaps Lenine could have found a way to preserve his father's legacy, but Kyura wasn't clever enough. He could barely sleep at night. And he dared not test how long he could oppose war before one of his relatives was successfully assassinated. He refused to sacrifice his family for peace when most of his fool subjects wanted war anyway. His only choices were to give in or to give up.

"The Zaldeaan Realm goes to war," he declared woodenly. "Send out the call to rally the levies."

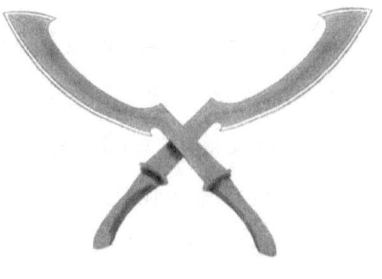

CHAPTER 9

RAIN BEGINS TO FALL

RUARNON: *Tarlah City*

K ing Kyura will declare war," Regent Omah announced to the Tarlahn Royal Council from the head of the table, two weeks after Ruarnon's parents' abduction.

Worried faces blurred before Ruarnon. The Council's theories on who tried to kill Ruarnon and who succeeded in abducting their parents ranged from high officials within the court to Kyura's relatives, the Zaldeaan provincial governors. The Council had as little evidence for one candidate as for the next. And probably no idea who had succeeded in pushing Kyura to war, or how. Ruarnon turned to Omah, their mouth hanging open in bewilderment.

"He fears his army siding with a rival candidate for his throne if he refuses to declare war," Omah explained. "That they will depose him and invade us. There is evidence of a plot to promote war. Kyura fears its hidden architect becoming apparent when they usurp him. Governor Iomar tried pleading after Kyura decided to declare war. Kyura was heard screaming and carried back to his chambers by his bodyguards. He was inconsolable, unable to see beyond his fears and insecurities. If we try to reason with him further, we may have a mad king on the throne."

Ruarnon sat stunned.

"Is that worse than another member of his family claiming the regency?" Companion Pamoran asked.

"I do not trust Syenne, Derlan, or Iagl," Monin replied. "They are the most likely regents or successors, and any one of them may lead the Realm to war against us."

"Our second ambassador refuses to negotiate further with Kyura," Omah added.

"Then it is a moot point," said Companion Pamoran. "If he will not negotiate, and with our messages by ship and bird being cut off before they reach Kyura, we can neither negotiate nor influence the rule of the Realm."

Ruarnon saw pain stir in Uncle Omah's eyes. Aunt Telena squeezed his hand. Ruarnon slumped. Lenaris' claims that their people would be willing to fight, combined with their fears their allies would not come, that Tarlah would fall and everyone around this table would be executed, made Ruarnon so dizzy they had to clutch the tabletop to feel that something in Umarinaris was steady.

They stood automatically when the meeting finished, filing out with the rest. Every event they'd read in history—devastating battle tactics, bloody sieges, the massacre the first time Tarlah City fell—went crashing through their mind. It was too terrible to be true.

They were barely aware of a servant calling them to the throne room, or taking their place near the dais as a Zaldeaan official arrived. Ruarnon noted the man's surprise on seeing Omah and Telena seated on silver plated chairs before the king and queen's empty thrones. If King Kyura's official didn't know of Ruarnon's parents' abduction, did Kyura?

Ruarnon spent the reception and recitation of Kyura's declaration of war worrying about who had taken their parents and whether Mother and Father still lived. But Ruarnon tried to wrench their thoughts back to their duties when most people had left and Uncle Omah stood and approached them.

"You'll be crowned Regent now?" Ruarnon asked. "I suppose I will have to start my co-regency early."

Omah bowed his head. "It is also time to tell the people we are at war and to announce your co-regency. As Junior Regent, you will continue to attend Council meetings, and Companion Tor will guide you. I do not expect you to formulate policy or implement it, but you will set an example for our subjects. If you need to rage, do it in private. Talk to Lenaris, myself, or your aunt behind closed doors if you are concerned.

"From now on, every corridor in which a single servant can see you is your stage and the language of your body, face, and words will govern the mood of our people alongside mine. If you appear calm, it will ease our subjects' anxiety. If you are optimistic, it will give them hope. If you are brave, it will give them courage. If you demonstrate that you have faith in them, they will believe in themselves and each other. My challenge is to lead by example whenever you are in public. Can you do this?"

Ruarnon forced a smile. "I used to resent Father sometimes. But he was preparing me for this all along." Ruarnon's fists clenched as facts from *The Bloody Occupation* leapt to mind. "If I don't dwell on the fact that the most frightening things I've read about may soon unfold, then yes, I can."

Omah didn't speak. A hundred thoughts seemed to flicker across his face. His eyes lowered sadly, but his lips turned to smile, and Ruarnon saw regret too.

"It has to be you," Omah said quietly. "You are Heir, child of the captured king and queen. If you can be brave, so can anyone. In theory, my sister Merlah could be Co-Regent. She is older and has valuable experience, but her duty is with your Uncle Kar. And you should know, some believe I am behind your parents' disappearance. Our co-regency will give them confidence that the succession will prevail according to tradition."

"Anyone who thinks that about you has straw for brains," Ruarnon assured him, responding instinctively to the hurt in their uncle's eyes. "And I suppose it makes sense for Aunt Merlah to stay with Uncle Kar and help command South Harbour, in case southern Tarlah is attacked by Zaldeaan ships. But we should lead our subjects by showing them how wrong they are, instead of publicly accusing them of foolishness."

For a moment fear, uncertainty, or guilt, became pronounced in Omah's eyes, and then he smiled. "I hope that when you are Ruler, your policy will be guided by the former and not the latter."

Ruarnon smiled at the first joke their uncle had made in weeks. Omah was only eight years older than Lenaris, but he had the same ageless wisdom as King Urmillian.

"Has anyone said you rule as well as my father?" Ruarnon asked.

Omah smiled and shook his head. "We were a king's great-nephews, and no one foresaw my brother becoming king, even had the Rebellion succeeded. Urmillian had much to learn after his coronation, and he didn't want it forgotten. He asked me to guide you, should anything happen to him. Have I succeeded so far?"

The vulnerability on their uncle's young face was such a surprise, such a contrast to the grave wisdom he displayed as Regent. It contrasted with Ruarnon's father's unfailing calm and understanding. It showed Ruarnon that kings were human. Kings still felt. Kings had doubts. They were not so different.

Ruarnon reflected on recent conversations with their uncle and replied, "You picked up my teaching where father left off."

Omah smiled again.

"Have you doubted all along? I never realised."

"If one person can see you, you are on stage. I did not think I could be Uncle Omah and Regent both. And you have Aunt Telena. What you need from me is Senior Regent."

Ruarnon nodded slowly. Becoming Co-Regent was their way forwards from their parent's abduction, and they needed help.

"Are you still Omah sometimes?" Ruarnon asked.

"When Telena and I are in our anteroom, we are the Regent and his Wife Advisor, but in the rest of our chambers, we are Omah and Telena. No matter what the regency demands, you need time as yourself. I think King Kyura lost who he was, becoming only Kyura the peace-loving king, frightened of traitors sabotaging the Peace, and it destroyed him."

"Benevolence, the people are ready," a voice called across the empty throne room.

Omah turned to Tor in acknowledgement, and Ruarnon saw that his face was determined, focused, and purposeful again. It wasn't a mask. Their uncle selected the face he needed, wore it, and became it.

Ruarnon exhaled deeply as they straightened their shoulders and followed their uncle. Omah looked back and smiled approvingly. The pair turned firm faces down the corridor, chins held high as they walked to the edge of a balcony overlooking a crowded courtyard.

Ruarnon gazed over the stone railing at people wearing silks, gold jewellery and precious stones, linens and copper jewellery, or bronze helmets, leather tunics, and swords. Officials, scribes, servants, soldiers: every castle inhabitant had come, from wizened crones to newborn babes. Beyond, the city's residents crowded from the courtyard gates down North Road into the city. They waited in silence, their expectant faces uplifted to Regent Omah.

"Good people of Tarlah City," Omah announced in a clear, carrying voice, "You know of the expulsion of our officials from Zaldeaa City, the attempted murder before they left, and that our Rulers have been indisposed for four weeks. The reason behind these events is that some Zaldeaans desired another conquest of Tarlah, but their king did not.

"The enemy tried to manipulate us to violate King Kyomi's Peace. To this end, they drugged our guards and abducted our Ruler. We refused to do the enemy's bidding. So warlords sought followers and gained the upper hand. It is my regretful duty to inform you that King Kyura has declared war. In four weeks, on the first day of winter, we march."

Among the crowd, young faces paled, eyes widening in fear. Older servants, officials, and their families looked grimmer with Omah's every word, and Ruarnon's heart grew heavy.

"In light of these events, it pleases me to announce that Heir Ruarnon shall take up the Junior Regency. We shall lead you together in war."

Hundreds of faces turned to Ruarnon. They held their breath, bracing against far too much attention, as the crowd's cheers and clapping filled the courtyard. Wondering what their people could see in them that was of comfort was an effective distraction. But as faces continued to smile, Ruarnon realised they gave their people hope as the shadow of war moved over Tarlah. Their uncle's words sounded again in their mind, "If you are brave, it will give them courage."

Instinctively, Ruarnon raised their right hand in salute, symbolising *Tarlah stands*, a message of defiance from the Wars. Doubt hardened to determination, uncertainty to grim commitment as arms returned the salute.

The salute broke into enthusiastic cheers, and Omah smiled at Ruarnon. Then Ruarnon saw her. Lenaris clapped near the front, her eyes shining with tears, her expression set with determination. Arlian paled behind her, looking nervously through the crowd. Other officials' children they attended lessons with stared in shock, and tears came to Ruarnon's eyes as their generation struggled with the fact that the safe world they knew had ended.

"I recommend that all children, elderly, and sick be evacuated from the capital soon," Regent Omah announced, "as a precaution."

That sent murmuring through the crowd, as parents reached to hold children. But Ruarnon saw nearby soldiers' jaws clench and eyes gaze steadily, upright postures indicating firm resolution.

"We shall prepare to meet the enemy as we always have, with the message that Tarlah does not belong to the Zaldeaan Realm."

Soldiers roared. The people cheered and determined salutes rose to both Co-Regents.

An hour later, Ruarnon returned to the throne room with their brown hair bound in a Tarlahn braid, their co-regents' red silk tunic rippling in the breeze. They kept their posture straight as they walked down a red-carpeted aisle between high officials clad in silks and silver chains. Ruarnon's gaze fell on the dais and their aunt and uncle surveying the room from bronze-framed thrones emanating sunbursts. Companion Pamoran and his father Monin flanked the royal couple, and Companion Tor stood before them with a pair of servants, all turning to Ruarnon.

Omah descended the dais, and when Ruarnon halted beside him, Tor asked, "Will you, Omah of Tarlah, swear the Senior Regent's oath?"

"I will," Regent Omah replied, his voice pitched to carry across the seated crowd. "I swear that I shall lead Tarlah by example, and to the best of my ability, in war and peace. By the Ancestors, I so swear."

Tor raised the gold circlet and placed it on Regent Omah's head. The court's applause echoed through the room. Omah turned a gracious, solemn smile to them. Tor motioned, and Ruarnon steeled themself as they knelt, their face a mask of calm, their feelings fluttering in confusion beneath.

"Will you, Heir Ruarnon of Tarlah, child of King Urmillian, swear the co-regent's oath?"

Ruarnon pushed aside the memory of their shock and how Captain Arleath had ordered them to move to safety when they were attacked in the Zaldeaan palace. They tried to let go of the soldier knocking them off their horse, ruining their attempt to delay the carriage and rescue their parents. With Tarlah at war, there was no room for regrets or hesitation, only decisive action.

"I will," Ruarnon replied, looking up. "I swear that I will lead by example, giving my knowledge and abilities as they are to the Royal Council for the governing of Tarlah. I swear to expand my knowledge, pursue wisdom, and develop my leadership in preparation for sole regency. I swear to support and co-operate with the Senior Regent on the rule of Tarlah, in peace and war. By the Ancestors, I so swear."

Tor placed the silver Co-Regent's circlet on Ruarnon's head and the court applauded.

A few days later, Ruarnon woke early. Dread of parting with their friends kept them tossing and turning in their bed, until they wandered to the battlements at sunrise. From the walls, they gazed down into Tarlah City. Banging rose from a side street. The first rays of sunlight lit school doors being boarded shut. Outside the house with the glass window, the woman who had scolded children for playing Throwing Stones stood among anxious families. A groom harnessed two horses to a carriage beside them. The wealthy homeowner raised her voice in exasperation.

"I have no children to send! Get your children into my carriage so Garas can evacuate them to my sister's country house before they get bored, start playing Throwing Stones, and break my window!"

Her words produced smiles and tears. Parents hugged their children, some clinging to them, others helping them onto the carriage. The wealthy woman exchanged a sad smile with the little girl who almost threw a stone near her precious window. Then the girl's father lifted her aboard, kissing her forehead. Two silver-haired women climbed aboard. The father closed the carriage door and parents waved tearfully at small hands and faces poking through the window. The carriage trundled down the cobbled road.

Slowly, Ruarnon's eyes followed it past other families: wealthy parents and servants loading carriages, donkey carts, and handcarts with small children, babies, satchels, and young women or older people to look after them. So many were evacuating the city, uncertainty hovering over them like a cloud.

A small boy in a crowded cart looked around nervously. Ruarnon waved, and the boy turned, tapping his companions and pointing excitedly. Other children saw, and waved to Ruarnon too. The first rays of sunlight fell on the silver Co-Regent's circlet on their head, and a hush fell as adults recognised the Heir and bowed. Ruarnon sighed. It wasn't so uncomfortable when they weren't looking at Ruarnon's face. But they did when they rose again. Ruarnon dismissed the adults swiftly with a salute: *Tarlah stands*. Adults saluted solemnly while children smiled. Ruarnon returned their smiles as parents continued loading children into carriages and carts, which streamed down North and Centre Road, to East, West, South, or North Gates.

"Ruarnon!"

Lenaris stood before a small crowd in the castle courtyard. Ruarnon descended to the main castle steps, biting back reluctance, as the Companions and high officials said goodbye to their families, while nearer the gate, linen-clad servants loaded their children into wagons. Ruarnon said goodbye to Drake and teary younger friends, and their mothers, then turned to Lenaris. Lenaris' face screwed up with emotion, and she reached for Ruarnon and held them firmly. "I wanted to fight," she whispered in their ear. "But my younger sisters are worried about Father, and Mother did not want them worrying about me as well. I will help care for them."

"I did not expect you to be able to stay," Ruarnon whispered back.

She surprised them by kissing their forehead, then climbed into a carriage with her sisters and mother, leaving a void behind her.

Ruarnon blinked back tears, trying not to think how they'd manage without her.

The carriages began to move, one after another. Ruarnon, the Companions, high officials, and their spouses waved goodbye to the young and the elderly as their carriages joined the traffic departing the city. Part of Ruarnon's life went with them.

The departure left only one other person aged under twenty on the palace steps: Arlian. The Censar's son bowed his head to Ruarnon, and Ruarnon bowed solemnly back. Arlian, the scoundrel of every lesson Ruarnon had attended, intended to fight.

"Does Your Benevolence wish to continue your lessons over the coming month?"

Ruarnon started at Companion Tor's voice. Their friends were gone, they were Co-Regent, and Umarinaris had changed.

"What can you teach me of battle tactics?" they asked.

"A good deal," Tor replied with a grim smile.

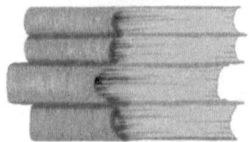

CHAPTER 10

CHANGE

LINH: Four Weeks After Declaration of War, Week Two on Myleth Island

L inh hurried down the main corridor of Myleth Island's castle with Fiona. Troy and Michael strode ahead. Linh's gaze crossed the Umarinaris Book on its reading stand when they entered the library, seeking Nuard beyond. He sat on a wooden chair before scroll-laden shelves, wearing a sympathetic smile. Linh's shoulders sagged. She prepared for disappointment, after a week of wondering whether their only known way home would be confirmed or not. Nuard motioned them to wooden seats on either side of the small room, but Troy stood with his arms crossed, while the others sat.

"I am sorry," said Nuard. "A message arrived from Imperial City this afternoon. The Elite Guard have histories that record them studying an archway, until several died trying to operate it, and further study was banned. No Elite Guard has approached that island's archway for over eighty years. The Elite Guard captain does not believe any of her people could have brought you here."

Linh pulled her feet up onto her chair and hugged her knees. If operating archways could kill an Elite Guard, and they didn't know how to do it, her greatest hope of getting back to Australia was dashed.

"But," said Fiona, "if the Elite Guard are the Guardians' descendants, and the Guardians used the archways to fight the Sorcery War, why don't the Elite Guard know how to operate them?"

Nuard shook his head. "Much was forgotten by the time the Elite Guard formed, under the reigns of the early emperors. The knowledge was probably lost before the Wars of Unity."

"Does that mean no one on this side of Umarinaris can help us?" Troy asked, wringing his hands.

"The Elite Guard Captain believes someone outside our empire may have reached the island you arrived here on, by travelling through an archway to its castle, then opened the archway to your world. Their histories report that not all Guardians sailed this way. If others have descendants in the Far West or the ocean in between, they may be able to help you."

Linh grit her teeth. "How do we find people who may or may not exist, and who could be *anywhere*?"

"Not necessarily. The continent of our former colony Tarlah is also home to the reclusive North Landers, with whom the Elite Guard once had direct contact. The Elite Guard Captain believes their settlement was founded by evacuation from the Far West via an archway. They may remember how to operate the archways. We believe there is at least one archway there."

Hope sparked inside Linh at this reason based on history, instead of myth and rumour, but it was faint, as Tarlah was far away, and how and when could they get there?

"Tell us the bad news," Michael asked. "Why couldn't you confirm whether they have an archway or know how to operate it?"

"There has been no contact with the North Lands since the Sea Wars, from which our emperor retreated during the rebellion on one of our major islands. Timbalen ships have not sailed near Tarlah in force for twenty years, so few merchants dare risk Zaldeaan piracy to trade there, and the Elite Guard have not left this empire since before then."

Linh stood, her limbs tingling, as dizziness washed over her. "Are you telling us our best plan is to sail with a rare Timbalen merchant to Tarlah, hoping we're not attacked by Zaldeaan pirates, then travel north through the kingdom of your allies' enemies, in the hope the North Landers can operate archways to send us home?"

"King Urmillian can contact the North Lands on your behalf. I can write to him, but as he does not know who I am, a merchant's letter about children from myths may be taken for a hoax. My letter may not reach the king, and if it does, with an uneasy peace already on his plate, he may dismiss it as a sailor's tall story."

"Would he believe *us* if we sailed there?" Michael asked.

"If you gained an audience and spoke to him, the fact we gave you passage to Tarlah may open his mind to the possibility that what you tell him is true."

Maybe and *might*. How could that be the most they had to go on to send them on a quest halfway across the known world? Linh's temper flared and her hands balled into fists. "Please excuse me," she said. "I need to shoot something."

She strode from the room, her fists clenching and unclenching at the near-total uncertainty of their situation. For a moment, her rapid heartbeat paced the echo of her footsteps through the empty corridor. Then footsteps echoed behind her. "Do you mind company?"

Linh started. She'd expected Fiona to follow, not Troy.

Venting steam in front of him didn't appeal, but his fists were clenched too, his knuckles turning white. It wouldn't be fair to hog the archery practice boards Nuard's daughter Familon let them use when Troy needed to vent too.

"Why not?" she replied as they turned down a corridor with daylight streaming in from its end.

"Linh?" Fiona called.

"Come with us," said Linh. "It looks nice out. You could sit in the shade."

She turned back and Fiona smiled. Michael wandered after her, his distant gaze suggesting he was lost in thought. He'd become more withdrawn over the past week on Myleth Island.

The castle's back gate beckoned. Troy opened it and Linh squinted against bright sunlight reflecting off golden fields on either side, as they walked down a narrow dirt track. Crossing fields beneath a vast blue sky with wispy clouds floating lazily across it gave Linh an illusion of freedom, but any journey that didn't end at her front door felt too short.

She flung open the crate in the archery yard and she and Troy strapped quivers to their waists, selected bows, then turned to target boards. Linh drew and nocked her arrow, yanking the bowstring as far back as her frustration allowed, then loosed. Her arrow shot towards the bull's eye, striking the ring around it.

Her lips twitched in a small smile. Getting home looked even more complicated than she had anticipated, and there was nothing she could do about it, but at least being able to shoot well made her feel like she had control over *something*. Straightening to draw her bow made her breathe more deeply, while knocking and loosing arrows in the same set of motions, again and again, gradually eased the tension in her torso. She was grateful Familon had taught them to shoot. It was good stress relief.

A little while later, she turned to Troy's target board, wondering why arrows thudded into it only sporadically. One of his arrows was lodged in a tree trunk. Another sailed through the branches. Linh laughed.

Troy tried to glare, but his lips betrayed him with a smile. "Just because you're a great shot in a temper doesn't mean we all are."

Linh met his gaze with a smile. He seemed to be either reckless and not taking anything seriously, or else took it too seriously. Both could annoy her, but today he was making her smile, and smiling eased tension best.

"Have you finished murdering the forest?"

Michael stood in the grass behind them, a few metres from Fiona.

"Maybe," Troy replied. "Got any revelations you'd like to share?"

Michael scowled at the ground. "Whatever Red Cloak was doing on Oval Island, he hasn't bothered us for a week. We could be shot of him. And we can't expect anyone else to share Nuard's enthusiasm or generosity in helping us get home. I think travel's necessary. I just don't know how far."

Linh's shoulders tensed. The other Timbalen scholars talked about Tarlah like it was the far side of the moon. She didn't like to think how hard it might be to leave Myleth Island, let alone reach Tarlah.

"You are early," Familon called from the path through the fields. "And not in the best of spirits," she added, her piercing gaze sweeping over them. "But if you are going to continue training, I should prefer you not decorate our trees with indentations."

She turned to Troy, her mouth set firmly, but her brows slightly raised. Linh suspected that was amusement glinting in her eyes. Troy grinned.

Michael and Fiona gathered their equipment, and Linh loosed more arrows.

On Linh's right, Familon instructed, "Focus, Michael. You are good at this when you put your mind to it."

Linh turned. Michael's arrows were scattered across his board. Maybe they should talk to him more.

Linh loosed another arrow, and Troy shook his head, as it thudded near the bull's eye. "How long did you protest about weapons being dangerous?"

Linh declined to comment.

"About four hours," Michael answered for her.

Linh's brows contracted. "Even *you* got tired after an hour's swimming at the beach," she said to Troy.

"But Michael was right," said Troy. "Helping the villagers mend fishing nets *is* safer."

Troy smirked, and Linh glared at him. Michael shook his head.

"This isn't any different from school camp," said Fiona, and Linh smiled at her friend backing her up.

"Yeah, but sword fighting?" Troy asked. "You both surprised me with that. I mean, Michael's a fast learner at anything, but I didn't think that would be your thing."

Linh's left eyebrow rose. She hadn't anticipated gentle Fiona wanting to duel. When Linh reluctantly picked up a sword and stood opposite Troy, wondering if it could be that hard, Troy had smiled nervously. When they had duelled, he'd sweated a lot, given it was a short bout, and he'd sidestepped to dodge her blow several times. Duelling had seemed an excellent way to pay him back for teasing her, and when she had decided she was happy to duel, Fiona had joined in.

One of Troy's arrows thudded into the outer ring of the target board, and Linh brows rose. She supposed he *was* capable, when he wasn't showing off, or restlessly impatient.

"Draw with all your strength, Fiona," said Familon, as she stepped beside them.

Fiona straightened, fitting an arrow to her bowstring, and her features tightened with concentration as she drew. She loosed. Her arrow whizzed through a grassy clearing towards the line of target boards. It hit the edge of the bull's eye, her first to do so.

"Well done, Fi!" said Linh, hugging her, while Troy grinned.

"I had my doubts," said Familon, "especially with how hesitant you were with a sword, but you have come a long way this week, Fiona."

Fiona's eyes shone.

"Now we require Troy's horse to do consistently as he wishes and your time here will have been well spent."

Troy gave her an innocent smile, and Familon eyed him sharply. Linh suspected Troy's horse did what he wanted all the time, even when it diverted from Familon's instructions. But today, riding was no longer a distraction from waiting to see whether the Elite Guard could help them get home or not. Now, they might have to leave Myleth Island and the Timbalen Empire.

Linh gripped her bow tightly, reluctant to leave the generous hospitality Nuard had shown them and the safety of Myleth Island. Would a captain and crew they had never met be so decent and kind, all the way across the ocean to Tarlah?

"Familon," Michael asked, "what chance do you think a letter asking about archways has of reaching King Urmillian?"

Familon studied Michael thoughtfully. "A message sent by a merchant to Tarlah should reach the castle easily enough, if the ship doesn't sink. But if someone in the North Lands or Far West can help you, then you will need to go to them. They have no reason to sail out here and send you back through Ghost Island's archway."

Linh slumped. They couldn't be sure there *was* an archway in the North Lands, let alone someone who could operate it. But there was little point staying near an archway they now knew no one here could operate.

"How long would we have to wait for a reply from King Urmillian?" Troy asked.

"A season and a half. We have three seasons, and the reply would have to wait for the season in which the winds change again, before it could sail back."

Troy dropped his bow. "Months just to confirm whether or not we should sail to Tarlah?"

"Our families will think we're dead by then," Fiona whispered, fidgeting with her bow.

Linh's shoulders tightened. "I've been trying not to think how they feel already. It's been eight days. There'll be a police-organised manhunt searching for us by now."

Linh's free hand balled into a fist. She'd never felt so helpless or frustrated. And she couldn't even be sure Red Cloak was to blame.

"Is there any chance some Elite Guard *do* know how to operate archways?" Michael asked.

Familon sighed. "If such people exist and the Elite Guard has yet to identify them, you have no chance of doing so."

Linh sat heavily on the grass, and Fiona sat beside her. She met her friend's gaze and saw the same revelation in Fiona's eyes. If they wanted to get home, and avoid putting their families through hell with worry, they had to leave the Timbalen Empire, asap.

Troy stared into the distance. "What are the odds of us making it to Tarlah, King Urmillian sending a message to the North Landers, and them being able to help us?"

Familon sighed. "I believe they are greater than those of calamity falling from clear skies on this empire, you fixing it, and the Guardians re-appearing to send you home when you are done."

Troy laughed until tears glistened in his eyes. Linh and Fiona exchanged bitter-sweet smiles. Seeking a way home in the North Lands sounded like a wild goose chase to Linh, but Familon affirming that it was a more likely route than their unqualified saving of the empire from non-existent peril was somehow reassuring. Sailing halfway across Umarinaris seemed almost sensible compared to that.

Linh and Fiona rode across the field, trotting being the fastest speed Linh wanted to go, while seated insecurely on a saddle blanket in an empire yet to invent stirrups. They had a plan. Compared to the last eight days, it was almost like having control over her life again. But even with that feeling, she still liked riding with Fiona in the afternoons. With Nuard searching for a captain to take them to Tarlah, archery and sword fighting lessons felt more like self-defence training now, and they made her anxious. But feeling the wind on her face afterwards and inhaling the sea breeze as their horses trotted along was still relaxing.

They turned into the cool shade of the forest. Long, curved leaves rustled together overhead, dry ones crunching under the horse's hooves, fallen twigs snapping beneath them.

"Not bad. You can pretty much mount a horse now," Michael's voice said from around a bend in the dirt trail.

"Sorry I can't compete with people who've been riding horses on cattle stations since they were six," said Troy.

"I was five," Michael corrected, and Linh smiled. Michael was so serious all the time that she wasn't sure if he was teasing or just being blunt.

The boys turned their horses down the road, and Fiona and Linh caught them up.

"And how are you today?" Troy called to a bird with vermillion feathers perched high up a nearby tree.

The bird's penetrating blue eyes fixed on him.

"It might decide it's sick of your attempts to befriend it and burn you up with its gaze," Linh warned.

"Or claw my face off?" Troy asked. "How did the supposedly more civilised scholars at the castle come up with the more violent myth?"

Linh rolled her eyes. "Because they're too well-educated to believe in a bird wielding eye-laser magic."

Troy's brows furrowed. "That doesn't seem to stop them believing that it's centuries old and guarding a relic from the Sorcery War."

Linh suspected the myths had developed because the bird behaved as if it guarded something, and because nothing ever happened on Myleth Island.

Trees thinned ahead, revealing a patch of grass, then sandhills beneath the warmth of late afternoon sunshine. Linh dismounted, leading her horse onto the sand. The wind blew against her face and ruffled the linen pants and tunic Nuard had given her. She envied its freedom to cross oceans so swiftly.

"Hail the Empire!"

Linh frowned at sandhills blocking her view. The East Islanders didn't trade with Myleth Island directly, and no one from further afield would come here.

"Hail!" the man called again.

Fiona ran ahead, and Linh and Troy jogged behind her, letting their horses graze at the edge of the forest. Linh crested a sandhill. A man stumbled across wet sand before breaking waves, dripping wet. Waves behind him washed a wooden barrel ashore. Objects bobbed beyond. Two people clung to barrels, and three clutched a large wooden crate. Beyond the debris, a sailing ship sat low in the water, waves washing over its deck.

"Why is it sinking?" Linh asked.

"Must've struck a reef," Michael replied.

"Are you all right?" Troy called.

"Tell the Emperor," the man said hoarsely, "Tarlah calls for aid."

He collapsed.

Linh's heart pounded against her chest.

"I'll get Nuard!" Fiona yelled, sprinting away.

Troy rolled the man into the recovery position, Michael reaching for his pulse. A bell tolled behind them, repetitively, and Linh saw a fishing boat trailing netting change its course, presumably looking for survivors.

"His heart's still beating," Michael said. "He's still breathing and his airways are clear."

"Is there anything else we can do?" Linh asked, clutching at her robes.

Michael shook his head, and Troy's neck flushed, his hands balling into fists.

"Raging against the world doesn't help," Michael said quietly. "It hasn't helped us, and it won't revive this man."

"How can you be so calm?" Linh asked.

"You two aren't calm because you refuse to accept it," Michael replied. "Too much has happened to my mob for me to deny anything. I've got family I've never met because they were taken away by the government as kids during the Stolen Generations and we couldn't track them down. Other crap happened, and people died. Fighting it does no good, and panicking doesn't get you anywhere."

"How do you just accept that?" Linh asked. She clutched at her robes with her other hand and squeezed, but it failed to relieve the weight pressing down on her chest.

"Tell yourself that's how it is, instead of dwelling on what you want when it can't be," Michael replied, his jaw set. "Worrying doesn't change anything. Focusing on what you want when you can't have it just makes you miserable."

Yes, it did. But how did she accept having no idea how they could get home and having limited options for blindly seeking one? Or that the man in front of her could be dying, and there was nothing she could do to stop it?

"I wonder what his story is," Troy said softly.

Linh studied the Tarlahn. His blonde braid dripped seawater. The broad chest beneath his leather tunic rose and dipped slowly. An empty sheath hung from his belt, and his feet were bare. At least fifty meters out to sea, two boats rowed towards the shipwreck, making for more people in the water.

A while later, Fiona returned, followed by two men carrying a canvas and timber stretcher. They lifted the unconscious Tarlahn onto it and hurried back to the castle.

"Nuard's coming. He'll want to speak to us. Come on," Fiona urged.

They mounted their horses and trotted across the sand, overtaking the stretcher. The forest ended on Linh's right and the castle's high walls drew nearer ahead. They dismounted, entering the Rose Gate, then strode past roses of all colours to Nuard, who stood halfway up the garden path.

"What happened to the Tarlahn?" Nuard asked.

"He just collapsed," answered Fiona. "After saying Tarlah calls for aid."

Nuard blinked, and his face drained of colour.

"Who is he?" Linh asked.

"From Fiona's description, a Tarlahn soldier. For too long have we abandoned them. The Zaldeaans must think us truly gone."

Nuard turned and strode away.

Troy's eyes widened. "Does that mean there's war in Tarlah? That our best base to seek someone who can help us get home is a war zone?"

"The Umarinaris Book might tell us more," Fiona suggested.

Michael nodded, and Fiona led the way through the castle's narrow, quiet stone corridors. The library was deserted, its walls lined with shelves containing papyrus scrolls, the Umarinaris Book lying open on its reading stand as usual.

Fiona turned the page recording their arrival and gasped. The pages beyond had been blank for over a week. Now, writing filled the next page and the one after. Linh frowned. Like every spoken word she'd heard on Myleth Island, the words were in English. How could someone in Umarinaris write in *English*? Had someone else from Earth reached Umarinaris before Linh and her classmates? But that still didn't explain why Myleth Island's inhabitants spoke and understood English.

"Why would it tell Nuard what's happening in Tarlah?" Troy asked, his brows climbing towards his curly, flyaway fringe.

"The emperor has an Umarinaris Book too," Linh reminded. "Maybe someone's trying to persuade the emperor to send aid."

"You're kidding," said Troy.

Linh's brows furrowed in confusion.

"If the empire aids Tarlah, the next ships to sail past here will be the navy sailing to war," Michael explained.

Linh's shoulders slumped. "I don't know if any merchant ships will sail that way now, until the war's over."

"We're not sure there is one yet," Fiona reminded.

"Can you read it out loud?" Michael asked behind her.

Fiona nodded and began to read the Umarinaris Book.

Chapter 11

Preparation in Tarlah

Ethlin: *One Week after the Declaration of War*

Ethlin grit her teeth as General Takanis attacked. The woman moved with the force and skill of a man, like her absent mentor Lenaris but more solidly built. Ethlin leapt, ducked, and scrambled aside, finding it best to dodge Takanis' blows altogether until she could get her own in. She dodged the fifth blow in a row, and the General barked a laugh.

"Esira seems to speed you through the air, girl!" said Takanis, stepping back. "If you dodge so well in battle, you may keep your enemies busy until your comrades have killed them."

Ethlin managed to smile at the compliment, but the idea of relying on others to kill her opponents in battle frightened her.

She needed to be more aggressive. If she dodged and danced too much, someone would stab her in the back.

When the General moved on, she agreed to spar with a tall, wiry man whose stance told her he was a veteran. He struck out with his spear butt, probing, and she deflected and stabbed at his legs. He spun aside, smiling, and their spearheads clashed.

"Be on guard for back blows," a voice advised behind them.

Ethlin danced aside from a thrust and nicked her opponent with her spear tip, his calf reddening. He grinned, his eyes brightening at a challenge, and he attacked more swiftly. Ethlin's arms began to ache from meeting the force of his blows with her spear.

"Be mindful of footwork!" the same voice called. "If your enemy controls where you move, opponents you cannot see may cut you down."

Well and good, but did whoever that was have to keep interrupting?

Ethlin grit her teeth as her opponent's spear butt crashed over her helmet. Her opponent changed his stance, attacking alternately with butt and spearhead. She pivoted, dodging and blocking, suspecting he was waiting for her to fall behind so he could stab at her. She held her spear in both hands like a staff, ignoring sweat pouring down her back. Kitchen-earned callouses on her palms served her well now, buffering the impact of his spear each time it slammed against hers.

Someone in too-shiny armour corrected weapon grips and encouraged levied soldiers duelling veterans on her right.

"Would Your Benevolence honour us with a demonstration?" General Aza's voice called.

Ethlin's training partner and everyone training around them paused. Iron-helmeted General Aza emerged, and Ethlin realised the comments distracting her had come from the Heir, who smiled nervously. She didn't blame them. General Aza was big, broad, and incredibly strong.

"It would be my pleasure," Heir Ruarnon replied.

The joy of challenge flared in General Aza's eyes. An elite soldier handed Heir Ruarnon a spear, and Ethlin's opponent nodded to a circle forming around the Heir and the General. She and her opponent moved to watch. Heir Ruarnon threw themself into motion, thrusting at General Aza's thigh. General Aza's spear moved to deflect. Heir Ruarnon slammed their spear butt lefthanded into General Aza's shoulder. The Heir ducked the General's spear butt, knocked his point aside and almost fell. Then the Heir turned, catching themself, ducked a spear thrust again and twisted their spear point to where General Aza's armour left their armpit exposed.

General Aza barked a laugh, and Ethlin's mouth dropped open. The General was far bigger and probably more robust than the Heir, but the Heir had bested him. Surely she could fight like that against bigger opponents?

"That people," said General Aza, "is how it is done. Defend first. Distract the enemy if you can. But ultimately, aim for weak points."

Encouraged, Ethlin threw herself back into training. She relished the chance to train with General Takanis and Arlian whenever it came, and trained with bigger opponents as often as possible. She and Arlian spoke less in their daily rendezvous in the Royal Training Courtyard, spending more time resting wearily in each other's arms after long days of training. She was becoming a good soldier, but they both knew training was very different to actual war, and nerves about the coming battle made them quiet.

Heir Ruarnon trained and encouraged levied soldiers as often as possible, but battle tactics lessons also claimed their time. Today, Companion Tor laid out model equipment across the table in his study: mobile wooden siege towers pulled by bullocks, iron-tipped battering rams, and a power sling.

"When the front row raises their shields," Tor explained, placing miniature wooden soldiers' shields side by side, "they form a shield wall. Strong men holding that wall and spears positioned overhead can bring down riders. But,"—he positioned mounted miniature soldiers opposite—"if the cavalry charge from both sides and enough horses breach the shield wall, horses can ride foot soldiers down and cause a rout, a nasty defeat. That is the challenge we will devise tactics to counter in the Royal Council."

In the next Royal Council meeting, the table was covered in model siege equipment, cavalry, and infantry.

"We know the enemy has greater numbers," said General Aza. "And their greatest advantage is their cavalry, which is enough to ride our infantry down unless we make effective use of our chariots and deception to bring down enemy riders."

Many tactics meetings followed. They gave Ruarnon hope that strong tactics could overcome superior Zaldeaan numbers. However, Ruarnon still lay awake at night imagining a blood-spattered field—when they weren't worrying about who had their parents and how their parents faired now that war was coming. The approach of war in all its uncertainty loomed like a storm front, its winds of fear whispering whenever they were alone.

Ruarnon's uncle took them aside after a Royal Council meeting, the day before battle. When Tor stepped out of the Golden Meeting Hall, leaving an empty room behind, Uncle Omah smiled. "We have located your parents, Ruarnon!"

Hope blossomed in Ruarnon's chest, slowly banishing half-acknowledged fears.

"A spy traced food to a secret passage in the palace, which our Elites are investigating. I hope to implement the rescue when King Kyura's army reaches the southern provinces and moves well clear of your parents' passage to Edesinia. A small Zaldeaan fishing vessel has been purchased for their homeward voyage."

Ruarnon couldn't stop smiling. War was almost upon Tarlah, but their parents were alive, and a plan was finally in place to recover them. Part of Ruarnon would remain anxious until they reached Edesinia, but they were hopeful of that.

Then Omah's features hardened, becoming grave and withdrawn, *Regent* Omah's expression. Ruarnon's joy receded.

"I intend to lead one of the cavalry charges. We have no surety our allies will come, and the Zaldeaan army has always been larger. Being more experienced, they have made more effective use of strategy. With that and King Kyura's sudden end to the Peace, the levied soldiers are nervous. My presence will show faith in them and strengthen morale."

Ruarnon nodded.

Omah met their gaze. "With your parents captured, your Aunt Merlah in South Harbour, and my life in danger, we cannot endanger you."

Ruarnon's eyes widened. "I have no younger siblings to care for. What am I to do?"

Omah sighed. "Were you not the last heir in our dynasty's line, I would have you ride with General Aza, who will command the infantry and have a good view of the battlefield. As it is, you must remain at a safe distance. You and your bodyguards will be stationed atop the hills before Death Belt Desert."

"After all my training?" Ruarnon stared, then turned away, pacing. "The idea of fighting haunts me, and I don't think I will be free of it till I confront it. But it is more than that." They turned to meet Omah's gaze. "Uncle, I have trained soldiers at arms. I mentored them, I helped them believe in themselves, and you want me to sit back and watch them fight?"

Omah eyed them patiently. "You have done well, Ruarnon. With the signing of the Peace less than a year after your birth, your parents dared hope you would never have to confront war. By the time I was your age, my father had died leading the rebellion. War or the contagion that tore through both armies during the Piracy War slew all my uncles, and grief, contagion, or childbirth killed my aunts. You have been fortunate, but fortune retreats from us now. You are right. Tarlah needs a leader, and I will lead. But as the last of our dynasty, you cannot fulfil your Co-Regent duty of supporting me in the field of battle. You must look to your duty of learning from tactics instead."

The least of their duties? When so much was at stake? Ruarnon met their uncle's gaze again, but their heated reply died on their lips. Omah's stark eyes said he could die in battle, and he didn't want Ruarnon killed too. Ruarnon turned away, unable to confront the possibility of losing their uncle within a month of their parents' abduction.

"I would like to show you something," Omah added, and from his tone, Ruarnon wasn't sure if he was speaking as Uncle or Regent.

They followed Omah to the Royal Writing Room. Daylight streamed onto the map table, strewn with diagrams outlining phalanx manoeuvres. Through the window, the city was visible. Adults walked down South Road. Every street table at the public dining house was full. People walked in and out of shops, a wealthy woman followed by a servant carrying a pile of purchases.

Ruarnon gaped. Not only had they chosen to stay, they were in the streets, in full view, going about their business as if it were an ordinary day.

"Are they not afraid?" Ruarnon asked.

"Of course they are," Omah replied. "They know that Tarlah City will come under siege if we fail. The armourers, smiths, and cartwrights would support the army under siege, but everyone else would evacuate. These are uncertain times, but they are defiant, Ruarnon. Each person on the streets is delivering their own message; that the Zaldeaan army does not frighten them and its presence nearby will not interrupt their lives."

Ruarnon turned to South Road with wonder. The history of war they studied was tactics, weaponry, and leadership. It said nothing of the spirit of the people.

"Urmillian may have been your age when he became Co-Regent," said Omah, "but he did not face war until he was twenty, and he was not of the Generation of Peace. You must dread war. Sometimes I see it, yet every time you have faced signs of war, you have gritted your teeth and done so. You have won the hearts of young soldiers and the respect of veterans. You are becoming an excellent leader, Ruarnon."

They were surprised to see Omah look hesitant, his mouth firm and eyes solemn.

"If the worst should happen, Tor will watch over you as Companion and father both. He would have done so had I not asked, being your father's closest friend. If you have fears or worries you do not wish to make public, go to him or my wife. I should tell you that Telena values you as her own child. She has always wanted children, but I, unfortunately, cannot give them to her. If the worst should happen, remember that you have them, and you are not alone."

Ruarnon opened their mouth and found they couldn't speak. Seeing Uncle Omah calmly contemplating what Ruarnon needed to know if he died made Ruarnon want to flinch away. No man should have to prepare for such a thing, least of all one as young as Uncle Omah.

"I know it is not easy, but I should like to know that you will remember," Omah pressed gently.

Ruarnon nodded. Their voice was hoarse, but they managed the words, "I will, Uncle."

Then Omah stepped forwards, kissed their forehead, and held them.

"I am not supposed to have favourites as an uncle, and it is not fair when we only see Coroth at the Festival of the Gods—once a year is hardly enough to judge—but you are my favourite."

"You are my favourite uncle," Ruarnon said, as they stepped apart. "And not just because once a year is hardly enough to get to know Uncle Kar. It has been only two months, yet anyone would think it was you who has been ruling for twenty years."

"I hope so," Omah said with a faint smile. "Now, I am sure you have done your best to prepare. Your last duty will be to sleep well, so you are alert to observe and analyse the battle at daybreak."

Ruarnon doubted they would sleep a wink with the fate of their home and the lives of most people they knew hanging in the balance, but they would try.

"Good night, Uncle."

"Good night, Ruarnon."

Apprehension gripped Ruarnon's shoulders, as their uncle sat and looked at his maps, and Ruarnon walked to their chambers to rest. It would be surreal riding to battle in the small hours before the desert heat of the day could defeat both armies. To abandon everyone they'd trained with in favour of their duty to stay safe. They had no idea how to reconcile that conflict, but they couldn't argue with their uncle's earnestness. And after so much time worrying and waiting for the war to arrive, their body sagged with weariness. A servant gave them a glass of deep red wine, and they hardly noticed the taste, as they drained the goblet and sleep descended on them.

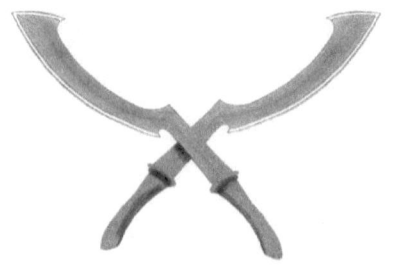

CHAPTER 12

BATTLE

RUARNON: *Tarlah City*

H ours before dawn, Ruarnon strode down a corridor through Tarlah Castle, their torso weighed down by a bronze cuirass secured by interlocking plates fitted with large pins. A short sword hung heavily at their waist, a quiver at their left hip, and a leather riding kilt swayed above bronze grieves as they walked. They carried a bronze helmet in their left hand and a bow in their right, and were flanked by heavily armed and armoured guards. The corridor stretched before them and their retinue like a dark tunnel.

Linen-clad servants bowed as they passed, and Ruarnon breathed slowly to counter their racing heart. They kept their head high and tried to project confidence, not the nervous uncertainty that made their stomach churn. Part of Ruarnon wanted to hide. To go back to sleep and wake from this nightmare. A smaller part wished the battle was over, but dread of the outcome made their mind flinch away, as uncertainty tighten their chest.

Ruarnon met Captain Arleath and their eight other bodyguards at the torch-lit courtyard steps. Grooms handed over reins, and Ruarnon and their guards mounted horses. Ruarnon forced their trembling hands to grip the reins tightly. Then the army distracted them.

Dozens of spear units stood or marched onto North Road; all five thousand elite soldiers would join the battle. Moonlight glinted off polished iron sword hilts and spear tips, off bronze helmets, cuirasses and bronze-plated, oval-shaped wooden shields. Apprehension perched on Ruarnon's shoulders, as war mobilised around them.

Silence descended, as Regent Omah strode into torchlight at the edge of the steps in full iron plate armour. "After fifteen years working as guards or building roads and bridges, some of you may fear you have lost skills honed in service of your king, while others have never put such skills to use. King Kyura seems to think you have spent over a decade twiddling your thumbs. That he can snatch Tarlah from us. Now is your chance to remember old skills, put new ones to use, and prove your mettle. Show Kyura his folly!"

The simplicity caught Ruarnon by surprise, but the soldiers cheered, seeming in their element.

Omah mounted his horse, and Ruarnon rode with him across the courtyard. Every balcony overlooking North Road was full. People peered through windows lit by oil lamps' flickering glow and a small crowd gathered at the nearest intersection. Right arms raised in salute as Ruarnon rode past: *Tarlah stands*. General Aza and the elite infantry returned the salute. Tarlah City's remaining inhabitants bowed their heads in respect.

Ruarnon gazed down a side street to find it crowded with people in boiled leather tunics and dented helmets. They carried hide bucklers, bronze swords, and spears handed down through generations: levied soldiers. Young soldiers gazed at elites with awe, while the generation who fought beside them in the Piracy War nodded to companions at arms. Ruarnon tried not to consider what awaited them all in Death Belt Desert.

Ruarnon rode through North Gate onto River Road beneath a dark sky full of stars, into a familiar yet strangely foreign world. Behind them, infantry halted and elite cavalry joined the column, as it moved towards Serpent River. Around Ruarnon, hilly farmland stretched across plains watered by canals reflecting starlight, while a distant town glowed with oil lamps. Ahead of them, the Serpent River marked the edge of Tarlah, and hills on the far side cast dark shadows.

Ruarnon turned alongside Serpent River, and apprehension tightened their chest and made their breathing shallow as they rode across the bridge. They tried to smile as Companions Tor and Pamoran clapped them on the shoulder and Omah nodded solemnly. Then Captain Arleath led

Ruarnon and their guards onto a narrow track through the hills, while Ruarnon's uncle led the army north.

At the first bend, Ruarnon looked back. Omah, the Companions, generals and elite cavalry and infantry wound along a road through hills. Behind them, moonlight glinted off armoured infantry down River Road, and distant, tiny chariots rolled out of Tarlah City. Ruarnon bowed their head and prayed to the Ancestors to watch over their people.

Captain Arleath led them to a hilltop, where they stopped beside their guards and gazed across Death Belt Desert, countless acres of dull soil dimly lit by moonlight. Tarlahn cavalry phalanxes formed up on its edge, infantry assembling in a column three phalanxes wide beyond, stretching back into the hills.

Beyond the Tarlahn army, the barren plains of Death Belt Desert stretched to the horizon. In the distance, a black shadow blotted the desert plains, King Kyura's army.

Ethlin shifted from foot to foot in her infantry line. Her boiled leather vest and the short sword Head Cook had given her weren't too heavy, but she wished she'd had more time to train with them and with the awkwardly unfamiliar rectangular shield in her left hand. Arlian had wanted to join her, but General Aza wouldn't hear of it. As a high official's son, he rode with General Takanis' cavalry.

Ethlin reached for the necklace hanging under her leather vest with her spear hand, from which hung a bracelet, where it couldn't be knocked off her wrist and lost during the fighting. Arlian hadn't told his parents he was courting her yet, but he hadn't wanted her going into battle without a promise bracelet. She hadn't taken it off since he asked for her hand in marriage. It was her main source of comfort, as Regent Omah raised his spear above a phalanx ahead and other captains raised theirs, signalling readiness.

The Regent, General Takanis, and Tarlahn cavalry charged. Opposite, the dark line of enemy cavalry became clearer as it advanced. Polished bronze armour and helmets reflected the pale grey pre-dawn light. Enemy cavalry surged, chariots close behind.

Regent Omah nodded to a captain, who led two cavalry phalanxes to the left. Omah veered right with two more. General Takanis and the remaining cavalry surged to meet the enemy head-on in the centre. Ethlin prayed to the Ancestors that the Tarlahns held the enemy riders off. That they didn't charge her.

An arrow glanced off Regent Omah's helmet. Ethlin gaped as another lodged in his chest plate. The Regent rode on, and both sides cried defiance. Spears thrust, swords slashed, and horses screamed. General Takanis' cavalry clashed with the enemy, and riders were thrown from their horses. Spears and swords clashed and horses kicked in a writing mass. For a moment, Ethlin's gut twisted, and she thought only of Arlian.

Enemy cavalry charged past Tarlahn riders. Veterans around Ethlin braced. The phalanx before her angled spears forwards, the frontline lowering pikes. This was it. Ethlin's heart pounded faster than the charging horses. She gripped her spear and shield tightly, as arrows soared over her.

Enemy riders fell and horses crashed to the ground, but more rode on. The phalanx before Ethlin stilled. Her grip on spear and shield became rigid. Zaldeaan horses screamed as they were impaled. Other war horses scrambled over pikes. Ethlin stared aghast, as they rode infantry down. Throwing spears hurtled towards riders, and thrusting spears stabbed at horses. Impaled riders toppled from saddles and spearmen battled rampaging horses. Everything beyond the front line of Ethlin's phalanx gave way to deadly chaos.

Hooves thudded nearby. Blood spurted, and soldiers before Ethlin fell. Her breathing became ragged. The rider's blood tipped spear was knocked aside. The horse screamed, as a pike drove home in its breast. Horse and rider toppled. Ethlin jumped as the man's helmet crashed to her feet. Her limbs tingled as if her legs wanted to run. But death lay ahead, and shields and close-packed infantry barred the way behind.

"Steady," said a veteran on her left. "Hold your ground and try to stab anything that comes near you."

Men screamed before her. Another rider charged her way. Ethlin's gaze locked on his horse. She gritted her teeth and hurled her spear with all her might. The horse screamed as the spear pierced its head. It bucked, and thrusting spears took its rider down. Then it collapsed, thrashing, knocking down another Tarlahn, whom comrades dragged aside before the horse kicked him to death.

Then the horse was still. Soldiers before her were still. But more horses and men were screaming. More cavalry mounted a shield wall ahead, skilled riders using lances to knock pikes aside.

"Shield wall!" Ethlin's captain barked.

Ethlin put her shield forward, resting it on the ground. She managed to keep it still, but her fingers trembled. Soldiers placed theirs on either side, ducking below their shields. Most raised their spears too. Ethlin drew her short sword and braced her shield against her shoulder as General Takanis had taught her, her breathing coming in ragged gasps.

Hooves thudded again, and more people screamed. Something heavy hit Ethlin's shield, and she gritted her teeth. A horse whinnied, where the veteran had crouched, on her left. Iron glinted, and she slashed, deflecting a spear aimed at her neck with her sword. Soldiers yelled around her, and thrusting spears drove the rider aside. Ethlin knew the veteran on her left was dead, ridden down, but she couldn't bear to look.

"Cavalryman!" someone warned.

Ethlin's blood boiled. How dare they kill the veteran! She stood, raising her shield. Her companions kept theirs in place, and the cavalryman ran for her, thrusting his spear. Ethlin danced sideways, knocking his spear aside with her shield. She rushed in, cutting his thighs with her short sword. He screamed. She straightened, and his spear stuck fast in her shield. Ethlin dropped her shield, ducked as she ran past his left arm and cut his throat.

She turned. Two cavalrymen were charging her.

"Take my spear!" a comrade yelled.

Ethlin switched the sword to her left hand and caught the spear with her right. She heard hooves. The fallen cavalrymen attacked Tarlahns out of formation on her left. The rider behind them directed his horse towards her.

"Stand your ground," Lenaris had told her. But her timing must be perfect.

She crouched while the rider charged. Time slowed and silence reigned. Her skin prickled with goosebumps. Then she jumped sideways, thrusting her spear up into the horse's breast. She let go, raising her sword left-handed to deflect a spear thrust. The spear struck her helmet, and she stumbled, head aching.

Sound came back. People yelled and jostled around her. Shields knocked her limbs as they moved past. A man screamed. The rider had turned and was charging her again. Ethlin drew her right arm back and threw her sword. It sailed into his throat. He slumped, and a Tarlahn hauled him to the ground and led his horse away.

"The first attack is broken! Tarlah stands!"

People shouted around Ethlin. Right arms raised in the exhilaration of having fought and survived: *Tarlah stands*! But in Ethlin's mind, beautiful four-legged creatures screamed, as they died, and there was a terrible cracking as the bones of a man who had shown her kindness were crushed beneath hooves. Why had she *ever* wanted to be part of *this*?

A firm hand clapped her upper arm. "You stopped the only two horses to charge us," her captain said. "It's called battle shock, but it passes. Can you return to us?"

Ethlin thought of the man on her other side, who had given her his spear, leaving himself nearly defenceless. Of people who had stepped forwards to protect her from the second rider when she was struck on the head. No one could save all of them, but she would save as many as she could.

"Yes," she replied softly.

Captains shouted orders. Soldiers parted on her right, and horses were led past, then Zaldeaans at spear point. Soldiers were regrouping before her. Those who survived the skirmish formed three lines before her unit. There was a wait and then an order that set her entire body tingling: "Forward march!"

Her breathing came in short gasps as they marched towards the cavalry battle. Towards kicking, bucking warhorses and their spear-wielding riders.

"Veterans! Aim at enemy soldiers! Throw spears at will!" a captain cried.

Horses shifted, spears soared, and braid-less Zaldeaan riders toppled. Arrows soared into the mass, their whizz drowned out by shouts, weapons clashing and horses trampling and screaming. Ethlin kept her shield between those on either side of her and braced her spear against whatever tried to charge through it.

Ruarnon hunched forwards in anticipation atop their horse and the hill, as their uncle's army pounded Zaldeaan cavalry and chariots. Throwing spears felled Zaldeaan riders trying to escape. Encircled Zaldeaans threw down weapons. Riders fought on or fled at the rear, but throwing spears brought down more enemies, until the rest surrendered. Ruarnon smiled, and their shoulders relaxed a little. The cavalry battle was won.

Tarlahn cavalry retreated. Tarlahn riders waved a red and a black flag to the enemy, who halted, while Tarlahn infantry moved the wounded and dead down Tarlahn lines towards wagons and surgeons in green linens. On the far side, Zaldeaan infantry moved the fallen from the chariot-cavalry battle, moving figures with Tarlahn braids and without.

Ruarnon tensed at the sight of so many dead. Had the soldiers they had trained with and mentored survived?

The enemy didn't withdraw. Giant chariot and cavalry units assembled on either side of the Zaldeaan army. Enemy infantry phalanxes stood four across and four deep, vastly outnumbering Tarlahn infantry. But Regent Omah commanded four cavalry phalanxes and four chariot phalanxes, the most powerful units. The odds favoured Tarlah. Ruarnon fought the urge to hold their breath, hoping that would be enough.

Tarlahn riders lowered flags, and both armies charged. Arrows arced ahead of them, crossing midway. Riders on both sides ducked behind round shields. Arrows rained on Tarlahn spearmen's shields, and defenceless enemy chariot archers fell. Cavalry and chariots collided in a confused mass. Ruarnon's breaths came in short gasps, as they struggled to tell who, if anyone, had the upper hand.

Enemy infantry advanced on the edge of Ruarnon's vision, but something moved behind, a mass visible in the pre-dawn light at the far edge of the desert. More enemy cavalry. Ruarnon's jaw dropped. Who kept those soldiers back while enemy cavalry was slaughtered?

Ruarnon shook themself. Fighting beyond this point would be horrendously costly. Their uncle needed to retreat, now, before his army was encircled.

Two men in iron helmets on horseback and their guards retreated to a sandhill: Omah and Companion Tor.

"Warn my uncle of the additional enemy cavalry," Ruarnon ordered.

One of their bodyguards bowed in his saddle and rode downhill.

Opposite Omah and Tor, Zaldeaan riders approached, led by a golden-helmed rider. King Kyura? Ruarnon shivered. Let it be a warmonger. Let Omah strike off his head!

Ruarnon's grip on their saddle tightened, as enemy infantry advanced around the cavalry and chariot battle. Tarlahn and Zaldeaan infantry would clash soon. Time to retreat had almost run out.

Ruarnon's messenger guard raised a horn to wind a warning. Arrows felled him, before the horn touched his lips. He toppled from his horse. Ruarnon gaped, as rider and horn hit the slope and lay still.

The enemy commander's sword struck Regent Omah's. The commander struck again and again. Omah only defended, barely getting his shield up and swaying in his saddle. He was injured, and Companion Tor battled multiple enemies on either side. Mounted guards clashed around them, and horses kicked, a distraction to delay Tarlahn retreat, and maximise Tarlahn casualties.

Closer by, a man wearing green crawled up the slope—a man with loose hair, a Zaldeaan. There were probably others.

"Shoot them!" Ruarnon ordered.

Ruarnon seized three arrows from their quiver and scanned the grass carefully, spotting more men crawling up the slope. They loosed each arrow expertly, one after another, and felled three archers.

Ruarnon's guards' arrows soared. But there was no time to waste.

Ruarnon heeled their horse. Captain Arleath protested and rode after them.

Ruarnon gazed at their uncle. Omah's head turned as his opponent's sword glanced off his helmet. Omah ducked another blow and struck the commander's sword arm with his shield. The commander dropped his shield and took his sword in his left hand. He rained blows with it: a true warlord.

Ruarnon ducked arrows and caught some on their shield, swatting at them distractedly.

Omah struggled against left-handed strokes falling from unfamiliar angles. Companion Tor moved beside him and struck at the warlord. Tor and the warlord fought fiercely.

"Aza! Retreat! Encirclement!" Ruarnon bawled as blades clashed behind them and Captain Arleath attacked enemy soldiers charging them on foot.

Backline Tarlahn infantry turned towards Ruarnon. Ruarnon struck an approaching Zaldeaan in the face with their shield, knocking the man down.

Raised spears passed a signal down the Tarlahn infantry column.

Captain Arleath reined in beside Ruarnon. "Well-timed, Benevolence," he said. "You dodged their first flight of arrows, and your guards took down the archers before they got a second chance."

Ruarnon nodded mutely, their heart still hammering against their chest. It wasn't enough. Omah's strength was failing and he was outmatched. And Companion Tor,

Ruarnon's favourite tutor, was struggling. Ruarnon heeled their horse around the infantry column, riding towards Omah. Someone shouted, and they heard Tarlahn chariots roll after them.

Ahead, Omah's sword clashed with a guard. Omah held him off but struggled to land an offensive blow. He slammed his shield and sword into the guard's sword arm. Then he thrust, and the man fell off his horse.

Captain Arleath's spear clashed with riders. Ruarnon deflected a spear left-handed, their gaze fixed on their uncle as they charged desperately towards him.

A guard stabbed Companion Tor in the shoulder. Tor struck at the guard and the warlord struck at Omah, knocking his sword wide. Omah brought his shield desperately forwards. His sword glanced back as the warlord's struck it.

Ruarnon lodged their spear in an approaching Zaldeaan rider's side, seized their bow from their saddle, and aimed at the warlord. He was just beyond range. Ruarnon held the bow taut as they charged, gripping their horses' flanks with their knees for balance.

Omah swung at the warlord's neck. His sword didn't come out of the warlord's armour.

The warlord was within range. But if Ruarnon missed, they'd hit their uncle. They hesitated.

Omah pulled frantically on his sword hilt. It wrenched free. The warlord's sword smashed Omah's shield aside, and

Omah was knocked sideways in his saddle. Ruarnon loosed their arrow.

The warlord thrust his sword into Omah's chest. Ruarnon's arrow pierced the warlord's face.

Ruarnon stared. They were too late. They didn't notice Captain Arleath seize their reins and slow their horse, nor Zaldeaan guards noticing the pair of them.

It was impossible, piercing an iron breastplate like that... but their uncle's armour was already damaged...

Zaldeaan guards' heads flew.

The warlord withdrew his sword, swaying in his saddle. Tor slashed off his head.

Ruarnon's horse jerked around, as Captain Arleath led their horses away. Behind them, the warlords' guards fled. Tor turned to Omah. Omah leant forwards in his saddle. His right arm, its sword gone, pointed to where new enemy cavalry had almost joined the battle.

Tor raised a horn and winded it. The deep sound echoed from sandhills beyond the fighting. Tarlahn infantry in front of the fighting halted, turned, and retreated in formation, following the rear lines.

Ruarnon turned desperately to their uncle. Omah's arm fell limply, and he sagged. Tor touched his neck. A Tarlahn guard seized Tor's reins and pulled his horse away. A second guard snatched at Omah's reins and missed. The guards and Tor were retreating, before Ruarnon accepted that Tor had been checking Omah's pulse.

Enemy cavalry charged round enemy infantry, some riding straight for Ruarnon and Arleath. A second guard seized Ruarnon's uncle's reins and led Omah's horse forwards. Then the guard slid sideways off his horse, a spear sticking out of his back.

Ruarnon blinked tears from their eyes as the guard fell and both horses stopped. Two enemy riders reached the horses, leading both back to the Zaldeaan army, Omah sitting limply in his saddle. Ruarnon didn't want to take their eyes off their uncle, despite the pain from twisting their neck to see. But the battle now lay to the right of them. They wrenched their gaze to the fighting.

Tarlahn cavalry fought in a line, holding off the enemy— infantry disengaged under cover of chariot archer fire— chariots formed a defensive corridor—the whole infantry column was withdrawing between chariots behind Ruarnon and Arleath—chariots turned to retreat, archers still firing at the enemy.

Part of Ruarnon was still with Companion Tor checking their uncle's pulse, imagining he had one and that Tor was about to bring Omah home. But the guards had been more desperate to save Tor... because Tor was still alive.

Ruarnon blinked away more tears, which splashed down their face as the last row of Tarlahn infantry broke into a trot and new enemy cavalry approached Tarlahn cavalry from both sides. Ruarnon barely heard the second horn blowing, as they and Arleath charged around the retreating infantry.

The battle was lost.

Ruarnon noticed little, as Captain Arleath led them ahead of the retreating army down empty River Road, which mirrored the gulf inside Ruarnon. Immediate threats were gone. The crushing weight of defeat remained.

They didn't question when the captain led them off the main road. They observed nothing, until they entered the forest. A sound rang out so many times over the city's eastern walls that it finally penetrated Ruarnon's awareness. A bell, tolling, again and again. There was a shout, repeated until they made out the words, "All persons are to evacuate, by order of the Regent."

The Regent was gone, and as Ruarnon watched, hundreds of brave spirits Uncle Omah had admired for their steadfastness flowed out of East Gate.

As the trees thinned before them, Ruarnon saw the middle-aged and older members of their generation marching. They carried packs and satchels, or pulled handcarts, wearing labourers' linens, merchants and shop keepers' silks, crafts people's leathers, most on foot, the wealthy on horseback, all trailed by the dark shadow of uncertainty.

Ruarnon's horse halted, sensing their mood.

"The city has not fallen yet," Captain Arleath said softly. "Your uncle's men still defend its walls."

Ruarnon's brows furrowed as they wondered why the captain wasn't taking them into the city. Dread stirred in the pit of their stomach as they noticed a clearing on the right, into which the stream of anxious, frightened, or resolute evacuees flowed. A woman stood in its centre, attracting bows as she signed her blessing to uncertain couples, families, and friends as they passed. The Captain had taken Ruarnon to Aunt Telena. They would have to tell her.

Ruarnon's heels nudged the horse of their own accord. They rode into the centre of the clearing, where a carriage was parked behind their aunt, and bronze-armoured, heavily armed guards stood. So intent was Telena on a large cluster of passing young people that she took a moment to notice Ruarnon. Her face was pale and drawn, but it lit with a smile when she saw Ruarnon. Her smile lasted several moments after her eyes met theirs, until tears filled them. Ruarnon dismounted and flung their arms around her, lifting her back into the carriage.

"I tried to save him. But I could not get a clear shot with my bow, and I feared wounding him. By the time I could shoot, I was too late."

The words poured from them with tears. Aunt Telena straightened to eye them with concern. "You fought? You approached the battlefield?"

Ruarnon sniffed and nodded.

"Thank the Ancestors you're safe!"

She flung her arms around them. They rested their head on her shoulder, as she steered them to a padded bench.

Captain Noma, Companion Tor's younger sister, knocked on the door.

"Enter," Aunt Telena's voice said softly, somehow retaining a tone of command, despite being cracked.

Captain Noma entered the carriage and closed its door, sitting opposite them. She hunched wearily, her young face drawn, prematurely lined like Tor's, though there was no hint of grey in the blonde curls straying from her braid.

"I am very sorry, Ruarnon, and not just for Regent Omah," she said. "Our rescue attempt failed. The servant who had access to your parents through the secret passageways was too frightened to be bribed, and more frightened of the enemy's threats than ours. He refused to admit anyone. Our elites drugged the guards to force entry, but they were detected. Several of our elites were killed, and the rest were eventually captured."

Ruarnon leant back into a cushion, feeling weak. "Did they see my parents?"

"No."

Ruarnon slumped.

"The enemy's determination to hold onto our rulers suggests they serve a purpose beyond the war."

"Will they threaten my parents to force our surrender?" Ruarnon asked, staring unseeing across the carriage.

"I suspect every warrior who holds to the Warriors Creed will understand that such a cowardly threat would offend our allies' pride, perhaps enough to goad them into war, even if they lack the resources to fight."

Ruarnon nodded. "Companion Tor?"

Anger flashed in Noma's eyes, and Ruarnon realised they were red-rimmed from crying. "A little lower, and that thrust would have pierced my brother's lung. The surgeons say he will recover. Companion Pamoran has taken charge for now."

Ruarnon nodded mutely. *They* should take charge. But they couldn't think. Perspective eluded them. Everything was dark and uncertain, and until they found their way out, they were incapable.

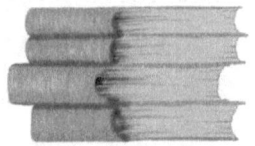

CHAPTER 13

DEPARTING MYLETH ISLAND

LINH: *Myleth Island*

What happened to Tarlah?" Linh asked, hugging herself in an armchair in the library.

"That battle happened weeks after Omah sent the ship that's wrecked outside for aid," Michael replied. "I think the Umarinaris Book's up to date, and that battle was fought today."

"So Tarlah was on the brink of war when we got here," Troy said, slumping against a shelf.

"There's still time," said Fiona. "Time for the Timbalens to set sail and drive the Zaldeaans out before they take Tarlah City."

Troy's brows furrowed. "What's wrong?" he asked her.

"It's not history," Fiona replied with a sniff. "It's not dates and figures and speculation on the distant past. We just read how someone feels about a battle they watched. About hundreds of people who died, including their uncle."

Linh's attention wandered. In her mind's eye, she remembered lying in bed as a little girl when her mother's screams woke her. Frightened, little Linh had climbed out of bed and run down the hall. Before she reached Ba's door, her mother started screaming in Vietnamese.

"*A'nh! A'nh! Thuc day! Thuc day A'nh!*"

Ba had stepped into the hallway, tying up her dressing gown.

"What's Mummy saying, Ba?"

Tears shone in Ba's eyes, and Ba reached to take her hand, explaining in Vietnamese. "When we lived in Vietnam, there was a war. One day your mother found her sister, my little A'nh, lying in the woods. She thought A'nh was sleeping and tried to wake her up. But A'nh wouldn't wake. Wars are terrible things. We are so lucky Australia doesn't have them."

Linh remembered the horror she later felt when she realised the war hadn't sent her aunt A'nh into a deep sleep, but that the eight-year-old had probably been shot dead.

"I thought the war was a long time ago. Is Mummy still sad?" little Linh had asked, as Ba led her back to bed.

"Sometimes she feels very sad. Sometimes I feel sad too. But we will look after her, and she will be all right."

That wasn't the only time as a child that Linh woke to her mother's night terrors. The death of the aunt Linh never met haunted her mother for decades. And Ruarnon had just had the same experience, seeing a loved one killed before their eyes. It was awful. And she felt for them. But she and her classmates had planned to visit Tarlah to ask if the reclusive North Landers could help send them home. Now, *Tarlah* was a war zone.

Linh shifted in her chair, but no position made her comfortable

"It's hard to take in," Troy was saying, his head bowed. "War's always been so far from home. I never imagined how it feels."

"Ruarnon's facing it alone," said Michael, sitting up straight and turning to meet their gazes as he spoke. "That's not good for you. I should know. If there was a chance we could support them while we searched for a way home, would you do it?"

Linh shivered.

"What would our families say?" Fiona asked, wringing her hands. "Wouldn't your parents worry as much as ours?"

Michael turned away, his voice hard-edged when he replied. "My parents haven't worried about anything for years. And they didn't worry about much when they were alive either. They practically left me to raise my younger sister. Until the car crash.

"That was a long time ago, but I was old enough to realise they expected nothing of me and didn't believe they could accomplish anything themselves. That's why they drank so much alcohol: to cure despair."

Linh's brows furrowed.

"But, your parents..." Troy faltered.

"The people I call Mum and Dad are my auntie and uncle. They taught me to believe in myself and pursue things I think matter. This is *our* choice, and it matters. We know what Ruarnon's going through. If you had a chance to be there for them, bearing in mind we need to get to Tarlah anyway, would you take it?"

Linh's jaw dropped, and she caught Troy's widening features and exchanged a significant look with him. Did they not know Michael *at all*?

"I might," Fiona replied quietly. "My parents wouldn't like me going, but I live with seven brothers and sisters. Someone's always hurt or sick, and there's always something I can do to help them feel better. I don't like sitting around doing nothing while people suffer."

Linh sighed. That was hardly surprising, but she needed to make Fiona see reason.

Troy got in first. "Even if we *could* cheer Ruarnon up while they carry the world on their shoulders, it's not our problem, and it's not safe."

"I spent my childhood watching what war did to my mother," Linh said quietly. "I saw her freeze up every time cars back-fired in the street because she thought it was gunfire. I found her and Ba looking at photos from before they fled Vietnam and Ba wondering if her other daughter would look like me if she'd lived past eight. I've seen the damage war does to people who survive it, and it scares me more than any of you can understand. We *can't* go to Tarlah till the war's over."

Michael bit his lip. "We've no way of knowing when the war will end or when merchants will sail for Tarlah again. The war could drag on, the Zaldeaans could win, and even if the Timbalens aid Tarlah and *they* win, we'd still have to wait for the winds to change, for word it's safe to sail to reach the empire's merchants. At best, we'll be sitting here waiting for months. At worst..." He shook his head.

Linh shivered. At worst, the Zaldeaans won the war, and the Timbalens stopped trading with or sailing to Tarlah altogether.

Troy groaned and sank to the floor. "So for all we know, if the Timbalens *do* send aid and we *don't* sail with them, we could be passing up our only chance to get home, for who knows how many *years*? And we've no way of knowing whether we're passing up that chance. But if we are... My little brother might not recognise me by then! My little sister will think I've abandoned them, just like dad and my mum will think I'm dead. I can't do that to them. And to be honest, if we're testing how long being helplessly stuck in limbo takes to break us, I'm not gonna last long!"

He was right. Linh's mother's mental health had never been good. Anxiety about where Linh was would only make it worse. They'd had a plan for two days, and Linh had felt like she had some control over her life. But waiting for the war to end would mean surrendering that control and waiting for external circumstances to dictate her fate. Whole months of being stranded, with no way of knowing when it would end and being helpless to change that.

She tugged on her ponytail. "Is there no one else who could open the archways?"

Fiona shook her head. "Familon says the East Islanders have no special abilities, and no one knows where the Island of the Guardians is located—if it isn't just a myth."

Linh banged her fist on the floor.

"We don't have to stick together," said Michael.

"You're going?" Troy asked.

"If the Timbalens are going, and we're allowed, yes. God knows my family have been through enough. I swore I wouldn't burden them the way my parents burdened me. And nothing in life being certain, I'd rather risk danger acting to get home, then wait in safety until I realise I've let my only chance for the next few years slip through my fingers."

He met Troy's gaze and his eyes filled with pain. "You're worried about depression?" Michael asked. "Well, I'm already slipping into it. I'm not sitting around with nothing to ward it off while it takes hold."

Troy stood and clapped him on the shoulder. "Me neither."

In a fairytale in Linh's head, they sailed with the Timbalen army, met Heir Ruarnon and gave them company and moral support when they needed it, a long way from the battlefield, then Ruarnon sent them by ship to the North

Lands, and a Guardian met them and opened an archway. In reality, getting home any time soon was likely to be far more dangerous. But if everything went pear-shaped in Tarlah, skirting a warzone now was better than never seeing most of the people she loved ever again. There was no way of knowing whether she risked that if she stayed here.

"I don't want to risk being cut off from home and everyone I love for years," she said softly, and Fiona nodded.

Linh heard footsteps and Familon arrived. "His Greatness Yarath intends to answer Tarlah's call for aid. He is rallying our fleet. They will set sail for Tarlah within days, and his Greatness has offered you a place onboard."

Troy smiled nervously.

"Familon," Linh asked, "if we travel with them, can we avoid the fighting?"

"Our fleet is far greater than the Zaldeaan one. They may attack us at sea to delay our landing, but their land army is stronger, and historically they have preferred to fight us on land. If you remain on board the ships, there is a reasonable chance you will avoid the fighting."

"Is Tarlah on the coast?" Fiona asked.

Familon shook her head. "It lies further inland. Zaldeaans attacking the city will be too far away to attack our ships."

Linh straightened her shoulders and took a deep breath. "We'd like to sail with them."

Linh heaved her pack over her shoulders, and she, Fiona, Michael, and Troy set off down a sunlit stone corridor. Everyone was quiet. Linh's chest was tight.

Troy's knuckles were white, as he gripped his pack straps with both hands. "The Myths of the Strangers didn't mention sea monsters, so that should be ok," he said, with an attempt at a grin.

"I know it's not what you always wanted," Fiona said bracingly, and Linh wondered what bad news they hadn't already identified, "to be stuck on a ship with Troy for four weeks or more, but I think you can handle it."

Troy turned to Fiona, wide-eyed, and she blushed. Then he burst out laughing at her having a go at him, when she didn't usually tease anyone. Michael smiled, and Linh couldn't help laughing, shaking her head. She might have killed Troy, had she found herself stuck with him for over a week once, but things were beginning to change.

They walked down the hillside, through the village to the beach and a pier stretching over shallow green water to deeper blue sea. Nuard and Familon stood at the pier's end, their pastel togas blowing in the wind.

"We have a parting gift for you," said Familon.

She held up a thick leather belt with a scabbard attached and an iron sword hilt protruding from it. She and Nuard handed a sword to everyone. Linh's shoulders tensed as she received hers.

"Thank you," Fiona said on their behalf.

Troy smiled, but Linh handled her sword with less enthusiasm.

"Look!" Fiona cried, pointing across the sea.

Five ships sailed into view, their high wooden decks towering over the water, three sets of sails filling the sky above each.

"Those floating castles are sea-worthy?" Troy asked doubtfully.

The foredecks were triangular, carved green serpent's heads rising majestically from their prows with fangs bared. The aft decks were rectangular, with green serpents' tails rising from their sterns. All five ships furled sails and dropped anchor. The foremost lowered a rowboat of soldiers in gleaming bronze armour and a man in a green silk tunic on a raised chair. When the boat reached the pier, soldiers raised a ladder, and the cloaked man climbed up.

"Good morning, all," he said. "I am Commander Imphin."

He was tall, with a tanned, weathered-looking face, long white-blonde hair braided behind his head, and pale grey eyes.

"May Esira shine upon you and your fleet, Commander," Nuard replied with a bow, while Familon stared at the ship.

The Commander follower her gaze. "This fleet is of the newest design, and the voyage to Tarlah will be its longest yet," he said proudly. "His Greatness intends to liberate and re-establish trade with Tarlah, then perhaps sail onward, seeking our lost homeland in the Far West."

Linh's heart sped up. If the North Lands yielded no archways or no one who could operate them, the Far West would be next on their list. Could their journey be *that* simple?

"But for now, Tarlah beckons, and the *Timara* awaits. Are you ready to depart?" Imphin asked.

"Thanks for everything," Fiona said to Nuard and Familon. "And for our weapons training, though I hope we won't need it."

Linh reluctantly shook hands with the scholar who had made them so welcome, and his daughter whose lessons had distracted them, and provided stress relief. It was strange, exciting, and frightening, knowing this may be the last time she saw Familon or Nuard.

She followed the others down the ramp to the boat's back bench and sat between soldiers holding oars. Commander Imphin's flagship was more imposing from the waterline, with its giant serpent's head towering to an imaginary life-size above her. Soldiers rowed them towards it, then secured cables, which lifted the boat alongside the ship's bulwarks. Linh peered through portholes, down a long piece of wood, to a wooden box reinforced with iron, with two halves of an enormous bow poking sideways from it and wooden levers rising beyond.

"Are those *machines*?" she asked.

"Power bows," Commander Imphin replied.

Linh blinked against sunlight, as the boat drew level with the railing and they climbed out. Cabins rose at either end of the deck, where stairs went up to the fore and rear decks, from which masts rose. Every timber surface was varnished and reflected sunlight. Crewmembers loosened lines neatly tied to belaying pins, and the mainsail unfurled, flapping downwards before the mainmast overheard.

Linh craned her neck and stared, as three men sitting on a yard lowered the topsail, perhaps thirty metres or more above deck. Sails on all three masts gradually filled with wind, and they glided ahead of the fleet.

"Have you not seen sailing vessels before?" Commander Imphin asked, and Troy shook his head.

Linh wasn't sure what frightened her more, the possibility of falling or the standard of medical care the sailors would receive if they survived.

The commander nodded to a young woman. "Mairatha will show you to your cabin and familiarise you with the ship's routines. We shall see each other later."

Linh returned to the railing when he departed, and the others followed. Myleth Island's pier was small and distant already, the figures of Nuard and Familon waving on it. Linh waved back. As they sailed on, the pier disappeared into the island, the island shrunk, and she shivered, as the only place they knew in Umarinaris vanished below the horizon.

"Would you like to go to your cabin?" Mairatha asked.

"Yes, please," Fiona replied, and they followed her to a small hatch, down the ladder through the boat deck, to a deck lined with power bows. Hammocks hung from its ceiling at different heights, some occupied by burly off-duty men, and storage trunks or barrels were jammed into every crevice on either side of narrow walkways behind the power bows.

"The crew and soldiers sleep in the main hall, but you have a private cabin," said Mairatha, leading them to the back wall. She opened a door, and Linh blinked against the daylight filtering in through a glass window. Four hammocks hung from the ceiling, two trunks stood against the back wall beneath a glass window, and a wide strip of linen hung from one corner beside the door. It was small and cramped but clean and private.

"There is a chamber pot behind the curtain," Mairatha explained, "and I can show you to the lavatory in the rear balcony, the wash space, and kitchens after you have unpacked?"

"Thank you," said Fiona, and Mairatha backed out.

"Not exactly the space I imagined when I thought of sailing," Troy commented, ducking to avoid banging his head on the low ceiling.

"At least we have privacy," said Fiona.

"Is that what the curtain in the corner's for?" Troy asked.

Linh smiled grimly. "No, that's where the pot that functions as a toilet is. And the lavatory she mentioned on the rear deck is probably what we know as a drop dunny."

"Awesome. Don't suppose you know how bathing works?" Troy asked.

"Probably in seawater on deck, with your clothes on," Linh guessed.

"This is worse than camping," said Troy, shaking his head.

"You could swim back to Myleth Island," Michael offered.

Everyone laughed, as Troy said, "I'll take my chances on board."

Linh sighed. That was exactly what they were doing.

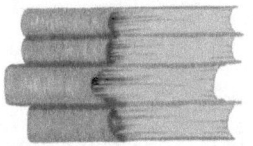

CHApter 14

Across the Western Ocean

Linh: *the Western Ocean*

Linh leant on the foredeck, watching Troy arm wrestle –Boormar, a soldier he'd befriended– over a barrel stood on its end.

"Leave enough of him for the girl," said Boormar's friend, Captain Doorna, nodding at Fiona, who blushed.

"Was that an attempt at sabotage?" Michael asked, quirking his eyebrow.

Captain Doorna winked, but Troy just grinned at Boormar, undistracted. Linh shook her head. The soldiers seemed to consider Troy one of their own. His size and willingness to arm wrestle them probably helped.

"You're still not sure about the soldiers, are you?" Michael asked quietly, as he moved beside her.

Linh shook her head. "They keep going quiet if Fiona or I walk past. Like they're talking about us."

Michael smiled. "It's usually because they don't want you to overhear them swearing or saying something rude."

Linh's eyes widened.

"Seriously," said Michael. "They don't want to 'offend the little girls.'"

Linh sighed, relaxing into the railing. Maybe the men were all right. 'Little girls' was patronising, but at least they weren't a threat.

Footsteps thumped behind her,+ as Commander Imphin approached. "The captain promises a change in scenery. We should reach Timraith Island late this afternoon. We will stop to trade for supplies and let the crew rest. You will be free to explore."

"So it won't be under attack?" Linh asked.

Imphin blinked. "Timraith Island is neither large nor wealthy, nor of strategic importance. Pirates are more likely to attack it than the Zaldeaan navy is."

Linh climbed into a rowboat with her friends, Commander Imphin, and a dozen soldiers a few hours later. Three boats rowed towards a low-lying, sandy-shored island lined with palm trees: a tropical paradise.

For a while, all they heard was the splash of paddles and creak of oars in oarlocks, but Linh noticed a subtle change in Commander Imphin's expression, and the soldiers sat upright, scanning the shore. The weather had cleared and it was warm, yet no one was swimming, not even small children. The beach looked deserted. Where was everyone?

When the boat reached the shallows, the soldiers pulled it to dry sand, where Commander Imphin, Linh, and her friends walked beyond breaking waves towards silence.

"Does this quiet seem strange to you?" Captain Doorna asked, as he and his men walked towards them from the second boat.

"Strange indeed," replied the other, grey-haired captain, as he led his men from the third boat. "There were boats this side of the island last I was here. Perhaps they relocated after the Piracy War, but things may not be as they ought."

Commander Imphin said nothing, and strode down a dirt trail through the vegetation. Linh and her friends followed, the soldiers encircling them. As they moved amongst palms and bright flowers, the soldiers scanned their surroundings with hands on sword hilts or spears in hand, and Linh's shoulders tensed. Her ears strained to pick up movement, but the only sound was breaking waves. It became fainter, until she heard only footsteps and the beating of her heart.

They marched through greenery along a dirt track, ending at a village of stick huts with thatched roofs.

"Captain Doorna, escort the children back to my ship," Commander Imphin ordered.

Soldiers behind him parted. Linh's jaw clenched, as she and her friends turned around and Doorna's guards encircled them. Michael was pale. What had he seen?

Doorna led them swiftly back down the trail.

"What's going on?" asked Troy. "I thought the Zaldeaans wouldn't come here?

"The island is unsafe," Doorna replied evasively.

Linh shivered. If he wasn't naming the Zaldeaans as the threat, was it something else?

Michael swallowed and said, "I saw someone lying on the ground. They weren't moving."

Linh stopped in her tracks, and Fiona gasped.

"They were *dead*?" Troy asked, his voice higher pitched than usual.

"Yes," Doorna replied reluctantly.

Was that why Commander Imphin had sent them away?

Dark half-thoughts made Linh's heart hammer against her chest in the tense silence that followed.

A faint breeze rustling leaves nearby made soldiers turn alertly with swords in hand, as if they thought whoever attacked the village could still be here. Linh stared through tropical plants on both sides of the trail, straining her senses to detect movement, until she relaxed slightly at the sound of waves breaking against the shore.

"There!" Michael yelled.

Linh spun.

"Hsssss!"

`The sound came from a large leaf lifting. A grey-skinned, short, vaguely humanoid creature leapt through the bushes, armed with a pointed stick. It charged the nearest soldier. The soldier slashed with his sword and it fell.

Linh hurried to keep up with the others. The wild pulse of blood through her veins echoed in her ears, as she tried to process the violent creature and its brutal death. She strained to hear other creatures' approach, but heard only the beat of her own heart.

"What was that thing?" Troy asked.

"Chaos Spawn," a soldier muttered. His eyes were wide.

The tight grip the soldiers maintained on their weapons suggested they were afraid. That scared Linh even more.

"Why would it attack *us*?" she asked.

"Shhh!" Doorna ordered.

Silence weighed on them as they walked onto the sand, towards the boats metres away. The sight made Linh relax, until Troy's mouth dropped open. Soldiers rushed to his left, blocking three grey creatures leaping from the undergrowth. All three carried crude wooden spears.

Everyone froze. The first creature thrust a spear at the nearest soldier. The soldier's blow knocked the spear from its hands, cutting the creature's shoulder. The creature ignored the gash and raised a five-fingered, clawed hand. The soldier slashed off its head. Other creatures ran at his companions, and their swords clashed with spears.

Linh gaped in revulsion. The things seemed more intent on attacking than concerned for their own safety, ignoring wounds and fighting on against armed opponents bare-handed when they were disarmed.

"Everyone into the boat!" Doorna commanded.

Linh blinked. The other creatures lay dead on the sand. A soldier pushed her gently and she splashed into the shallows with her friends. They hurried onto boat benches, and she sat gratefully between armed soldiers. More soldiers pushed the boat into deeper water. It rocked as they climbed aboard, seizing their oars.

Linh heard a screech before the oars splashed into the water, and saw another creature fall dead on the beach, a spear in its chest. The soldiers rowed with forceful strokes, and the boat gained speed as more grey-skinned creatures ran onto the beach, five bursting from greenery. One hurled a spear at them. The weapon splashed harmlessly into the waves.

All five creatures waded into the shallows, fanning out. They stumbled in up to their shoulders and began flailing. They struggled and ignored each other. A wave swept over them, and they went under. Linh bit her lip, waiting for them to surface again, but they didn't. They couldn't swim. They had drowned.

"Thanks be to Esla," said Captain Doorna. "Row to Commander Imphin's ship."

Linh's pounding heart gradually slowed, as she stared back at a deceptively deserted beach. They quickly reached Commander Imphin's ship, and the boat was hauled up.

Boormar leant over the side, calling, "What are your orders Captain?"

"Have the other boat readied and filled with armed men. Commander Imphin needs aid."

The boat drew level with the deck. Hands reached to help Linh out. She backed out of the soldiers' way and Fiona moved beside her, as soldiers climbed into their boat.

Mairatha stepped out of the crowd and asked, "What is wrong?"

"We were attacked," said Troy. "Some grey-dwarf things with spears are loose on the island, and they attacked when we were leaving. I don't think there's anyone left," he added softly, his gaze downcast. "Those creatures seem to have overrun the island."

Linh shuddered. She heard Fiona sniff and put an arm around her, then identified the background retching as Michael throwing up over the railing. Troy placed a reassuring hand on his back. What had he seen?

"Can you be sure of this?" Boormar asked.

"I think the village was full of bodies," Michael replied softly. "I saw one. Commander Imphin told us to leave because he didn't want us to see."

"You have never seen a dead person before?"

Michael shook his head. "Never. And not one that was..."

"Murdered," Troy finished. "Those little bastards."

"Come inside," said Mairatha.

Linh followed the others into a room off deck. Daylight shone through a window, and Mairatha ushered them to chairs around a table built into a wall. Linh stared into the distance, then became aware of a wooden cup of tea in her hand, which she vaguely remembered accepting. She didn't drink tea.

"Are any of you injured?" Mairatha asked, hovering beside the table.

"No," Troy replied. "Those soldiers know what they were doing."

"Those creatures were unnatural," said Michael. "Animals that can't swim *never* try. But those things..."

"Drowned themselves," Linh finished. "And attacked for *no* reason."

"I didn't notice any wildlife," Michael added.

Linh shuddered again.

"They're horrible," said Fiona, tearing up. "All those people..."

Linh hugged her. The creatures had killed the wildlife, which somehow disturbed her more deeply than murder. What could anyone or thing gain from that? It sounded like mindless violence, and Michael was right: it was entirely unnatural.

"Have you heard of anything like what we're describing?" Michael asked Mairatha, who shook her head and smoothed her skirts, pale-faced.

"Maybe they only exist on that island," Troy suggested.

"Those things and people don't coexist," Linh objected. "They must have come from somewhere else."

But where? And how had anyone made the creatures want to kill more than they wanted to survive?

Commander Imphin returned later, and Mairatha led him to what Linh belatedly realised was his sitting room. The commander surveyed their faces and asked, "How did you know?"

"Mic saw one of the bodies," Troy replied. "And Doorna's guards killed creatures which attacked us on our way here."

"Chaos take those damars!" Commander Imphin cursed. "I would never have brought you if I knew creatures like that were here. I have never seen anything like it."

"Were there survivors?" Michael asked.

Commander Imphin shook his head. "The attack surprised the villagers. Most do not seem to have realised they were in danger."

Linh sunk into her chair.

Lines formed between Commander Imphin's brows, and he kept talking. "Someone knew the creatures were loose. We found damars shot with arrows on a beach, facing the island, as if shot from the sea. There was timber and bits of broken wooden crate around them."

"What does 'damar' mean?" Troy asked.

"Creature of evil," Imphin replied. "My men named them so."

"Who would ship creatures like that?" Fiona asked.

Imphin shook his head. "Perhaps someone in the Far West."

Linh shivered. As if the prospect of sitting on board, hoping Zaldeaans didn't attack their ship as the army disembarked wasn't stressful enough, there could be murderous creatures in cages being shipped around these waters.

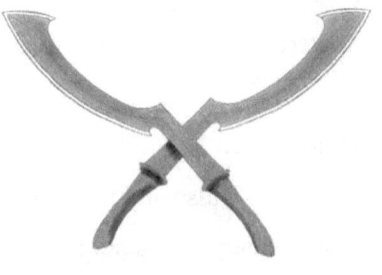

CHAPTER 15

AFTER THE BATTLE

RUARNON: *Tarlah City*

In Tarlah Castle, Ruarnon lay on their back in bed. Moonlight from their balcony shone on frescoes of their ancestors around the walls. It was late. They should be sleeping. But every time they closed their eyes, they saw figures falling off horses. Cut down by swords. Shot with arrows and exposed by retreat. The dead. Hundreds of them. Ruarnon's uncle was one of many who had gone to war and wouldn't be returning.

Ruarnon sat on the edge of their bed, rubbing weary eyes and failing to shut down their overworked mind. They rose, pacing past their double bed and ivory inlaid writing desk. The Zaldeaan Realm had built an empire on the corpses of its enemies. They must have drunk rivers of blood, and still they thirsted for more. Ruarnon's heart sped up with anger. Why hadn't King Kyura executed the warmongers in his court? Why hadn't Uncle Omah... Ruarnon froze. In their mind's eye, Uncle Omah sat atop his horse, hunched forwards, his sword arm wide, shield lowered, the warlord's sword piercing his middle.

Ruarnon flopped on their bed. They wanted to go back to when Tor checked Omah's pulse and have him seize Omah's reins and lead Omah to safety. For a surgeon to tend to Omah. To tell Aunt Telena her husband hadn't died.

Memories whirred through Ruarnon's mind. Uncle Omah in shining iron armour, leading a cavalry charge through a shower of arrows. Uncle Omah in red silks, calmly discussing the war in the Golden Meeting Hall. Uncle Omah's pride at the defiance of those who showed faith in the army by remaining in the city until the battle was lost.

Ruarnon remembered the man who had smiled as he expressed hope Ruarnon would rule with patience and diplomacy, instead of frustration at the occasional foolishness of their subjects. Their mentor after their father's abduction, their uncle, friend, and partner in ruling Tarlah. How could he be gone?

Eventually, Ruarnon sunk into a fitful sleep. They rode on horseback at great speed, away from Death Belt Desert. Uncle Omah was in danger. They had to find him, had to warn him. They left their horse in the stables and ran through corridor after corridor, until their mother stepped in front of them near the gardens.

"I have to find Father! I have to tell him not to let Uncle Omah go!" Ruarnon shouted.

"But your uncle isn't going anywhere," said Corina. "He is in the gardens with your father, discussing kingship."

That didn't sound right. But there they were, beyond Mother, on a balcony overlooking the gardens—Ruarnon's golden-haired father talking amicably with his younger brother. Ruarnon ran to them and seized their uncle round the middle. Uncle Omah laughed and hugged them back.

"I thought you were going," Ruarnon said with relief.

"I can't go anywhere," said Uncle Omah. "I promised your father I would guide you if anything happens to him."

"Even if he left," said King Urmillian, "You would still have Aunt Telena and my friend, Companion Tor. You would not be alone."

Umarinaris came back to Ruarnon slowly the following day. A servant sat beside their bed, and they smelled fruit. They blinked once or a hundred times, then finally sat up. A concerned face came into focus, and the servant passed them a breakfast tray.

"Companion Pamoran says your presence is required in the Golden Meeting Hall," the servant said hesitantly.

A summons from Pamoran. It sounded wrong. Ruarnon tried to distract themself with breakfast, then stood and let their servants dress them.

"We are finished," the second servant said uncertainly.

Ruarnon blinked, They were staring at the wall. There was no excuse to delay. But the Golden Meeting Hall seemed so far away. They didn't feel like walking, yet it felt terribly close, and they didn't want to go because something painful awaited them. But they *had* to go.

Ruarnon walked slowly, one of their servants hastening to open the door, the other wishing them luck. But replying required thinking and opening their mouth to form words, and Ruarnon couldn't do that just now, so they nodded and wandered distractedly to the Golden Meeting Hall.

Dread grew within them when they sighted the doorway, but they had to appear in command, so they took a deep breath and walked through.

As Ruarnon strode in, it struck them why they didn't want to be there. It wasn't the two men standing to one side, it was someone who should be there but wasn't. Someone who would never enter the room again. Someone who had once run the Royal Council, but would do so no longer.

Ruarnon clenched their fists. They couldn't rage yet. They had to do that in private; it was important.

They strode towards two men at the end of the table talking. Companion Tor should be there. He was Head Companion, King Urmillian's greatest friend, and he should be Regent... but he couldn't because he was wounded. Captain Noma, his younger sister, must be here to replace him.

Ruarnon suppressed the urge to hit something and announced, "As heir, Co-Regent and nearest kin to the king, I, Ruarnon of Tarlah name Companion Pamoran as my father's Regent, until my father returns or I assume the regency."

Pamoran and Noma bowed in reply.

"I shall do my best, Benevolence," Pamoran said gravely.

Ruarnon vaguely remembered seeing a lone chariot with retreating infantry rushing past it. Pamoran had overseen the retreat until the last moment. He was the right choice.

"If Your Benevolence wishes to rest," said Noma, "my brother will also be absent for several meetings."

Ruarnon considered it. They could go back to their room and smash everything they owned. They could go to the training yard and fire arrows until they split one down the middle with another or their muscles became rigid with fatigue. None of it would do any good. Fighting did no good. Decisions would be made here. They couldn't set an example for anyone now, but Tarlah was under siege, and the Council would decide how to fight back. That seemed the closest to happiness they could feel now, so that was what they would aim for.

"I wish to see how the Council prepares for a siege," they said.

The Companions inclined their heads, but Noma looked concerned. If Tor were present, Ruarnon might have said more, but they hardly knew Noma and felt the need to prove themself to Regent Pamoran, the warrior, so they kept their silence, despite their reluctance when Pamoran sat in Omah's seat.

Advisor Monin entered, blinking at Ruarnon, then bowed his head gravely. Aunt Telena arrived wearing a black veil from head to toe, and took her seat on Pamoran's other side. The veil symbolised the world becoming dark in the eyes of those who had lost someone they loved... but Ruarnon had spoken to Uncle Omah yesterday. Omah had been at every Council meeting Ruarnon attended. It felt like he was late, checking battle diagrams or watching people evacuate from the Royal Writing Room. Just because he wasn't here didn't mean he was dead.

Ruarnon had a sudden urge to run to the Royal Writing Room. Their legs tightened to push off their chair, but a hollow feeling in their chest stopped them. The rational part of their brain told them that a visit to the Royal Writing Room, Uncle Omah's quarters, or that scouring the castle and Tarlah City would be painful. Reluctantly, they relaxed their legs, unsure if they were committed to being at the meeting. But they didn't know where else to go or what else to do.

"Welcome to the first Council of the Regency of Pamoran, may it be the last," said a grave, firm voice, and Ruarnon turned as Pamoran continued. "We shall begin with a report from Companion Noma."

Noma's first few sentences were clear, but her voice grew quieter and more distant the longer she spoke of evacuees and enemy patrols leaving them alone. Ruarnon listened until their eyes became unfocused, and they gazed into the distance, unhearing.

Gradually, sight and sound became clearer, perhaps as they woke from a daze. Pamoran led a discussion, and then officials were summoned. Pamoran gave them orders and demonstrated that he was in charge, until Ruarnon couldn't deny that Pamoran was Senior Regent and their uncle was gone. They didn't hear their aunt calling for refreshments, but when she took them by the arm and steered them towards a door to a small private courtyard, they realised they were crying.

"He is really..." said Ruarnon, their vision blurring with tears. "He is gone. I just want to speak to him again. I do not care what we speak about... if he spends hours lecturing me about kingship or gives me new challenges as Co-Regent. I just want to see him again."

"I know dear," their aunt said softly. "I feel the same way."

And she held them for a long time until the tears stopped.

"Take some time for yourself," Aunt Telena advised. "Give yourself time to feel, to accept what you don't want to. The enemy is camping in the forest preparing siege equipment and it will be at least a week before they are ready to act. The Council can prepare Tarlah for siege until you are ready to join them." She sighed. "Ruarnon, you may need to take up sole regency until your parents are recovered. I suggest you return to the Council ready to speak boldly, wisely, and to leave certain men in no doubt that they will be advising you, not making decisions for you."

Ruarnon was too drained to care about that now. They needed rest.

"Will you sit in, in my place?" they asked.

She smiled sadly. "Yes. I will."

"Thank you." Ruarnon returned to their rooms and slumped in a chair. Servants came bustling in, asking if they needed anything. What they needed was confirmation that their parents were alive, but spies had been unable to provide that. They shook their head and motioned the servants out. Then they sat and gazed unseeing at the wall, until their exhausted mind regained the capacity to have thoughts. What did they do while adults solved Umarinaris' problems, and all they could think about was the uncle and friend they had loved, and the pain of being forced to let him go?

In such a short time, they had learnt so much from Omah... That was it! They stood, tore open a drawer in a cabinet and rummaged for a scroll of parchment, a stylus, and ink. Uncle Omah couldn't relay their father's lessons anymore, but Ruarnon could commit to writing everything Omah and Urmillian had taught them. They could preserve their father and uncle's teachings for themself and future rulers. Ruarnon sat at their desk and began to write feverishly, ignoring ink stains on their hands.

CHAPTER 16

EAVESDROPPING

ETHLIN: *Tarlah City*

Ethlin didn't rest the day after the battle, not until she saw Arlian walking across the Royal Training Courtyard, instead of sneaking up on her like usual. His anxious gaze roved her figure, hesitating at her bandaged wrist, then he smiled, realising she was whole, her only injury a sprained wrist. She ran to embrace him and he kissed her eagerly, then smoothed hairs that had strayed from her braid.

"I was very fortunate," he said solemnly. "General Takanis fought with my older brothers in the Piracy War. She knows I am my father's last living son, so she insisted I ride with her. If I had gone with the Regent... Most of their guards were killed, and Companion Tor is lucky to be alive. One of my friends lost their uncle yesterday, and another nearly lost his father."

Tears started in Arlian's eyes, and Ethlin hugged him tightly. For all Arlian complained about how dull Tor's son Drake was, and joked about Ruarnon being an old midlun at sixteen, she suspected he was secretly fond of the high-ranking Tarlahn youths he took lessons with.

She straightened. Were those footsteps?

"Behind here," she whispered, leading Arlian around the columns at the back of the courtyard.

His brows creased as they crouched, which made Ethlin realise it was strange for anyone to be training the day after the battle, on an official day of rest.

"Why here?" asked a deep male voice.

"It is the last place in all Tarlah Castle anyone would go after a battle," a gruff, slightly hoarse, elderly male voice replied softly. "They made you Regent?"

"I am young and a soldier at heart. Who better?"

"You do realise that if their parents are not recovered, you would be well-placed to be king?"

Ethlin stifled a gasp. Arlian tensed and silently motioned her to be still. There was a long pause from the courtyard. Ethlin's muscles began to ache as she sat too long in the same position. But she didn't dare move, for fear of being overheard.

"I held one boy's hand through war," the gruff, elderly voice continued. "But Urmillian risked being executed every time he picked up a spear to train. He was raised in occupied Tarlah, dreaming of our independence, and he helped fight for his throne and people. Ruarnon has fought for nothing and is a midlun to boot. I'll not coddle them through war."

"What do you mean to do, Father?"

"A midlun's sensitivity is the last quality we need in a wartime leader, and the fact Ruarnon is still a child will only make them more reluctant about necessary sacrifices."

"Perhaps. Tor and my brother will have trained them the same way any of us were, but they are different, and Tor believes their greatest strength is their mind. I wonder if that will be a tactical advantage."

There was a pause, in which Ethlin could almost feel the older man's frown radiating across the courtyard.

"They are fond of Lenaris, are they not?" the elderly voice asked. "Recall her to comfort them in their grief. Inform her she is the best marriage match they could make in Tarlah. Have them promised to each other to distract Ruarnon while you rule us through war. Tell them her father will stand in for theirs, so long as Urmillian is missing, and they may have their co-regency with you. Then lead us through this war, the next, whatever it takes, until we are both in our graves, and you, Lenaris and I have them prepared to lead Tarlah at war."

"And we so happen to put your future great-grandson, my grandson, on the throne in the process?"

Ethlin's heart skipped a beat.

"Why not?" Monin replied. "My tactics won Tarlah's independence in the rebellion. The people owe me their freedom and the fair treatment they receive. Tradition and nostalgia placed a youth on the throne because they happened to be related to the previous king. He was unqualified and unfit, like his heir It is a foolish system, and you are in a position to change it."

"Ruarnon tried to stop the carriage themselves, then attacked Omah's attackers with arrows on the field, close enough to battle to get themself killed," said Pamoran. "The youth is brave. But they are a youth. I will speak to Lenaris."

"Speak to her? Not instruct her?"

"You know I wanted sons, yet she is more capable than most sons in Tarlah, and has a will to match mine. She will not be led, but she can be persuaded."

"You give the girl too much licence."

"Her confidence and independence are what they admire about her. It will give Ruarnon cause to listen to her."

"Since when was the warrior Pamoran a strategist of the heart?"

"Since I was allowed to finish raising my daughters during the Peace."

There was another pause, then finally the Regent and his father departed. Arlian held up a hand, straining his ears until he was sure they were beyond hearing. Then he exhaled deeply and Ethlin leaned back and stretched her aching legs. Her mind wasn't so easily relieved.

"What do we do?" she asked Arlian.

Arlian sighed. "If anyone else were involved, I would tell Lenaris. But they want to place her at the heart of this."

He frowned; an expression unfamiliar to Ethlin.

"Leave it with me. I will consider whom to tell. And do not speak a word of this to anyone, not even your sister. If Advisor Monin would criticise and seek to control Ruarnon... It is dangerous knowledge. Do not let anyone know you possess it."

He looked earnestly into her eyes, and Ethlin sighed. He usually spoke casually to her. But now he sounded like the young man of status his mother had raised, the way he spoke when he was anxious.

"I promise," said Ethlin.

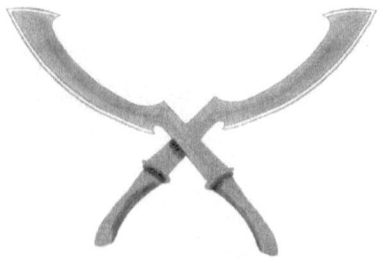

CHAPTER 17

REGENCY

RUARNON: *Tarlah City, the Siege of Tarlah, Day One*

R uarnon nocked another arrow to their bow and loosed. It whizzed across the Royal Training Courtyard, thunking into the centre of the target board.

"I am glad you can still shoot."

Ruarnon's breath caught. Lenaris entered the courtyard in a fitted leather tunic and kilt and greeted them with a smile. Ruarnon ran to hug her. She hugged them back, but there was something reluctant about the set of her mouth.

"What brings you back?" Ruarnon asked.

"Father suggested you needed me more. I'm so sorry about your uncle."

Ruarnon grimaced.

"I suspect it wasn't Father," she added. "I think Grandfather had something to do with it. He may want me to influence you."

Ruarnon's face fell when they saw the conflict in her eyes. Ruarnon stood too close to the throne. Everything unfolding around them may be about politics now.

Lenaris straightened. "I'm happy to discuss anything Father or Monin suggest, but if *I* advise you, it will be what *I* think."

Ruarnon gave her a small smile. "Monin's being daft if he thinks you'll be his game piece. Would you like to duel?"

Lenaris returned their smile, took her spear, and stood poised with the same controlled grace as Companion Pamoran. Ruarnon swiped with their spear. Lenaris danced wide. They parried her counterblow, and the dance of lunging to attack, sidestepping, and pivoting to best defend or attack began.

The pair trained regularly from then on, and Ruarnon recalled stories of Omah as they discussed Omah and Ruarnon's father's ideas about kingship and Ruarnon recorded them.

But Ruarnon was late for one training session.

"Ruarnon!"

The whisperer behind the pillar was Arlian. Ruarnon's brows rose when Arlian motioned them over. Arlian was flushed and breathing too fast.

"What is wrong?" Ruarnon asked.

"I overheard Monin plotting with Pamoran. They want you to marry Lenaris and her to convince you to give Pamoran the regency until the war is over." Arlian's gaze fell to the ground, and he continued in a rush, "Monin doubts your ability as Co-Regent because of your age, inexperience, and because you are midlun."

Ruarnon's breath caught. "*Marry* Lenaris? She suspected they wanted to influence me, but..." The rest began to sink in. "Monin said me being a midlun was a problem?"

"He thinks it will mean you're too soft to make hard decisions during war," Arlian said, shifting awkwardly.

Ruarnon shook their head. "Thank you. It was brave of you to seek me out."

"What will you do?" Arlian asked.

Ruarnon's heart raced. They only intended to side-line Ruarnon, but the plot bordered on treason, especially if it involved a long regency for Pamoran, even if it was for the sake of Tarlah...

"*Not* marry Lenaris," Ruarnon replied dazedly. "We're not made for each other that way. And not let them know that I know, so there's no risk of them tracing my knowledge back to you."

Arlian exhaled deeply.

"I'll have to claim the regency and show them who's in charge, like Tor and Aunt Telena advised."

Arlian gaped, then smiled. "I stuck around for the fighting and I'm happy to leave the politicking to you, but it's the same kind of courage. Monin probably doesn't think Lenaris should be a Companion because she's female, and I suspect he only accepts Captain Noma on the Council because she's Tor's sister, but he's kind of blind in some ways."

Ruarnon laughed. Arlian was known for being irreverent, but it was a relief to hear someone speak freely.

"Best," Arlian added, clapping them on the arm.

Ruarnon bowed their head. Arlian jogged away and Ruarnon entered the Royal Training Courtyard. Lenaris met their gaze with a smile. She didn't know about the marriage proposal yet, they were sure of it.

"I think it's time," Ruarnon said. "Aunt Telena said I should return when I'm ready to lead. I don't feel ready to step into Uncle Omah's sandals, but putting it off won't do any good."

"I don't think Omah felt ready to step in for your father's sandals," said Lenaris. "I think he related better to Drake and me, as Tor and Pamoran's children. I wonder if he felt like the king's kid brother."

Ruarnon felt their eyebrows rise.

"Hold your ground with my grandfather. Appeal to reason. Father may back off if you do, even if you disagree with Grandfather."

Ruarnon sighed. "Father and Uncle Omah taught me well enough. But I was never quite good enough for my father. Leading experienced men like your father and grandfather will be the biggest act of my life. What if they see straight through me?"

Lenaris shook her head. "If you give them good reasons, stick to those reasons and push everyone to accept, and you counter the Zaldeaans and act as you say you will, they will accept that you are the co-regent you swore to be."

Ruarnon's head spun. Play a game until they were so well-versed in the rules, such a good performer, that the game became a reality. It fit Omah's metaphor of the stage. But the act... Fireflies burst into flight in their stomach, an entire swarm fluttering madly.

"I barely have battle experience," they said, voicing their most significant doubt.

"Your quietness and thoughtfulness reassure people," said Lenaris. "Arlian mentioned it when Father trained all of us."

"Arlian?" Ruarnon asked with raised brows.

"Exactly. The last person to publicly admit respecting authority. You have a way of quietly standing your ground and meeting every challenge my father throws at you. That doesn't just position you well in dealing with the Royal Council; it makes your presence calming to your soldiers as they defend the city."

Pamoran wouldn't have that effect. He'd energise the army. Inspire it. But he was the wrong man to calm nervous levied soldiers, especially inexperienced youth. Ruarnon could do that. They knew exactly how levied soldiers felt, because they felt it themself.

"You think I compliment him?" Ruarnon asked.

Lenaris bit her lip. "I think you could rein him in, as I suspect your father did. Father likes action, but I worry he's too used to danger, too eager to throw himself into the thick of it."

Ruarnon remembered the last chariot to retreat from the battlefield. Pamoran was brave, self-sacrificing, but also liable to get himself and possibly others killed. Was he a force best channelled?

Tor would be best as Regent, but he was too severely wounded to take on the role for some time. But Ruarnon knew much of what Tor knew and how Tor thought. Could Ruarnon's calm and strategic thinking balance Pamoran's bravery?

Ruarnon rubbed their chin. They would come of age in six months and could claim the regency then. But why wait? Why give Monin six months to try to sway Ruarnon to his will? Or Pamoran six months to taste power? If Ruarnon claimed the regency now, if they played the role Urmillian and Omah had schooled them in, having the final say as Regent, but letting the Council guide them, could they ensure their reign was more stable and their advisors more united than Kyura's?

"Do you think it could come to factions, divide our people?" Ruarnon asked.

"Not as the Zaldeaans did," Lenaris replied.

"But is there a risk of rivalry?"

"I wonder if Tor would back you out of loyalty to you and your father. But my presence is a sign that two factions could develop. Just because we are not as power-hungry and self-centred as the Zaldeaans does not mean the Royal Council couldn't be divided on the question of your leadership." Lenaris smiled. "You don't have to speak as loudly and as often or to enjoy being the centre of attention as much as your father, to be king. Omah was quieter, but the people still respected him."

Ruarnon smiled. They would take decisive action in dangerous times, and hope their advisors would unite to support them instead of competing and risking undermining Ruarnon's efforts to defend Tarlah. Surely most would see that was more important and focus on advising Ruarnon, instead of worrying about whether a midlun was up to the job?

But they might worry. Because if a midlun could rule, theoretically a woman could too, and Ruarnon doubted Tarlah could handle that again just yet. After all, Aunt Merlah was Father's older sister, but she stood aside in favour of Urmillian when their father died. But none of that changed what Ruarnon needed to do.

"I'll claim the regency. I wish you could be there to see it."

Lenaris smiled. "Don't make eye contact with my grandfather if you can avoid it."

"Have you ever contended with his will?"

Lenaris' smile turned wry. "I suspect I do so every time I pick up a spear. If he wanted me to sway your policies, he should have anticipated this is how I would do so."

Ruarnon shook their head. "I wish I had your will sometimes. You've always been so sure of yourself."

"What the kingdom thinks of me doesn't need to concern me. Perhaps that allows me to trust my judgement more. Perhaps that's what you need to do."

Ruarnon nodded. They were so used to trusting and following their father, uncle, or Companion Tor. But when they claimed the regency, they must trust themself. They couldn't lead the Royal Council if they let self-doubt make them hesitate. This was going to be the performance of their life.

A week after Omah's death, Ruarnon strode apprehensively towards the Golden Meeting Hall, their posture the upright stance of the regent, their heart pounding against their ribs. Their grief was still raw, and they weren't looking forward to entering a room that may prod it, nor doing so while Tor was wounded and absent. But it was time.

Ruarnon entered the Golden Meeting Hall with their head held high, glad that the Council wasn't in session and noting that General Aza was also present, and they would have to convince not only the Council, but also the head of Tarlah's army. Conversations around the room faded. Ruarnon's heart thudded against their chest, but Aunt Telena nodded encouragingly. Ruarnon laced their hands behind their back to stop them from shaking. "I feel it is time to begin my regency."

Newly appointed Companion Noma blinked. Anger flashed in Monin's eyes, but Pamoran's lips twitched. Ruarnon could ask him to act as Co-Regent. By not doing so, they were telling the Council they intended to lead. Ruarnon had the strangest feeling Pamoran approved.

"Benevolence, you are grieving," said Monin. "And inexperienced at war. This is no time to have an apprentice at the helm."

His motives may be pure, but the plot Arlian had reported was not. Ruarnon didn't need Lenaris' warnings to see that they could not give ground to Monin. Whatever arguments Monin made, Ruarnon had to counter them outright. Their chest tightened as they drew on Tor's teachings. "I am young and inexperienced. I trust this Council will advise me well and that we will defend Tarlah to the best of this Council's ability."

"Wartime decisions are difficult to learn, let alone to make," Pamoran said, and Ruarnon respected him for saying what he thought to Ruarnon's face.

"I decided to kill archers hunting my guards and the warlord attacking my uncle easily enough," Ruarnon countered. "I have killed with my own hands. I won't hesitate to do so by proxy defending this city."

Pamoran inclined his head slightly. He knew every word of that was true, and he seemed to respect Ruarnon's actions in battle. Maybe Ruarnon had more to offer in war than they thought?

They'd just gained an advantage in the Council's debate. It was time to drive their position home. But Aunt Telena was eyeing their Uncle's chair at the head of the meeting table pointedly. Ruarnon took a deep breath and gestured everyone to sit, pretending their chest didn't feel about to burst with nerves as they approached Uncle Omah's chair and sat in it, leaving Pamoran the chair on their left, which in the previous meeting had been Ruarnon's co-regent's seat.

Monin's brows rose as he sat, but were Pamoran's lips twitching in the hint of a smile? Ruarnon had no time to consider.

"If the Zaldeaans breach the walls and take this city," they addressed the Council, sitting up straight as they peered down the table, "I assume we will be beheaded, like Tarlah's leaders during the Bloody Occupation. I should like to know the Council's thoughts on how to prevent that."

A storm raged in Monin's eyes. He thought Ruarnon a child at play, as Tor had warned. But Ruarnon was speaking as Regent and Heir. Surely defying Ruarnon now would be treason?

"We suspect the enemy is modifying their siege equipment," Companion Noma reported, and Ruarnon's shoulders relaxed slightly at the woman taking them seriously.

230

"Our reinforced walls are too strong to be rammed like last time. They are constructing an iron-tipped ram to force the gate. And they have power bows, though they are not yet set to assault the city."

Thought of weapons capable of hurling boulders into their people's homes made Ruarnon's stomach churn. But they kept their breathing steady, schooling themself to be calm, knowing the Council would watch their reactions as closely as Urmillian had.

"How is our gate defended?" they asked.

"With signal fire," Noma replied.

Apparently, being a junior member of the Council meant Noma got lesser tasks, like telling Ruarnon things everyone else knew.

"The gate is the weakest point, but few will wish to enter the city that way, if we light a fire across North Road," Noma continued.

Ruarnon noted how the woman repositioned her hands as she spoke: a sign of discomfort? Would a cruel Zaldeaan general drive invading soldiers through fire to attack Tarlah Castle? If the enemy entered the city, house to house fighting would follow. That would be chaotic and involve many casualties.

"Have you considered additional obstacles?" Ruarnon asked.

Monin watched them intently, taking their measure. Omah hadn't expected them to devise tactics. But with no word from

Tarlah's allies, the enemy at the gates, and the lives of everyone at Tarlah Castle at stake, Ruarnon was determined to defend the city by every possible means.

"Furniture can be an obstacle, or carts," Pamoran replied. "But it can be burned, and the Zaldeaans have weeks to clear it before Planting Season will require their levied farmers return home."

Monin glared at Pamoran, and Ruarnon suppressed a smirk at Monin's frustration that Pamoran was taking them seriously.

"What about earth and stone from the gold mines?" Ruarnon asked. "If we set the signal fire atop it, would they be able to clear it?"

Monin's mouth opened, then shut.

"We would need to give the order to shift rubble immediately to get it in place before the enemy attack," General Aza replied.

"But does the Council think it effective?" Ruarnon pressed, projecting authority they didn't feel, grateful that their father had pushed them so hard. Concealing their feelings from Urmillian had taught them to keep their hands still and to ignore the rapid thudding of their heart, which right now was declaring them an imposter.

Noma looked to the others. To Ruarnon's surprise, General Aza bowed his head in acknowledgement with Aunt Telena, followed by Pamoran, hastily followed by Noma, Monin seeming deliberate in bowing his head last.

Ruarnon almost smiled in relief at the Council's approval of their first tactic. "Which other locations in the city does the Council think are vulnerable?" they asked.

"Anywhere along the eastern wall may be tunnelled under from the forest," General Aza reported. "General Takanis' second cavalry raid disrupted one attempt at tunnels, and we are yet to see signs of a second. Tunnels and the gates are the only likely points for the enemy to gain entrance."

"What of the enemy's siege towers?" Ruarnon asked.

"Our walls are too strong to be rammed by siege towers," Aza replied. "The enemy towers are still under construction, already higher than the last siege."

Digging tunnels was slow, especially in secrecy. And gates could be barred with rubble. If siege towers could lift soldiers to the height of the ramparts, the enemy could fight defenders from atop them and enter over the walls. It had never been done before, and it would be bloody fighting, with high casualties. But Planting Season was coming. Tarlah City had to fall before Zaldeaan levied farmers worried about planting next year's crops at home and dissension arose in the enemy ranks.

"What if the enemy plan to put infantry in their towers and use them to assault our wall defenders directly?" Ruarnon asked.

"We can place many more archers atop the walls than they can place soldiers atop their towers," Monin objected. "Any general who gave that order would be positioning his men as target practice."

"Then how does the enemy plan to capture Tarlah City?" Ruarnon asked. "Betrayal would be a death sentence to most of us, and I doubt Kyura will accept having defied his father's Peace in vain."

"Enemy generals were prepared to lose cavalry on the battlefield to lure us into encirclement," Pamoran added. "I agree this generation of Zaldeaans is willing to make sacrifices to seize victory. We will do well to prepare against all means to take the city."

Heads around the table bowed in acceptance to Pamoran. Fireflies stirred in Ruarnon's belly as they wondered how long it would take the Council to trust their suggestions by merit, not the sanction of another council member.

The Council was all eyeing Ruarnon expectantly. Pamoran had said to defend the walls against all means of attack...

"What options do we have for countering towers with soldiers that assault our wall defenders hand to hand?"

When their plans were complete, Ruarnon dismissed the Council, then exhaled deeply and sunk back into their chair. If they kept acting the part of Regent well enough, perhaps eventually they would *feel* like the regent.

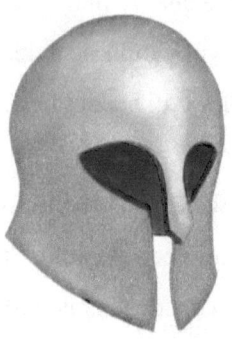

CHAPTER 18

A NEW THREAT

10 MAR: the Zaldeaan Realm, the Siege of Tarlah, Day One

A ir streamed past, as Iomar rode through the countryside, grain fields stretching left and right, as his horse galloped along a cart track. This had always been his favourite way to ease tension, and with his father ruling as regent in Zaldeaa City and Kyura fighting a war he opposed in Tarlah, Iomar needed this more than ever. But it wasn't to last. As he and his bodyguards neared a town nestled against Wilder's Forest, a few bowshots from the coast, he reined in.

"What is that noise?" he asked.

"Shouts," his captain replied. "From beyond the village."

Iomar looked up to where a group of children had lined up to play throwing stones beyond the last cottage.

"Get inside!" the woman running towards them from the fields yelled. "It isn't safe! The west coast is under attack!"

Iomar's breath caught. That was impossible. She sounded panicked but sure of herself. And her dress was torn and darkened by patches of sweat.

"And who is going to attack us?" asked an old man shuffling around the cottage. "The Tarlahns are under siege. Go back to your home and rest, woman, you must be tired from overwork in your husband's absence. Go care for your children."

"They are dead." Her gaze was unfocused, but her tone was firm.

Iomar heeled his horse forwards. "Who killed them?" he called, his bodyguards following.

"Grey-skinned creatures, Excellency. They were wielding spears. Hissing, screeching, clawing. No one knows where they came from. But I kept encountering them as I ran from the coast."

An attack by *monsters*? He studied her pale, sweaty features. Her gaze was distant, her hands clutched at her skirts, and her spirit seemed far away, as though distancing herself from reality. Which suggested she had seen or experienced something terrible, but monsters?

"Where?" Iomar asked.

"Near the coast. They seemed to come from everywhere." She staggered and sat abruptly.

"How far have you run?" Iomar asked.

"Since this morning," she replied.

"Get her to the castle," he told one of his guards.

"Your Excellency, how could such creatures exist?" Iomar's captain asked quietly, as two of his guards helped the woman onto one of their horses.

Iomar shivered. "She is pale as death and has just collapsed with exhaustion. She claimed her children were dead, and she was concerned about protecting these children. I would rather march every man I have to the coast for no good reason, than wait for messengers while some ungodly thing kills my people. Give my soldiers the order to assemble and tell the captain they are to meet us here as soon as possible."

"Excellency, there is someone else," the old man called, pointing further north at Wilder Forest.

A broadly built cart-horse trotted out from underneath trees, towing a cart filled with children. While Iomar waited for his soldiers, a woman rode out of the forest further south, slumped in her saddle. Urgent barking rose, and two dogs emerged nearby, whining when the older man approached them.

"Seize every horse in and near the castle," Iomar ordered the rest of his guards. "We mount as many soldiers as we can."

Within the hour, Iomar and his men rode out. They passed villages near his castle where children played happily and farmers' wives tended their fields in peace. But it was different near the forest. There wasn't a single bird call.

Nothing rustled the leaves of the undergrowth. Then something crashed through the plants. Two-thirds the height of a human, the two-legged creature wore only a loincloth as it charged them. It ran with a crude spear raised, hissing and spitting through a mouth full of fanged teeth. Its eyes glowed yellow in the darkness of the shade. Iomar grimaced, raised his bow, and shot it in the heart. It fell dead.

As his soldiers rode closer to inspect the impossible creature, Iomar kept one of his best riders back. "Cut off one of the creatures' hands," he said quietly. "Deliver it to my father. Tell him we are under attack."

"There isn't time to starve the city into surrender," Kyura told his First General in his field tent. "How do you propose to take the city?"

Companion Karmarn eyed the general from a cushion on the tent floor on Kyura's right. Aoran paced on Kyura's left. Neither would like how the siege unfolded.

Kyura wouldn't, either. Karmarn had needed to restrain him from bodily assaulting his Cavalry General for his wasteful tactics in the field battle. But those tactics had very nearly let them encircle the Tarlahns, almost achieving total victory. Kyura grit his teeth. Now was not the time to be squeamish about the loss of life. He had to fight his desire to end this repulsive madness a little longer, until the job was done.

"Diversion," the First General replied. "Assault the northern walls with power slings, power bows, and siege towers, and the gate with a fire cauldron and ram. When their entire army is engaged, begin the true assault."

Kyura clenched his teeth at the bloody skirmishing that would involve. But the diversion must be convincing. He must appear to be committing everything he had to the northern walls, to persuade the Tarlahns to throw everything they had north, leaving his other forces free to take the city.

"See to it," Kyura ordered.

"Highest," said Karmarn when the First General had left and one of Kyura's guards signalled they could speak privately.

The worry in Karmarn's eyes made Kyura want to flinch away. "What is it?"

"The army will follow you loyally, whether or not this conquest succeeds. But the generals are becoming too confident. You are giving them too much power. They are all but Co-Regents, now that the First General commands your army."

Kyura's hands balled into fists. "I will not sully Father's Peace further by commanding the army that violates it! My hands are filthy enough with blood as it is. I want this war over, those who agitated for it found and arrested, my throne secured, and to move on from this blight on our kingdom's history!"

"Kyura," said Aoran, and Kyura blinked at the lack of a title in Karmarn's presence. "Karmarn and I think we saw the First General receiving a report from home this afternoon. We worry that the generals control the army and the siege camp and information going in and out. If they control information, your position becomes even weaker."

"Find out what was in that report," Kyura ordered, dismissing them before his fury at how his attempt to gain control of his army had only weakened him further erupted.

"Highest," said a woman's voice from the tent flap.

"What?" he asked.

"Do you require company this evening?"

Her tone wasn't quite neutral. There was a hint of seduction. Was that the generals' plan? Distract him with women while they took over his army, his camp, and all but ruled in his name? How in Chaos did he take charge of the First General now?

Kyura winced at the sharpening pains in his head and summoned a physician. Companion Karmarn would warn him to be careful with how much medicine he took. Too much could make him drowsy, distracting him, making it easier for his generals to take over. How had he made such a mess of things?

The physician's herbal drinks eased Kyura's head pains over the next few days. Still, when Aoran's report on intelligence entering the camp finally came, no medication was enough to calm the stress it caused.

"*Attack?*" Kyura asked, sinking into his camp chair in his command tent. "Who in Chaos' name could be attacking our shores?"

"It was only one ship," Aoran reported, as he sat on the camp chair Karmarn unfolded opposite Kyura. "But something went wrong in countering it."

"We have enough guards to defeat one ship," Kyura objected.

"Regent Derlan is vague in his report, but it sounds as though he has failed to contain some attackers, who have fled the city guard and begun attacking inland. He was asking for our aid."

Kyura's goblet of wine slipped through his fingers and split on the carpet lining his tent floor. "Impossible. We command the best soldiers on this continent. Nothing short of superior numbers and superior weaponry could overpower our city guard."

"It is unclear what happened. Some reports Regent Derlan received spoke of invaders fleeing into the night and slaying the inhabitants of fishing villages. Others spoke of soldiers killing them with ease. The more hysterical reports claim the invaders are not human. That their manner of fighting, movement, and attacking villagers is erratic because they are Chaos Spawn."

Spawned by the god who supposedly created sorcerers and caused the ancient, mythical Sorcery War and had never been heard from by humans since? "Madness."

"Kyura," Aoran added, his extended, open palms imploring. "Iomar met them. He sent Regent Derlan a hand. It was too small and thick fingered to be human. The skin was grey, and it had long claws. The letter described it, but the finger Regent Derlan tried to send began to decay, and the fool messenger disposed of it. Regent Derlan is convinced that the Western Shore is in grave danger and that he needs more men to protect it."

"Take a thousand soldiers back to the Zaldeaan Realm," Kyura ordered Karmarn. "We outnumber Tarlah confidently without them, and I will *not* see our coast left vulnerable."

"Highest, the generals must also be told of this," Karmarn cautioned.

Kyura took a deep breath. It was time to show his generals who was in charge. If their arrogance had had anything to do with levied soldiers marching to war without orders to do so... "Summon the First General."

Kyura moved to his gilt travel throne while Aoran fetched his crown. He sat upright, his limbs tingling and threatening to tremble with the rage seeking to burst free of him.

"Highest," the First General said with a short bow as he entered, his face sobering when he saw Kyura's expression.

Kyura thought swiftly. He didn't just need to establish his authority with the generals; he needed to behave as if it was still intact, then bend them to his will.

"While you are busy overseeing the siege of Tarlah, I shall oversee the defence of the Western Coast of the Zaldeaan Realm," Kyura announced. "A small distraction to you, no doubt, yet, with the bulk of our army on the far side of the continent, one that requires the attention of a senior person in government."

There was a slight hesitation in the First General's expression. Nerves? Even now, Kyura could have him killed. He could accuse the General, rightfully, of concealing information from the king and usurping his power. But to do so would admit Kyura's weakness to the entire army. He needed to rein the General in without letting the army know he had lost control. Behaving as though the concealment of the attack on the western coast had never happened would let Kyura continue to act as the ultimate authority. And signal that danger awaited, should the General overstep again.

"I shall be overseeing the western defences. Your preparations for the siege must continue with a thousand men fewer than you anticipated."

The General's eyebrows rose before he could contain his surprise. "With some adaption, I believe my assault can succeed without those men."

"I shall leave you to adapt it, then. Dismissed."

When his footsteps faded beyond hearing, Kyura exhaled with relief.

"It would be good for you to lose your temper with rogues more often, Highest," Companion Karmarn said with a quirk of his lips.

Aoran beamed, and Kyura laughed with relief. "I didn't think the man would take me so seriously. He made me feel so powerless. But I still wield power here. I see that now. I will protect our coast. Take your men, Karmarn, and aid Uncle Derlan."

Companion Karmarn swept a bow and retreated swiftly.

"What do you think attacked our shores?" Aoran asked Kyura.

"How did you find out?" Kyura asked.

"Iomar tried to contact us directly, in case his father didn't take him seriously. Someone diverted the letters, but a servant saw them and told me."

Kyura managed a smile. "So my servants are loyal." His mirth faded swiftly. "If my uncle did not say clearly, then I do not believe it is a regular army. I wonder if he was vague because he feared the generals wouldn't believe him."

Derlan had fought in the Piracy Wars. The generals ought to trust his judgement as a military man. If his report was unbelievable, then what in Chaos had Iomar fought?

A week later, Ruarnon's Royal Council was rocked by a report from their Spymaster. Ruarnon would have to warn their Aunt Merlah in South Harbour, order soldiers to patrol Tarlah's southern coast, and warn the Urai tribes of the southwestern jungle, despite the Unspoken Agreement, of monsters roaming the Zaldeaan Realm.

The Spymaster's report was shocking, but word of Governor Kia closing her gates and putting archers on her walls convinced the Royal Council that the threat was real.

"I have heard tales in west Zaldeaan coastal towns of men, women, children, and livestock being murdered," he said, ashen-faced.

Noma shifted in her seat, and Ruarnon tasted bile.

"Regent Derlan has ordered the evacuation of the entire western coast. Hunters and retired soldiers are taking up arms to support its defence."

"How many murder reports have you heard?" Pamoran demanded.

"Eight independent reports have been verified. But tales of brutality are widespread. My spies report their neighbours boarding up their windows as far from the western shore as Zaldeaa City. Terror of invaders, still rumoured to be grey-skinned Chaos Spawn, is gripping the entire Realm, and the three provincial capitals nearest to the coast have barred their gates and massed archers on their walls. Women are taking up bows for the first time in Zaldeaan history. The City Guard must be utterly outnumbered."

Ruarnon wasn't sure what to make of the first reports of Chaos Spawn since the Sorcery War, centuries ago. Yet the entire Realm was on edge, and something unnatural appeared to be behind it.

"I cannot verify the enemy numbers because their forces are scattered, but multiple spies' reports suggest the invaders breached the city guards' attempt to defend the coast and are making their way inland. A thousand soldiers from the Zaldeaan army have reached the west coast. However, more ships of Chaos Spawn are still arriving, keeping Karmarn's soldiers busy containing them, so the enemy forces moving inland roam unchecked. Sheer numbers may be the reason for their success."

Ruarnon sat in stunned silence. No one had set sail from the Far West to these waters since the Sorcery War, the last people to do so immigrating to city-states the Zaldeaan Realm had conquered centuries ago. It was hard to believe anyone could be invading from across the ocean, let alone crazed murderers. But as Ruarnon's mind grappled with the idea, the implications became clear. The Zaldeaan people were in crisis. The only question was whether Kyura would abandon the siege of Tarlah City immediately to protect his coast or launch his assault to seize Tarlah first.

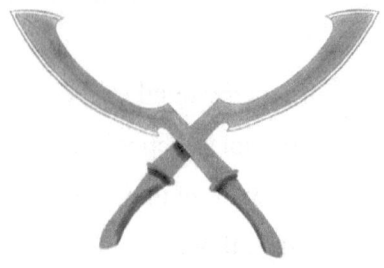

CHAPTER 19

DESPERATION

RUARNON: *Tarlah City, the Siege of Tarlah, Day Nine*

R uarnon's eyes flew open. Pale grey light drifted through the window hangings, and the tolling of a bell cut the air. It was distant, but a nearer bell began tolling, repeatedly. When a servant withdrew the window hangings, twin blue fires burned at North Gate and a third flame rose from a watchtower in the city centre. The Zaldeaan army was assaulting the walls.

Ruarnon leapt out of bed, calling for servants to help with their armour. The cuirass the servants fastened to Ruarnon's torso was iron this time, as were the discs of the kilt and the helmet they seized off the hook on the wall. Ruarnon was Regent now. The Tarlahn army was about to enact strategies Ruarnon had devised and their Council had overseen. Knowing both had failed their uncle and the Tarlahn army on

Death Belt Desert, Ruarnon sent a quick prayer to the Ancestors that it would hold the enemy off until Tarlah's Timbalen allies arrived.

They buckled on their sword belt and quiver, took up their bow, then forced down some pastries and water delivered by a kitchen servant, careful not to show the dread inside them to their nervous servants as they said goodbye. Their spearmen and archer bodyguards bowed in the hallway, and Captain Arleath stepped forwards. "Companion Pamoran requested Your Benevolence have a full guard until the assault ends."

"Does *he* have a guard of ten?" Ruarnon smiled as they led their guards towards the stairs.

Captain Arleath was saved an awkward answer by Ruarnon spotting Pamoran descending the stairs alone, calling, "Our allies have been sighted, Benevolence. They ought to be here by sunset."

Ruarnon exhaled deeply as they approached the stairs. One day. That was how long their defences must hold.

"I am sure your guards are adequate, but would Your Benevolence care for company?"

Ruarnon's face split in a smile, and some of the tension left their torso as Lenaris approached, a bronze cuirass hugging her figure, a leather strap kilt flapping against her thighs, her shins guarded by bronze greaves and a bronze helmet tucked under her arm. She was smiling too, and she moved with the same eagerness, the same anticipation shining in her eyes as her father's.

"Always," Ruarnon replied.

She smiled fiercely. Ruarnon's bodyguards shifted, the men looking alert, the women smiling and raising their chins to Lenaris.

"Who will be showing who how fighting is done, if needed?" she asked Captain Arleath, her gaze sweeping the other nine guards who circled them as they descended the stairs.

The captain smiled. "I am sure Companion Pamoran and Companion Tor will be content to have both their proteges standing beside Their Benevolence during the siege assault."

Ruarnon liked Tor's son, but Drake was very much a scholar, so the Treasurer's son Arleath had benefited from intensive arms training from Companion Tor instead. Marching to battle with highly skilled companions on either side of them made Ruarnon feel better.

In the courtyard, General Takanis saluted Ruarnon with her right arm raised as her horse charged past: *Tarlah stands*.

The infantry were pouring into the courtyard, assembling in phalanxes on the command of captains shouting orders. They all knew what to do. If only Ruarnon were as confident in their role.

"Chin up and smile," Lenaris whispered in their ear. "Treat it like a military parade."

Ruarnon straightened and tried to channel the chaotic tumbling of nerves in their belly into inspecting their surroundings as they entered the stables. Everyone mounted their horses, and Ruarnon's guards flanked the group as they, Pamoran, and Lenaris crossed the courtyard, then rode down North Road. Hide and bamboo screens rose above the northern walls, silhouetted by a blazing sunrise. More daylight shone as a bamboo screen fell. Another section swayed as a distant crash echoed across the city.

Companion Pamoran smiled approvingly at Lenaris, then turned to Ruarnon. "The enemy is attacking the battlements with power slings," he explained, "aiming at ten specific locations. You were right about why their siege towers are so high."

Ruarnon swallowed awkwardly. Monin had been incredulous about a youth of the Generation of Peace and a midlun thinking they could predict how reckless Zaldeaan generals could be. But Ruarnon knew Kyura might try anything, if he was as desperate to take the city as Ruarnon was to defend it.

"Are we firing back?"

"The enemy's power slings have been moved, and we are adjusting our power slings to reach them, but our power bows are already piercing the bronze shields protecting enemy power sling crews."

They reached the watchtower on the corner of Middle and North Roads, and Ruarnon reined in as Pamoran called, "May the Ancestors watch over you," and bowed his head to his daughter and Ruarnon. Lenaris bowed back.

Ruarnon replied, "And you," then Pamoran rode on alone.

Ruarnon, Lenaris, and their guards dismounted. They tied their reins to a rail at the watchtower base, then Ruarnon led the way to the tower top, where messengers and a barrel of signal flags stood. General Takanis and Companion Pamoran would command one side of the northern walls each, individual captains controlling their units in the chaos of battle. General Aza stood in a watchtower nearby, overseeing all gates, ready to command reinforcements to defend against surprise attacks elsewhere. Only a distant position would let Ruarnon see it all, revise tactics, and direct reinforcements.

They stepped up to a crenellation, gazing through it over rooftops to the northern walls.

"What do you need to watch for?" Lenaris asked, her gaze locked on theirs.

"Where my soldiers and the enemy are positioned along the northern walls. I need to anticipate where we'll need reinforcements."

She nodded, and Ruarnon knew she'd draw their attention to anything they missed. They studied everything intently, drumming their fingers on the crenellations before them.

Their rubble and earthen barricade rose a dozen paces inside the gate, barring the far end of North Road above the height of a man. Blue signal fire rose along the length of the barricade. On either side, defensive screens were hoisted atop the walls, while on rooftops, power sling crews worked. Wooden power bow frames angled upwards; fitted ropes reinforced a giant bow protruding horizontally, while a sling hung across the power bow's diagonal structure. Two men operated levers, pulling the claw that the drew sling and rock back along ratchets.

Ruarnon shivered and turned to the northern battlements. Tarlahns in full armour formed a bronze shield wall on either side of North Gate, archers poised behind them. Opposite, ten siege towers loomed. Ruarnon raised a flag to signal reinforcements up the gate towers and summon more from the castle, hoping to put enough Tarlahns between the siege towers and the battlement stairs.

Beyond the northern walls, oxen-drawn siege towers advanced. Enemy archers in bronze helmets carried bows, a quiver at one hip and a sword at the other. A cauldron of fire glowed beneath a pole hanging from a chariot, which soldiers pushed towards North Gate. Additional soldiers shielded a man working bellows to fan the flames in the cauldron. The battering ram rolled, its triangular tip plated with iron, its sides and triangular roof of ox hide glistening with water. The enemy was arrayed before Tarlah City, better equipped than ever.

"That cauldron and style of ram, they're both new?" Lenaris asked.

Ruarnon nodded. "The gate is doomed, but I hope my other plan defends North Road."

A lone cry drew Ruarnon's attention. An enemy soldier shielding the fire cauldron fell, a power bow bolt in his middle. Another fell on his right. More bolts were fired at the cauldron crew, and cries rose. Enemy bolts hurtled at the gate towers, where soldiers yelled.

Shadows moved on the edge of Ruarnon's vision. Enemy power slings behind earthen mounds loosed rocks bigger than their head. Cracks cut the air. Bamboo and hide screens atop the battlements swayed, as rocks struck the outer facing of the walls. Ruarnon tensed, resisting the urge to grip their sword.

Captain Arleath watched them, as did messengers and their guards. They had an act to maintain, childhood nightmare unfolding before their eyes or not. Lenaris glanced at them, but there was little they could say in front of the others.

Rocks pounded the ground and shattered enemy power slings beyond the walls. Bolts shot between siege towers and wall towers, from gate towers to cauldron. Shouts and screams pierced Ruarnon's ears. Cool pre-dawn winds on their face wafted the iron scent of blood. It was ceaseless noise, movement, and chaos assaulting Ruarnon's senses until every muscle in their body felt tense.

A shadow passing overhead caught their eye. The boulder smashed through a mud-brick apartment. Debris rose again as a second rock crashed through a second rooftop. Ruarnon gritted their teeth, as their people's homes were destroyed.

Something glowed at the corner of Ruarnon's eye. The fire cauldron was entering Tarlahn arrow range at a run. Tarlahn arrows pelted its crew, and their shields bristled. Small and medium-sized rocks joined the deadly rain, as the cauldron fire drew nearer. The rocks bounced off armour or evoked screams when they struck flesh. Orange glowed, as the cauldron set the gate alight.

"Abandon the arch!" General Takanis boomed.

Lenaris took a step closer. Her steady presence was reassuring, as arrows soared from the walls and archers fled the gate arch, dragging injured comrades. A flame soared above the gate arch, retreated, and rose again. The enemy must be flinging pitch to encourage the fire to climb the gate timbers. Smoke rose, thickening as more wood caught alight.

Another crack split the air, and Ruarnon's knuckles turned white where they gripped the battlements before them. Timbers flew. An iron point pierced the gates, which were blackening from the bottom up. The point withdrew, moments passed, then it punched through again. Two large rocks smashed through the gate top, and a large fragment broke free and fell into the city, into fires burning atop Ruarnon's barricade.

Ruarnon tensed at the ram's blows, until the gate shattered. Burning bits of timber and charcoal chunks sprayed onto North Road. Cheers rose from the far side.

"But have you won?" Lenaris asked, leaning over the tower wall.

Enemy archers advanced in formation, a bronze shield wall before them, a bronze shield roof overhead, a column of phalanxes rushing to enter the city.

Ruarnon waited with bated breath. The smoke cleared, revealing the burning barricade of earth and stone rising above the advancing enemy and flames flickering far above their heads. A command was shouted in Migryan. The enemy retreated. Ruarnon and Lenaris exchanged triumphant smiles.

Ethlin braced herself between comrades in boiled leather armour bearing rectangular shields and spears. This time, an ox hide screen blocked her view of the enemy and oncoming death. The screen rippled, as arrows struck its far side. It tore when enemy crossbow bolts hit it and lodged themselves in her companions.

Ethlin shuddered and gripped her spear, as several people fell on her right. Heavy breathing and panting filled the air. She didn't know where to look: at the approach of death through the screens, the frightened eyes of young soldiers on her right, or the steely gaze of veterans on her left, whose detachment from death was hardly reassuring.

"Steady," a captain called. "Shields up and hold them steady."

Ethlin exhaled slowly as giant wheels of siege towers creaked beyond the bamboo screen. Tarlahn axes struck the screen and her shoulders tensed at losing its protection. Burning torches set the screen alight as it fell back.

The burning screen crashed onto a siege tower ramp. Flames kept enemy infantry back, but they stood so close she could make out every wide featured face through the orange glow—even the anger burning in the eyes of the large man opposite her. Ethlin shivered despite the fire's warmth.

The enemy raised shields as Tarlahn arrows soared over the flames and thudded into them. A few unwary Zaldeaans cried out, making Ethlin flinch. She braced her shield against return fire from the tower's archery deck above the infantry. Kill or be killed. The meaning of war had never been so clear.

Tarlahn axemen hacked at the near end of the siege ramp, wood splintered, and the burning ramp swung uselessly. The screen fell from view and nothing stood between three rows of Ethlin's comrades and a front line of frighteningly broad Zaldeaan infantry, armed with spears and shields, baring their teeth in menacing grins.

Ethlin flinched at arrows whizzing overhead, bombarding the Zaldeaan archery deck. Then enemy infantry raised their shield wall and a timber plank slid across the divide, forming an impromptu ramp.

"Brace!" her captain called.

Shields thudded either side of Ethlin in readiness.

"Behind me, girl," a voice whispered.

The man beside her had his shield turned sideways. She stepped beside him, and more shields turned, giving her a narrow corridor to retreat. Care-lined grim faces bowed her past, and she moved quickly as footsteps thudded and men roared behind her.

Bronze clashed with bronze. Ethlin cringed, stepping behind the back line to a narrow, empty stretch of the battlement, facing the way she had come. Tarlahn lines braced, resting their shields on the backs of the soldiers before them, lending their support to the front lines shoving against Zaldeaan infantry. On Ethlin's left, a girl stood biting her lip. Ethlin gave her a weak smile, wondering if the veterans had sent them back to protect them.

A roar rose over groans and the clang of bronze on bronze, and Ethlin gaped. A bare-chested, tattooed Zaldeaan man leapt the shield wall. His shield smashed spears aside as he landed among the Tarlahn second line, kicking Tarlahns down and felling more with swift spear thrusts, roaring as he fought. He could kill many quickly. But she had an idea.

Ethlin climbed onto the waist-high wall behind her, swallowing awkwardly as she glimpsed rooftops below, then turned to the berserker. She clenched her teeth, raised her spear, and hurtled it into the berserker's shoulder. He kept fighting, until a Tarlahn gripped her spear, angled it downwards and rammed it deeper into his chest.

"More throwing spears!" Ethlin's captain called.

The girl she'd smiled at seized Ethlin's wrist and pulled her down. A spear clanked off the wall behind her as she landed on the battlements. Arrows whizzed after it, soaring through empty air.

"Thanks," Ethlin gasped, stumbling to her feet.

"We'll need to get up there, throw our spears and get down quickly," the girl said with a shaky smile, her clear blue eyes a mix of fear and the crazy sense of adventure which had made Ethlin want to be a soldier.

"The captain asked for spears for us," Ethlin said, dazed by the prospect of playing an essential role in defending the walls.

"Not just us," said the girl.

More shields flashed sideways, letting another young woman, several young men, and a youthful midlun through: people who weren't big enough for shoving matches against enemy shields but could throw spears at charging enemies a dozen feet away.

"We could jump and throw if they spot us standing on the battlements," a young man called.

"Jump down as soon as you've thrown," Ethlin suggested. "Then find a foothold to stand on slightly above ground in the back wall so that we can see better, but the enemy can't see us well."

From their pale faces, none of Ethlin's new comrades fancied being spear or arrow targets. But they could help defend the people shielding them from the enemy charge. Her captain kept them supplied with throwing spears, and Ethlin and her young comrades watched the enemy and timed their attacks between volleys of arrows, dodging the odd thrown spear.

But as berserkers fractured Tarlahn lines and Zaldeaans pressed behind them to gain ground on the walls, the space Ethlin and her new comrades had to move in shrank.

"Target only the berserkers," she called to the other spear throwers, over the groans of soldiers not so far ahead.

She glanced left and right and saw berserkers attacking and puncturing Tarlahn shields all down the left side of the northern battlements. Zaldeaans leapt spears or rammed Tarlahn shields, pressing forwards. Ethlin and the others stood between shorter Tarlahns for a better view, hurling spear after spear over their infantry comrades. The enemy kept coming, and everything was shouts, screams, the grate of weapons on armour, and clash of spear tips.

"Ethlin!" Someone was moving around the girl she had befriended on her right.

Her face split in a smile as Arlian approached.

"General Takanis wants you all to come with me," he said. "The berserkers are getting too mixed in with our soldiers. But you can use the same tactic at East Gate if it's assaulted."

Ethlin turned to her captain. "Dismissed," he said, waving them off.

Arlian led the way to the gate tower, Ethlin's companions following. "I'm glad to get you away from the fighting," he said, "at least for a while."

"I'd rather wonder if East Gate will be attacked than stand up here watching when it's no longer safe to throw spears. I'm not fond of killing, but watching the enemy kill my companions is worse."

Arlian slipped his arm around her neck as they walked, where she could feel his skin on hers, above her leather armour. General Takanis had a dozen horses waiting for them at the bottom, and Arlian had less skilled riders mount behind more experienced ones. Ethlin mounted behind Arlian, holding onto his bronze armoured waist with her left arm. Her right arm ached from endless spear throwing.

As their horses' hooves clacked away from the walls into the quiet city, it was easier to hear the ringing in her ears, caused by continual screaming and the clashing of weapons. It was good to ride away from the deafening noise and inhale air untainted by the iron tang of blood. To ride down North Road lying empty, the calm behind the storm.

Ruarnon fought the urge to fidget. Their reinforcements had captured and set fire to the siege towers at either end of the walls. Eight siege towers remained. They had done all they could to reinforce their defenders. Now they could only wait, watching the endless shoving and jostling and berserkers cutting their way onto the battlements.

"The power slings," Lenaris said softly.

A trail of wreckage lay across rooftops on the left. Rocks punched holes two rooftops in front of Tarlahn power slings.

Enemy power sling operators must be observing where Tarlahn rocks emerged above the walls. Their estimate of where Tarlahn power slings were stationed, and their aim, was getting more accurate. If the enemy destroyed those power slings, what would they target next? Ruarnon's reinforcements were massed on the far left and right on the wall. If the enemy brought the guard towers above those soldiers down...

"Assault power slings only!" Ruarnon shouted, and men by the nearest power slings saluted with right arms raised.

Ruarnon's order was shouted across the rooftops, and they nodded in thanks to Lenaris. Their gaze scanned the battlements. Before all eight functional siege towers, the enemy used the same tactics. Spears thrust, berserkers broke away, wounding Tarlahns, while enemy shield walls advanced into gaps in Tarlahn lines. Enemies advanced across battlements, reinforced by ladder hatches in their siege towers. They outnumbered and were overpowering defenders in the middle section of the northern walls.

Ruarnon gripped their sword hilt tightly. They had no way of getting soldiers to the middle of the battlements. The enemy flung occasional ladders up the walls, but Ruarnon's soldiers pushed the ladders back.

Shouts close by distracted Ruarnon. Two enemy ladders rested beside the left gate tower. Enemy soldiers climbed off under arrow fire. Fighting spilled onto the gate arch as the right gate tower guards charged. General Takanis ran her opponent through and advanced, yelling obscenities.

A large soldier climbed down a ladder with a man slung over his shoulder, while his comrades held off Tarlahn guards. General Takanis cursed at the top of her lungs and fought ferociously. Ruarnon stared. Enemies on the gate arch were soon cut down, but both ladders had disappeared by then. General Takanis waved a red flag knotted in the middle. The enemy had Companion Pamoran.

"Father," Lenaris said softly. "Why capture him alive during battle? What does the enemy want from him?"

She wrung her hands. Ruarnon shook their head and leaned heavily against the crenellations. "It makes less sense than capturing my parents."

Pamoran was the best military leader Tarlah could have under siege, and his support in Council meetings had encouraged and inspired Ruarnon, whereas Monin made them doubt themself. The prospect of leading Tarlah without Pamoran made the ground feel like it was rushing up to meet Ruarnon.

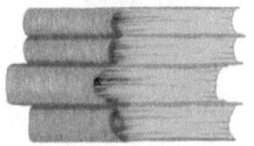

CHAPTER 20

AUSSIES IN TARLAH

LINH: *Timbalen Fleet, Assault of Tarlah City*

L inh clutched the main deck's railing as the Timbalen fleet approached Tarlah's eastern shore.

"I suppose we wait here while both sides butcher each other, to find out how it went?" Troy asked bitterly.

The infantry were buckling on armour around them, and Linh expected to be sent back to her cabin at any moment.

"Danger to port! Zaldeaan ships!" a voice cried.

Linh tensed. Green forest shores lay a few kilometres ahead. Closer rose four vessels, sitting nearer the waterline, propelled by multiple rows of oars, moving like giant insects crawling across the water.

"Triremes! Archers ready! Power bows ready! Prepare for battle!"

Troy gaped. "Those tubs are going to attack five sea giants?"

Boormar shook his head. "It's not about size. They're equipped with rams. They'll try to damage or sink us."

Captain Doorna shuffled through soldiers towards them. "The fleet will stop and fight. We have the firepower to destroy the triremes before they damage our ships, but we're larger and less manoeuvrable, so we defend each other best if we fight together."

Linh's heart leapt into her mouth.

A strange noise, like wobbling wood, sounded across the port side. Arrows made of iron tore through the air, hitting distant figures on Zaldeaan trireme decks. Distant cries tore at Linh's heart. Her breath caught, as small figures—Zaldeaans——toppled overboard, and some floated, unmoving. Her heart raced and adrenaline flooded her bloodstream, urging her to move. They were dead. She'd just watched people get killed...

"How do we get out of here?" she asked.

"You don't have to stay on board," Captain Doorna assured her. "I'm escorting our messenger to Tarlah Castle. The sailors are raising my boat above deck now, and the commander has permitted you to accompany me. We'll walk to the city's southern side, the opposite side from the main assault, though we may have to dodge Zaldeaan patrols. But you must decide swiftly. We leave as soon as my boat and men are ready."

Linh was vaguely aware of pulleys lifting the boat through a hatch, but the pressure building in her head was distracting. Wood wobbled again. She didn't want to look, but her eyes were drawn to multiple metal arrows tearing through the air. A scream pierced her ears as one found its target on a Zaldeaan trireme on her left and a man fell overboard. She made out his head and limbs. The triremes were getting closer.

Horror tightened her chest and constricted her throat. "I'm out of here."

Troy's brows furrowed. "Zaldeaans could still attack us in the woods."

"What if the city falls?" Michael asked Captain Doorna.

"Breaching the city with the attacks the Tarlahns described by message bird will take hours. We will reach them before then. Once we surround the enemy and smash them against the walls, with Tarlahns raining arrows from above, I don't like their chances."

"Do you think the city's less dangerous than being on a ship while it's attacked at sea?" Troy asked Michael, who nodded.

"I don't care," Linh replied, her hands balling into fists. Troy's brows furrowed, and Linh's eyes glazed with tears. "I'm not staying anywhere near screams of the dying, wondering if that's how my uncles sounded and their faces looked when they were gunned down in the jungles of Vietnam."

She shivered. She'd wondered. She'd imagined what fighting and fleeing would be like. But she'd never heard anything as visceral as the screams of men dying nearby to complete the picture. She dreaded even more the sight of their faces as they died. The triremes might be close enough for her to see that soon. She couldn't stand it.

Fiona took her hand, her ordinarily rosy cheeks drained of colour.

"I'll go with you."

Linh blinked in surprise at Michael's words.

Troy's brown eyes were wide with confusion, his mouth open to protest, but Michael seemed to understand how she felt.

"This way," said Captain Doorna. He opened a trunk on deck and handed them each bronze chest and back armour plates. It hung well past Fiona and Linh's knees—too long. They put on leather kilts underneath and strapped on a bronze helmet padded on the inside.

Captain Doorna buckled on Linh's armour faster than her shaking fingers could manage; then he helped Fiona while Boormar helped Michael and a protesting Troy.

"If both are dangerous, but one's less dangerous..."

"We go the way Linh finds less traumatising," Michael finished for him. "This isn't just about physical risk for her."

Linh sighed. Michael *did* understand. What had he been through to be so aware and so instinctively protective of her mental health?

Mairatha emerged from the crowd, hugging four swords before her, Familon's parting gift. Linh was grateful to take a reminder of a safe place with her, but she buckled it on with shaking fingers, her stomach roiling at the possibility that she may have to use the sword to defend herself today.

"All aboard!" Boormar called, gesturing to the boat suspended beside a gap in the main deck's railing.

He handed Michael an oar, and Michael moved to the far end of a bench, while sailors held the boat steady and soldiers boarded.

"Hop in the middle," Boormar told the girls. "You should fit between the soldiers, and your arms aren't long enough to row."

Linh sat between Michael and Fiona, Troy biting his lip as he boarded with his oar beside Fiona. It was snug, but as wood wobbled and more screams cut the air, making Linh shudder, she was glad of that.

Captain Doorna, Boormar, and a soldier with a yellow collar rising from his armour, the messenger, boarded, then their boat was lowered towards the sea so fast that Linh gripped the bottom of her seat, while Troy went pale and stared ahead without blinking. Then they hit the water, bobbing in the waves. The soldiers detached the pulleys and began rowing fiercely towards the shore.

"How do we get into the castle if the city's under siege?" Troy asked.

"There's a device," Doorna replied. "The Tarlahns are well equipped for a siege."

Linh flinched. The whizz of crossbow bolts and distant cries sounded over the groan of oars in oarlocks on either side of her and splashes of paddles in the water. She took shallow breaths, noting the archers in the bow and stern, each sitting with bow raised and three arrows in hand. Could Zaldeaan arrows reach them as they rowed to shore? She trembled, wondering whether she'd made the right decision. But she couldn't sit in her cabin listening to screams of the dying draw nearer or wait until enemy archers hit the *Timara*'s deck, and men above her started screaming too. She crossed her arms and sat hunched in on herself, trying not to think about it.

People cheered. Linh turned back. Fire burned on the nearest trireme's deck. Arrows pelted both ways. Linh turned away. More screams and splashes as dead and wounded soldiers fell into the sea. Oars splashed around her, raising spray in unison, pulling the boat across the waves. Linh clenched her fists, urging them to row faster. The salty sea air swept into her face as their boat glided towards shore, yells, the whizz of arrows, and splashes continuing from embattled ships behind her.

"Shit!" cried Troy.

Linh turned back. More triremes approached, gliding towards the fleet, all of which had turned and halted to fight, arrows and iron bolts whizzing between them. Linh wrenched her gaze away, hunching against the cries of the wounded and dying. Would those have been less audible from her cabin? Was sailing towards a city under siege, towards more fighting, the best idea?

Her heart gradually slowed as they neared the shore, and she feared Troy was right about their safest choice. But it was too late now. Their boat was rocking as it glided through breakers towards a sandy shore. The soldiers pulled them to dry sand and Linh's shoulders relaxed as she climbed out. The messenger eyed her and her classmates curiously, as their guards took up swords, spears, and shields. Then Captain Doorna led everyone swiftly across the beach, the guards moving protectively around them, and Linh and Fiona had to trot to keep up.

They climbed sand hills, then stepped under dainty-leafed trees, the soldiers entering the forest with a hand on their sword hilts, four with bows and an arrow in hand. The forest was hilly, made up of short dainty-leafed trees and tall trees with broad leaves, blocking her view in all directions. Their guards scanned the trees for Zaldeaans and her shoulders tensed. But all she heard as they walked was birds flapping away.

They followed an animal track between stunted trees, until they reached a clearing with footprints pointing towards them. Linh exhaled. Tracks from the city's evacuation? Were they near Tarlah City already?

Sporadic bird calls gave way to distant shouts as they crossed the clearing. Patches of the wall became visible between branches ahead. Linh gazed up at battlements on which tens of soldiers surveyed all directions. Apprehension settled around her like a cloak.

A woman in boiled leather armour hailed them from the walls as they stepped from the trees. "Greetings! Your arrival is most timely."

"Greetings! We bring word from Commander Imphin of the Timbalen fleet," said the messenger.

"We'll haul you up using the lift."

Linh started at soldiers flinging a small wooden platform with a rope railing over the wall. The soldiers turned a capstan to lower it via ropes attached. Fiona smiled sympathetically. Linh shook her head as the platform landed. She concentrated on the wall as she stepped onto the platform, hoping that view would help her breakfast stay put. Troy stared at the wall too.

"It's fascinating how the stones are wedged together like a puzzle, and it stands up without mortar," he commented, his face pale.

It was interesting to Linh and Fiona, but not normally to Troy.

"Like the view of the sea was better on the foredeck than from the fighting top on the ship?" Fiona asked.

"Absolutely," said Troy, flinching as the platform went up slightly faster on one side.

Linh managed a nervous smile, and he blushed. It almost felt silly being this discomforted by heights after travelling via rowboat away from enemy arrows. Logically, she knew this lift was less likely to kill her. But logic had never reassured her when it came to heights.

She exhaled with relief when she stepped onto the solid stone wall at the top, but a second lift awaited them.

"You have to see this!" said Fiona. "It's the best view we'll get of Tarlah."

Linh gritted her teeth and gazed across the city. The outer walls of Tarlah Castle and its towers rose nearby, red flags atop them flapping in the breeze. Left and right, the sun beamed down on multi-storey, rectangular, mud-brick apartments lining streets in grid patterns, with a wide road dividing the city beyond. The rooftops were flat, and those near the palace were covered in colourful pot plant gardens. It was breath-taking. Linh's legs shook, but she kept her gaze on distant points of the well-preserved, ancient, mud-brick city, which held her spellbound until the lift touched the ground.

They waited beside the outer city walls for their Timbalen guards, then Captain Doorna gestured them to chariots tethered to two horses each. "Choose a partner and a chariot. We will squeeze a guard on behind you."

The captain and a pair of guards stepped onto the first chariot. Troy, Michael, and Boormar took the second. Then Linh and Fiona climbed onto a small, open-backed, two-wheeled chariot, Linh holding the handrail across the front. A guard braced his feet against both sides behind them, taking and flicking the reins.

As warm air rushed past her, Linh sensed silence left and right of the wide road, from empty streets and abandoned homes. There were background noises, the crash of boulders hitting unseen targets and cries over the hum of war on the far side of the city, making her shiver.

"On the left!" Michael cried.

Linh gaped. Two bronze armoured soldiers rushed out from between houses, raising spears as they charged Doorna's chariot. They were attacking... They were Zaldeaans. *Inside* the city. Unknown to the South Gate guards. How was that possible?

Both Zaldeaans thrust spears at Doorna's chariot. The captain ducked and stabbed back. "Get to the castle!" he yelled. "The city walls are breached!"

But there were only two Zaldeaans... Footsteps slapped down the lane. More Zaldeaan soldiers ran onto South Road behind her chariot. An ambush? How?

An arrow whizzed. Boormar stood facing backwards in the chariot behind Linh, his knees wedged against the chariot's sides while he loosed arrows. Linh gasped as arrows impaled Zaldeaan torsos. Zaldeaans fell to the ground, where blood pooled. War: she'd entered it now.

"Breach!" came a shout from behind. "Archers, target the Zaldeaans!"

Tarlahns ran along the city wall, several houses back. Around Linh, grand yellow mud-brick apartments rose to three stories on all sides. How many of them concealed Zaldeaans?

"Everyone down!" Doorna bellowed.

Michael and Troy ducked a spear. It struck one of the horses pulling Linh's chariot. The horse screamed, slowing. The other horse pulled ahead, dragging its companion. More spears from an alley on their left followed. One struck a horse pulling Michael and Troy's chariot. The horse reared, snapping its wooden yoke, throwing both boys into the air. The wounded horse collapsed, and the second horse bolted, dragging remnants of chariot away, as Michael and Troy hit the pavement.

Linh's guard halted her chariot and leapt down, handing Fiona the reins and cutting the wounded horse free. The wounded horse stumbled aside as footsteps thudded down the road. Enemy soldiers poured out from a laneway behind them.

Troy lay on the ground, blinking. Boormar seized him under both armpits and hauled him up, revealing the flattened side of his bronze helmet, which had probably saved his life. Linh started at bright red blood on his elbows, palms, and knees.

She heard pitiful sounds from a wounded horse and saw Michael struggling to sit up; his helmet also squashed. Captain Doorna and the guards ran past Linh, forming a defensive line behind her chariot. They were going to fight. She leapt off her chariot and ran forwards.

"Get the boys out of here!" Captain Doorna yelled. "Go with the messenger!"

The yellow collared man claimed Doorna's chariot and turned to her impatiently.

Linh flung an arm around Troy's middle and said, "You're coming with me!"

"But I never do what you tell me," he mumbled.

"Get moving!" she ordered, pulling him towards Doorna's chariot with all her strength. He smiled, wobbling and stumbling. Then he tried to step over the chariot. She had to guide his feet onto it, while Fiona helped Michael. Linh stepped onto the platform snuggly beside Troy, behind the messenger, supporting Troy's wavering figure with her left arm. Fiona supported Michael behind her. They barely fit on. The messenger eyed the reins uncertainly. This was no time for hesitation.

Linh seized the reins and flapped them urgently with her right hand. "Move, horse!" she yelled.

The horse stamped its hooves and remained where it stood. This was no time for animal stubbornness. One horse would be slow enough as it was. Linh drew her sword and smacked the horse on the rump. It screamed, and the chariot surged forwards, Troy stopping Linh from falling. She gripped the railing by putting her forearm through it, then sheathed her sword, held the railing and turned back.

A trail of the fallen lay behind charging Zaldeaans. Boormar shot from behind Doorna's defensive line. Every other soldier stood with a spear in hand. The first three enemy soldiers approached. The Timbalens stabbed and danced aside. Linh shivered.

"Get the Heir!" a voice bellowed.

Linh turned ahead to a small group of soldiers exiting another laneway on her left.

"Which of you is the Heir?" a soldier demanded.

Emotion rose, and Linh rode it. "Fuck off!"

Troy shakily drew his sword. Linh clenched her jaw, tied the reins to the handrail, held the handrail with her left hand and drew her sword. Fiona drew her sword, and Michael slowly drew his as they neared the enemy soldiers.

"The big one, he's got jungle colouring—runs in the queen's family," a voice called.

Troy frowned. A soldier reached for him. Linh clubbed the soldier's helmet with the flat of her blade, and he stumbled at the impact, which vibrated up her arm.

"Girl bodyguard?" another asked.

"Don't underestimate her," Troy warned.

The Zaldeaans leapt at the chariot as it began to overtake them. Iron flashed in the sunlight and Linh ducked. Her heart thudded against her chest. The wooden shaft of a spear followed a spearhead past her face. Troy roared and slashed. The spearman cried out.

Four soldiers sprinted behind the chariot. One threw a spear at Fiona. Linh gaped as Fiona screamed and knocked it from the sky.

A second spear sailed towards Linh, and she ducked, knocking it aside, Troy yelling as its haft struck his head before it clattered to the road. Another soldier raised a spear, and Troy raised his sword. "Try it, and I'll throw this at you!" he yelled.

Dark brows contracted. They seemed puzzled that anyone would do anything so unorthodox with a sword, but Linh was all for throwing them if that worked, so she raised hers threateningly, and the Zaldeaans hesitated, allowing the chariot to pull out of range.

Linh swayed as the chariot slowed. Arrows whizzed, then a voice called, "Tarlah stands!"

Gates in a high stone wall rose before her, creaking open.

"Tarlah stands! Welcome!" a return cry came from behind gates. But the chariot was approaching too swiftly.

"Stop the chariot," Michael murmured.

Linh snatched the reins from the hesitant messenger and yanked them back. She swayed, Troy's arm stopping her from falling as the chariot slowed abruptly, Fiona keeping Michael on behind her.

"You can be a bit gentler," said Michael.

"Bloody calm know-it-all!" Linh retorted.

Troy laughed. Linh glared. Michael was smiling. That cheeky bastard; he *had* been teasing Troy and her the whole time on Myleth Island.

"Not bad, Troy," said Michael. "Scaring Zaldeaans off when you've got a concussion."

Troy laughed nervously, saying, "Fiona and Linh saved me at least once. We're damned lucky we weren't wounded. My head bloody hurts!"

"We may like to get off now," the messenger suggested. "I have a message to deliver, and you may need to explain to Companion Noma what you're doing inside Tarlah Castle."

Linh and Fiona helped Michael and Troy stagger out of the chariot. Another horse's hooves clattered into the courtyard—a chariot, with several Timbalen soldiers on board.

"Did you defeat the Zaldeaans?" Fiona asked.

"They won't be bothering anyone," the chariot driver said gruffly as he helped the men on his chariot off.

"Thanks," said Michael.

"Boormar!" Troy cried.

Boormar sat hunched on the chariot's rear, clutching a stab wound. "Don't walk into spears, kids, bad idea!" he said with a pained smile.

"I'll remember," Troy replied. "Don't do faceplants on roads, either!"

Boormar flashed his teeth, and his eyes shone with mirth, but tension across his face showed his pain.

"Is Doorna all right?" asked Fiona.

"He's fine. But I fancy a physician, and you have a messenger to accompany."

The messenger was already walking towards terraced gardens of flowering trees ahead.

"Tell Companion Noma who you are," Boormar gasped. "Tell her they thought Troy was Heir Ruarnon, and Their Benevolence is in danger."

The messenger paled, and Linh and Fiona, supporting Michael and Troy, headed swiftly after him, Troy waving goodbye over his shoulder.

"Who do we say we are to Companion Noma?" Linh asked, butterflies fluttering in her stomach as the gardens passed too quickly and a door in the castle wall beyond opened to the messenger.

"Tell them we're visitors from afar," Michael replied. "His Greatness Emperor Yarath sent us because he believes we're foretold of in a prophecy, which grants us a role in the affairs of Tarlah. That should convince Tarlahns, who only seem to worship their Ancestors."

Linh shook her head. Even concussed and struggling to walk in a straight line, Michael was still perceptive, if slower than usual.

Troy smiled approvingly. "I've been a bad influence on you, Micky. That's what I'd say if I understood what the hell's going on."

"Are you all right, Troy?" Fiona asked.

"He's concussed," Linh replied. "I could barely get him onto our chariot."

Fiona grimaced. "I don't think you're going to get an icepack here."

"And I thought there was nothing to miss about school," said Troy.

Linh shook her head and gazed through the open door at a corridor with frescoes of bright, multicolour buildings lining its walls, lit by burning torches. Maybe there was beauty in Umarinaris beyond its wars.

Chapter 21

Breach

Ethlin: *Assault of Tarlah City*

A round Ethlin, distant shouts echoed over rooftops and reverberated off walls of empty apartments. There was so much chaos at the city's northern end, but eerie silence reigned here up on the walls beside East Gate. She suspected General Takanis wanted the Censar's last son to survive the siege, and was grateful for a reprieve, even if it meant listening to distant crashes of power slings hurling boulders through rooftops.

"General Aza is at the intersection of North and Middle Roads, and so are two units of reserves," Arlian said quietly. "I think he anticipates an attack from the forest at East Gate."

Ethlin smiled. They both liked speed and daring. But training with Arlian had shown her that he enjoyed tactics just as much. He had a head for it. Perhaps being educated helped.

"And instead of sending some hapless underling to sit bored and find out, you wanted to escort us there yourself?" she asked with a smile.

"I can't let hapless underlings have all the fun," he replied with a grin.

Ethlin's face fell, as she remembered the man who had tried to reassure her as they awaited an enemy charge on Death Belt Desert, going silent because he had been killed beside her.

The mirth faded from Arlian's face. "If there is fighting at another gate, I'd rather fight beside you than on the northern wall."

Ethlin eyed West Gate periodically. East Gate was more likely to be attacked. The forest offered cover to approaching soldiers, and carefully targeted Tarlahn patrols watching it could be removed. But the gates remained closed and everything stayed quiet and still. There was a legitimate reason for sending them here, but Ethlin suspected Takanis was taking advantage of it to be kind to young soldiers.

"Attack! Siege tower attack!"

The cry came from West Gate. Ethlin frowned. The siege tower approaching the western walls was unusual. A giant, hide-covered crosspiece stuck out the front, long enough to cross the walls.

"Hold your positions!" East Gate's captain called to her soldiers along the wall.

Fire arrows glowed, as they soared at the siege tower through the dawn. A second tower approached, and a third. Archers on the battlements beside West Gate fired desperately. The first tower's protrusion moved over the battlements. A rope dropped from it, and enemy soldiers slid down into the city. A second rope fell, and more soldiers slid down.

"Reinforcements to West Gate!" the west gate captain cried. "West Gate is breached!"

"Go!" Ethlin's captain ordered archers down East Gate's stairs. The women sprinted along Middle Road. But they had a long way to run. Arlian turned anxiously to the captain.

"Stay here and be on your guard," she ordered.

If the enemy secured entrance at West Gate, it would attack the northern walls from inside the city. The Tarlahn army could be routed and the city would fall. Arlian had taught Ethlin enough tactics for that to be clear. And Generals Takanis and Aza had been right: the Zaldeaans weren't depending on fighting their way across the northern walls to take the city; they were occupying the Tarlahn army while entering in force elsewhere.

The second and third oddly shaped enemy siege tower wheeled before the western battlements, hide corridors extending over them, more ropes lowering, more Zaldeaans sliding into the city. Sacks were lowered too. Zaldeaans picked up bows and shot at archers atop West Gate's walls.

Cries rent the air, and Ethlin gasped as Tarlahns plummeted off the battlements.

A roar cut through the city. Grey and even white-haired Tarlahn braids swung above old, dented armour, as retired soldiers burst from houses near West Gate, loosing arrows, waving spears, and attacking the enemy.

"That's the reinforcements?" she asked. "Did the regent order them to stay?"

"Some," Arlian replied. "I suspect most ignored the order to evacuate," he added with a grin.

A younger infantry unit turned the corner of North and Centre Roads, running towards West Gate. A second followed. The central reinforcement units must be stationed near the junction, halfway between East and West Gate.

Ethlin turned to the western walls and gasped. No Tarlahns defended them. Zaldeaans stepped freely from siege towers onto the battlements and ran down West Gate's tower stairs. Zaldeaans attacked a shield wall of Tarlahn veterans and reinforcements on the road. The Tarlahn line barred the road, but soon, Zaldeaans were attacking the entire line. More Zaldeaans kept sliding down the ladders and climbing from tower to battlement stairs to the road.

"They will be overrun," Arlian said worriedly. "The reinforcements are not coming fast enough."

"I have signalled more," said the captain.

Ethlin twisted her spear in her hands. Neither of them had bows. There were shields in East Gate's towers if they needed them...

Pottery smashed. Ethlin's head snapped towards the house it came from. Arlian raised an eyebrow.

"Something smashed," she said.

"That's impossible," he objected. "There's no one inside these buildings. From the numbers, I suspect every retired soldier is fighting at West Gate."

Ethlin knew that sound. Things got broken in the kitchens often enough. She crept down the gate tower stairs and towards the house. She stayed in the shadows of the building opposite and squinting through the pale light of dawn. The man standing in the parlour beyond the window had free-flowing hair.

Ethlin strained her ears. She never expected to be grateful for the walloping a cook gave her the first time she shirked her duties in the kitchen, but the hearing she had developed since made her sure others were moving, gathering in the first floor of the house opposite.

"There are people in the house," she whispered back to Arlian, who crept behind her. "I saw a man with loose hair."

Arlian shivered. "They *did* tunnel in through the forest. They must have climbed trees to estimate the distance and tunnelled under a house so we couldn't see them come in."

Their captain led the remaining East Gate archers towards them. "Just that building?" she asked.

284

Ethlin bent double and crept along the road. Someone grunted in the house next door. She stiffened and held two fingers up to the captain. Then she bent beneath the windows and hurried back to Arlian, her hands tingling with fear. A messenger atop East Gate waved a flag signalling for reinforcements. But if Ethlin, Arlian, their captain, and East Gate's remaining soldiers didn't block both doors and fight like Chaos himself, she would be dead before the reinforcements arrived.

Arlian cupped her face in his hand and kissed her. Another soldier passed them shields, and the captain led everyone forwards. Ethlin heard a whizz and tugged Arlian down. An arrow shot over their heads.

"Low and make for the doors!" the captain ordered.

Arlian ran and Ethlin sprinted beside him. More arrows whizzed, and soldiers cried out around her. The doors remained closed. She and Arlian paused at a corner. A door creaked around it. She and Arlian crept along the front wall, bent below its windows. The enemy was sneaking into a side street from both houses.

Ethlin's spear took the lead soldier in the throat. Others turned. Arrows whizzed and felled them. Someone shouted, but Ethlin didn't understand. Her captain thrust her spear into Ethlin's hand. "Don't throw it."

Soldiers poured from both houses, roaring, spears out, shields deflecting arrows. Ethlin ducked a thrust and rammed her spear into a soldier's thigh. She withdrew while he screamed in pain and stabbed him in the neck. He fell, revealing more Tarlahns meeting Zaldeaans, her comrades fighting two or three opponents at once.

She and Arlian fought with their spears, side by side. Another attacker approached her, and another. They kept pouring out of the house and the one beyond. Maybe the attack on West Gate was a diversion too. Perhaps this force was meant to take the city.

Ethlin grimaced as a spear sliced her elbow, and struck her opponent in the face with her butt. "Hold your ground," Lenaris had said, and that was what she would do.

Ruarnon

Boulders crashed into houses before Ruarnon. Battle roared, and Tarlahns gained ground atop the walls slowly enough for Ruarnon to wonder if the glory-seeking followers of the Warrior's Creed had the patience to push all day. The sun was well into the sky now. Sweat glistened on arms holding shields. The heat caused some to stumble, weaken, and give ground. Determination, aggression, and endless shoving might take the wall before the end of the day.

Ruarnon eyed the city behind them nervously. The noise was deafening at North Gate. Was that city bells calling for help elsewhere? Their question was soon answered. There was movement atop the watchtower at the intersection of North and Centre Roads. It stilled. A brown flag was thrown into the air. A thrown flag meant, 'Send reinforcements; we are dying and the building is falling.'

Ruarnon leaned over the battlements. "All reserves to me!" they yelled. "West or East Gate is under full assault! Captains, ready every messenger's horse. Mount them with archers!"

Captain Arleath gave them a single nod. Ruarnon turned and rushed down the tower stairs, hearing their guards running after them while Lenaris paced them.

"Ruarnon, Arlian is down there! I saw him leading younger soldiers that way."

Ruarnon bit their lip.

"They may be in the side streets," Arleath cautioned. "We must be wary of every street as we ride."

Ruarnon gave a curt nod, then flung themself into their saddle. They kicked their horse into motion, then seized their bow. If the enemy were inside the city, elite archers were needed. Ruarnon was one of those, as were Lenaris, Arleath, and their bodyguards. Delaying the enemy with arrows before they reached critical mass and assaulted the walls from inside, or Tarlah Castle itself, was crucial for Tarlah to stand. They would buy as much time as they could. Where in Chaos were the Timbalens?

Ruarnon, Lenaris, and Captain Arleath charged down North Road in a perverse reversal of the pursuit of the carriage that took Ruarnon's parents. They would *not* be too late this time!

Their horse's hooves ate up the paved road. The intersection of North and Centre Roads drew nearer. Ruarnon drew three arrows and held their bow ready.

Shouts sounded west of Centre Road. Ruarnon stared at grey-braided soldiers fighting Zaldeaans. Many casualties lay scattered around them. General Aza's archers moved on nearby rooftops, firing at three siege towers that branched over the battlements and trailed ropes into the city. Ruarnon's retired soldiers and the mid-city reinforcements were outnumbered.

"I fear it's East Gate, Benevolence," General Aza called from the watchtower. "The captain there left only a single soldier in view on the walls. They must be overrun."

Ruarnon heeled their horse down a road running parallel to Centre Road, towards East Gate. How long had it taken the enemy to reach the middle of the city? When had the captain led her soldiers to fight Zaldeaans? How many had breached the walls?

Arleath flung up a hand, and Ruarnon, Lenaris, and their guards slowed their horses. Weapons clashed ahead. The guards branched out, several dismounting to scout between buildings. Mounted archers slowed behind Ruarnon, but they'd outridden the foot soldier reinforcements. Ruarnon and the mounted soldiers around them would have to contain the breach, until the foot soldiers arrived.

Ethlin wiped blood from her face. Arlian was missing an ear. His head was bleeding badly. She worried, in between ducking, dodging, catching blows on her spear, stabbing, and the sting of metal cutting her limbs, the side of her neck, and once, her forehead. The strength she had built in kitchens and training kept her upright. It stopped her from being wounded anywhere vital.

She didn't feel pain. There was only need. Only Arlian fighting beside her. Their captain behind. Only her companions falling around her, one by one. They were crying out, spasming or dying silently. There was only this road. The screams echoing off the walls. The endless rush of Zaldeaans from two doors. The greybeards and older women on her left were tiring. The ever-thinning line of Tarlahns standing between the enemy and its goal, to take Tarlah City. She. Would. Stand. Her. Ground.

Ruarnon rounded a bend in a side street. Ten heads with free-flowing hair turned towards them. Lenaris' first arrow killed a man before Ruarnon raised their bow and loosed a trio of arrows, one after another, into enemy necks between armoured chests and heads. The enemy charged. Ruarnon's guards loosed arrows, and Ruarnon loosed into gaps in oncoming enemy soldiers armour. There were so many enemies. Ruarnon and their guards shot up to point-blank range.

Then Ruarnon swung their bow onto their saddle and drew a double-bladed spear. They caught the nearest enemy under the chin with the right blade. The left end cut a soldier's face on their other side. Ruarnon leapt from their horse and kicked at shields. They landed, danced under spearheads, and sliced with both ends of their blades, pivoting, ducking, reaching, kicking, slicing in a frenzy.

Their guards stayed back, holding ground on one side, while Lenaris fought in a bloody maelstrom on the other side. Arrows soared overhead into charging enemies. Zaldeaans roared, and their charge towards Ruarnon became all out.

Ruarnon fought three men and stepped forwards to reach new opponents with every kill. Arleath advanced on their left and the Lenaris advanced on their right, with a speed and aggression Ruarnon had never been able to match.

The arrow fire increased, confusing and distracting enemies. Ruarnon and their companions cut into Zaldeaans swiftly, momentum carrying them beyond wounded opponents, Ruarnon's guards finishing off those they left behind.

Captain Arleath halted Ruarnon as the arrows intensified. Lenaris had already stopped, while Zaldeaan foot soldiers paused before her. Ruarnon couldn't help smiling at that.

The enemy raised shields overhead. Lenaris led the
Tarlahn charge, Ruarnon, Arleath and their guards struggling
to keep up with her. Ruarnon's spear became slick with sweat
in their hands as they fought on. They were vaguely aware
they were bleeding, but they didn't care.

Ethlin stumbled. Why was there a spear in her chest? She
thrust her spear into the throat of the offending Zaldeaan.
Then the ground came to meet her. Arlian cried out, and his
spear cut the air. The captain's short sword slit throats as she
danced among the enemy, unshielded. They were protecting
Ethlin. But they were supposed to be guarding the road. They
were holding their ground. Lenaris would be proud. Arlian's
family would be proud. They would let her marry him now.

Ruarnon's urgency was flagging. Their motions were
slowing. Captain Arleath steered them back from the front
line. Lenaris and their bodyguards cut down Zaldeaans before
them. Archers loosed arrows into the street beyond. Zaldeaans
running forwards stumbled over bodies across the road.
Ruarnon's archers must have felled over a hundred enemies.
There were only twenty archers on the rooftops, every
surviving archer from East and West Gate, Ruarnon suspected.

More soldiers were fighting either side and ahead now. The reinforcements who had followed Ruarnon on foot had entered the fray. After a while, it became clear the Tarlahns were reclaiming the street. Zaldeaans retreated towards a house, trying to shield themselves in formation. Ruarnon's bodyguards hurled spears into the cracks, then pried the formation open with their swords. The reinforcements charged it and pushed the enemy aside.

Ruarnon looked down a few buildings before East Gate. A Zaldeaan fell, revealing two soldiers.

"Arlian!" Ruarnon sprinted forward, ducking spears, hamstringing enemies who dared get in their way.

Sounds of a scuffle on their right told them Lenaris was fighting her way forward too.

Arlian fell to his knees. "Isn't she beautiful?" Arlian asked, gesturing to a fallen soldier beside him with a messy brown braid, beautiful deep brown eyes, and a smile on her lifeless face. "Tell father I want to marry her."

Arlian collapsed. He wore bronze armour, unlike his unfortunate betrothed. But his thigh was wounded, gushing blood. His face was pale. And the hilt of a short sword stuck out of his armpit. Lenaris knelt beside him, taking his hand, her face stricken.

"Did we do well today?" he asked her.

"You were marvellous. Both of you," she replied, her eyes filling with tears.

"Arlian?" Ruarnon asked, their voice cracked as they knelt beside the body of the boy who could smile at anything, whom Lenaris rebuked for never taking life seriously. But Arlian's face had stilled, his chest no longer rose and fell, and his eyes were glazing over. Ruarnon turned back to the girl and realised that beneath the blood, the pendant hanging from her neck was a Promise Bracelet.

"I will tell your father. And bury you together," Ruarnon said.

They closed Arlian's eyes, while Lenaris wept. Then they and Lenaris washed the betrothed's faces with their tears.

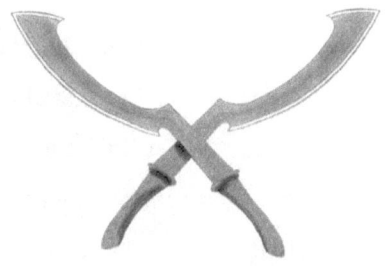

CHAPTER 22

THE MEETING OF ALLIES

RUARNON: *Assault of Tarlah City*

They helped me stop half the soldiers who tunnelled into these homes," said a woman behind Ruarnon.

Ruarnon took a deep breath and pulled themself away from memory of Arlian and his lover kissing at the Festival of Life. From an Umarinaris in which they had not been too late to save someone they cared about. Again. They wiped their face on their sleeve and turned. The woman's arms were covered in blood, her face pale, but she still stood.

"I taught them," said Lenaris. "I was training them both in secret. He taught her well, but she would likely have died in battle sooner, if not for my teaching."

Ruarnon placed a hand on her neck, the closest thing to a hug anyone could feel with armour on.

"I am sorry for your loss," said Captain Arleath, bowing his head. "The reinforcements can contain the Zaldeaans now, Benevolence."

Ruarnon sighed and stood. Their childhood companion and his lover lay dead, Lenaris was devastated at losing both her students, but time never stood still for the regent. At least fifty Zaldeaans still fought their reinforcements. The entire street was littered with bodies, more Tarlahns around Arlian, where his companions had been outnumbered, tens up and down the street embedded with arrows, and swerving lines down the road of Zaldeaans with other wounds. Ruarnon shuddered. Had they, Lenaris and Arleath truly cut down so many?

"This street likely has more casualties than any siege tower," Arleath added.

"It was how the enemy planned to take the city," said Ruarnon. "I suspect Arlian figured it out. That will be why he got himself stationed halfway across the city. It was why we stationed General Aza, two units of reinforcements, and the retired soldiers here. But I didn't have enough soldiers to defend these gates against so many. We've barely held. And I've left no reinforcements on the northern walls. They could fall soon, one tower at a time."

Lenaris gasped.

Thought of the walls and Zaldeaans pushing Tarlahns across them and probing towards tower stairs spurred Ruarnon back onto their horse. Lenaris rushed to hers, and the pair rode back down North Road to North Gate together.

"I'm not sure what our numbers are," Ruarnon told Lenaris, "or if my captains pulled men from the walls to join my reinforcements at East Gate."

They couldn't bear to say the rest of that thought aloud. What if Arlian and his betrothed and a few brave others had died holding off the enemy's true attack force, only for its diversion attack to succeed?

When they reached the watchtower, Ruarnon and Lenaris hurried up its stairs. At the tower top, Companion Tor turned to them. He looked thinner and paler than Ruarnon remembered, his care lines deeper, but his light blue eyes shone.

"You are well enough for this?" Ruarnon asked.

Tor smiled, leaning against the battlements on one side, holding a crutch with his other arm. "I hear you have been commanding soldiers defeating a breach of the walls. I would say you are like your father, but your leadership reminded me of someone else."

Ruarnon smiled painfully. Thought of their uncle still saddened them, but they were happy to be compared with Uncle Omah.

"My sister tells me that the Timbalen army will reach our walls at any moment," Tor added. "The Fourth Zaldeaan-Tarlahn war is almost over."

Ruarnon slumped, exchanging a relieved smile with Lenaris. The northern walls weren't breached, and soon their allies would drive the enemy away.

"I, I need a moment," Lenaris told them.

Ruarnon bowed their head in understanding, and she retreated down the stairs.

"There is a change on the walls," Ruarnon noted. "Between the third and second left siege towers. The enemy have merged."

Tor sighed. "Soldiers trapped in between cut their way out. I do not think the Zaldeaans would have accepted their surrender. Most made it out alive."

There was a pause, then Tor's expression changed completely, as he said, "I am sorry I failed Omah."

His gaze was dark.

"You nearly died trying to protect him! And *he* chose to fight."

"He had his father's instincts. I fought with your grandfather in the uprising against the Zaldeaans. The mob were angry but scared. Roused, but they needed a leader, and your grandfather died providing them with one. Our levied soldiers were much the same. Omah led them well. We must send an envoy to the Zaldeaans after the fighting. His body must be recovered, and his spirit guided by the priests into his bust."

"Do you believe that?" Ruarnon asked.

"I believe a face reminds me what I know of a person, and that can be of enormous help in difficult times."

Ruarnon nodded.

"But look to the walls," said Tor.

It was getting quieter. Then they heard a drum, DOM-DOM, DOM-DOM.

"TIMBALENS! TIM-BA-LENS!"

DOM-DOM. DOM-DOM.

Sudden movement rippled beside the second left siege tower, men turning and walking back into it. The opposing front lines pressed together, but rear Zaldeaan lines returned to siege tower tops and down ladder hatches. The fourth left siege tower was retreating. A few Tarlahns leapt off its ramp.

DOM-DOM. DOM-DOM.

"TIM-BA-LENS!"

Front enemy lines retreated as back lines threw their shields onto shooting decks or beside ladder hatches and flung themselves down ladders. Ruarnon watched, not daring to believe it was over. It seemed like a truce, which they supposed it was. Apparently, with their west coast under attack, even Zaldeaan generals wouldn't risk fighting the Timbalens as well.

Bodies were exposed on the battlements, more Tarlahn than Zaldeaan where Tarlahns had been squeezed between larger groups of enemy soldiers on the left, and more Zaldeaan than Tarlahn near both ends of the battlements where Tarlahn reinforcements had broken enemy lines.

Tarlahn front lines kept their shield walls in place as the enemy retreated. Were they still 'the enemy' now that the invasion was over? Slowly, Ruarnon smiled.

Zaldeaan phalanxes retreated behind siege towers, reaching their camp, where their baggage train awaited. It was over. The enemy were leaving.

Soldiers appeared around the eastern and western corners of the northern walls, yellow banners of the Timbalen Empire at their head. The last Zaldeaans climbed onto the siege towers, the functional eight moved back, and Ruarnon was so happy to see them leave that they laughed. Only then did discipline collapse. Soldiers cheered, throwing their helmets into the air, embraced, kissed, and others waved at Zaldeaans, smiling grimly, or made rude gestures.

"Come, you ought to congratulate them," said Tor.

Ruarnon smiled and followed Tor down the watchtower stairs, nearer the walls, and up the right gate tower. Soldiers cheered when they saw Ruarnon and were so noisy that Ruarnon gave up trying to address them and saluted instead. Soldiers returned the salute, then continued cheering and talking eagerly amongst themselves.

"Benevolence, our allies have almost reached the gate!" a voice called.

Ruarnon tried to recover their command voice.

"Tell them we will convey their leaders over the walls in the lifts," Ruarnon said hoarsely.

"That will do for now, but you will need to receive their commander formally," Tor advised.

Ruarnon nodded. "How will the dead be organised?"

"They will be moved to the marketplace where comrades, captains, or returned family members will identify them," Takanis replied. "The unidentified will have their portraits sketched, and graves marked, so the priests will know which grave to summon their spirits to their busts from."

As hadn't occurred for Uncle Omah. Ruarnon sighed.

"Do not burden yourself with the dead, Ruarnon," Tor advised. "They number less than half the total slain on the battlefield and depend on the living to celebrate the liberation of Tarlah."

Ruarnon nodded. "Then I will prepare to meet the Timbalen Commander."

Tor inclined his head, and Ruarnon retreated down the gate tower stairs, their guards approaching as they mounted their horse.

"You have done well," Ruarnon told them, "As you did helping me escape the enemy weeks ago. I would not want you to miss soldier-organised celebrations I am ignorant of, so take your orders from General Takanis for now."

Their guards and Captain Arleath smiled broadly and bowed atop their horses. Then Ruarnon rode down North Road, safe in blessed peace and personal space, in their own home at last.

But they didn't prepare to meet the Timbalen Commander immediately. They took their time walking back to their chambers, past smiling servants whispering excitedly, continuing to smile as they bowed at Ruarnon. Ruarnon tried to return the smiles, but could only manage a half-smile.

The war was over. They had led soldiers to defend a breach. Successfully. After fifteen years of absence, the Timbalens had returned in force, and Tarlah's future seemed bright again. But Arlian was dead. Omah was dead. There were people, many of them, whose bodies Ruarnon had seen on the battlefield, atop the northern walls and in the streets, who should share this celebration, but were gone now. And on top of the exertion of fighting and supervising battle, it weighed on all Ruarnon's limbs and was exhausting. So when they reached their chambers, they sent an invitation to the Timbalen Commander, then lay down and let sleep refresh them.

Later that afternoon, Ruarnon walked to the castle courtyard with Aunt Telena. They wore their finest clothes, she a Timbalen style green silk tunic with an emerald necklace, her hair intricately braided into a bun decorated with emeralds, they in their red and gold tunic with the golden Regent's circlet atop their head. Ruarnon and Telena watched carriages moving down North Road from atop the steps, some turning to large mud-brick homes near the castle, others

coming up the hill and entering the courtyard. Companions
Tor and Noma, high officials, and low officials assembled in
their finest clothes to greet their families.

Companion Tor greeted his family while Lenaris told her
sisters and mother of her father's abduction.

The Companions' wives rushed to Aunt Telena as high
officials greeted families emerging from carriages beyond.
Two stood weeping.

Ruarnon turned from the couple, shivering at the memory
of Tarlahn bodies scattered across the road beyond Arlian's
body. Many more would have died had Tarlah fallen, but the
price the soldiers had paid to protect the city still weighed
heavily on Ruarnon's heart.

Ruarnon exhaled, but their torso remained tense, their
chest tight. Their parents were gone, and it wasn't their fault.
Their uncle had died, and it wasn't their fault, despite how
Ruarnon had failed to save all three. Now Arlian was dead,
and Ruarnon hadn't been able to save him, either. There may
have been nothing they could do for Arlian or Ethlin. That
somehow made it worse.

"It should be easier now," Lenaris said quietly, as she
approached. "The empire will secure our independence. Kyura
will have to accept a truce."

"Kyura is still at war against invaders we know little
about," Ruarnon said quietly. "But we haven't time to discuss
that now."

Lenaris eyed them darkly and nodded. Ruarnon led Lenaris to a high table set atop a wooden dais, where they were served wine, and the Companions, their families, and Generals Aza and Takanis took their seats. The castle's occupants gathered in the courtyard below.

A tall blond man with a weathered face approached Ruarnon's table, flanked by two men in yellow cloaks, Elite Guard. Ruarnon had grown up with stories of their strange abilities, not quite comparable to the North Landers beyond the Zaldeaan Realm, but both men were of average height and build, blond-haired and blue-eyed, and looked ordinary enough.

Ruarnon stood to greet Commander Imphin. "Thank you again for your assistance today."

The commander inclined his head and said quietly, "It will not just be today. His Greatness intends to resume trade with the Far West in the future, and we shall garrison soldiers and retain ships here as long as need be to secure Tarlah by land and water."

Ruarnon managed to limit their surprise to a blink. That implied the Timbalen Empire was secure beyond all doubt, its emperor more confident than ever, and that perhaps this time, the Timbalen Empire could be relied upon.

"I will be glad to discuss details with you tomorrow," Ruarnon said. "For now, will you and your guests join us?"

Behind Imphin, four youths stood hesitantly. Tor had told Ruarnon of youths attacked after the breach, whom he thought may be akin to characters of Timbalęn folklore from unknown lands. It seemed prudent to invite them.

"May I present to Your Benevolence: Troy, Michael, Fiona, and Linh," said Commander Imphin, following Ruarnon's gaze.

The short girl with freckles and golden-brown hair bowed, the others copying awkwardly, as though they knew what bowing was but weren't used to doing it.

"Welcome," Ruarnon said. "I gather that you come from afar. What brings you to our shores?"

Commander Imphin cleared his throat, and Ruarnon wondered if the man doubted his own people's legends.

"We're puzzled by Timbalens and what they suggest about why we're here," said Michael. "I don't see how we can answer why someone in Zaldeaa City wants your parents alive, who is invading the Zaldeaan Realm, or what will happen there now, though I don't think this is over. We came because the Timbalens believe that the North Landers, or people further west, may be the only ones who can help us get home."

Ruarnon's brows furrowed. Did they hope the North Landers could help them travel home by magic? Had the emperor sent them all this way believing that was possible? Or did he indulge them because he could afford to spend resources on curiosity and testing his people's myths? Ruarnon shook their head. Timbalens were prone to fancy...

The two girls beside Michael had already turned away, scanning Ruarnon's people as if they'd never seen Tarlahn tunics or even braided hair before. Tarlah seemed far stranger to them than it did to the commander or his guards. And Michael's serious, brown-eyed gaze suggested he was in earnest to get home.

"We may be able to help you contact the North Landers, but it will take time, as it may not be safe to send messengers overland or by sea until the Zaldeaans defeat their invaders. Even then, it may be dangerous to travel through or sail past the Zaldeaan Realm when Zaldeaans are resentful over losing the war."

The curly-haired youth grit his teeth, and the golden-haired girl sighed, but Michael just nodded, as calm in the face of adversity as Ruarnon aspired to be. They looked a similar age to Ruarnon too. If they were stuck in Tarlah a while, perhaps it was time for Ruarnon to consider Regent's Companions...

Ruarnon bowed their head and gestured the youths to seats beside Commander Imphin, but remained standing to address the castle families seated below. Silence fell. Some mouths smiled, couples holding hands, parents resting small children on their knees. Other eyes were red-rimmed at tables with empty chairs, where the fallen would have sat. The mood was solemn.

"Welcome. It pleases me to see many of you returned to your homes under Tarlahn rule. But as I bore witness to..."

Ruarnon blinked, and for a moment, they were cutting their way through Zaldeaans, desperately searching for Tarlahn soldiers surrounded by enemies before they were all slain. Ruarnon's chest tightened with the fear that had spurred them towards Arlian. They tore their focus away from the past, gripping their goblet tightly. "Many lives were laid down to hold the city before our allies arrived. May their spirits make their way to the Ancestors."

Ruarnon raised their goblet. As one, the crowd intoned, "May they be at peace with the Ancestors," and drank a solemn toast to the dead.

Ruarnon wasn't sure if they wanted to mourn the dead, to celebrate holding the enemy back, or to retreat to their favourite quiet corner of the library and read for hours. But they suspected regents never had that kind of space or peace. As always, duty called and Ruarnon had a pre-prepared speech to recite.

"We have fought, weathered a siege, and with the aid of our allies, banished our enemies. In a time we all hoped would be of peace, you have weathered war well. Today, our army destroyed four siege towers. They stood their ground atop the walls and kept the enemy back under gruelling conditions. Then the mere sight of our allies drove the enemy away. Our allies have agreed to remain until the kingdom's safety is assured. To our allies and Tarlah's independence!"

Fierce smiles met that toast, and some people cheered. Others toasted quietly, grateful for their safety but solemn or heartsick at the loss of friends or family.

"There are a few people whose efforts I wish to single out, especially those who gave their lives to protect us. First, my uncle, second son of a king's nephew, whom no one intended to rule. He did so with devotion, clarity, calm, determination, and bravery. To my uncle, Regent Omah!"

Ruarnon's heart warmed when their aunt managed to smile through her tears, and everyone drank. They proposed toasts to General Takanis, Commander Imphin, the retired soldiers who defeated enemies who breached West Gate and the eastern wall, and to Arlian and Ethlin.

"Omah would have made that toast too," said Aunt Telena, "though your father may not have approved. To Omah," and they drank, as servants flocked around their table, delivering platters of meats, pastries, vegetables, and fruits.

Ruarnon switched seats to talk to Lenaris and noticed their aunt talking to the four youths, whom she put at ease. They listened to friends' tales and appreciated being surrounded with happy, familiar faces who had good things to talk about once more. It was a reprieve from the memory of Arlian's gaze at the lover he was too severely wounded and disoriented to realise was already dead. It let Ruarnon push aside things that would haunt their dreams and appreciate pleasant things while they were awake.

The dinner was soon over, followed by recitations of poetry and re-enactments of heroic deeds by the Ancestors to the tunes of lutes under a starlit sky. It was late when the crowds dispersed, and for the first time since their parents were abducted, Ruarnon slept soundly.

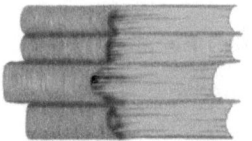

Chapter 23

Next Steps

Linh: *Tarlah City, Day of Rest After Siege*

From the shade of steps beneath a roof on the edge of a courtyard, Linh didn't feel the joy shining in Lenaris' eyes as she duelled another youth the day after the siege was lifted. Nor did Linh feel the peace in Ruarnon's relaxed posture as they watched Lenaris several steps away.

"We need to speak to Ruarnon about the damars," she told her friends.

"It's supposed to be a day of rest," Fiona said from the steps on her right. "Lenaris said the Royal Council is meeting tomorrow."

"I'm sure Commander Imphin intends to tell them," said Linh, "but this can't wait. Damars have been attacking the Zaldeaan Realm for nine days and the Zaldeaans don't seem to be getting anywhere against them, despite being experienced warriors. I'm worried the Zaldeaan city guards are vastly outnumbered and damars are running beyond them to civilians."

"I think it could be more than that," said Michael. "The damars spread out when they attacked us on the beach. They entered the water separately. They don't work together, even when they're dying. So would they stand and fight a pitched battle with the city guard?"

"As soon as a damar went for the guards on the beach," said Troy, "the other two tried to move around him. The guards who fought them had to block their path."

"They seem like hunters to me," Michael added. "The speed they ran with and the way they kept spreading out, it's like each of them was seeking its own prey. Only they don't hunt to eat; they hunt to kill. Like someone made them as an attack force, to kill, as fast as they can, over the greatest distances they can run."

Linh's mind rebelled against the idea. But the chilling logic of it matched what she had witnessed. And suggested why the mighty Zaldeaan army had failed.

"If you're right," she said, "dealing with them isn't about fighting. It's about containing them. If they outnumbered the city guard, and they all split up, the city guard wouldn't have known which ones to chase. And we know how heavy bronze armour is. I couldn't run for an hour in it, let alone nine days. And damars are fast. The ones the guard didn't catch up to and kill early on might have been running further and further ahead ever since."

"And the best, and possibly most of the horses, are with the army," Fiona added. "So most city guards might have to hunt them on foot."

"How do you fight them if they're everywhere?" Troy wondered.

"The same way we did," Michael replied. "They must have heard us. You send out a large party of soldiers, make lots of noise, and they come running. You keep making noise, killing those who approach and they'll keep coming. We've already seen that they don't fear death."

Linh shook her head. "I don't think an army used to conventional tactics is going to think of that. The Zaldeaan army will probably split into smaller groups and hunt damars randomly. It could still take days to find them all. But we can make sure the Zaldeaans know Michael's strategy because we can tell Ruarnon to tell them. And if we don't do it now and the Zaldeaans keep using ineffective strategies to fight the damars, they'll keep spreading and attacking civilians. They might even reach Tarlah."

Her friends agreed, and she turned to Ruarnon, who watched Lenaris from steps on their left. Ruarnon had probably invited her and her friends out of politeness. Hopefully the fact they were strangers of unclear status wouldn't affect how Ruarnon received her news.

"Heir Ruarnon," she asked, "can we have a word in private?"

Ruarnon studied her and seemed to pick up her mood. "Of course," they replied, and they led her and her friends to a distant corner.

"I know this is supposed to be a day of rest, and you're probably exhausted and that you don't really know who we are," Linh said in a rush, "but we know something you don't, about the invaders attacking the Zaldeaan Realm. Has Commander Imphin told you what they are?"

Ruarnon's frown deepened. "You feel it cannot wait?"

"The Zaldeaans are the best and most experienced soldiers on this continent, aren't they?" Linh asked.

Ruarnon nodded.

"Aren't you surprised they couldn't fight off a few hundred invaders?"

"I assumed the invaders staggered their arrival to conceal their numbers and ensure that the Zaldeaans underestimated them."

"I thought so too, but the invaders *aren't* an army. We think they're more like hunters, targeting prey individually. We suspect only a few would have stayed to fight while the rest ran ahead. And they're fast. We wouldn't have stood a chance if we had to run away from them. The only reason we weren't hurt was because our guards were walking around with swords in their hands and were trained soldiers who didn't lose their nerve when they saw what was attacking us."

"You speak as if these invaders are not human," said Ruarnon. "How can this be?"

"Do your people have the same myths of the Sorcery War as the Timbalen Empire?" Michael asked.

"Yes, but that is ancient mythology, as distant and unknown to us as Creation itself. Are you suggesting a sorcerer bred these invaders using magic?" Ruarnon turned away, then continued softly, "The Sorcery War was fought in the Far West, and it looks like damars sailed from the West, but a sorcerer breeding monsters? In this era?"

"That's the only explanation we can think of," Michael replied.

"Where did you encounter them?"

"On Timraith Island."

Ruarnon gaped. Several emotions flashed across their face before they said slowly, "The Timraith Islanders were attacked? But we received no word... Were they overrun?"

Fiona nodded sadly.

"The reports from the Zaldeaan Coast," Ruarnon added distractedly, "reports of Chaos Spawn and murder..." Ruarnon shivered, leaning on their knees. "Timraith Island is part of Tarlah," they said, their voice cracked. "Those were *my* people."

"We're sorry," said Fiona. "The Timbalens arrived too late."

"Those creatures roam the Zaldeaan Realm, and the Zaldeaan army is still sailing home."

Ruarnon stood. "Follow me," they said, striding up the steps, and Linh and her friends hurried after them. "I will not have the fate of the Islanders befall the children, elderly, and women the Zaldeaan army left behind. The Zaldeaan army must divide to contain damars."

"You plan to tell the Zaldeaans what we know?" Michael asked, as they followed Ruarnon into a corridor.

"We can do more than that," said Troy. "We think we know how to fight them."

They entered a room, and scribes seated at a long wooden table stood and bowed. Ruarnon motioned one to join them, Linh, and her friends at a table. The scribe produced a new scroll, a quill, and ink and eyed Ruarnon expectantly.

Linh and Michael repeated their experiences and suspicions, pausing for Ruarnon to dictate a letter.

"Thank you," Ruarnon said earnestly, meeting Linh's gaze when they finished.

"Least we could do," said Troy with a shrug.

Ruarnon's brows furrowed as they asked, "Where exactly do you come from, and how did you come to be in the Timbalen Empire seeking your way home?"

"Put it this way," Michael replied. "If you set sail looking for our homeland, you'll never get there."

"What do you mean?" Ruarnon asked.

"Do they have the Myths of the Strangers here?" Fiona asked.

Ruarnon nodded. Linh saw understanding in their eyes, and they shook their head. "They are known here as the inventions of bored Timbalens who do not have the shadow of war or its outbreak to occupy their time. But the Timbalens believe you are Strangers? And you do not know your purpose?"

Fiona explained Red Cloak, and the archways, and Linh admired her friend's ability to ignore Ruarnon's piercing gaze and open-mouthed surprise.

When no one cried 'April Fool,' Ruarnon shook their head. "Perhaps my people should give our allies more credit. The tales never made sense to me, but there's always been enough happening in lands we know for me to wonder why someone would invent people and lands beyond that or claim people from so far away had visited the Timbalen Empire when they hadn't. But I'd thought that if the stories were true, it would be people from faraway places you *can* sail to."

Linh shook her head. "Every landmass you can sail to from our country has been sailed to and mapped out already. Tarlah and the Timbalen Empire weren't among them."

Ruarnon's mouth fell open. "You have mapped *every* ocean reachable from your homeland? The Timbalen maps are best, but they are vague about Tarlah and guesswork for anywhere further west. It would appear Umarinaris is bigger than I had thought. But if it is so large, if there are unconnected oceans with their own landmasses, I still struggle with the idea that magic gateways could let anyone travel between them."

"It's easier to believe when you see your surroundings change instantly and completely around you," Troy assured them.

"It sounds like your journey so far has been hard on you," said Ruarnon. "You are welcome to rest here, until I can safely send a messenger to the North Lands."

"Thank you," said Fiona.

Ruarnon: Tarlah City

Ruarnon summoned Commander Imphin as soon as they said goodbye to the four youths. The Commander confirmed Linh and her friends' descriptions of the damars and seemed to share their opinions on the creatures' natures. Ruarnon left the interview breathing deeply to slow their racing heart and tried not to panic as they walked to the castle battlements. They gripped the stone crenellations, gazing out across the city. Voices crying their wares in the marketplace, the hum of conversation, and the creak of wheels as people moved down South Road were calming, but Tarlah's safety didn't make the fact that creatures from the worst myths of the Sorcery War were loose in the Zaldeaan Realm any less shocking.

Linh and her friends had spoken so compellingly, and the haunted look in Imphin's eyes, the way his gaze became distant and his posture slumped when he spoke of the creatures left no doubt in Ruarnon's mind that something terrible had landed further north. It had slain an entire island of Ruarnon's subjects, and more Zaldeaan children, elderly, and women were vulnerable to it while they waited for the Zaldeaan army to return.

"What's wrong?"

Ruarnon started at Lenaris' voice, chewed their lip, then told her.

Lenaris halted. "Chaos Spawn? The worst of the myths of the Sorcery War are roaming across the Zaldeaan Realm?"

Ruarnon nodded.

"You'll have a hard time convincing my grandfather," said Lenaris. "He won't believe it unless you send scouts to capture a creature and bring it back here."

"What if the creatures escape the Realm?" Ruarnon asked, their fears brimming over. "What if they reach our northern fields?"

"The council will agree to increase border patrols, especially so soon after the war with the Zaldeaans."

"The creatures have slain an entire island of our people already." Ruarnon turned away. "So many died in the war, and those creatures are still killing people. I want it to end."

"Kyura will stop them soon," Lenaris said as she stepped beside Ruarnon.

Ruarnon shook their head. "So we sit and wait."

"It's not like we can aid the Zaldeaans," Lenaris added. "They won't want our soldiers on their soil, and there's no way I'd trust them. They've no one to blame for that but themselves."

Ruarnon said nothing. She was right. The latest Zaldeaan-Tarlahn battle had ceased, but the war itself was never over. Bitterness soured Ruarnon's thoughts. People were still dying, Tarlah's future was still uncertain beyond Timbalen convenience, and there seemed to be nothing Ruarnon could do about either.

CHAPTER 24

THE FALL

KYURA: *the Zaldeaan Realm, Four Days After the Siege of*

Tarlah

K yura sat tensely in his carriage, barely aware of
scrunching Regent Derlan's letter, until its
contents became illegible. The words still burned
in his mind.

"Kyura?" Aoran said cautiously.

Kyura should have brought Companion Armar with him.
He needed Karmarn. He needed his wife. Why were the
people he needed most dead or absent? He needed Syenne too.
He shouldn't have had her investigating his uncle. He should
have asked her to secure lines of information into his camp.

It was bad enough that the generals had concealed the
approach of the Timbalens. The First General's head arriving
in Zaldeaa City before the rest of his body ought to inform

warmongers of his feelings about that. Syenne's people were about to make arrests, and Zaldeaa City would soon see many executions. But that wasn't what worried Kyura. He gritted his teeth and withdrew Iagl's letter from his satchel on the seat beside him.

Kyura,

Your communications are being blocked. Iomar has tried to contact you. Kia has also written. The invasions are far worse than we thought. Father has had to evacuate the coast. Iomar and Kia's people have retreated into their cities and barred the gates. The invaders are not human. Monsters roam inland. You must bring the army home. Hang the generals— all of them—and come home.

Iomar and I shall support you.

Love,

Iagl

Kyura had torn the letter into ten pieces before he was conscious of his actions. He continued ripping, until the pieces were so small he could no longer hold them, then dropped them back into the satchel. If someone loved him still, perhaps he should keep a record of that. He may need to remind himself of it in the dark days to come.

His carriage had charged through the desert tunnel at full speed on receiving that message, followed by his cavalry. The infantry would march to the western coast and take ship. Regent Derlan had sent ships before Kyura had a chance to request them.

Now the high hills of Derlan's province rolled past. A hiss cut the air, followed by a screech. Kyura drew the curtains as a grey creature ran through the trees towards them, shrieking defiance and raising a simple stick. An archer felled it with a single arrow and it lay twitching as it died. The thing wore no armour. Its weapon was simple. How could these creatures have killed half as many as Regent Derlan claimed?

More screeches rent the air. Hisses too. Before the carriage. Behind it. From either side. As his column raced through the forest towards the shores of Kia's province, bowstrings twanged relentlessly and soldiers cried out. They had to stop twice. Soldiers dismounted and cut the creatures down with swords to defend the horses.

This must be how so many had died. Sound attracted the creatures, and fear and horror paralysed their prey, until they struck. They paralysed Kyura's subjects to their deaths while the army sought glory in Tarlah.

"Did we issue arrest warrants for the Spymaster yet?" Kyura asked, trying to distract himself as his soldiers carved a path to the coast through Chaos Spawn.

"Yes, Highest," Aoran replied. "Syenne has arrested him, the Vizier, the Rural Overseer, and she wrote that we should arrest the First General."

Kyura shivered as he removed Syenne's letter from his satchel.

The Vizier confessed. Uncle Derlan led the conspiracy. His every warning of rumours on the street were the rumours he had his spies plant. It was Derlan who suggested increasing the prize monies of the Military Games to the Second General, and who persuaded the Treasurer to sign off on it. The Vizier directed the staged conversation between himself, the Rural Overseer, and First General, to persuade you to war, but it followed Uncle Derlan's instructions.

Derlan has fled the palace. I have claimed the regency. I will support Iomar and Kia. We will defend the west coast together and deal with Derlan when you get home.

Iomar's words came back to Kyura: "I doubt he came here out of compassion. He has his interests." Iomar had been right.

"Why are there so many creatures still in this forest!" Kyura shouted, his eyes filling with tears.

"People around here have boarded up their homes," Aoran said, his voice cracking as he took Kyura's hand. "Karmarn ordered the bulk of the army to stay on their ships and kill many creatures at sea before they could land and add to this."

"Do I trust Karmarn?" It pained Kyura to ask. But his guards were killing so many creatures. The brutes had spread so far. So fast. How many of his people had been skewered by these fiends?

"Yes, you trust your uncle and Iomar and Iagl. They're coming to meet us, both of them. Hold on, Kyura. Please hold on a bit longer."

Kyura must have slept on Aoran's shoulder. He was leaning against it when he woke, listening to Aoran's gentle snores. They'd stopped moving. The carriage must have reached the Western Shore. Kyura dreaded what he would see here. But he would not be kept in the dark, not deprived of information any longer. He stood shakily and opened the carriage door.

"Highest! My family! They have been trapped in the woods without food for three days!"

"We need medicine. Highest! The Herbalists have run out, and many are wounded!"

Kyura stumbled. His guards circled him, trying to keep people back. This wasn't Kia's capital. It wasn't even a city. He could only see a few houses. But a small crowd gathered behind his soldiers, who were shooting fiends charging through the trees at his people. Why had his people come out of hiding when it wasn't safe? Were they so desperate?

"You need to put him down," a woman's voice said across the clearing. "There is nothing more you can do for him."

She was speaking to a young woman cradling a small boy whose unnaturally pale features said he had been dead for hours.

Kyura reached out, as if running his hands along the edge of his baby's cot.

"If it's a boy, we'll call him Kyomi, after your father," Lenine had said. "And if it's a girl, we should name her after your mother."

Kyura's mother had died giving birth to him. He knew how dangerous childbirth was. He should have got better physicians. He should have let the herbalist woman in. He should have done more to save Lenine. To save them both.

He should have listened to Syenne and Karmarn and arrested whoever he suspected. Without waiting for proof. Before so many people died and he wasn't here to protect the pleading, weeping, desperate souls flocking towards him on this cursed shore where Chaos-spawned fiends shrieked for blood.

Kyura staggered towards a physician stand. Aoran cried out and rushed towards him. He should have listened to Syenne and Aoran, and Karmarn. He should never have gone to war. And now that woman was sobbing over her dead infant son, and hundreds more were dead.

"It's my fault. I should have stopped it. I've failed everyone." Kyura's muscles gave out, and he collapsed into the physician's table. Guards were shouting, running. Aoran was calling. But it was too late. Everything was ruined.

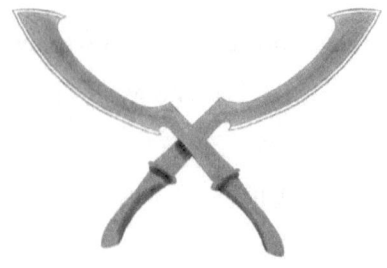

CHAPTER 25

AMBASSADOR ARMAR'S TIDINGS

RUARNON: *Tarlah City, One Week After the Siege of Tarlah*

Ruarnon gazed over Tarlah City. A week on from the siege, crowds filled the streets and marketplace again. Children's laughter and the hum of conversation replaced the cries of the siege assault. Before North Gate, soldiers lifted rubble onto carts to clear the barricade, while in the forest, the occasional tree fell, cut down as timber for a new gate. Everything was setting itself right again. It brought Ruarnon contentment, affirming that war was over, but part of Ruarnon was tense about the latest report on their parents.

"I have word of Our Benevolences," the Spymaster had told the Royal Council. "A blonde man and a dark-haired woman were carried out of the Zaldeaan palace in the dead of night during the siege here, looking pale and sweaty."

"Could they have been drugged?" Tor had asked.

"I believe that likely. I could not ascertain where they were taken, by whom, or for what purpose."

"To keep them secret and alive, I should think," Monin had said.

The Council had agreed. So while life went on for the inhabitants of Tarlah City, it was as uncertain for Ruarnon's parents as before war was declared. Meanwhile, the Urai Ambassador reported that the jungle coast was safe, but survivors of an invader shipwreck had wandered into the desert and north through the jungle, where they were dragged away by wild animals. Tarlah was well, but Ruarnon and Tor were increasingly convinced that damars were the savage hunters Linh and Imphin claimed.

A carriage entered the castle gates with an escort, and Ruarnon studied it. It stopped in the courtyard, and Ambassador Armar stepped out. Ruarnon gaped. The Zaldeaan army's ships had arrived in the Zaldeaan Realm the day before yesterday. Why had Armar departed as soon as the army began battling damars?

Ruarnon sent a messenger to summon the Council, then went to the throne room. Since their uncle's coronation as Senior Regent, no one had sat on the portable bronze throne before their father's. Ruarnon approached the dais with a pang of loss, followed by nervous uncertainty about what this visit would bring.

They sat, wrestling with tingling nerves as guards in full bronze armour lined the red carpet before the throne. Companions Tor and Noma, Monin, and Commander Imphin took their places on either side of the dais, Ruarnon's aunt standing beside them, their four young guests standing uncertainly beside her. Monin scowled. It wasn't appropriate for strangers to be in the room while Ruarnon received a Zaldeaan Ambassador, but Armar entered the throne room before anyone could send the youths out. The openly troubled look on Armar's face distracted even Monin and commanded Ruarnon's full attention.

Armar stopped some distance before the throne and knelt.

"Welcome, Ambassador Armar," Ruarnon greeted him. "How have you come so soon?"

"Greetings, Your Benevolence," Armar replied, lifting his eyes but stopping short of Ruarnon's face. His Timbalen sounded fluent, but his clipped accent was clearly Migryan. "I bring tidings from Zaldeaa City. Firstly, King Kyura is dead."

Ruarnon tensed.

Armar added, "He took his own life the day I set sail."

Ruarnon's mouth fell open. The idea shocked them more than monsters invading the Zaldeaan Realm.

"Governor Syenne claimed the throne and sent soldiers to arrest all suspected warmongers and traitors. We also searched our Spymaster's quarters, where strange documents came to light. He was, as we suspected, the war faction's tool, but they were not his only masters. Our Spymaster was in the pay of a stranger. Our scholars decoded a letter found with a collection of silver dishes, payment for his efforts in persuading King Kyura to conquer Tarlah, signed by a man called Narz."

Syenne may want a peace treaty, but why was she blaming an outsider for manipulating Kyura to war?

"The traitors we have questioned are adamant that abducting Your Benevolences' parents was the Spymaster's idea. But he knew how proud your allies are, and I would expect him to have realised the risk of a blatant attack on Tarlahn sovereignty provoking the Timbalens to intervene. I suspect the suggestion to abduct your parents originated with Narz and that he saw in the war between our kingdoms the opportunity to gain his own ends. We suspect Narz is a foreign king."

Ruarnon's brows furrowed.

"We have yet to learn where Their Benevolences were kept in the palace or moved to weeks ago."

"Warmongers took them without your knowledge?" Ruarnon asked.

Armar sighed. "This was not a warmonger plot. Only two generals were prepared to betray the king to initiate war, and they were following orders. Governor Syenne believes Governor Derlan murdered her father and intended to press Highest to war, or else kill him, seize the throne, and conquer Tarlah himself. Had Governor Syenne had her way, Derlan would have been assassinated early in Highest's reign. But she could not prove King Kyomi was murdered.

"Knowing Governor Syenne suspected him, and that proof of his treachery might prompt the king to act, I believe Derlan acted on the Spymaster's advice and had your parents abducted to distract Highest. When Highest didn't move against him then, he was emboldened and had the Second General send soldiers on a 'marching exercise' towards Tarlah, in the wake of rumours he started about Tarlah being ripe for conquest. He also attempted to infiltrate King Kyura's servants, but Governor Syenne's assassins slew his assassins."

Ruarnon's head spun at the full extent of Derlan's betrayal.

Armar continued. "Governor Syenne has executed our Vizier, Rural Overseer, and the Spymaster. Immediately after the Spymaster's death, a dozen soldiers and three servants were murdered just before the Vizier's execution. We suspect that those who helped abduct, feed, or move Your Benevolence's parents are dead, while none of the traitors we have arrested knows their whereabouts. As for the governors, I received a report during my voyage of a provincial army mobilising in the south. I suspect Governor Derlan is marching to war against Governor Syenne. Another report confirmed that she has left Zaldeaa City, perhaps to rally her provincial army."

Hadn't that bastard done enough damage to his people yet?

"What is the state of affairs in Zaldeaa City?" Tor asked.

"Grave. We were overrun before Companion Karmarn arrived with a thousand men, at which point many ships attacked. I sent word to Highest, and he launched his assault on Tarlah City, determined to secure the southern border before he took the army home, but the Timbalens arrived first.

"Highest Kyura arrived on the west coast the day that the ninth enemy ship landed on our shores. Sight of the dead and the fear and grief of survivors led him to despair. He blamed himself for needless deaths of battle, the assault, and failing to bring the army home immediately. He seized medicine from a physician's table and ingested a fatal dose. It killed him before the physician had time to prepare an antidote."

Armar's eyes were pools of darkness, worry battling urgency, battling insecurity, battling a need to stay calm in their depths, and his posture was rigid and tense. Why did Zaldeaan tradition make men rulers and not women? Governor Syenne could have prevented everything. And now Kyura was dead, and the Zaldeaan Realm was in turmoil, suffering a fate only Derlan deserved.

Ruarnon shivered. Kyura had gone to war believing it would secure control of his army and his court. He hadn't acted decisively against those who opposed him. He had made the mistakes Ruarnon feared making. It had destroyed him. And so many people had died because of it. Far too many. They were *still* dying.

Ruarnon dragged their mind back to the present. "Did you receive my advice on how to combat damars?"

"It came too late. Karmarn and the army sailed to meet damarian ships offshore, and our ships attacked with power bows and arrows, but a report swore by Esla herself that not a single arrow or bolt hit its target. All arrows and bolts hit an invisible barrier and fell into the sea. Our ships sailed past and continued west, out of sight. They did not attack the four damar-filled vessels sailing towards our coastline."

"You would have us believe that your entire navy was bewitched?" Tor asked. "By whom?"

"Most of the damarian vessels had men on board. I assume they were sorcerers working for Narz."

"How much do you know of Narz?" Tor asked.

"We presume he is a North Lander king. We know that the North Landers have strange abilities, sorcery powers according to folklore, and they may have created the damars."

But why, having acknowledged Zaldeaan overlordship for centuries, would the North Landers suddenly breed such horrid creatures and desire to destroy the Zaldeaan Realm?

Ruarnon pushed the thought aside. "What do you ask of us and in whose name?" they asked.

"For aid against damars, in my name and on behalf of my people. The palace is held by Highest's guards, who answer to his closest friend, my son Aoran. Captain Nish of the City Guard now controls the city, and should you come to our aid, he is prepared to hand it over."

Ruarnon stared.

"Why would he do that?"

"Is it true you rode into battle to defend your uncle? And that you led the main charge on the breach during the siege?"

There was conflict in Armar's eyes, and Ruarnon couldn't fathom it. "Yes."

"You are of the Generation of Peace, yet you can fight to defend your people. You choose to do so. That is what the Zaldeaan Realm needs. Syenne is too clever and too strong. I do not trust her. Derlan would ally with Chaos himself if it benefited him. I do not pretend to know what Iagl wants. And while their hearts are in the right place, Iomar and Kia do not command armies as great as yours."

If the Zaldeaan army had indeed vanished at sea, Ruarnon had the power. And they cared about people. And had a loyal army and advisors who supported them. Did Armar hope that if Ruarnon could find it in their heart to care for their enemies, they could succeed where Kyura had failed?

"I will discuss it with my Council and inform you of our reply as soon as possible," Ruarnon heard themself say. But their mind was in chaos. The damarian invasion appeared to have turned everything they knew about the Zaldeaan Realm and the entire status quo on its head. They struggled to gather their thoughts as they and their Council walked to the Golden Meeting Hall.

"I suggest we wait for the Spymaster," Tor advised quietly as they sat.

Ruarnon nodded and waited in a daze.

"I bring strange reports," the Spymaster told the Council when he arrived. "A spy in Governor Kia's capital reports that the Zaldeaan army went to sea, failed to fight damarian ships, then sailed beyond the horizon. This was witnessed from the coast, as Governor Kia led her provincial soldiers to aid the army onshore."

"When was this?" Ruarnon asked.

"The day before yesterday."

"What is the state of the countryside?"

"Families on remote farms hide inside their homes. Those that did not take cover near the west coast are dead or fled to Governor Kia or Iomar's cities. The Western Coast is in a state of devastation."

"Then their army is stranded offshore," said Monin. "More likely by ordinary sabotage than sorcery, damaged rudders leaving them unable to steer perhaps, North Lander archers shooting down messenger birds, and setting fire to boats trying to reach shore—if Narz is a North Lander king."

That sent a ripple of unease around the table.

"We must send a ship to confirm their location," said Tor, and Ruarnon nodded and sent a messenger with orders for a ship from South Harbour to sail around the southern coast to investigate Zaldeaan waters.

"Benevolence," said Monin, "it may be wise to have cavalry patrol River Road, lest any of these creatures survive a journey across the desert."

"I should like to do more than that," said Ruarnon.

"Taking in Zaldeaan refugees will likely earn them the enmity of our people for the war," Tor cautioned.

Tarlah was safer than ever. Damars overran the Zaldeaan Realm and its army was temporarily missing. All Ruarnon's Council anticipated was responding to any threat damars posed to Tarlah. All Ruarnon's duty required was to secure Tarlah. But the Zaldeaans had just returned to war at the first opportunity, after the most genuine peace between the two kingdoms. And who knew how long the Timbalen Empire and its extra soldiers would be available to guard Tarlah this time.

"This Council's advice is to secure Tarlah, dependent on Timbalen aide, and leave the Zaldeaans to their fate?"

"The capital is being offered to Your Benevolence now," Tor replied. "But it may not be long before the Zaldeaan army overcome their predicament and return to slay damars. We could not hope to hold the capital against the Zaldeaan army. Were Your Benevolence considering that, I should advise you to wait for our spies to confirm that the Zaldeaan army is out of commission."

"It cannot be," said Monin. "North Landers have never fought the Zaldeaan Realm because they have never possessed the strength to do so. If Narz is a North Lander king, he holds the army at bay by trickery. It is only a matter of time before they overcome him and wreak vengeance."

"It may not be North Landers attacking," the Spymaster said hesitantly, and all heads turned, some eyebrows rising. "I have heard strange reports from the far north of the Zaldeaan

Realm. Descriptions of great fires burning along the border. Some claim that the fire also burns along the North Lander coast."

"Why would the North Landers bow to the Zaldeaan Realm all these years if they can work magic?" Monin objected.

"Why are they defending their kingdoms with sorcery if one of *their* kings invaded the Zaldeaan Realm with damars?" Ruarnon countered.

"They have always presented a united front to the Zaldeaan Realm," Tor replied. "For one of their kings to unilaterally attack the Zaldeaan Realm would be bizarre enough, let alone for the other kings to feel they need to protect their borders against one of their own."

Ruarnon sighed. North Landers creating the damars contradicted most of what little Ruarnon knew of them. It made far less sense than Ambassador Armar wanted to believe. But the idea that some unknown ruler had bred an army of monsters in the west to attack the Zaldeaan Realm was so bizarre that none of their advisors was prepared to comment on it. But that wasn't what mattered now. What mattered was how to respond to the damarian threat. And how relations with the Zaldeaan Realm would proceed. When they focused on that, Ruarnon saw a possibility.

"How much of a threat to us is the Zaldeaan army under Companion Karmarn's command?" Ruarnon asked. "You all trust his loyalty to peace?"

"If Derlan claims the throne, the army will obey him," Monin replied. "It may resist or defy Syenne, but it is likely Derlan's for the claiming."

"And if Derlan murdered the Peacemaker? If that charge is laid and the order for his arrest given?" Ruarnon asked, wanting the man who may bear ultimate responsibility for the war and wretched state of his kingdom to be brought to justice.

"The people may think it is a lie started by Syenne to strengthen her claim," Monin warned.

There had to be a way to stop the army from falling to Derlan's command. "What if I asked Karmarn to keep the army offshore while I march mine through the Zaldeaan Realm, destroy the damars, and occupy Zaldeaa City? If we could have Derlan executed or assassinated, who would the army obey?"

Stunned silence followed. Ruarnon kept their hands below the table to conceal their shaking. They were frightened and exhilarated by the possibility that after sitting helplessly through one war, they might be able to end two. If they or Syenne failed to kill or defeat Derlan, the Zaldeaan army could come sailing back to fight the Tarlahn army. But if Kyura's treacherous uncle were killed, surely Syenne would succeed? Would she restore her father's Peace?

"Syenne may not survive determined attempts on her life if she were crowned king," Monin cautioned, and others nodded. "A man would have a better chance. Governor Iagl would win most Zaldeaan approval. But he is Derlan's son, and his allegiance is questionable. His brother Iomar approves of peace, but he is not a military man and has no standing in the army. He may have as much trouble as Syenne gaining approval or countering popular rebellion."

"Karmarn can hold the regency, but with his royal blood unacknowledged, he may face popular protest," Tor added.

"Can he marry one of Kyura's sisters?" Ruarnon asked.

From the shocked, awkward expressions on their advisors' faces, Ruarnon gathered Karmarn was already married.

"May I call a break?" Tor asked.

Ruarnon's brows furrowed as their advisors stood without waiting for their reply.

"Karmarn is not merely Kyomi's half-brother," Tor said as the door closed behind the last advisor. "The reason this Council trusts him, and the reason he is already married, is because Companion Karmarn is your Uncle Kar. He married your Aunt Merlah to secure the peace treaty between Kyomi and your father."

Ruarnon gaped. "They never lived in South Harbour?"

But Ruarnon's aunt and uncle had always been referred to as living there. Yet Ruarnon had never visited them in South Harbour. Uncle Kar, Aunt Merlah, and cousin Coroth had always come to Tarlah, once a year, as far back as Ruarnon could remember. They were so used to it by now that they didn't question it. Now they did wonder, why hadn't they visited Uncle Kar? South Harbour was only a two-day journey on horseback, hardly far enough for their aunt, uncle, and cousin to visit only annually. But if the family lived in the Zaldeaan Realm, and Uncle Kar was Zaldeaan, his marriage to a Tarlahn would not be popular, which may make travel through the Realm dangerous for Aunt Merlah. Which may be why they visited so rarely.

Anger simmered. Did Ruarnon's whole Council know, but no one had bothered to tell Ruarnon who their family was?

"Your parents did not wish you to experience the heartache of fighting a war against your uncle and cousin. As it was, Coroth was given exemption from the army to protect your aunt, who was attacked after the war was declared. Your uncle avoided fighting by continuing his role as King's Companion."

It made Ruarnon dizzy. All of it. And they resented being lied to. But it made sense.

"My Uncle Kar, Companion Karmarn, was our second Ambassador to the Zaldeaan Realm, whom Uncle Omah spoke of? Did he act as our spy in Kyura's court? That's why the Council trusts him so much?"

"Yes."

"Then we should trust him to keep the army at bay while I occupy the Zaldeaan Realm. And he would be my preferred choice as Regent. Call the others back."

Tor inclined his head, and Ruarnon blinked, realising they'd just given their former tutor their first command. The rest of the Council returned, eyeing Ruarnon speculatively.

338

"I propose occupying the Zaldeaan Realm, asking my Uncle Karmarn to keep the army at bay, and with our control of both armies, reckoning with the governors to have Karmarn's Regency accepted."

Monin eyed Ruarnon with his mouth open. "There is great risk Derlan will succeed in communicating with the army and summon it to him by private channels. We cannot be sure this will work, and if we are wrong, the Zaldeaan army will attack us. Even if it did not, if you let the Governors live, they will scheme to seize the crown. Karmarn will be under constant threat of assassination and seen as a Tarlahn pawn."

"I know how the Zaldeaans ruled us," Ruarnon said. "They killed our leaders and ruled by the sword. But with the exception of Derlan, this is the Peacemaker's family, likely to support peace. I propose offering the governors a bargain. They retain their positions if they accept Karmarn as regent. If they betray him, they are executed for treason."

"That is the firm hand Zaldeaans need," Monin said. "But I wonder if things are bad enough in the Zaldeaan Realm for this plan to work."

"I would prefer to judge that in person, in the Zaldeaan Realm," said Ruarnon.

"And endanger yourself?" Monin asked.

"I am not sending our army to fight damars without me."

"Then you risk your capture if Derlan gains control of the Zaldeaan army," Monin countered.

Ruarnon groaned. Why did everything have to be so complicated? But the Zaldeaan Realm had never been this weak. And never had Tarlah had a better chance to secure long-term peace, despite the risks.

"How good are our scouts?" Ruarnon asked. "Our spies? Can they keep us well-informed enough of the Zaldeaan armies' movements to evade the army, should it come ashore?"

"If the Zaldeaan army is ordered to attack us," Monin replied, "it will sail as close to us as it can. The deeper into the Zaldeaan Realm Your Benevolence went, the harder it would be to retreat, or evade an attack."

The Spymaster blanched when Ruarnon turned to him. "Benevolence... I... It takes time to verify reports. Sometimes false rumours are reported, perhaps started by the enemy. I would be nervous of the Zaldeaans drawing too close before I was sure of their location and could send a warning."

"Our scouts may manage, if they are not killed in ambushes," General Aza said.

"I do not advise such an expedition," said Monin. "It would be a terrible risk to our army."

"What are your thoughts?" Ruarnon asked their Companions, their hands clenched under the table to mask their tension.

"No Tarlahn king has considered such an expedition for decades," Companion Noma replied, shaking her head.

Tor eyed an empty chair near the head of the table. "Pamoran may have approved. But with respect to him, we know how reckless he can be."

"Benevolence, this is not some youthful fancy to hand your father more than he left you on his return?" Monin asked.

"I hadn't considered father," Ruarnon replied. They lowered their head, knowing that in their shoes, their father would be unlikely to attempt it.

"Omah may have considered it," Tor added, earning a stern look from Monin.

"You would not please either by risking the worst defeat our army has ever faced," Monin admonished.

Ruarnon slumped. But they remembered what Aunt Telena said about their speeches when the siege was lifted: Urmillian might not have toasted wayward serving girls who died containing a breach of the walls, but Omah would have. Ruarnon had aspired to become like their father as king. But Omah may have been different. Pamoran certainly would have. Which leader did Ruarnon need to be to secure Tarlah's independence?

"Another break," they said.

This time they left the room. No Tarlahn had ever dreamed of occupying the Zaldeaan Realm without military backing from the Timbalen Empire, and even then, not for a century. The thought that they may have the power and ability to decide the kingship of the Zaldeaan Realm made Ruarnon dizzy. As did the risk of Derlan summoning the Zaldeaan army and ambushing the Tarlahn army on its own soil.

They looked for Lenaris in the royal training courtyard, letting their shoulders relax. They could drop the confident act, show their worry, and discuss their fears openly with her. Perhaps when they stopped acting, it would feel real. They hoped so, because the consequences, needless deaths in the Zaldeaan Realm, and the possibility of Derlan seizing the throne, of a shattering defeat of Ruarnon's army on Zaldeaan soil, or, maybe, Tarlahn occupation of the Zaldeaan Realm, would be too real when they came.

But when Ruarnon stepped into the courtyard, it wasn't Lenaris standing with her back to them, her arrows thunking into a target board on the far side. It was Linh. Michael stood to her left, drilling with a spear. Troy attacked a wooden dummy with enough force to carve shavings off it with his sword. Fiona sat on the steps before Ruarnon, hugging her knees with her back to them. What were they doing in the Royal Training Courtyard?

Troy paused in his attempts to reshape the wooden dummy. "What do you reckon the chances of the Tarlahn army aiding the people they were fighting a week ago are?"

"I suspect those chances will increase if Tarlahn soldiers meet damars," Michael replied. "No one would want to risk things like that getting near their family."

"What if they're too cautious?" Fiona asked from the steps. "What if they say no because they're worried it's a trap or something?"

Ruarnon halted. Instinct said to raise their mask of regent's calm. But the conversation was distracting. Most Tarlahns were careful not to be overheard commenting on anything important in front of Ruarnon, let alone Royal Council policy. Yet here these youths stood with their backs to the courtyard entrance, speaking freely. It defied Tarlahn sensibilities. And it tempted Ruarnon to talk of things not meant for ears outside their Royal Council.

"Oh, um, hey, Ruarnon!" Troy called. "Your aunt said we could train here. She, uh, thought it might be good if we spent more time with you."

Ruarnon frowned. Aunt Telena was thinking of that *now*?

"Maybe she, um, hoped we could be friends, or something," Troy added, blushing.

Ruarnon smiled. Most people watched their words in the presence of royalty. The way Troy blurted out whatever he was thinking was refreshing. But why, now of all times, would their aunt want them to make new friends? Omah's words came back to Ruarnon: "I think Kyura forgot who he was." And what Omah had said about just being himself, not Regent Omah, with Aunt Telena. Ruarnon had done nothing but be Regent so far. And while these youths were strangers, they were not Ruarnon's subjects. Ruarnon need not lead them nor present a perfect face to them.

Was that why Aunt Telena wanted them to spend time together? Had she brought them to the throne room with her because she thought they would make good Regent's Companions?

"Now isn't the best time to chat," Ruarnon said. "Though I would welcome new training partners on a quiet day."

"Are we right about your army?" Michael asked. "And your people being cautious about aiding the Zaldeaans?"

Michael's serious expression was impossible to read, but Fiona's freckled face clouded with worry, and Linh braced her feet as if preparing for a terrible reply. It was an inappropriate question, but Ruarnon's instinct as host was to put them at ease. Ruarnon couldn't say too much, but if Aunt Telena thought these were potential Kings' Companions...

"I would like to send my army north," Ruarnon replied. "But the risk of being encircled by the Zaldeaan army is great, even if scouts report on their location to help us evade them."

"Then what happens to the Zaldeaans, with their army missing?" Fiona asked, still hugging her knees.

Ruarnon sighed. "They stay in their homes until their army escapes. They risk running out of fresh water, then food."

Fiona's lip trembled.

"And you don't know if Narz will call the creatures off?" Troy asked.

Ruarnon sighed. Troy shouldn't know that name, but with Aunt Telena having brought these youths to the throne room for Ambassador Armar's visit, they already knew too much.

"We are unsure who Narz is or what he wants. But if the Zaldeaan army is detained for too long, people will starve while Governor Derlan fights Governor Syenne for the throne. The Zaldeaans may be better off if I conquer them."

"You haven't decided?" Michael asked.

"When you could protect people from monsters and prevent or end a civil war?" Fiona added.

"If Derlan gains control of the Zaldeaan army at sea, it will move faster than my army on land. They will be able to position themselves to ambush us. Their provincial armies can help, and if that happens, we could suffer crippling defeat. I could save the Zaldeaan Realm or lead my army to its destruction. Scout reports may or may not be able to help me know which outcome is more likely."

"How close can you get to the Zaldeaan western shore without endangering your army?" Michael asked. "If you invade, the closer your army is when you get the all clear, the sooner it can attack damars and make it safe for Zaldeaans to leave their homes."

"Are you suggesting I march my army without confirmation that the Zaldeaan army is securely detained offshore?" Ruarnon asked.

"Hide them in the tunnel under Death Belt Desert!" Linh said eagerly. "Then the Zaldeaans won't know your army is on their border. And if they find out, you retreat through the tunnel. Surely Derlan won't chase you out of the Zaldeaan Realm with the succession up for grabs?"

Ruarnon's mouth wanted to drop open, but they resisted. Only Lenaris spoke so frankly to them. Linh was bold and eager, and hers was a good suggestion. If Aunt Telena did intend these youths as Kings' Companions, she appeared to have chosen them well.

"He may not," Ruarnon said. "He appears to be mobilising his army against Syenne. The tunnel is the safest place to station my army while my scouts locate the Zaldeaan army. It is probably the least risky of multiple dangerous options for leaving Tarlah."

"Then do it," said Linh. "The longer your Council debates, the longer Zaldeaans cower in their homes and risk life and limb to get drinking water and food."

Ruarnon stared. No Tarlahn would speak to them like that. Their Council would be shocked and offended. But she was right. Tarlahn logic could identify the best course of action, but it could also delay action while people suffer. In their mind's eye, Ruarnon saw a sword pierce Uncle Omah's chest, Arlian and Ethlin lying dead on a side road, faceless villagers of all ages dead and undefended on Timraith Island's sandy shores.

They'd sat, helpless to prevent hundreds of deaths, watching men debate, since the war began. They'd felt bitter about people continuing to die after the war. This wasn't what their father would do. Perhaps even Omah would hesitate. But perhaps leading like either was no longer the best way to proceed because it might not allow Ruarnon to save the lives they could save.

Positioning their army in the tunnel under the desert was the best way to prepare to occupy the Zaldeaan Realm without risking ambush. Wherever these youths came from, it appeared their ideas could help Ruarnon develop their plans.

"We'll march to the border," Ruarnon decided. "This afternoon, if my army can prepare fast enough."

Ruarnon turned to leave the courtyard, then turned back, making another decision. "You are welcome to accompany us if you wish."

Linh's face tensed. Troy grinned nervously. "Can we get back to you on that?"

Ruarnon bowed their head. "Of course."

They strode back to the Golden Meeting Hall, where their advisors broke off conversations, then took their seats without being asked.

"I do not wish to give damars more opportunity to spread," Ruarnon announced. "I want our scouts dispatched. Our army mobilised. We will march through the tunnel under Death Belt Desert in force. If reports suggest it is unwise to proceed at the border, we turn back."

Monin's face went blank. Was he in shock? If so, it was probably best to continue before he recovered.

"Summon General Takanis and tell me what I need to know to evade ambush and successfully drive out as many damars as possible. I would also hear your advice on dealing with the governors if we get the opportunity before the Zaldeaan army returns. I would like to attempt negotiations with the governors who supported peace."

Tor was smiling. He smoothed it away and began giving advice, and Monin hurried to join in. This wasn't the decision Ruarnon's father would have made. But it was leading decisively, Omah's leadership style. And it was working. Perhaps there was much Ruarnon could do to save lives after all.

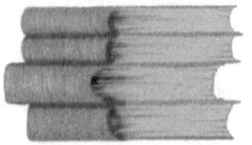

CHAPTER 26

LOOK AND LEAP

LINH: *Tarlah City, One Week After the Siege*

Linh bit her lip. It wasn't a good time to ask, but there wasn't going to be one. So when Heir Ruarnon stepped out of the Golden Meeting Hall, she and her friends were waiting to speak to them.

"Heir Ruarnon, sorry to ask you now," she began, internally squirming at raising such a minor issue when Ruarnon had just pushed their advisors to invade the Zaldeaan Realm, "but we wondered if you knew anything about magic archways. If there are myths about the North Landers being able to operate them? That's how we think we got here and why we think they may be able to send us home."

Ruarnon's brows furrowed. "I have heard strange tales of them, but none mentioning magical gateways. I had intended to send a messenger, but if that is what you want to ask, it may be best if you travel to the North Lands yourselves. They are secretive people, and they may hesitate to put such information in writing."

Troy's and Fiona's faces fell.

"The Zaldeaan capital is far north, not far from the border. If you accompany me, I can send you on with an escort of guards once the area is clear of damars."

Linh's stomach dropped. That sounded even more dangerous than sailing to Tarlah had been.

"There has been little I could do to recover my parents," Ruarnon added, "so I will do what I can to reunite you with yours."

Fiona's eyes filled with tears. To Linh's surprise, tears shone in Ruarnon's eyes as well. Troy clapped them on the shoulder. Ruarnon blinked uncertainly, then smiled and clapped Troy's shoulder.

Relief flooded Linh at the sincerity on Ruarnon's face. Whatever happened, it seemed they cared, and that suggested they may help Linh and her friends after the Timbalens sailed home and the emperor lost interest.

Tor cleared his throat, and everyone started, seeing that they weren't alone. Ruarnon bowed their head, and Linh smiled and everyone bowed back. Then Tor and Ruarnon turned down the corridor, and Troy led Linh, Fiona, and Michael through the castle, until they stumbled across the gardens. They sat on the edge of steps going down to terraced lawns of tall and exotic evergreen trees with bright flowers.

"I didn't realise they'd be so heartfelt," said Fiona, wiping her eyes.

"I guess they get it," said Troy.

"Despite that, they might worry we were hoping to go home instead of helping them in the Zaldeaan Realm," Michael added.

Linh tensed. They'd agreed to ask Ruarnon about possible ways home easily enough. But for this war, they were contemplating marching with the invading army. There was no question of witnessing violence. They might need to defend themselves.

"We should stay in Tarlah," she said. "Wait till this war's over. This is probably more dangerous than sailing here was, and we can't just row away from danger this time."

Troy nodded.

"It'll be harder to get a group of armed guards to escort us from Tarlah City to the North Lands after the Tarlahn army marches," said Michael. "We'd have to wait till it suited Ruarnon. Until their aunt goes to visit them, or something."

"Insufferable waiting, having no say over your own life, or risking your life: which do you hate more?" Troy asked, shaking his head and standing to pace across the terrace.

"Ruarnon wants to destroy the damars and secure peace with Tarlah," said Fiona. "They're sympathetic to Zaldeaan commoners, but we'd be their only advisors mainly concerned about Zaldeaans. We could be the difference between more

Zaldeaans dying needlessly or not. We've just proved we can do that."

Linh saw nothing but earnest sincerity in Fiona's eyes. Was there no limit to the extent she'd put people in need before herself? Worse, Fiona was right. None of it sat well with Linh. She didn't know the Zaldeaans. She didn't owe them anything. But she'd met damars. Ruarnon had warned that Derlan might prioritise war with Syenne over defending his people. And she was getting an idea of how cautious Tarlahns were. She and her friends' advice may be just what Ruarnon needed to save as many lives as possible in the Zaldeaan Realm.

"I want to go," Fiona said, meeting Linh's eyes.

Linh shut her eyes and took a deep breath, exhaling slowly. Instinct shouted at her not to go, but waiting in Tarlah while her best friend marched to war? The sight of fighting and death would get to Fiona. Linh couldn't let her face it alone.

"It's not our war, again," Troy said gently.

"Damars don't stand a chance against soldiers," Fiona countered. "We'd be with an army that outnumbers them."

"There's still a risk of the Zaldeaan army escaping and attacking us," said Michael.

Troy shook his head. "It's like trying to predict when lockdowns would end back home. Or, when borders did open, whether you should risk getting stuck interstate or overseas because borders kept changing all the time. We can't be sure how likely or unlikely we are to get caught in the fighting. All we know is we're potentially risking our lives."

"But we can be sure it's our best chance to get near the border until we-don't-know-when," said Michael. "It's the same choice as last time: risk your life, or stay in safety knowing you might be delayed for weeks or even months waiting for your next chance to get home."

"You're making me want to go, to stick it to the universe and take control of my life," Troy asserted, shaking his head. His eyes were shining, his mouth smiling, but his features twisted halfway between amusement and annoyance. His eyes were tearing up. He was tired of this choice. And Troy didn't do well with waiting or being stuck somewhere when he wanted to travel. Their journey so far had proved that.

"This is life and death," Linh said, eyeing Fiona. "You realise that applies to us too?"

Fiona's mouth tightened, but she nodded.

"If we go as Ruarnon's guests," said Michael, "we'd be almost as well protected as them."

"As you said, they're risking having their army ambushed by a stronger one on its home soil," Troy pointed out. "That's not very safe."

"I'm not fighting Zaldeaans," Linh insisted. "But knowing what damars are like and what they've done, if the Tarlahns give me a bow, I might shoot a few myself."

Troy blinked. "Same," he said grimly.

"We shouldn't go unless we're prepared to fight," Michael warned.

"Are you?" Troy asked.

Michael nodded. Fiona shivered, but to Linh's surprise, she replied, "If I have to. I'll go to help by advising Ruarnon. Their Council don't understand what they're facing and where damars are concerned, we do."

Linh said a silent prayer to her grandmother's ancestors and every god she could name. "I've proven I can persuade Ruarnon to act to protect Zaldeaans. I don't want people dying because I wasn't there to do that. I also don't want to die."

Troy grinned. "I can't imagine you letting anyone kill you."

Linh laughed. But she saw his point and took comfort in it. Fiona was quiet and often went with what everyone else did, but she was taking a stand this time. She'd never done that before, and Linh could tell she wouldn't back down. She'd just march quietly off after the army, leaving Linh running after her.

Troy walked away.

Linh frowned and asked, "Where are you going?"

"To ask if Lenaris will help us train. Everyone thinks she's the most skilled person with a sword in Tarlah, and apparently we'd all benefit from being her students."

Michael smiled, and he, Linh, and Fiona went with Troy.

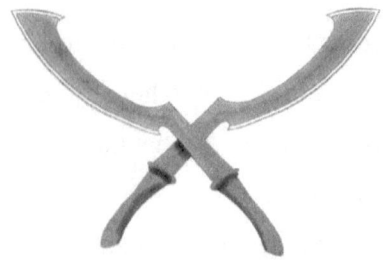

CHAPTER 27

THE ZALDEAANREALM

RUARNON: *Tarlah City, Nine Days After the Siege*

Ruarnon walked down a corridor towards the main castle courtyard in an iron cuirass, with an iron scale apron over leather pants, their sword at their right hip and a quiver of arrows on their left. Their stomach writhed. What would their army make of being told they were about to battle monsters to protect their enemies?

Ruarnon stepped through an archway onto the courtyard steps, above phalanxes of Elites equipped with bronze armour, swords, and spears or quivers and bows. They scanned the crowd for their friends, guests, Companions Tor and Noma, and a scholar who would translate Migryan for them. Then they stepped to the edge of the balcony where Monin, Regent in Ruarnon's absence, inclined his head slightly. Silence fell, and Ruarnon addressed the crowd.

"On their way here, our allies discovered that the Timraith Islanders are no more. They were slain, down to the last child. The invaders who slew them were not human. They are called damars, and are like short humans, but stronger, grey in colour, with clawed hands, sharp teeth, and yellow eyes. Their target is the Zaldeaan Realm.

"Damars have slaughtered their way through villages on the west Zaldeaan coast. When the Zaldeaan army confronted them, it went missing at sea. We believe city guards and provincial soldiers trying to contain the creatures were severely outnumbered and overrun. The Zaldeaans have abandoned their coast, three cities have barred their gates, and damars roam inland unchecked. The sight of their atrocities prompted King Kyura to take his own life, and now the provincial armies are at war over the succession."

Before Ruarnon, line upon line of soldiers gaped in stunned silence. Ruarnon paused. Older faces among the armoured crowd eyed them critically. Younger ones appeared puzzled. Few seemed horrified. None were convinced. Soldiers turned to Ruarnon's advisors, perhaps hoping they were joking. Expressions creased with worry when the Companions remained solemn.

"We are assembled today, not for revenge, pride, or glory, but to confront and eliminate damars, to avenge the Timraith Islanders, and to protect farmers, villagers, and Tarlah itself. This is our chance to prove to the Zaldeaans that we are just as brave, strong, and capable as they are. Show them your discipline, before the battle with damars, during, and after it. I would have you prove our worth as a kingdom beyond Zaldeaan ability to question. I would have a second Peace, on our terms, twice as long as the one that preceded it!"

They couldn't promise more than that. Their incursion in the Zaldeaan Realm might only be a favour to the Zaldeaans, a bargaining chip in peace negotiations at the end of the Succession War. But they would make the Zaldeaan Realm respect Tarlah. When warmongers spoke of glory and conquest in the future, they wanted the Zaldeaan people to remember who aided them at their darkest hour. To consider war with enemies they respected and were indebted to. They dared hope this invasion would position the Zaldeaan masses to baulk at the notion of war with Tarlah.

Soldiers turned and whispered to each other, some whispers carrying above the crowd.

"What do they mean?"

"Monsters? *Real, live* monsters?"

"We're fighting *in* the Zaldeaan Realm?"

There were many frowns and uncertain looks. Ruarnon thought back to Omah's simple speech before the battle. "My uncle asked you to remember old skills and put new ones to use. I would have you use those skills in the Zaldeaan Realm to eliminate monsters before they spread beyond it. Who will march with me?"

Young soldiers blinked nervously. Gazes shifted to General Aza.

"Or should we leave you behind?" Aza barked.

"I'll not be left behind by a sixteen-year-old!" a veteran cried.

"Let's get moving!" another called.

They shifted restlessly. Ruarnon saluted the soldiers. Tens of soldiers saluted instantly, a hundred within a moment. Their faces were grim, smiles nervous, feet shifting impatiently. Ruarnon hoped marching would settle the soldiers and give them time to prepare.

Ruarnon mounted their horse and rode with Captain Arleath and their bodyguards to the head of the column, between Tor and Noma, then led their army towards heralds reading their speech to bewildered Tarlahns lining North Road. Colourful silks and white linens shone in the first rays of daylight. Many saluted, but just as many eyed Ruarnon with furrowed brows.

Ruarnon's Companions and Lenaris sat their horses more alertly than the army had when it last left Tarlah City. Generals Aza's and Takanis' stiff postures suggested they registered the uncertainty of the crowds lining the streets and the confused murmurs of conversation among the army as it marched.

Ruarnon gripped their reins tightly as they passed through North Gate. Then they led the army onto River Road, towards the bridge over Serpent River. Behind them, Timbalens remained in Tarlah City, securing it. Ruarnon remembered their silent parting with their uncle as they crossed the bridge.

The pain the memory stirred didn't recede until they rode towards the tunnel and their thoughts turned to their parents. Did Governor Derlan hold Urmillian and Corina captive now? Getting them back would be difficult, but it felt good to follow their path, and Ruarnon hoped to find them at its end.

Daylight shone into the tunnel from its Zaldeaan end. After four days marching under the narrow Death Belt Desert, hundreds of footsteps cut off behind Ruarnon as the army halted. A scout rode towards them as they wondered whether the Zaldeaan army was far away enough that they could begin their war against the damars.

"Greetings, Benevolence," the scout said with a bow. "Derlan's army has left these lands, and there is no word of the Zaldeaan army being sighted near the coast, let alone on land. Only damars move in the open here."

Ruarnon exhaled, relieved that the main army wouldn't restrict their movements and that they wouldn't need to deal with provincial armies yet. But nervous energy still rushed through them, and their muscles braced for a fight.

"What do you suggest?" Ruarnon asked Generals Aza and Takanis.

"I'll survey the terrain," Aza replied. "If it is favourable, I suggest we make our stand outside and summon and slay as many beasts as we can, stationing scouts ahead to keep watch."

Ruarnon nodded approval, and both generals moved off.

"We are not in much external danger here," Tor said quietly, "but this battle will be a shock to the soldiers and a test of their morale. I would make that your focus for now."

Ruarnon nodded. They thanked the scout and signalled their party closer. Their bodyguards formed a semi-circle, five with bows and arrows in hand, the rest holding throwing spears, all with swords at their hips. Ruarnon heeled their horse out to a hillside sloping down to trickling water on their left, while a road curved round an upward slope on their right. In all directions, tree and flower-covered hills concealed the horizon of a country greener and wetter than anywhere in Tarlah.

Ruarnon moved left, while spearmen formed a shield wall under General Aza's direction on the right, and General Takanis led the cavalry ahead. Lenaris, Tor, and Noma kept an eye on their four younger guests while Companion Armar sat stiffly beside them. Beyond, a nervous man clutched a book like a shield: the scholar. Ruarnon wasn't sure the front of the column was the best place for either, but with damars roaming the countryside, nowhere was safe.

General Aza bordered the road with a bronze shield wall on both sides, then rows of infantry holding thrusting spears, with archers in the middle. Takanis led riders who would fell damars that fled. It seemed like good tactics, but Ruarnon's worries about why Karmarn's thousand soldiers had failed to contain damars made them tense.

General Aza drew his horn and winded it. Its deep call carried down the valley. A screech rose from trees on the left. Screeches echoed back. Little grey bodies waded through grasses and splashed into the stream. Muscles tensed down Ruarnon's arms, and they squeezed their reins. Damars raised sticks and hissed, then rushed uphill towards their column.

"Left front loose!" cried a captain.

A volley of arrows arced off the road. Creatures fell onto the hillside or splashed into the stream, shrieking as deadly rain fell among them. They wore no armour, only loincloths. They looked easy to kill, and it made Ruarnon's stomach churn unpleasantly.

Two damars rose and tried to climb the hill with arrows embedded in their shoulders. They were moving *towards* the army. They walked into more arrows until they collapsed, dead. Ruarnon gaped as more creatures fell around them, thrashing on the grassy slope. Those that could move hissed and ran to the road, charging Ruarnon's soldiers. Soldiers cried out. Spears thrust with more force than was necessary, soldiers struggling to extract them from dead damars.

"Hold positions!" General Aza yelled.

The front line held, but as damars fell, shields wavered, and restless soldiers shifted. Armoured men and women jerked upright, tensing as more damars shrieked in the distance. Hissing in the trees signalled packs approaching. They burst from the trees and splashed into the river, towards bodies of dead damars scattered up the hillside.

"Have they no sense at all?" a soldier cried.

"Loose!" a captain barked.

Ruarnon tracked the deadly rain distractedly. Arrows struck grey heads, necks, and shoulders. Creatures with limbs impaled with arrows tried to rise and attack again. Ruarnon stared. Troy gripped his spear with white knuckles, and his friends grimaced with distaste. Fiona was particularly pale, but neither she nor her friends seemed shocked. Was this how the creatures normally behaved?

A dozen damars burst into the stream and were shot down. General Aza winded his horn again, and it produced more screeches down the valley. Ruarnon shook their head. Why did the creatures summon each other to slaughter?

"That screech came from above," Michael warned.

Ruarnon started and turned their horse. There was a sheer drop from the hilltop above the tunnel exit.

"They can't be mad enough to—" Troy stopped mid-word as a hiss sounded.

Ruarnon removed their bow from its saddle strap and fit an arrow to the string. A screeching damar plummeted towards them. Troy cried out as the creature glanced off his shield. It hit the ground. Ruarnon loosed an arrow into its neck. It thrashed. More arrows struck it, and it stilled.

"There's more!" Michael warned.

"Into the tunnel!" Lenaris ordered, steering her horse aside for them to retreat, while Ruarnon's guards formed up between them and the incline. Three creatures stepped into the air overhead. Ruarnon loosed an arrow. Others followed. The three creatures screeched as they landed, snapping arrow shafts.

"Back up, Benevolence!" Tor ordered.

Ruarnon steered their horse back as guards and Lenaris loosed arrows at creatures rushing off the incline, one after another. Hissing monsters stepped willingly to their deaths. How could they defy Earth Goddess Mijora so?

By the time the incline cleared, cold sweat trickled down Ruarnon's back, and their entire body was tense. The road between their guards and the steep slope was piled with damars. The creatures' only defence was tough hides, long claws, and sticks, yet still they attacked, uncaring if they lived or died. Every fibre of Ruarnon's being wanted to scream in protest at the creatures' wrongness.

Archers loosed a volley at a damar pack uphill on Ruarnon's right. Creatures rolled to the road, leaping to charge the shield wall, ignoring spear thrusts. One damar hissed defiance with two spearheads in its middle. The infantry shouted in shock and revulsion, fighting with more force than necessary.

"Last pack archers! Finish them!" General Aza yelled.

Bowstrings twanged, then the whizz of arrows, hissing, and screeching ceased, replaced with panting, gasps, and curses.

"All clear among the infantry, Benevolence!" General Aza yelled. "Captain, get those bodies piled on the hilltop and burn them. Make sure none are left in the water. We don't want them fouling it."

A captain saluted and led a dozen spearmen onto the grey body-scattered hillside, while archers drew bowstrings as taut as their faces, scouring the valley for damars. General Aza strode towards Ruarnon, his gaze dark, his posture rigid. Around them, archers' faces paled, their features wide with shock or narrowing with anger. The creatures' behaviour suggested they *were* Chaos Spawn. How did Ruarnon bolster morale against such an enemy?

"Takanis' riders did not move, Benevolence," Aza said quietly. "And these killers are not trained to fight. If we wait here, with those fiends sneaking up on us, it will prey on the soldiers' minds."

Ruarnon nodded. "I want to march towards the west coast. Killing as many of those things as we can."

"We do not know the whereabouts of Governor Kia's provincial army," General Aza cautioned. "But in the presence of those fiends, if we keep our soldiers back and make our intentions clear, I doubt she will wish to fight us. If you offer her an alliance, and Governor Iomar, they may accept."

"We must be wary of Derlan attacking from behind," said Tor. "If he sets aside his war with Syenne to drive us out."

Aza grimaced. "That dog may try to pin us between damars and his soldiers; Iagl's too, if he can persuade him. And we cannot be sure Syenne will appreciate our presence. I will have scouts survey our rear as we march."

"What is our destination?" Tor asked.

"Governors Kia and Iomar have the direst need of your aid," Companion Armar replied. "I suggest staying within their western provinces, keeping well east of Derlan's army marching north through Syenne's province."

"Between Derlan's army and the Zaldeaan army at sea?" Tor asked.

"I would rather that than stay here while my army's morale fractures," Ruarnon replied.

General Aza inclined his head.

"Tell the captains to ready the soldiers to march," Ruarnon ordered.

Aza moved off.

Lenaris called the youths and the scholar out of the tunnel, and they rode beside Ruarnon, behind their bodyguards and the vanguard. Ruarnon was careful to sit straight, trying to lead with grim confidence. Lenaris glanced at their hands. They were fidgeting compulsively with their reins. How had Omah and Pamoran ridden so calmly to battle?

Ruarnon wanted to tell Lenaris their horror of damars, their concern for morale, and how difficult it was to look calm when the sight of damars put them off as much as it did their soldiers. But they couldn't. The reverse of Omah's teaching was that displaying fears and worries would intensify the army's insecurities.

They rode across eerily quiet hilltops. Ruarnon gripped their horse's flanks to vent tension discreetly, but their mind raced in the silence. For the first time since Omah's death, they remembered their father's advice to reflect on what they were fighting for. Ordinary Zaldeaans in farmhouses and towns would live with the same fear, until Ruarnon's soldiers freed them. They tried to focus on that.

The army rounded the bend, the stream turned, and the valley opened out. Water trickled on their left and wind whispering through trees atop a hill on their right.

"Where are we?" they asked Companion Armar.

"The middle of the foothills, Your Benevolence, before the mountains barring Death Belt Desert. Those creatures will have taken at least two days to get here. More have breached containment. The first wave may have reached the eastern shore."

Armar's skin was a similar grey to the damars, and he spoke woodenly. Ruarnon turned away, troubled by inklings of what he must be feeling.

The river rounded another bend, and the road forked. Wooden fences and bluestone houses rose on the right. A scream rent the air. General Takanis called a halt. Ruarnon tensed, scanning the ground for damars. More cries rose and a warning bell tolled.

"Secure the village!" Ruarnon ordered General Takanis.

A child wailed. Linh swore and rode off, her friends haring after her.

Linh: The Zaldeaan Realm

Linh ignored shouts, shrieks, and bluestone cottages on her left. Ahead, a small foot disappeared behind a tree. She reined in as three small, frightened faces peered out from behind a tree trunk.

"You have to go back to the village!" she ordered.

"Scary things are coming," said a little girl.

"But Myah keeps us safe," one of the boys objected.

"Myah?" Linh asked.

"Don't you know anything?" piped up the second boy. "Myah is the forest goddess, and this is her sacred tree, and it's the safest place in Umarinaris!"

For a moment, Linh gaped at their foolishness. Then it occurred to her that these kids couldn't be older than six and might be completely naive. They needed to be taken home before they got themselves killed.

"You need to go inside," she said, dismounting and planning to lead them to the nearest house by the hand if she had to.

The little girl gasped and backed away as Linh approached.

"I think the goddess might want you to go home, so your mums don't get worried," said Troy.

The first boy's face fell.

"And the longer we stand here, the more worried they're going to get. I think you need to get home quickly. Who wants to ride with me?"

The first boy eyed Fiona's horse, and she smiled at him. The boy let Troy help him mount in front of her.

"Horses are higher up than scary things, and they travel fast," Troy added to the girl.

She hesitated, then ran towards him, and he lifted her to Michael's horse, where Michael scooped an arm around her shivering frame.

"Sorry the foreigners don't trust you," the second boy said to the tree. "I don't think they mean to be rude."

Linh stamped her foot with impatience, but Troy scooped him up swiftly, and they both mounted again.

"Keep watch," Michael told her quietly. "I hear fighting on the other side of the village. Damars might get through."

Linh shook herself and scanned gaps between buildings carefully as they rode clear of the trees towards houses.

"Ilza? Ilza!" a woman called.

"Mummy!" the little girl called from Michael's horse.

"Over here!" Michael called, nudging his horse forwards. "I've got Ilza!"

A woman tore around the corner and cried out with relief.

"They ran off. They were scared," Troy explained as Michael passed Ilza into the woman's arms.

Another door opened. A woman poked her head, bow and arrow out.

"Do you know who these boys' parents are?" Fiona asked.

The woman's face widened with shock. She dropped her bow and arrow wordlessly and ran forwards, grabbing one boy in each arm, nodding in thanks and ran back inside, the door slamming behind her.

"Thank you so much," said Ilza's mother, and she knocked on a door on the right, which admitted her and a waving Ilza, then slammed behind them.

A whimper rose from a house, then singing, as her friends scanned the area with arrows to bowstrings, and everyone realised how exposed they were.

Where are you going, across the sea?
I sail for Safe Haven, my family and me.
Long is the journey, dark are the nights,
But worth more than gold is Safe Haven's sight.
Safe Haven, oh, Safe Haven.

Linh shivered. Nuard had told them that song, once sung by refugees sailing to Umarinaris' end, the future Timbalen Empire, at the end of the Sorcery War. Did the Zaldeaan Realm seem that dangerous to Zaldeaans now?

A woman screamed, and a damar hissed between homes down the main dirt road ahead. A man yelled, "Get inside, woman! It isn't safe!"

"Help! They're chasing me!" the woman yelled, running into view across the road.

"Get inside, I say!" a Tarlahn soldier yelled behind her.

"Tarlahns are attacking! Help!"

"He's saying get inside!" Troy shouted in exasperation.

The woman turned to Troy, her face wide with shock as a door behind her opened, and an old woman said, "Inside, Liliss, like the boy says."

"Like *I* say?" asked Troy as the door closed.

The soldier stared at him. Goosebumps rose up Linh's arms.

"Who are you?" the soldier asked, glaring with suspicion and keeping his distance. "She didn't understand *me* when I spoke Timbalen... but she understood *you*."

"What language do they speak?"

"Migryan, of course."

"Let's get back to Ruarnon," Linh whispered.

Troy frowned, but Michael said firmly, "Listen to Linh," and they turned out of the village, Troy looking wrong-footed.

"Remember how we wondered about Nuard appearing to speak English?" Michael continued quietly. "Apparently, Zaldeaans hear Migryan when we speak, while Tarlahns hear Timbalen."

"What?" Troy asked. "How's that even possible?"

"Maybe bringing us here wasn't Red Cloak's only experiment," Michael replied.

Linh shivered at the idea that something had got inside her brain and influenced her ability to process information.

"When Tarlahns hear us speaking Timbalen, yet Zaldeaans understand us," Michael continued, "it freaks them out. We'll have to avoid speaking where both can hear us."

"That might not be possible in Zaldeaa City," Fiona cautioned.

"We need to try," said Michael. "It won't help Ruarnon if word gets around that their friends speak two different languages simultaneously and Zaldeaans or Tarlahns suspect we're sorcerers."

"I'll keep my mouth shut, then," Troy said as they rode back to Ruarnon.

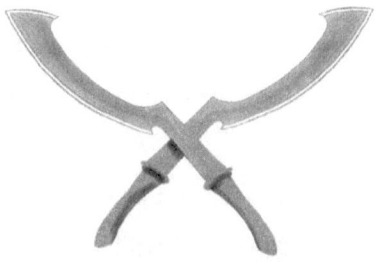

Chapter 28

The Western Shore

Ruarnon: the Zaldeaan Realm, Five Days March From Tarlah

The next afternoon the road wove through dense forest, and Ruarnon felt exposed. Trees, leafy shrubs, and their shadows might conceal damars, allowing the creatures to creep close unseen, then charge with speed and mindless violence. It made Ruarnon tense, and they noted rigid postures, white knuckles gripping weapons, and a heavy silence among the vanguard, whose wary eyes scanned the undergrowth.

Then the trees thinned, and they rode onto low, open, grassy hills with rivulets running through them. Further east lay villages and a flock of grazing sheep.

"This is the river Ila," said Armar. "Further north, it divides Governor Syenne's province from Governor Kia's, and Governor Iomar's from the Heart of the Zaldeaan Realm."

Damars hissed. Archers tracked them with bows drawn while Ruarnon scanned the plains and spotted a low rise between rivulets.

"General Aza, I want the front phalanxes to form a human fortress on that rise, with a shield wall around it and three rows of spearmen around the edge, then archers ten lines deep. I want the soldiers to feel reassured by each other's presence and to hold the high ground with archers ready should Derlan sneak up on us."

Ruarnon wanted to recreate the shield walls their soldiers had fought confidently in on Tarlah's northern walls. They hoped the reassuring presence of comrades either side of and behind them would not only provide collective protection but reassure soldiers. They and the Council wondered if, in pursuing monsters in small groups and without formation, probably beyond the hearing of their captains' orders, it was not the Zaldeaan city guards' physical strength that had failed, but their nerve and confidence.

Ruarnon and their companions rode to the centre of the first formation at the height of the rise. Ruarnon breathed shallowly, trying to focus beyond the press of bodies around them, over rows of helmeted heads, bows and spear tips, across the riverbed.

Bowstrings twanged as scattered damars ran into range. Archers picked creatures off, felling them well before the bronze shield walls. Hisses and screeches passed along the river branches and down the road. Packs approached from the west side of the valley; a third came from the east and more from the north.

"Loose!" captains cried.

A volley soared and arced down. A few damars stumbled into the second volley with an arrow in the chest, shoulder, or arm. Charging damars didn't help each other, keeping their eyes on prey and trying to reach it till wounds from more volleys felled them. They lacked the animal instincts of a pack as well as survival. Surely, they were created by sorcery?

Packs alerted by screeches approached in all directions. Archers released volley after volley, grimacing, their postures rigid. Captains began to rotate lines, allowing outer shield wall soldiers to rest and stretch taut muscles in the centre. For a moment, Ruarnon wondered what it would be like to walk around, exposed, hunting damars on foot, alert to attack from all directions for hours on end. Sheer exhaustion might have weakened Zaldeaan attempts to stop the creatures from spreading.

Archers on the hill provided cover fire, while runners retrieved arrows. There was no risk of running out of arrows, and the shield walls and human fortress rings proved sound defences for the army. The only threat Ruarnon could see was postures gradually slackening with fatigue. Time passed, and no word of Derlan or the Zaldeaan main army arrived. Ruarnon gradually relaxed.

General Takanis sent outriders and horns blew in all directions. It was some time before riders returned, and packs emerged from trees and along rivulets to the west. Some were shot down, but more came, until every western facing unit had a pack to itself. Damars pressed closer, and Ruarnon heard bodies thud against shields. Soldiers thrust spears, and a woman shrieked as a damar tried to climb her shield, the woman behind her kicking it off.

Damars stabbed at bronze shields, blunting their sticks. They seemed oblivious to destroying their weapons and not harming Tarlahns. Some reached and clawed blindly behind shields. They had no idea how to fight against a shield formation, making Ruarnon sure the Zaldeaans had panicked and not confronted them with one.

Gradually, the damars fell. The air smelled of sweat, soldiers slumped with fatigue. Ruarnon felt wrung out. But with the right tactics, it seemed damars could be destroyed.

"I know they're horrid, but are we going to slaughter them all?"

Ruarnon turned at Fiona's voice. She and Linh sat at the centre of the circles of soldiers, where they couldn't see the slaughter. The scholar sat beside them, hunched in on himself, reading.

"They're all picking humans to attack," Troy replied, sitting opposite the girls. "I thought I saw some running away, but they attacked the column instead of a shield wall on one of these hills."

"There's too many to capture," Michael added. "You'd have to build cages to stop them escaping. Hundreds of cages."

Something went out of Ruarnon. Something was lost. How had they found themself in a situation where they were orchestrating slaughter to save lives? It was kill or be attacked with damars, if not killed yourself. But the creatures were ineffective against professional soldiers fighting in formation. Narz must have known his killers would be killed, eventually. So why breed them at all? What was the point of them?

A cavalry unit escorted a scout towards Ruarnon, General Takanis riding with them, soldiers parting to admit both.

"I bring word from the ship searching the western seas, Your Benevolence," the scout reported. "We began searching the water within sight of land two days ago. Last night, we sighted a tiny ship tracking a fleet at a distance. We made out sails of four Zaldeaan battle transports. They are four days from the coast, sailing west."

Four days? What in Chaos were they doing?

"And the ship tracking them?" Tor asked.

"Zaldeaan in style, a fishing vessel rigged for speed. We think it set sail from Governor Kia's capital."

"What of the western ships?" General Takanis asked.

"We do not think the Zaldeaan ships sailed alone, though we were too far back to say how many vessels accompanied them. There was no sign of western ships along the coast either."

Ruarnon turned to their advisors, who formed a tight circle.

"This is too elaborate for a ruse," said General Aza.

"How does anyone force a fleet to sail against its will?" Ruarnon asked. "Armar, why do you think Karmarn took the fleet west?"

"The report I received mentioned lightning in a clear sky and balls of fire hovering over the sea," Armar replied. "Damars can be fought, but against sorcery, we have no weapons."

"Westerners threatened to attack the Zaldeaan Realm with sorcery and used it to coerce Karmarn into surrendering his army?" Tor asked sceptically.

"Certain death versus military service, I know what I'd pick," Troy commented from behind, raising eyebrows.

"Sorcery has been rumoured on this continent but never verified," Tor told him.

"I verify it now," said Linh, "it's over there." She pointed at a damar pack walking into a volley of arrows.

Ruarnon tried to shove aside waves of dizziness.

"The Zaldeaans are the best army on the continent," said General Takanis. "And they were assembled in full strength. If a westerner desired an army for conquest... He may have designed the damars for such and found them useless. Then conceived of using them to lure a competent army to sea and coerce it instead."

Dizziness resisted Ruarnon's attempts to shove it away.

"If Monin was right about ships being sabotaged by ordinary means," said General Aza, "*some* Zaldeaan soldiers ought to have made it to shore by now. But for the army to sail away, giving free rein to the damars it set out to fight, it must be beyond Zaldeaan control... unless it is confronting an even greater force. Someone has overpowered it, a feat I thought impossible."

The Zaldeaan army would respond to any physical threat by fighting. That was what they did. But it occurred to Ruarnon that there were two kingdoms the Zaldeaans hadn't fought, the Urai and the North Lands. And myth claimed North Landers could wield magic. Had a western sorcerer captured the Zaldeaans?

"You are certain there is no sign of ships in the seas?" Tor asked the scout. "There is no evidence they threaten the North Landers or us?"

The scout shook her head.

Had the damarian ships truly come from the west? It appeared they had what they wanted: the Zaldeaan army. Uncle Karmarn was gone. So was Derlan's best tool to usurp the throne. And the strongest power in the Zaldeaan Realm. In its absence, Ruarnon could challenge the governors for the Zaldeaan throne. They could occupy Zaldeaa City themself.

The ground seemed to shift beneath Ruarnon, and they braced their feet till the dizziness passed.

"How do you think Captain Nish and the city guard would receive me?" Ruarnon asked Armar.

"In our army's total absence, with a small bodyguard, from atop the city walls, with the gates shut. He and the people will fear retribution for the invasion of Tarlah."

Fear governed the Zaldeaan Realm. Now more than ever. And there was still a risk of Derlan or a combination of governors pinning Ruarnon's army against the walls of Zaldeaa City if they opposed Ruarnon's occupation.

"Nish cannot hold the throne indefinitely," Armar added. "He is not of royal blood. But to whom he opens the city gates and to whom Aoran opens the palace depends either on your occupation or the outcome of the Succession War."

"Regency is an unfamiliar concept to the Zaldeaan Realm," Tor added, "which has seen three Regents in a month. If I were advising a Zaldeaan Heir, I would say the Zaldeaan Realm needs a ruler."

"I would prefer one now, not after a protracted succession war," Companion Armar added. "If the battle between Syenne and Derlan is undecided, the other governors will finish killing damars and be drawn into the Succession War."

The Zaldeaan Realm needed what Ruarnon's father had trained them to be every day of their life: a leader. If Ruarnon was truly committed to ensuring no one else died, they had to end the Succession War. But could they *rule* the Zaldeaan Realm? Would the Zaldeaans tolerate a midlun ruler?

"A *Tarlahn* as Zaldeaan king?" Ruarnon asked.

"As a male-presenting midlun," said Tor, "and a warrior leading soldiers into battle, you resemble the most revered Zaldeaan kings, save that you are Tarlahn. They may insist on calling you 'he,' but correcting their pronoun use *and* asking them to accept a Tarlahn ruler *may* be more than they can handle. And you control the strongest army. In theory, you may be the best candidate for the Zaldeaan throne."

"Many Zaldeaan men will hate that," said General Takanis. "But I suspect they would hate Syenne as king even more. She's supposed to be weak, meek, and obedient, the model Zaldeaan woman. Instead, she has the tenacity to outdo most Zaldeaan men, and their brittle egos cannot stand it. The people may prefer you, even as a male-presenting midlun, to a woman."

"Iomar's relationship with my son defies our normal expectations of relationships between men," said Armar, "which says both or at least one ought to be a military man. Neither he nor Aoran has more than passable skill at fighting, nor are they as loud, aggressive, or assertive as many Zaldeaans think men should be. Iomar's people love him, but were he to claim the crown, I am not sure the rest of the nation, who do not know him well, would tolerate him. Whereas Your Benevolence has a quiet intensity that, accompanied with your decisive leadership, they may respect.

"As for Your Benevolence being midlun, many of the worst kind of men in my homeland like to dismiss most Tarlahn men as midluns, considering them less manly than Zaldeaan men, whom they consider to be 'true men.' So, Your Benevolence being an actual midlun may not be the barrier you think."

Ruarnon's mouth opened in surprise. Were Zaldeaans so prejudiced against male-presenting Tarlahns that Ruarnon, as an actual midlun, would appear no different from a Tarlahn man in Zaldeaan eyes? Perhaps being Tarlahn was Ruarnon's only likely reason to be hated as a potential ruler...

"Iagl, however, they consider the perfect man. I am concerned, but do not know enough of him to be sure of the extent to which he takes after his father and the 'truest' of Zaldeaan men—the ones who are tearing my country apart.

"Aiding Kia and Iomar against damars will probably win their loyalty for now. But I suspect you will have to confront and perhaps fight the others."

"Would they risk fighting us without their main army?" Ruarnon asked.

"They have never been so weak," General Aza replied, "but they are Zaldeaans. Proud warriors who hoped to conquer us as recently as two weeks ago. Most may temporarily unite to ambush us and drive us out. Especially given that Syenne may have lost her father and ultimately her brother to the cause of peace. She may hold that against Tarlah."

Ruarnon shivered, especially when Armar paled and bowed his head in acceptance of that assessment.

"If you leave," said Linh, "you'd abandon the Realm to civil war, and who knows how many more people the damars might kill while Derlan finishes screwing over his entire country to get what he wants."

"You can't risk that prick becoming king," Troy added.

"I'd rather kill him myself," said Ruarnon.

The moment they said it, they knew it was true. Too many people had been killed because of Derlan.

"But if I can't predict Iagl's actions or Syenne's, I can't make or rely on alliances with governors. My best option is to occupy Zaldeaa City, use it as a base to destroy the damars and see if I can hold it against the governors. What would you do?" Ruarnon asked General Aza.

"The same. Take a stable base to hunt the fiends and cut down any Zaldeaan who stopped me. I can almost hear Monin having palpitations at me saying that, but he hasn't met damars. They must be dealt with. And dealing with them may present an opportunity for alliances with governors. I'd want to attempt that before I went home."

Ruarnon nodded, turned to General Takanis, and said, "I would negotiate with Governor Syenne, and I suspect you are the best person to invite her to the table."

Takanis smiled and bowed.

Ruarnon smiled too. They suspected Syenne would find a woman general refreshing. And they had Iomar's lover's father travelling with them. Surely that would help with Iomar.

"Our aims have changed," Ruarnon said, projecting their voice to carry over silent bowstrings, as their soldiers scanned the plains for live damars and failed to spot any. "The Zaldeaan army is disabled, and its ships hijacked. The provincial armies war against damars or each other. We will continue to slay damars. But our new destination is Zaldeaa City. We will occupy the Zaldeaan capital, and I will claim its throne. I seek peace under Tarlahn rule."

Stunned silence greeted Ruarnon's words. Their advisors looked grave. Companion Armar sagged with relief. But the four youths were smiling unreservedly, all four of them.

Soldiers found their voices. "The new Regent! The new Tarlah! The new Peace!"

The lone cry slowly spread, until soldiers roared it so loudly that more damars appeared in the distance, drawn by the noise. Their army had had reservations when Ruarnon ordered it to march, but their soldiers had overcome them. Ruarnon possessed what Kyura had lacked, the loyalty of their army and its mandate to protect the Zaldeaan people. They smiled nervously and dared hope to succeed where Kyura had failed.

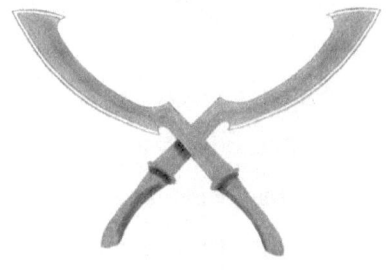

CHAPTER 29

DAMARIAN MARCH

RUARNON: *the Zaldeaan Realm, Six Days From Tarlah*

S ire, I don't mean to be rude, but your young
companions..."

Ruarnon's brows furrowed at Companion Armar
gripping his reins so hard his knuckles were white, as he eyed
Troy chatting happily to Michael.

"What about them?" Ruarnon asked.

"When they speak, you and your countrymen hear
Timbalen, but I hear Migryan. What sorcery is this? Where
did they come from?"

"Outside the Timbalen Empire," Ruarnon replied. "That
much I understand. They didn't have this ability with language
in their homeland. They believe they acquired it on their
journey, which involved travel through a magic castle."

Armar gaped. Ruarnon found that part hard to believe too.

"They are not Elite Guard? Or sorcerers?"

Ruarnon shook their head. "They are unlike Tarlahns and Zaldeaans both in many ways, but language appears to be their only incredible power."

"I suggest they not utter a word in the presence of Zaldeaans. Every time I become aware I'm hearing them speak another language than what the rest of you are hearing, it makes my blood run cold. They seem affable enough, but their ability is frightening."

"I'll try to monitor them more carefully and remind them," said Ruarnon.

How had they forgotten what Michael had told them only a day ago? Ruarnon was already thinking of Armar as one of their party, as their advisor. He'd hidden his discomfort and shock, but the youths appearing to speak two different languages simultaneously seemed to have shaken Armar up.

Ruarnon slowed to fall in beside the youths and reminded them not to speak near Zaldeaan settlements and to give Armar space.

"Crap," said Troy. "I forgot about him speaking Migryan, probably because we met him before we realised the Zaldeaans hear us differently."

"We'll be careful," Michael promised.

"Smile and wave," said Fiona. "That should be safe as our default."

The next day, scouts led Ruarnon and their army to a cart track leading from Governor Kia's capital to Governor Iomar's, southwest of Zaldeaa City, through forest and farmland. They rode towards a village with livestock penned between houses and archers on its rooftops. Dead damars lay around bluestone buildings, embedded with arrows. Hissing started again.

General Aza called a halt and winded his horn. "Draw! Loose!"

Arrows soared at a damar pack charging through the trees beside the road. Hissing announced more. More volleys were loosed until silence fell.

Zaldeaan archers atop the roofs lowered their weapons, cheering, and clapping. Ruarnon eyed the village sharply. Damars lay on every side; dead chickens were scattered about, as were the bodies of several women. They were nearing the western coast and places that had been under attack for three weeks.

The applause halted, cheers breaking off and faces on rooftops looking nervous, as Ruarnon's soldiers entered the village. Mouths dropped open. Ruarnon halted, wondering how to reassure them. Inspiration struck, and they raised both arms in a two-armed salute. Their soldiers gaped. Aza smiled, mimicking the salute, and their soldiers copied. Villagers stared in amazement and spoke a language Ruarnon didn't understand.

"They are surprised to see Tarlahns so far north, and say Umarinaris has turned on its head," the scholar translated. "They realise Your Benevolence means to conquer them but are relieved that order will be restored and they will be safe from damars."

Window shutters opened, and Zaldeaan elders and women stared, but children waved and smiled. The soldiers smiled back, and the four Aussie youths waved. Hope blossomed in women's eyes then, and the elderly bowed their heads in acceptance.

A hum of conversation began in the houses, in which hope and optimism were as audible as caution. Ruarnon suspected the caution was for whether the Tarlahns held the war against the Zaldeaan villagers. If Ruarnon could dispel that fear, the Zaldeaans might be glad of order, and in the short term, they might not care that a Tarlahn had restored it. Knowing they were making the right choice in occupying the capital warmed Ruarnon's heart.

A rider appeared on the trail ahead, a scout. Ruarnon motioned them to approach and report.

"Governor Kia and her soldiers are defending towns along the coast lacking defensive walls," the young man said. "Governor Iomar's soldiers have also been spotted, split into groups hunting damars across his province. Governor Derlan has laid siege to Governor Syenne's capital. There is no word yet on Governor Iagl's movements."

Ruarnon smiled. They *would* reach the capital. Ruarnon had their army continue marching northwest, stopping twice to summon and slaughter damar packs. They were disturbed by how many creatures came from the east—inland.

Another scout approached as they neared the edge of a forest. "Small party of Zaldeaans approaching, Benevolence. Governor Iomar is among them."

Ruarnon bowed their head, gazing nervously beyond paddocks and farmhouses towards the bluestone walls of a distant city. Grey sea mirrored a grey sky beyond, and a small party of Zaldeaan riders approached, felling damars with arrows as they rode. Despite knowing those were Iomar's soldiers and that Iomar's lover's father accompanied them, Ruarnon's hands tingled with nerves. They wanted to offer their first alliance, but the thought made their mind flit to their last diplomatic visit to the Zaldeaans. To someone who still hadn't been identified, who had sent assassins after them. And that was before they marched their army into the Realm, intending to occupy it. Ruarnon shuddered. Even if peace appealed to Iomar, how would he greet Ruarnon when an occupying army marched at Ruarnon's back?

The riders stopped beside the road, and Ruarnon studied them. Each wore full bronze armour, except the leader, whose helmet and cuirass were iron. He was young, blue-eyed with fair skin and his dark hair trimmed at the base of his elegant neck, around which a bloody bandage was wrapped.

Ruarnon braced themself, calling, "Governor Iomar?"

The riders bowed in their saddles. Ruarnon exhaled slightly.

"I am told Your Benevolence has been hunting damars?" Iomar asked, his accent heavier than Armar's, his Timbalen flawless.

"Your reports are correct," Ruarnon confirmed.

"Yet you left my cousin's city untouched?"

"I am here to end wars, not start them."

"Your Benevolence does not intend to seize the provincial capitals?"

Ruarnon considered their reply carefully. "I do not, aside from your father's—unless Syenne takes it from him first."

Iomar's face hardened. "That would be no less than he deserves."

There was resentment in his eyes, and fear of Derlan, Ruarnon suspected. That made the hair on the back of Ruarnon's neck stand up. If Derlan's own son feared him, and Derlan had betrayed his nephew, how on Mijora's earth could Ruarnon deal with the man?

"How do your men fare?" Ruarnon asked, gripping their horse's flanks unnecessarily tightly in an attempt to expel the worst of their anxiety.

"They are weary and bloodied," Iomar replied.

Ruarnon sensed how alertly the Zaldeaan soldiers sat their mounts or stood behind Iomar, their eyes scanning for any sign of Ruarnon's party reaching for weapons. One wrong move could lead to violence. Ruarnon's guts churned. They needed soldiers on both sides to trust each other. Before blood was spilt. But Ruarnon could think of only one way to build trust between strangers: make them work together and get to know each other. It was risky, but a shared workload, a clear purpose, could distract them from their differences. Perhaps unite them. There was only one clear task for that.

"Would they like to finish their work and accompany us north?"

Iomar's mouth opened in surprise. "Your Benevolence would permit this?"

"I wish to ensure the security of the Zaldeaan Realm, not snatch the duties of this province's protectors from them."

Ruarnon saw Tor's brows rise.

"I shall assemble my army, Your Benevolence. Where would you have us meet you?"

"Meet us here."

As soon as the Zaldeaans had ridden beyond earshot, Ruarnon's advisors converged on them.

"I approve, but this is sudden, Benevolence," General Aza cautioned.

"These are not the soldiers who fought us on Death Belt Desert nor our walls, and our soldiers know it," Tor asserted. "But if the strictest discipline is not maintained..."

"Tell my army these soldiers are with us to fulfil their duty to their people," Ruarnon ordered. "And that any person who cannot accept this may return to Tarlah and take up guard duty."

If Kyura's struggle to control his soldiers had taught Ruarnon anything, it was that it was best to be rid of soldiers who would cause trouble before trouble started. It *was* very soon after the battle, but Ruarnon's soldiers would reach the capital soon. Ruarnon wanted to see that Tarlahn soldiers *could* work with Zaldeaans. They had no desire to spark a rebellion like the one their father had fought in at fifteen.

Within half an hour, Governor Iomar approached with mounted guards, leading four infantry phalanxes. Many wore bandages, looked weary, and probably wished they had the support of their other half, who were with the army at sea. Yet they held heads high and kept a firm grip on spear and shield.

"Governor Iomar, will you translate for me?" Ruarnon asked.

Iomar nodded, and Ruarnon spoke. "I am aware of your struggles and proud of your efforts to fulfil your duty. Together, we shall end damars in this province, and you will return here for the rest you have earned."

Mouths opened in surprise as Iomar translated. They stood upright, alert, and cautious as they weighed their perceptions against Ruarnon, who saw a shift in their eyes. Their spear butts stamped the ground, the Zaldeaan sign of readiness. Not a salute, but...

"Fall in beside the head of my column," Ruarnon instructed.

Iomar repeated the order, and Zaldeaan soldiers blinked. Then the first row walked forwards, their captain issuing the command belatedly, other units following. Ruarnon exhaled heavily. These soldiers knew where power lay. Despite their misgivings, they seemed willing to respond to the familiarity of orders and to overlook Ruarnon's identity while Ruarnon aided them against damars. The need to defend against the immediate, widespread threat of damars might gain their allegiance. But when it became clear the damars were losing across the Realm, how many of these soldiers would then see Ruarnon's army as their people's greatest threat... And how would the Tarlahn army, who had lost comrades to the Zaldeaan army, greet Zaldeaan soldiers?

Ruarnon returned to the head of their army, determined to lead the newly allied soldiers as best they could, but they were distracted by smoke rising from where the gentle hills of Iomar's province met forested mountains further north.

"Is that the North Lander fire?" Ruarnon asked.

Iomar exhaled deeply. "Indeed. If only we were so gifted at defending ourselves."

"They *can* wield magic."

Iomar nodded. "We trade with them, but their merchants mostly come to my city. Their abilities are more than my people like to be reminded about living next to—not that they normally wield magic in front of outsiders."

"Why do you speak such good Timbalen?"

"It was Uncle Kyomi's idea. Had his Peace continued, he hoped I might take a Tarlahn husband."

Ruarnon blinked in surprise. In Tarlah, men, women and midluns could marry any gender. But Zaldeaan men did not marry men, let alone Tarlahn men. It seemed Kyomi wasn't just radical in promoting peace with Tarlah, he was radical in accepting his nephew's sexuality beyond the narrow limits of Zaldeaan culture.

And Urmillian and Kyomi had seen Uncle Kar and Aunt Merlah's marriage as the most powerful act of diplomacy, so Kyomi seeking more marriage ties between his family and Tarlah made sense for diplomatic reasons. If Kyomi had gone so far as to ensure his nephew learned Timbalen so he could speak to a possible Tarlahn husband in his language, then Kyomi's commitment to peace had run deeper than Ruarnon knew.

They followed the road through more villages and paddock-covered coastline, turning right alongside great forests and a fire of impressive height: the border with the North Lands. Damars rushed towards them in greater numbers, screeching and charging. Ruarnon called a halt and drew their bow.

Three packs made a beeline for the front of the column. Ruarnon nocked, drew, and loosed methodically. Captains ordered archers to fire. Damars crashed into the shield wall ahead, and spears thrust, felling a pack, a second and third streaming past to attack the column's sides.

Ruarnon turned back. Iomar's last phalanx gestured to Ruarnon's rear unit with hands or spears. They were boasting about killing the most damars. Ruarnon smiled, then saw Iomar's head lower as General Aza's horn sounded and more damar packs ran towards them.

"We never fought with such a formation," Iomar said quietly. "This is so efficient. They came so quickly, and the murders... We hunted however we could, one pack after another, many spreading beyond us too far to keep following, more attacking from behind. We had to fight our way to the castle to sleep at night."

"My generals and I planned this formation in the safety of Tarlah castle. We had a much easier time of it."

Iomar sighed.

Soldiers cleared the road of bodies, and they advanced towards cheering villagers, people lining the street as far as Ruarnon could see, smiling, waving, and throwing flowers. Young women blew kisses, making Ruarnon blush and Iomar smile. The people called out to their Governor but paused when they recognised the Tarlahn army. Ruarnon eyed the hesitant crowd. Zaldeaans cheered anew, growing louder, as General Aza and bemused Tarlahn soldiers saluted them with spears. Ruarnon's eyes widened in surprise. Were they so shaken by the damarian attacks that they didn't care who saved them?

The army followed the road into the northern forest again, halting for General Aza to wind his horn. Then Tarlahns and Zaldeaans competed to kill the most damars. Some refused to look at each other, a few were restrained by captains and sent away from the other army, and there was uneasiness and tension, but Ruarnon hoped they would accept each other in time.

"You wish for them to work together?" Iomar asked, following Ruarnon's gaze.

Ruarnon nodded.

"Then, Highest, send five hundred men to complete my province's army. Let them build on the bonds they are forming."

Ruarnon's shoulders tensed, and Tor shot them a warning look. Breaking off units of their army would leave those soldiers more vulnerable to Zaldeaan treachery—not that Ruarnon believed Iomar was capable of that. Iomar presented himself as earnest and sincere. And his plan fit with the vision forming in Ruarnon's mind for Tarlahn governance of the Zaldeaan Realm. This was an opportunity for Tarlahn soldiers to demonstrate to Zaldeaans that they came to protect, not harm.

"I shall," said Ruarnon. "The first four phalanxes behind me can march back with you. If we have missed damars here or in Governor Kia's province, they can help hunt them."

Both armies camped in the open, soldiers who would be garrisoned in Iomar's capital reluctantly setting up tents beside the Zaldeaans. Captains selected soldiers to remain with the army to avoid trouble, but most put a bold face on it. Ruarnon smiled at some Tarlahns arm-wrestling Zaldeaan comrades, a pastime the language barrier didn't affect. In the morning, those soldiers and Companion Noma, whom Ruarnon appointed commander under Iomar, bid them goodbye.

Iomar turned to Armar. "When you see Aoran, tell him I want him to come home."

Companion Armar smiled and bowed his head.

Ruarnon offered Iomar their hand, and Iomar smiled as he shook it. Then Ruarnon led their army into taller forests and the hilly landscape of the heart of the Zaldeaan Realm, towards Zaldeaa City and the boldest decision they had ever made.

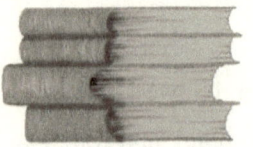

CHAPTER 30

ZALDEAA CITY

LINH: *the Zaldeaan Realm, Eight Days March From Tarlah*

Linh gazed beyond the vanguard. The hilltop before them sloped into a valley with forested, snow-capped mountains on its left, then the hilly plains of Governor Syenne's province on the right. Houses scattered the hillside below and opposite them, linked by a stone bridge over a river. Older men and women carrying bows walked among houses, keeping watch for damars, but each figure froze as the Tarlahn army turned down the slope.

"What's spooked them?" Troy asked.

"Governor Iomar reassured the others," Linh replied, "but these people have no reason to believe we won't harm them."

They followed the vanguard across the bridge and zig-zagged up the far side of the valley. Michael's brows narrowed. Bells tolled ahead. The bow-carrying villagers scattered, and doors slammed shut behind them.

"What does that mean?" Troy asked.

"We are the only likely attackers for bells to warn against," Tor replied.

Linh did *not* want to fight Zaldeaans... They were supposed to *save* them. She sat rigidly.

"Benevolence! A report! Several governors have combined provincial armies and are riding this way. They appear to be heading to Zaldeaa City," a rider called from behind them.

"Do you know which governors lead those armies?" Ruarnon asked.

The scout shook his head.

They crested the hilltop, and Linh gazed down a stone-paved road leading across a plateau towards the high bluestone walls of Zaldeaa City.

"It may be a trap," Aza warned.

Ruarnon raised their looking glass, and their grip tightened as they said, "Someone has set fire to the gate."

"Are you certain?" Armar asked.

"That's screaming," Michael asserted. "In the city."

"Sound the horns!" Ruarnon commanded.

Linh gazed ahead as horns were winded and the column advanced towards the city, past shuttered homes and more forest. Its gates were burning, the bottoms charred. Damars clustered before the gates, cracks of light flashing between them, the charred section of the gate destroyed and damars flocking into the city. She gaped.

Several creatures turned and rushed the column. Screeching began, and more damars turned. They spread across the road and between trees, charging the column from all sides. Battle would erupt a few soldiers before her, but screams meant people were in danger, and killing damars was a mercy to everything that breathed.

Linh was only half-aware of tying her reins to her saddle. Adrenaline flared as she unbuckled her bow, took an arrow from the quiver at her hip and fit an arrow to bowstring. On either side of her, Troy, Fiona, and Michael drew their bows.

Damars charged the vanguard, and archers loosed a volley. Linh aimed and loosed nervously, hitting a creature in the shoulder. It shrieked and ran on, shaking its crude spear. She flinched, but there wasn't time for being squeamish. She fit and drew her second arrow, loosing it into her target's throat. The sight made her grimace, but adrenaline spurred her on. Her third arrow hit a damar in the thigh, but it kept running. Her fourth hit a damar in the chest, and it fell.

Bodies thudded into the shield wall and Linh tensed. Spears thrust before her, and a damar tried to climb a shield. An archer shot it at point-blank range. Linh drew and loosed another arrow, envying the fluid way Ruarnon, Lenaris, and Tor released three arrows in swift succession.

Spearmen thrust at more damars, climbing shields, and the shield wall rippled ahead of her. Screeches rose. She drew and loosed again. Soldiers tried to shake damars off their shields and broke ranks. Her heart sped up as the shield wall broke before her and creatures ran through. Archers struck the creatures with bows or drew swords.

"Use your spears!" Lenaris shouted.

Linh hung her bow off her sword hilt and took her spear from its saddle holder. Lenaris and Tor's spears stabbed at creatures, protecting their horse's necks. On her right, Troy's horse reared, and he dropped his spear, clutching the reins as the horse kicked and a damar fell dead.

"Turn your horses sideways!" Michael yelled.

Linh turned her horse as the column halted. On her left, Michael knocked a spear from a damar's hand. The creature hissed, its many-fanged mouth opening wide, wild anger in its yellow eyes. Michael stabbed it with his spear. Another damar hissed as it ran towards Troy.

Adrenaline flooded Linh's bloodstream, and she thrust her spear at its chest, gritting her teeth as she met resistance. The creature shrieked and fell. It thrust its stick at her horse. Linh twisted the spear, and the creature stilled. She withdrew the bloodied spear, panting heavily and staring at the red liquid on the spear tip, the only natural thing about damars.

A creature clawed at Fiona's horse. Linh stabbed its chest instinctively, but it ignored the wound. Fiona stabbed it too, and it shuddered and fell. Linh withdrew her spear, but Fiona stared at the dead creature, her breathing out of control.

"You had to save your horse," Linh said gently.

Fiona bit her lip, then nodded.

Hissing nearby ceased, and the shield wall reformed. Just like that, the mayhem of death stopped. But Linh's muscles were still tense, her heart still crashed against her rib cage, and she still gripped her spear for dear life. It didn't feel over.

"I'll be happy if we *never* need to fight these things again," Troy said firmly.

"I'd be happy not fighting anything, but I don't think that will happen," said Michael. "People in the street didn't realise they were in danger. We just helped save them, and we'll need to do it again."

"Wish I had your perspective," Troy said, darkly eyeing the damar Linh and Fiona had killed.

In Linh's mind's eye, a damar fell, and her spear met resistance. She turned, trying to push the memory away. Archers behind her loosed arrows on both sides of the column. Under General Aza's command, shields bashed creatures, then spears thrust over them. Some damars snuck between moving shields and were stabbed by spearmen.

"Why *did* they burn their gates?" Lenaris asked grimly.

"Treachery," Armar replied softly, "To provoke my people to resist Tarlahn occupation. Unless, amid all the fighting and death, someone went mad. Either way, the rumour will spread faster than Regent Nish can deliver orders. Individual captains will command their guards as they see fit. There is every chance they will attack Your Benevolence."

"We should enter the city," Tor advised. "Slaying damars is our only hope of convincing them we did not let the creatures in, even if it means skirmishes with the city guard."

At Lenaris' prompting, Linh replaced her spear in its holder, and struggled to hold her bow steady as Ruarnon led the column forward. Would the Zaldeaans accept aid or panic at the sight of Tarlahns? She rode tensely, barely aware of sweat trickling down her back.

"Not an archer on the walls," General Aza commented, "but there is shouting in the city. I suspect the guards panicked once the creatures got inside and tried to fight them in the streets."

The burning gates opened. The sound of mingled shouts, screeches, and ringing bells drifted out.

"Report, soldier!" Armar ordered, and she noticed a man in the gate tower.

"Companion," the soldier replied with a bow, "people are saying Tarlahns breached the gates and let damars into the city! Or that it is the end of Umarinaris!"

The scholar translated for Ruarnon, who turned to address their army. "Someone opposing us has burned the gates. They may have spread lies about our purpose, but do not let yourselves be provoked. Act with discipline, slay damars, spare Zaldeaans who get in the way, and you will help establish Tarlahn rule."

Soldiers nodded grimly, saluting with both arms, and Linh shivered.

"Don't worry," said Troy. "If the Zaldeaans don't get why we're here, we can tell them, and they'll hear us in Zaldeaan."

"Unless Tarlahns hear us speaking Timbalen at the same time," Michael cautioned. "If they decide we're sorcerers, they'll go crazy for sure."

"Bloody hell, Mic," Troy objected. "You *had* to remind us that our only comfort isn't a comfort, didn't you?"

Michael blushed, and Linh shook her head at Troy's ability to joke at a time like this. Fiona managed a smile. Maybe Troy's ability to laugh in the darkness wasn't silly, after all; it seemed to make the others feel better.

They rode behind the vanguard between burning gates onto a wide main road lined with bluestone townhouses of two or more stories. The street was deserted, every door and wooden window shutter closed, but Linh heard the hum of hushed, anxious voices from inside, and occasional shouts or screeches in the distance. The bells had stopped.

The window shutters of upper stories opened above, and Zaldeaan women, children, and the elderly peeked down at the Tarlahn army. Nervous eyes followed them down the road, making Linh's skin tingle.

Ruarnon called a halt before a fork around a majestic apartment, and Linh's ears strained through thick silence. Shouts cut through the air.

"They're still coming in through North Gate!"

"Post archers on the walls!"

"It's the Tarlahns! They'll be here soon. Their army will kill everyone!"

"Shut that fool up!"

With shaking hands, Linh fit and drew an arrow against whatever emerged from either fork in the road. Ruarnon raised their bow, and Tarlahn horns were winded. More faces appeared in upper-story windows above the army, staring anxiously.

Screeches sounded down the left fork. The patter of approaching damarian footsteps echoed off walls. A first, second, and third damar moved into sight, running full-pelt, each carrying a wooden spear its height, long-pointed teeth bared in feral grins. Bows twanged, and all three fell. Linh kept her bow trained behind them. Damars she could handle. Let the Zaldeaans stay back...

"Archers, loose!" Ruarnon commanded.

The patter of feet and hisses echoed, and damars charged into view again. Bowstrings twanged and the damarian front line staggered or fell. More creatures came, shoving each other against houses and knocking each other down in the narrow space.

Linh's mouth firmed with determination, and she loosed her arrow a split second after Lenaris. She fit another as her target fell, and her friends' arrows joined the archers' second volley. She drew as damars thudded into shields, jabbing their spears.

"Forward shields!" Ruarnon cried.

Linh's arrow took a creature in the head as the shield wall jerked forwards, knocking creatures down. She froze.

"Again!" Ruarnon ordered.

The shield wall rammed the second row of creatures, thrusting spears felling more. An object moved in the corner of her vision. A large pot was falling towards the damarian hoard.

"Take that!" a boy yelled as the pot smashed on damars.

"Archers, hold fire!" Ruarnon ordered.

Pottery and wooden furniture flew out of windows beyond the shield wall, raining on damars. Thumps of damars striking the shield wall lessened. Linh smiled.

Then she saw more damars claw and bang spears futilely against doors and window shutters. Archers loosed arrows at them, as the thudding of damars against shields stopped and Zaldeaans ran out of household items to sacrifice. The next volley of arrows felled half the remaining damars. A last volley shot down the rest.

Linh exhaled deeply, panting, and stared down a street of damar corpses bristling with arrows. There were no more padding footsteps or screeches. No shouts from Zaldeaans defending the city. Both sections of the road beyond either side of the fork remained empty, and Linh realised they had slain most damars in the city. She sank into her saddle with relief. Fiona smiled as cheering erupted from Zaldeaan windows, and soldiers clapped each other's shoulders, some archers kissing. Linh smiled and returned Fiona's hug across their saddles.

"And some of us wondered what we could achieve here," Michael said to Troy without a hint of mockery.

Troy's face split into a broad grin, and he hugged Michael, who hugged him back.

"The nightmares might be worth this moment," Fiona said softly, her eyes shining, as Troy rode between her and Linh and hugged them one-armed. Linh smiled and hugged him back.

Ruarnon: Zaldeaa City

Ruarnon ordered their captains to relieve the front lines and their phalanxes to hold formation. As the new front line formed a shield wall, hisses and yelling rose on their left. Three damars rounded the bend, and Tarlahn archers shot them dead. Footsteps echoed behind the fallen creatures. Zaldeaans armed with spears marched into view, an armoured phalanx. The Zaldeaans froze, staring at Ruarnon's shield wall from within arrow range.

"Hold your fire!" Ruarnon yelled.

Between the shield wall, Tarlahn spears lowered. The Zaldeaans formed their own shield wall, but they didn't have archers.

"Lower your bows!"

The archers obeyed hesitantly. Ruarnon's soldiers stood tensely, defying their instinct to attack. The Zaldeaans stood poised to charge. A Zaldeaan rider rounded the bend, and

Ruarnon gaped. It couldn't be Governor Iomar. The man had blue eyes, Iomar's long slender face, dark hair cut in the same style, and wore the same iron armour. But there was no bandage on his neck, his mouth was open in surprise, and he looked willing to attack on instinct.

Ruarnon felt a moment of panic, knowing Iagl might do anything. So Ruarnon saluted with both arms to signal their intentions. Their soldiers reluctantly mirrored their salute with weapons in hand.

Governor Iagl stared.

Ruarnon's scholar appeared at their elbow, sweating profusely.

"They brought the damars!" the scholar translated a shout.

"We should kill them and drive them out!"

Iagl's shield wall rippled as the front line took a step forward.

"*No*," the scholar translated Iagl's command. "That salute means Tarlah and the Zaldeaan Realm stand. The right arm for Tarlah, the left for us. They do not mean to destroy us."

"Then who sent the damars? Who else would want us dead?" yelled a Zaldeaan.

"They did it to force our army home! It's how they ended the siege!" cried another.

"Then they came here to kill the damars and save us, I do not think," Iagl scorned.

The scholar paused as silence fell. Defensive claims rattled through Ruarnon's head. But they didn't need to defend themself; they needed to calm frightened, angry soldiers before flaring tempers erupted in pitched battle.

"A ship of damars wrecked on the coast of Timraith Island," Ruarnon said, and the scholar translated loudly. "The island was overrun, and our allies found over a hundred of my subjects slaughtered. I hate war, I hate warmongers, but I do not hate fishermen's children, farmers' wives, or the elderly. My army has toured the west coast from south to north to annihilate damars, *not* to fight Zaldeaans."

"Your whole army is here?" Iagl asked in Timbalen.

"It is." Ruarnon longed to add that they didn't want to fight, but the Council had warned them against displaying the unwillingness for violence that had let warmongers think they could reduce Kyura to a puppet. So they sat firm and waited tensely for Iagl's response.

"Stand down!" Iagl ordered.

Ruarnon gave their army the same order. Bronze shields and spear butts rested on the ground; points angled harmlessly skyward. The worst of the soldiers' tension vanished, but they stood alert for a change of command. Governor Iagl turned warily to Ruarnon. Ruarnon tensed as a distant horn blew repetitively.

General Takanis. The rear end of the Tarlahn column was under attack. The other governors were arriving, surrounding Ruarnon's army *inside* the city instead of pinning them *outside* it...

Ruarnon turned their horse. "Aza! Do not let them fight!" they ordered.

"Right step!" General Aza bellowed.

The column stepped to Ruarnon's left as they heeled their horse down the road. They ignored curious Zaldeaan faces in windows and their soldiers leaping aside before them. General Takanis commanded the rear, and she knew not to initiate hostilities, but if a governor's army attacked first...

Bluestone apartments flashed past, and soldiers ahead of Ruarnon rippled aside for an interminably long time. Their heart hammered beneath their armour, then finally the road turned and the city gates were in view.

Outside, Ruarnon's phalanxes stood in double rows with their backs to the city wall, front lines forming a shield wall and roof, spears and archers poised to attack. Opposite them stood three divisions of Zaldeaan soldiers, two with a mounted commander at their head. The commanders wore iron armour with strangely curved breastplates. Governor Kia and Governor Syenne.

Ruarnon's archers drew their bows, but the Zaldeaans weren't yet in range.

"Hold your fire!" Ruarnon yelled, riding forwards. "Hold your fire and stand your ground!"

General Takanis bellowed, "*Hold fire!*"

Ruarnon felt a strange tug at their right shoulder, which they ignored as their captains repeated the command. They breathed a sigh of relief, reining in beside General Takanis, behind their soldiers, wondering why the general gaped at them.

"The enemy has power bows! *Get down!*" Tor shouted.

A man in the Zaldeaan front line held a small power bow. The man fell backwards, a line sticking up from his chest.

"I said, hold your fire!" Ruarnon yelled confusedly.

"You are not my king yet!" a young man's voice yelled from the walls. The walls... A *Zaldeaan*?

Ruarnon felt strange. An iron bolt protruded from their shoulder. Then Tor was beside them, catching them as they slid out of the saddle. One of the women they had seen rode forwards alone.

"Don't let them fight!" Ruarnon insisted.

The woman came closer, sitting upright on her horse, her posture proud. She had the most determined pale face they had ever seen, and icy blue eyes.

"Let her through," they said softly.

Soldiers parted before them. Tor gasped, and Ruarnon realised they were leaning heavily against him. The woman dismounted. She strode through tense, sweating soldiers, coolly ignoring them, radiating strength.

"You should have been king," Ruarnon said.

Her eyes widened slightly. Then everything went black.

Linh's heart beat wildly.

"Fetch a healer!" Tor shouted, and one of Ruarnon's guards rode back along the Tarlahn column.

Governor Syenne advanced between the fourth line of Tarlahn archers. General Takanis stood mesmerised. Tor's distraught gaze was fixed on Ruarnon. Lenaris rushed to Ruarnon. The Tarlahns weren't ready to negotiate, and Syenne was almost close enough to hail.

Michael eyed Linh nervously, the offer to speak in his eyes. Memories flashed. Ba's text saying not to take risks. Linh's doubts that she and her friends could achieve anything in Tarlah. Her desire since Myleth Island to spare families the trauma hers had suffered. She shook her head and heeled her horse forwards. Syenne's stern gaze fixed on her.

"Good afternoon, Governor Syenne," she said, cloaking her nerves with determination to do whatever she could to halt the war in its tracks. She ignored General Takanis' gasp.

"You have the authority to speak on behalf of your Regent?" Syenne asked, her tone as smooth and iron as the curvaceous breastplate that made her gender clear.

Linh was vaguely aware of the shock on Tor's face and of Lenaris blinking in disbelief, while Takanis eyed Linh and discreetly shook her head in warning. Linh doubted Syenne's razor gaze missed any of it.

"Technically," Linh replied, ignoring sweat trickling down her back, "no. But I don't intend to let that stop me."

Syenne's eyes became less icy. Michael's face went slack; then he began to smile. That subtle change on Syenne's face: it couldn't be *amusement*?

"By what right do you speak on the Regent's behalf?" Syenne asked.

"I helped convince them to come here," Linh replied.

Syenne blinked. Linh wasn't sure if she was reacting to Linh's influence or Ruarnon being nonbinary. But that slight shift in Syenne's cold beauty seemed to be approval.

"Why did they come? Why did you advise them to?"

Linh heard a loud intake of breath around her, signalling that her answer would determine whether Syenne's armies attacked. Her reply had to be powerful and true; she could sense Syenne's ability to detect lies.

"When she was a child, my mother escaped a war with wounds that haven't healed over the decades since. Damars were dealing those wounds every day. I wanted Ruarnon to act on their desire to stop them, undeterred by their Council's caution."

"And?"

Linh exhaled nervously, but if Syenne knew when she was holding back...

"And I wouldn't have them sit in Tarlah while governors dealt their people those same wounds, fighting each other for the throne."

Tor gasped, and Linh realised she had just criticised the royal family to one of its most powerful members. Soldiers before her tensed. What had she done?

Syenne's lips twitched. Was that the hint of a smile? Or a trick of the light before she ordered a crossbow to take Linh out?

"As War Leader Syenne, I invite you, Councillor, and your Regent, War Leader Ruarnon, to a Council of War Leaders. My sister and nephews shall come, and I will come as War Leader of my province and my uncles'. As host, Ruarnon may station a hundred guards throughout the city and fifty in the palace, no more. We shall meet tomorrow morning."

Linh bowed her head in Tarlahn style and saw a flash of approval in Syenne's stern gaze before she turned, baring her back to an entire army as she strode calmly towards her horse.

"Leave him!"

Linh turned. Governor Iagl and Companion Armar had followed Ruarnon too. Iagl's order was directed at someone on the wall, where scuffling ceased and a young man's face appeared.

"Aoran!" Armar whispered.

"He upheld the conditions of the War Council by ensuring soldiers did not attack each other during the Council Truce!" Iagl yelled. "Release him!"

Aoran moved, but Armar looked worried.

"He should go to Tarlah," said Tor. "Lady Telena will happily host the man who saved her brother-by-law's child's life. I suspect only a knife in the back awaits him here."

"Iomar wanted him to come home," said Fiona.

Iagl turned to her in surprise; then his eyes lit up. "It is about time. I will have some of my men escort him to my brother."

Armar bowed his head in thanks, then rode to his son.

"You would do that for a man who shot your countryman?" Tor probed.

"I would do that for a friend," Iagl replied firmly.

Tor blinked, then asked, "What is a Council of War Leaders?"

"Before the Zaldeaan Realm was unified, it was a meeting of the kings of the city-states. It is held under the condition of truce, with all armies waiting outside the city. I shall send my men out East Gate, Syenne's armies will take this gate, Kia will wait outside North Gate, and my brother will join me. West Gate will be for your army to hold, and each of us will bring ten bodyguards to the Council."

"Have the army set up camp near West Gate," Tor ordered General Takanis. "Then take charge of the hunt for the remaining damars. Aza will take charge of organising the palace and city guards."

Tor turned back to Ruarnon, worry etched in every line of his face. Ruarnon looked paler, and blood was seeping through the hole in their armour. The bolt head had passed through their shoulder and out their back. The sight made Linh nauseous, and she was grateful when the Tarlahn healer arrived and obscured her view.

"You should take them to the palace," said Iagl.

Linh gaped. Armar had made Iagl sound like the epitome of toxic masculinity, yet he'd just shown concern for his brother's boyfriend and used Ruarnon's correct pronouns. Maybe Iagl was more complicated than anyone guessed...

"There is a North Lander healer at the palace," Iagl continued, "but it will not do for my people to think your Regent is wounded. I suggest you," and he nodded to Michael, "pose as them as you travel through the city. Let them see you healthy and in charge and know that a Council of War Leaders has been called. That will ensure calm for now."

Tor bowed his head, his expression reserved and hard to read. "It would be unwise for soldiers from both our armies to scour the city for damars."

"I leave that to you. I would like to question my men about the rumour that your people sent the damars and find out if it is linked to the gates being burned. If you find any Zaldeaans trying to leave the city, I suggest you arrest them for treason."

There was no mistaking the bitterness or anger in Iagl's tone. He turned and rode away, and Linh didn't relax until the clack of his horses' hooves was out of earshot.

"Nicely done," Michael said to her.

Fiona smiled, and Troy shook his head with a grin as if *he'd* never done anything reckless. Linh rolled her eyes and shook her head back at him, making him smile.

Tor turned to her. "That was the rashest act I have ever seen. Yet, with your conviction and boldness, she approved. I do not know where you four children came from, but you were right for that moment, and I thank you." He bowed his head.

"Tarlah's welcome," Linh said with a smile.

"Syenne is here with two armies," Michael added. "That suggests she won her war with Derlan."

Linh and her friends exchanged broad grins.

"I advise sending for the North Lander healer," Captain Arleath told Companion Tor. "And commandeering a secure house near the palace, with solid doors and windows overlooking the streets, to treat the Regent in."

Tor signalled a messenger, telling them to update General Aza, and sent a second messenger to the palace. Then Michael and Captain Arleath led everyone towards the palace, the healer supervising the guards carrying Ruarnon in a palanquin. There was no mistaking the palace. Its walls rose higher than the two-storey bluestone buildings on either side of it, and it was wider than any other building.

Six guards at the palace gates stared dead ahead, ignoring the Tarlahns. As they walked past, Linh gazed up a grand flight of steps towards high walls decorated with giant battle-axe reliefs. An archway of iron blades framed the entrance, and the lawns beyond were adorned with models of crossbows, catapults, and siege engines.

"Looks welcoming," Troy whispered.

"I'm happy not to go in there, today at least," Linh added.

"I'll be speaking to Companion Armar, the generals, and Zaldeaan Captain Nish about security arrangements before any of us enter," Companion Tor said quietly.

Captain Arleath selected a house ahead and knocked. The door opened a crack.

"Good afternoon," said Arleath, the scholar translating the conversation. "We would like to hire one of your bedrooms."

"My... My children are in them," the woman said hesitantly.

"You may like to send them next door," Arleath suggested. "Our colleague's wound isn't a fit sight for children's eyes."

A pouch jangled as Tor passed it to Arleath. The door opened as the homeowner took the money, admitting Ruarnon's bodyguards, who Linh assumed were searching the house. When Arleath gave the all-clear, Tor gestured everyone else to dismount and guards to take the horses round the back, then led everyone inside.

The Tarlahn healer directed the guards carrying Ruarnon's palanquin, and they sat Ruarnon on a bed indicated by the nervous homeowner, who stepped out. Linh and her friends waited while Lenaris and Tor removed Ruarnon's armour.

"Benevolence, the North Lander Healer, Xa, has arrived," Captain Arleath called.

Xa was short, wearing a fitted green silk gown over her cool bronze skin, and she had black hair and eyes, unlike anyone else Linh had seen since leaving Australia.

Xa studied Ruarnon with interest. "A person was shot outside the walls, trying to stop their army from fighting Governor Syenne's. Is this them?"

Tor frowned, and Fiona replied, "Yes."

"I will heal them," said Xa.

Tor nodded to Ruarnon's guards, and they moved back, letting Xa through. Lenaris and Tor removed Ruarnon's bloodstained tunic. Their wound was small but bleeding steadily. Xa reached out, holding her hands in the air above both sides of the wound. She closed her eyes as if meditating, then took a cloth from the Tarlahn healer's hand and wiped the blood from Ruarnon's torso. There was no wound. Linh stared at the small scar on Ruarnon's chest.

"You have just healed Regent Ruarnon, heir to the throne of Tarlah," said Tor. "You have my deepest thanks and that of all Tarlah." He bowed his head, looking grateful, but he seemed reluctant to take his eyes off a woman who could wield magic while she stood beside the Regent.

Xa smiled at Ruarnon, who blinked, looking groggy. "You will need to rest and to eat well, Benevolence."

Ruarnon looked down at their muscled chest, blinking at the scar, then stared at Xa in wonder. "Did you heal me?"

"If you take the throne of the Zaldeaan Realm, my people will happily call you Prime Ruler," she replied. Then she turned to Linh. "But I am afraid that the archways you seek are beyond my people's knowledge."

Linh's brows rose. How did Xa know who she was? And North Landers didn't... Linh slumped. Xa eyed her sympathetically.

Troy leaned back against a wall, grimacing and shaking his head in silent frustration. Linh's heart sank as she wondered how long they would be stuck in Tarlah.

"May I ask your status in the North Lands?" said Tor.

"The Zaldeaans see me as a healer. My people consider me to be their ambassador, and I speak on their behalf."

Michael frowned, and she wondered if they both suspected Xa spoke with such authority because unbeknown to the Zaldeaans, she was North Lander royalty.

"Thank you for your assistance," Tor said, bowing his head.

"You are welcome," Xa said, and she turned and left.

"How many of them do you think wield magic?" asked Troy when the front door closed behind Xa.

"A few," Michael replied. "Iomar hinted as much."

"Are they pacifists?" Fiona asked.

"That was Urmillian's theory," Tor replied. "That they keep to themselves to avoid conflict with outsiders and are bound by strict laws to use their powers only for defensive or healing purposes. They may be much easier to deal with than the Zaldeaan governors."

CHAPTER 31

The Council of War Leaders

Your attendance would be inappropriate," Tor said, in firmer tones than Ruarnon had ever heard the man use.

"Syenne thinks I'm one of Ruarnon's advisors," Linh objected. "I think she approved of a woman advising Ruarnon, and officially or not; I've done that."

"It may present well to Governors Syenne and Kia," said General Takanis.

"Not if they think Linh and Lenaris are only there for that reason," Michael countered.

"Having young female companions but no male companions may look suspicious," Troy added, "especially when women advisors are rare here. It might look more convincing if all four of us turn up."

Ruarnon suspected the gleam in Troy's eyes meant he was joking, and the twitch in Michael's lips was a smile. A Zaldeaan would probably smack them both and send them away, but while Tarlahns were used to reasoned debate, they were not used to youths being so confident or capable at it.

"Monin would have a fit," said Tor, shaking his head.

"He's not here, and we're not silly," Troy insisted. "We won't say anything at the meeting unless one of you asks us to."

"You'd have to not *do* anything unless asked, either," said Tor. "Have you any idea how historic this day is? There has never been a moment in Tarlahn history like it!"

"Exactly," Fiona said with a smile. "It would be a privilege to witness. The last thing we'd want to do is wreck it for you. And don't forget, we understand Migryan. The Zaldeaans won't expect that."

"That would be a serious advantage," said General Takanis.

"You won't be able to speak," Ruarnon warned, meeting their gazes. They bowed their heads in reply.

Their ability alone was reason enough to bring them. And letting them be privy to the meeting was an excellent way for Ruarnon to judge if they were appropriate companions. If they passed this test, they could stay on as Ruarnon's Companions while they awaited the chance to travel west seeking sorcerers and gateways home.

"Look to Lenaris for guidance," Ruarnon instructed. "You'll be there to observe only."

Ruarnon led the way, entering the circular War Leader Chamber with a tight chest and a stomach full of fireflies. Swords, spears, battle-axes, and arrows around the walls gleamed in the daylight from a tall, narrow glass window. Eight throne-like cushioned chairs stood in a circle in the centre, one for each king of the former city-states. It had been centuries since rulers sat here as equals, but it had worked before, and Ruarnon was determined to make it work again.

"Trust your instincts," Tor said quietly.

Ruarnon nodded mutely. That had worked well with Iomar, but Syenne was something else, and Ruarnon wasn't sure what to make of Iagl. Ruarnon worried that acting their part and trusting their instincts may not be enough for Zaldeaan politics.

Governor Iomar arrived first, in a sapphire blue silk tunic and pants of thin black fur, his straight brown locks held back by a solid silver circlet set with a large sapphire. The absence of armour and innocence of his blue eyes made him look much younger than his twin, though he had Iagl's narrow face. Guards entered around him, in full armour, armed with knives and swords.

Iomar approached Ruarnon and shook hands, smiling, his eyes dark with fatigue. Ruarnon returned his smile, and then Governor Iagl entered, identical, except that he strode confidently, looked better rested, and his darker blue eyes were harder to read, making him appear older. He shook hands formally with Ruarnon and his brother, then stood on Iomar's other side.

Governor Kia arrived next. Light brown hair flowed freely over her shoulders, and her brown eyes were sharp and curious. She stood as tall as Troy, bearing herself confidently in a fitted silk dress of sapphire blue. She greeted Ruarnon and her cousins politely and guardedly, and wore the same blue stone as her cousins in her silver circlet.

Governor Syenne came last. She wore a long dress of pale blue silk, which offset her fierce light blue eyes but didn't soften them, nor did the blonde hair hanging loosely below her shoulders. Her face was pale, her bone structure elegant but firm, and her circlet had a large, light green stone in the middle. She looked everyone sternly in the eye, then asked in flawless Timbalen, "Has anyone business before the Council of War Leaders begins?"

Ruarnon was painfully conscious of not knowing as much of these people or of King Kyura's reign as they should, which reminded them of how this Council would begin if it were in Tarlah.

"I have not had the opportunity to pay my respects," they said. "In Tarlah, where there is a body, one pays one's respects before business is tended to."

Syenne's brows narrowed slightly.

Iagl's tone was defiant as he said, "It is only fitting to honour the last War Leader of the Zaldeaan Realm before the meeting commences."

"As you wish," said Governor Syenne.

Iagl's features narrowed suspiciously as she led them out, her guards walking solemnly beside her, the other governors and their guards following. Ruarnon, their guards, and companions followed in silence, along bluestone passageways and whitewashed walls depicting frescoes of heroes battling mythical creatures.

Ruarnon gazed with interest as Syenne led them down a corridor decorated with frescoes of rivers or waterfalls, animals, and people travelling in boats with predators and prey standing side by side in unreal harmony. They exited the palace on a hilltop, crossing green lawns towards a bluestone building beside a river. A waterfall roared nearby, while sunlight glinted on gold lining the building's roof: a golden half sun, its rays stretching in all directions.

Syenne asked her guards to remain outside and entered the mortuary building alone, the other governors copying. Was that why they hesitated? Because custom had guards wait where they couldn't defend against knifings inside? Ruarnon nodded to Captain Arleath to stay, and the scholar stayed with him, but Tor, Lenaris, and the four youths accompanied them.

They turned down a corridor, then into a stone room with a double marble sarcophagus. On its right was an elaborately carved statue of a woman seated on a throne, a crown of gold set with diamonds and purple stones on her head, her eyes set with sapphires. On the left, a stone man sat on a throne beside her, with sapphire blue eyes and a gold crown upon his head patterned with emeralds, sapphires, and garnets. A round hole in the roof let sunlight shine on King Kyura's resting place and lit the frescoes of feasting, dancing, bright lakes, grassy flower and tree-covered shores, and a large group picnicking on a bank, each scene including the same woman and man, on the whitewashed walls.

Ruarnon studied the inscription but could only make out a few words here and there.

Michael saw them frowning. "Would you like me to read it?"

Ruarnon blinked. "You can *read* Migryan as well as be understood in it?"

"Apparently," Michael replied as he turned to the inscription.

May Her Majesty, the faithful and beloved Queen, wife of King Kyura II, and her child rejoice in the land of the dead. May they feast all day and dance all night with her beloved parents, Narmune and Tiglath. May Highest King Kyura join them there.

Ruarnon stared at the painting of the dark-haired woman and golden-haired man. Their eyes looked alive, and they were both smiling, looking so young. So this was the wife Kyura had been mourning when warmongers abducted Ruarnon's parents and tried to re-ignite the war...

"Queen Lenine died in childbirth, early in my brother's reign," Syenne stated matter-of-factly.

She was eyeing Ruarnon sharply, but they didn't care. She could see this as a battle of wills, but they wanted to understand their once-enemy. Even, strangely, to farewell the man they had never met, who had shared a similar wish for his people.

Michael read on.

May Evis welcome Queen Lenine and her child in the lands where the sun always shines. May she dwell there forever, with her beloved parents, late friends, and family in happiness and peace. May every day be the first day of spring. May she never grow hungry, nor thirsty. May she be robed in the finest clothes, crowned with the finest crowns, and exalted above all queens.

May the scent of fresh flowers dwell ever in her tomb and those who remain in this life never forget her memory, nor her name. In the name of the Mother, Fahria.

"There's an addition: *May her beloved husband King Kyura find her there and may they dwell together forever.* The inscription on the right requests the same for King Kyura."

"May the Ancestors guide them to the land of their people," Ruarnon said, feeling that the prayers described a place both deserved to go to in peace after King Kyura's painful struggles in life.

They felt the governors' eyes on them. The governors' faces were sternly masked. They were determined not to show one jot of emotion in front of Ruarnon. Kyura was their brother or cousin, and it occurred to Ruarnon that his death was barely two weeks past.

"I shall leave you in privacy," they said, but before they could leave the building, Troy called, "Ruarnon, you'd better come and see this one."

Ruarnon stepped into the room left of King Kyura's.

"It says..." Troy began.

Ruarnon's mouth opened as they turned to the statue. It had sapphires in its eyes, a Tarlahn braid hanging over one shoulder, a gold circlet on its head and wore a smile they hadn't seen since their last private conversation with Uncle Omah. The likeness was perfect.

"What does it say?" Ruarnon asked.

"May Regent Omah of Tarlah's spirit return to his kingdom, to the Golden Meeting Hall, to offer up his wisdom for the good of Tarlah throughout the Ages."

Uncle Omah was buried in a royal mortuary building. Not lost on the battlefield or in some anonymous mass grave. His spirit was here, with this beautiful statue decorating his tomb in Zaldeaan style with sensitivity to Tarlahn beliefs. His body was at peace, and the priest could now consecrate the gold bust of his head and bring his spirit home to Aunt Telena and the Golden the Meeting Hall. Uncle Karmarn must have asked this of Kyura for his brother-by-marriage. Kyura had approved. Ruarnon smiled and shed their first peaceful tears since their uncle's death.

It was a while before they dried their eyes, long enough that the governors seemed to think they had gone, as the murmuring from next door became raised voices.

"*Why?*" Governor Kia asked angrily. "We would have helped him!"

"So would *we!*" Governor Iagl retorted.

"Yes, all *men* together!"

Ruarnon shouldn't have left them alone...

"He supported you!" said Governor Iomar, his voice broken. "Do not speak of him like that!"

"He is right," Governor Syenne's calm voice affirmed.

"And now..." Iomar whispered. "What if the Gods don't welcome him? What if he... If he's left roaming the darkness?"

"I do not think that has happened," Syenne replied.

"Then what do you think *has* happened?" Iagl asked aggressively.

"Father will find him," Syenne replied softly. "He was always looking after him."

"If you worry his spirit wanders lost," Iagl said gently, to his brother, Ruarnon assumed, "Perhaps you can ask Ruarnon to lend you one of his priests, and they can call him here or wherever you think he would like."

"He would like to be with her," said Syenne, "and the child." Her voice cracked.

Ruarnon heard something hit something, and Iagl yelled, "It was not supposed to be this way! Aoran watched him so carefully! But he forgot that physicians' herbs, taken in the wrong combination, could be poison... And that bloody general..."

"What do you mean?" Syenne asked firmly.

"The First General blocked letters from reaching him in Tarlah," Iagl replied, all but shouting. "He didn't learn how serious the damar attacks were or that the Timbalens were coming... If Kyura hadn't killed that piece of shit first..."

Ruarnon wondered, as they heard several quiet gasps, how it had never occurred to them how deeply upsetting it would be to Kyura's family not only to have lost him but to know that he took his own life. The guilt they may feel at not having prevented it, and the regret that they hadn't saved him.

"Companion Pamoran tried to warn him the Timbalens were coming," Iagl added, "but the generals kept it from him!"

"Which generals?" Syenne asked quietly.

"I've already killed the other one!" Iagl replied heatedly. "Do you think I would let him live after the waste they caused? After what Iomar and Kia's people suffered because those fools wouldn't come home?"

"Kyura would not have wanted those who died on the battlefield to have died in vain," Syenne replied.

"So he sacrificed more and accomplished nothing!" Iagl snapped. "I went to see him. Iomar told me he had come to Kia's province, and we both went to visit, and by the time we reached him..."

There was a long silence, and Ruarnon wondered whether they should wait outside.

"This is the legacy of the Warrior Culture," Syenne said finally. "It killed our father and our brother."

"Then let us end it," Iomar said softly. "Let us honour their wishes."

"That's what *they* want!" Kia said, and Ruarnon sighed. They would have to talk to her.

They squared their shoulders, reminding themself that this was a dead man's grieving family and trying to keep their cool as their father would have. Ruarnon stepped out of their uncle's tomb and across to King Kyura's.

"You did this on purpose!" Kia accused as they stepped into sight.

"That man died trying to achieve something we are about to contemplate. Do you think it appropriate to ignore him?" Ruarnon asked firmly.

Kia and Iagl's faces were flushed with anger, but there was also a terrible sadness in Iagl's eyes. Iomar wept silently. Syenne looked as powerful as ever, though there was a terrible sadness in her eyes too.

"The efforts of those who came before us need to be remembered and understood before we make our own," Ruarnon continued. "Otherwise mistakes of the past are repeated, and foreseeable problems are not addressed."

"Is all you would have us do sit around and *talk*?" Kia asked.

"That suggestion and this young man have more wisdom than most War Leaders," said Syenne. "You know why Father made us governors. I resented him being sacrificed for a peace that benefits Tarlahns when we did not require it, but to ignore our brother's struggle is to dishonour his memory. And with him gone, our father's ideas live or die with us."

"And with us," Iagl insisted. "I still want to know how my father died, and I will never trust you. But if you would offer Iomar and I a truce, I would make it a formal peace."

Ruarnon tried to set aside their relief that Derlan was dead and make the most of the opportunity before them.

"I would have more than that," they asserted. "In Tarlah, the king's most sacred duty is to protect their people. Any man, woman, or midlun who would take their army to war for personal reasons is, by definition, a traitor. I would have you all sign an agreement to respect each other's positions as governors."

Kia stared. Syenne eyed Ruarnon critically. Iagl sighed, and Iomar smiled through his tears.

"You would have us as governors under you?" Syenne asked.

"Your people tried killing our leaders and ruling with beatings and beheadings. An angry mob massacred them. That is not how *I* would do things. I would have you rule your provinces, and my soldiers and yours patrol the Zaldeaan Realm's cities side by side. You lack guards, farmers, labourers, and artisans. I would call on volunteers from Tarlah to train your women in farming and craftsmanship and have our people work together. I would unite the Zaldeaan Realm and provide security, stability, and peace for its people as well as my own."

"You want what Uncle Kyomi wanted," Iomar said quietly. "I want it too."

"I will sign your agreement," said Iagl.

Ruarnon was speechless. Why would Iagl agree so quickly? Ruarnon's army might be four times the size of the combined Zaldeaan provincial armies. It would take genius levels of ambush for governors to have a hope of defeating Ruarnon in battle, and while that and Ruarnon's goodwill may be enough for Iomar, Ruarnon suspected Iagl's motives differed. Did Iagl see Ruarnon's rule in the Zaldeaan army's absence as a reprieve in the Succession War? As time to recover from his father's and cousin's deaths before fighting Syenne for the throne?

"Father's wishes and Kyura's said nothing about surrender," Kia objected. "How do we know they are worthy of our brother's throne?"

"Their soldiers' every instinct was to attack mine in the city," said Iagl. "Yet their word kept every person back."

"The Tarlahn army obeys their orders whether it agrees with them or not," said Syenne. "They are a great War Leader, but they are young."

"From what I understand, people question your ability to govern because you are a woman," said Ruarnon. "Yet that does not seem to have stopped you. Nor do I intend to let my age stand in my way."

Syenne's lips curled upwards in a hint of a smile, though her eyes shone fiercely. "Let us return to the Hall of the War Leaders and discuss this agreement of yours."

They were angry at King Kyura's death, had been divided into factions, and there was anger both ways, while Governor Kia was suspicious of Ruarnon. Only Governors Iomar and Iagl appeared to trust Ruarnon, they knew not how far, but Ruarnon hoped these things could be overcome. They led the governors back to the round hall, where they took their seats, each person's bodyguards standing an equal distance behind them.

"Before we can agree, points of contention must be dealt with," said Iagl. "I want the truth of Father's death."

"Derlan laid siege to Rindesh," Syenne reported calmly. "He gave me the opportunity to surrender before making a serious attempt to take my city by force. I replied by asking if he killed my father. His face did not lie as well as his tongue, as both our armies witnessed. One of his soldiers cut his throat. I pardoned the murderer as vengeance for the king, and his army swore their loyalty to me."

Iomar looked forlorn. Iagl's fists clenched, his knuckles going white, and he stared at the floor, breathing heavily. Ruarnon couldn't tell whether he was angry or violently upset.

Iomar sighed. "Father always underestimated me. He thought Iagl was the strong one. He probably thought two men enough to throw me down the stairs, but he was wrong."

Iagl jerked, turning pain-filled eyes to his twin. His fist struck stone again, drawing blood. He didn't seem to notice. "You are not sorry he is dead?"

Iomar shook his head. "If I were sorry about anything, it would be his death starting a blood feud between you and Syenne. I know it is not easy for you to accept, but he deserved what he got. He killed our uncle, and I believe he tried to kill me. My death would have cleared the way for you to be his heir once he obtained the throne."

Iagl's eyes blazed with anger. He glared at the floor, his features warped by wrath and pain. Ruarnon stared at Iomar. His *father* had tried to kill him? And he accepted it? He was right; he was a *lot* stronger than his father thought.

"Father was what his generation made him," Iomar said. "But Uncle Kyomi allowed me to be something different. Is his way something the rest of you would choose?"

"Do you think I can, brother?" Iagl asked.

"I do not doubt it," Iomar replied with a smile, and for the first time, Ruarnon saw Iagl smile.

Then Iomar turned to Kia. "Kyura said you were indisposed soon after the attempt on my life. I was worried."

Kia sighed. "I saw the Second General ordering your soldiers to march to war on Tarlah. He didn't recognise me, but he assumed I was a spy. I was wounded escaping his soldiers."

Ruarnon tensed, as Syenne explained, "Kyura had the Second General executed."

Kia turned sternly to Ruarnon. "I do not like surrendering without a fight."

"I could challenge you to a duel," Ruarnon offered.

Kia's eyes widened.

"I presume the armour you wore yesterday was not decoration?" they added.

She flushed, and Iagl chuckled, Iomar smiling.

She wasn't entirely won over, but instinct told Ruarnon to stand firm, so they added, "Do we need to find a place to duel, or will you sign?"

Kia's eyes flashed, but Ruarnon would have her jump one way or the other.

"I will sign," she replied with dignity.

"Then we need a document worthy of our signatures," said Syenne.

Ruarnon had a scholar bring out the Zaldeaan law code and Governor's oaths, and they spent hours drawing up something Linh called a 'constitution' for the Zaldeaan Realm, outlining rights and responsibilities of the governors, ordinary subjects, and legal reforms. It involved arguments, Iagl storming out to be calmed by Iomar, Kia losing her temper and Syenne threatening to draft the constitution without her, and Ruarnon having to battle Syenne's stern gaze on many points. Finally, it was drawn up, and to Ruarnon's astonishment, Syenne smiled at them approvingly. Had she been testing them?

"Your people hold their breath," Ruarnon said. "I would have you sign these documents publicly and the agreement read out, so they know how the Zaldeaan Realm shall be governed."

"Benevolence," Tor objected, "you have no speech to address the people with."

"Get the scroll out of my satchel," Iomar ordered one of his servants. "I brought a copy of the speech Uncle Kyomi made when he first announced the Peace. I think you should read it. And add words of your own."

Ruarnon nodded, and they and Tor read and added to the speech, as everyone took a very late lunch. Then Ruarnon asked Syenne quietly, "What will your people think of Tarlahn rule?"

"We always believed the Timbalens were the real power," she replied. "But half the Zaldeaan Realm has witnessed your soldiers' bravery against damars. I have seen it myself. As a youthful ruler who invaded to protect their militarily superior enemies from monsters, you are a legend made flesh. And as it is common knowledge here that Tarlahn male-presenting people are midluns, anyway,"—the curve of her lip acted like a wink—"and you ruling means Iagl and I aren't having our people kill each other to obtain the throne, I would say that for now, you are a desirable Zaldeaan ruler."

Her bluntness surprised Ruarnon, but not her words.

"What happens, should the army return?" Ruarnon asked.

Syenne eyed them appraisingly. "Kyura named me heir. Iagl would prefer to forget, but months or even years under Tarlahn rule may cool his blood enough for him to behave when the time comes. I dislike his temper, but his heart is in the right place, and I see much of Kyura in Iomar. I will not wound Iomar by feuding with Iagl if I can help it."

Should the army return and back a Zaldeaan king, Ruarnon suspected Syenne would be highly capable.

"The court is another matter. They may underestimate you and do as they please. Or charm you, only to stab you in the back. Don't let them get away with anything and assert yourself from the outset. I have executed the most dangerous members, but it's likely that some who opposed peace and who oppose Tarlah are still at large. Most of my uncle's associates have escaped and disappeared. If they resurface, they will likely cause trouble.

"I will continue investigating the plot to manipulate my brother to war and see if I can learn more of the plot to murder my father. But in the meantime, and as a Tarlahn, you need to be on guard against assassination."

Ruarnon's chest tightened. Someone had tried to kill them before they did anything to provoke Zaldeaans. Likely, many would attempt it now. That was frightening, but having a governor who could have led a war against them, informing and helping them prepare to meet these threats, was dizzying.

"Have your spies heard anything of a blonde man and a brunette woman hiding in the palace?" Ruarnon seized the opportunity to ask Syenne in private.

Syenne's brows furrowed. "Were the people you speak of smuggled out of the palace during the night, before the battle on the Red Desert?"

Ruarnon nodded.

"One of my spies saw them leaving, but I assumed they were illegal Zaldeaan slaves and stopped investigating when I was unable to identify them."

Ruarnon bit their lip. They suspected Syenne had the best intelligence in the palace. It may take widespread circulation of their parents' portraits throughout the Zaldeaan Realm to trace them now. They gestured to a messenger and gave orders to hire artists.

Syenne rose. "You present differently to Kyura and Iomar, but you appear to be kindred spirits. I will support you, but you cannot sit on my throne forever."

She stood, and Ruarnon's mouth fell open at the first warmth they had seen in her features. The flash in her eyes was fierce yet somehow teasing. It seemed she would be a solid ally to Ruarnon's rule, but only so long as it suited her. Ruarnon found themself admiring her, respecting her, and wary of her.

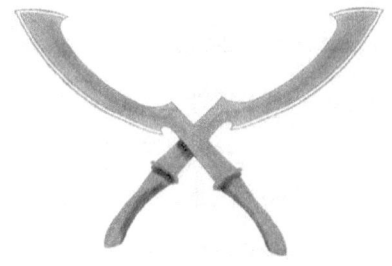

CHAPTER 32

The New Regent, the New Peace, the New Tarlah

L
ate that afternoon, Ruarnon led their companions, the governors, and guards to the steps before the plaza in front of the Zaldeaan palace. They wore plate armour under their tunic and black fur pants like Iomar and Iagl's, at Tor and Syenne's suggestion.

Heralds rang bells in the city streets, window shutters opened, women peered through doors, and children peaked around their woollen skirts. Ruarnon's soldiers stationed around the plaza remained still, and gradually the elders, women, and children crept past them.

The Zaldeaans wore homespun clothes; the elderly men wore their hair cut short, while the women's was worn long and out, in mourning for their king. Women gripped children's hands, and older men bit their lips. Fear and vulnerability in the absence of their army overshadowed the crowd. It was time to reassure them.

Ruarnon stepped forwards, and their scholar translated, the heralds repeating their words. "As you know, just over two weeks ago, Tarlah and this realm were at war. An ill-advised war, a blight on King Kyomi's Peace. But now the fourth Tarlahn-Zaldeaan war has ended. So too, is the War of King Kyura's Succession. My army, Governors Kia's, Iomar's, and Iagl's armies have slain most of the foul creatures that plagued you, and their remnants shall soon be destroyed.

"Behind me are the surviving governors of the Zaldeaan Realm. They are here to sign an agreement to end hostilities between them and swear to govern their provinces in accordance with the new laws I have made. You shall be informed of the laws in due course. For now, the governors have an agreement to sign."

Some eyes in the crowd scanned the gold ornaments in Ruarnon's braid, and those in the front row noted the kohl around their eyes and the spirals signalling that they were midlun. Some seemed curious, a few older men scowled, but mostly, the crowd seemed to hold its breath in anticipation. Governor Iomar came first, smiling, and signed his name with a flourish. The crowd clapped, fear in many eyes reducing. Governor Iagl followed to louder applause, then Kia and last of all Syenne, at which point the crowd relaxed and clapped with hopeful looks.

The people before Ruarnon were parting around a procession led by a tall, dark-haired woman. She wore ceremonial armour of silver and gold, and men in similarly rich, ornamental armour escorted her, carrying daggers and swords with jewelled hilts. The woman's guards stopped at the edge of the steps, and she ascended alone, eyeing them confidently.

"Heir Ruarnon, the light of Fahria has gone out," she announced in a carrying voice. "The people fear that Fahria's protection has left us, but you have restored it by slaying damars and ending the Succession War. Will you restore the light of Fahria?"

Fahria, Patron Goddess of Zaldeaa City, Mother Goddess of the Zaldeaans. Which made lighting her torch an act of kingship, as the High Priestess well knew she was offering... To lure Ruarnon to their assassination or to legitimise the rule of the most powerful person in the Zaldeaan Realm?

Ruarnon shot a sideways glance to Tor and Aza. Tor inclined his head slightly, while Aza scanned the crowd for potential threats. Killing Ruarnon now, when their entire army was camped outside a city gate controlled by Tarlahn soldiers, would be foolish. But Kyura hadn't responded to the damars based on what he thought, he'd been overwhelmed by how he felt. As may any Zaldeaan standing in the crowd before Ruarnon. But Ruarnon could not turn down a chance to legitimise their rule in the eyes of the Zaldeaan people.

"I shall," they replied to the High Priestess.

Noise rang in their ears. It was applause.

"Take what guards you wish," the High Priestess instructed. "All who defend her city are welcome in Fahria's Temple."

Tor met her gaze and Ruarnon wondered if they were agreeing that a large retinue of guards through the crowd would be prudent. Even more prudent may be travelling to the temple tonight, then lighting the fire after dark, after everyone had returned to their homes. But Zaldeaans had always told themselves Tarlahns were cowards. Ruarnon needed to show them they were wrong, especially to discourage the dissent that had brewed under Kyura's rule.

Tor chose bodyguards and additional archers. Then Ruarnon and their party followed the High Priestess into the applauding crowd. Ruarnon's heartbeat sped up as they walked past cheering women, children, and smiling older men. So many Zaldeaan faces. So close.

Ruarnon's bodyguards circled them, standing in pairs between Ruarnon and the crowd, keeping the crowd back. Ruarnon's instincts forced them to scan the huge sea of faces for danger, instead of gazing vaguely above the crowd. It made their insides squirm, but a quick scan of faces showed that most nearby ones were smiling, and most postures were relaxed.

On Ruarnon's right, a young woman and her small children smiled. The elderly couple behind the young family smiled nervously, while a greybeard behind them smirked.

The faces in the front row seemed happiest. Those further back were uncertain, or disapproving, but no one seemed to pose a threat. Until one of the priestess' guards collapsed.

Ruarnon heard a whizz. Arleath raised his shield and caught an arrow in it. Two guards raised shields as Lenaris raised her bow and loosed arrows. Guards caught arrows on their shields. Lenaris' arrows struck two men on a balcony opposite, who fell.

Ruarnon's heart pounded against their chest as they halted. Several onlookers cried out, pointing at the priestess' fallen guard. One of Ruarnon's guards cursed and tore her tunic to bandage her own arm, but no one else seemed harmed. The other bodyguards surveyed families either side of them, who backed up, mothers shielding young children's eyes from the body.

The priestess knelt, saying a prayer over her fallen guard, and two women came forward to carry the man's body away. The High Priestess turned to meet Ruarnon's gaze, her eyes wide with worry.

Ruarnon took a steadying breath. "I assume those arrows were meant for me," they said with forced calm.

She bowed her head.

"They are not the first, and I doubt they will be the last," Ruarnon added, fingering their sword hilt as they scanned nervous crowds backing up on both sides, and cheering people ahead, who seemed oblivious to the murder.

"I suggest we walk swiftly," the High Priestess replied. "You are too exposed here."

Ruarnon's guards moved closer, their shields forming a mobile circle, though none held their shields overhead. Ruarnon supposed that would have impaired the guards' vision and looked weak to the Zaldeaans.

The close press of bodies made Ruarnon's muscles tense. They walked faster, raising a hand to smiling members of the crowd in false confidence to mask their nerves, ignoring the churning of their stomach until finally, a dark, blue stone building like a mountain with a flat peak, rose high above the rooftops before them.

Ruarnon followed the High Priestess up an external flight of steps cut into the temple's sloping side, relaxing slightly as long steps brought them up out of the crowd. They climbed swiftly to a height several floors above street level. Guards flanked doors ahead, bearing ceremonial weapons. Ruarnon hesitated, realising that departing the threat of murderers hiding in the crowd behind may make them vulnerable to assassins indoors. But none of the temple guards stood with the alertness of Ruarnon's bodyguards, and their ceremonial weapons had dull blades.

Ruarnon crossed a floor of polished stone, and the temple guards eyed them curiously, some smiling. None seemed a threat, at least not today. Then Ruarnon followed the High Priestess up a spiral stone staircase with daylight shining down it.

"You are young," the Priestess said, "but you have the strength to unite our Realm. The War God has abandoned our men."

"And what of your women?"

The High Priestess smiled. "My people have not the wisdom of Tarlah. They will tolerate a midlun rather than suffer a female king. The Goddess cares not for Tarlahns nor Zaldeaans; she cares for the safety and security of her children. Your views are much the same, are they not?"

How did she know? Did priestesses have spies, as well as kings? She smiled. Then they stepped into daylight and cool air, on a platform of burned stone, the highest point in the city, far above the palace and slanted rooftops of other buildings. Another priestess passed a burning torch to the High Priestess, who gave it to Ruarnon.

"Throw it in the centre of the burned space."

Wondering if it was a clever trick to kill them and studying her knowing smile, Ruarnon threw the torch. Flames soared before them, a wave of heat warming them. Cheers and shouts rose from streets below as a large section of temple top burned, and Ruarnon stepped back from its heat.

"You are now officially Protector of Zaldeaa City," the High Priestess announced. "But you would be ruler, would you not?"

Ruarnon sighed. Tor had warned them the Zaldeaans might see them claiming regency instead of the crown as a half-measure, an invitation for opposition. They didn't want to provoke the Zaldeaans so soon after King Kyura's death by claiming the crown, but the people needed a *ruler*.

"I will if it ensures a Second Peace."

"Then you meet the conditions Highest King Kyura set before he went to war," said Syenne, stepping onto the roof behind them, with her retinue of guards and a servant carrying a box before her.

Ruarnon's mouth dropped open when the High Priestess removed a golden helm glittering with diamonds from the box, the Zaldeaan crown.

"Will you receive it from me and, by extension, from the Goddess Fahria?" the High Priestess asked.

"Do you think the Ancestors would mind?" Ruarnon asked Tor, and the High Priestess laughed.

"No, Ruarnon," Tor replied, "I do not think they would, knowing what this achieves for their descendants."

"I would be honoured," Ruarnon said, and the priestess inclined her head slightly, her face serious again.

They descended many steps, stopping above hundreds of Zaldeaans packed into the plaza, who watched Ruarnon expectantly.

"It is tradition for our kings to swear to lead by the sword. But I believe you wish to change that?"

"I can swear to rule by the new Laws of the Zaldeaan Realm."

"And their purpose is to ensure the safety of the Goddess' children?"

"It is, but I should like to add commitments I made to my Tarlahn subjects."

"That is well. Say your vows to the crowd."

Ruarnon turned, filled their lungs with air and projected their voice carefully. "I, Ruarnon, child of Urmillian, swear to govern the Zaldeaan Realm by the new Laws of the Zaldeaan Realm and to lead its people by example, in peace and war, to the best of my ability. By the Ancestors and the Goddess Fahria, I so swear."

The High Priestess placed the crown upon their head. Ruarnon scanned the crowd, nervous of more assassins' arrows. Tarlahn guards restrained and hauled cursing Zaldeaan men away at several points in the crowd. But many Zaldeaans were smiling. The people didn't cheer. Cheering a Tarlahn ruler probably felt unnatural to them, but so many smiled up at Ruarnon. It reminded them that since the Zaldeaan army had departed to invade Tarlah, the Zaldeaan people had spent nine days living in fear of damars rampaging across their kingdom, their king had died, Regent Derlan had been killed, Regent Karmarn had disappeared at sea, and to cap it all off, Captain Nish, whom Companion Armar thought in charge of the city, had vanished. These may have been the two most uncertain weeks in the Zaldeaan Realm's history. Ruarnon's coronation marked a formal, if only partial, end.

"A king has returned!" a man yelled.

"Long live the king!" the crowd chanted.

"A child of Fahria has been chosen!" another yelled.

"Long live the king!"

"A warrior shall lead us!" yelled a third.

"Long live the king!" they all chanted.

Ruarnon smiled. 'King,' not 'Ruler.'

"'King' is kind of catchy," Troy whispered.

"And they seem happy you're not offended by it," Michael added. "Calling you 'Ruler' might have been a little more change than they could handle just now."

Ruarnon's smile broadened. "With the amount of change I mean to introduce here, I will need to be *very* patient. Here's an opportunity to start."

There was a pause, just long enough for Ruarnon to appreciate that while they ticked two undesirable boxes of Zaldeaan kingship, they also ticked *all* the most desirable boxes... And now they were *ruler* of the Zaldeaan Realm. It made them dizzy, yet they couldn't stop smiling. Many faces smiled up at them still, though some Zaldeaans watched resentfully from doorways, having ignored the summons. Those before Ruarnon were happiest to have a king, whomever they were. Ruarnon would have to win over the rest.

"I am Arogar," a voice called, "speaker for the people. What says the king?"

"I say the words of another," Ruarnon replied, "and my words also. In our day, we carry lists of crimes the enemy has committed against us, of all we have lost to them. We speak of history, of victorious ancestors and traditions. So did those in the war before this and the war before that. Yet we see the death, poverty, suffering, and loss that war brings. We see that retribution does not undo victims' pain, that plunder does not compensate for poverty past, that victory cannot raise the dead.

"In these times, we face a choice. Shall we hold on to the list of wrongs, nursing the hatreds and prejudices that fuel the fires of war, damming our children and our children's children to the loss, suffering, and poverty we have endured, or shall we have the strength to bear the past, and seek a different solution to the greatest goal of our Ancestors: Peace?

"Peace is not merely the absence of war, it is the absence of hatred, anger, resentment, bitterness, and all that disturbs the spirit. If you want peace, let go of your hate, mourn your dead, respect their sacrifice, but remember that the enemy mourns too. Remember that for all the lies commanders tell their soldiers, all commoners are commoners alike, generals, generals' alike, and soldiers, soldiers' alike. Zaldeaan or Tarlah, it makes no difference. There is no claim you can make of your enemy that they cannot make of you, and until you accept this, until you untangle yourself from the deception of your anger, until you see how alike you are, you will never know peace."

Ruarnon concluded with their own words. "I am sure many of you lost loved ones in this war. I lost my uncle and Regent. But I ask you not to respond to your loss with anger. I ask you to allow yourselves to grieve. I ask that those who died in battle with Tarlah and the siege that followed, and any who died in the War of King Kyura's Succession be the last.

"I did not claim Lordship of this Realm to rob it, oppress it, or to take revenge. I took this Realm because I alone had a united army that could drive out the damars, end the War of King Kyura's Succession and restore security, as well as ensure a second Peace with Tarlah.

"Under me, your governors shall govern the Zaldeaan Realm. Alongside Tarlahns, your people will patrol the streets as guards and enforce the new Laws of the Zaldeaan Realm. Tarlahns and Zaldeaans are now both my subjects; both my people and I would see you work together to restore security, ensure your crops are planted, and restore trade between the two kingdoms. What say you?"

"Long live the king! Long live the king! Long live the king!"

A few shouted it, but much of the crowd at least murmured it, over and over. Ruarnon realised they were witnessing joy at the end of the terror and uncertainty of the damarian plague and the Succession War. The Zaldeaans welcomed them as ruler for the same reason as the High Priestess of Fahria: because they brought stability when no Zaldeaan had. It appeared that went a long way towards compensating for the fact they were Tarlahn and a midlun, for now.

The chanting and murmurs gradually faded, and Ruarnon dismissed the Zaldeaans with a two-armed salute. Tarlahn soldiers shifted uneasily, and Zaldeaans stared. But everyone seemed to understand. Tarlahn guards smiled and took up the salute. Some Zaldeaans took it up, and others copied, in ignorance, smiling enthusiasm of the moment, or open-mouthed at its meaning: *Tarlah and the Zaldeaan Realm stand.*

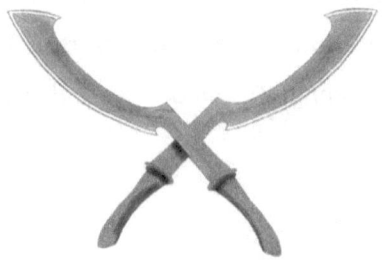

I n the days that followed, Ruarnon watched Tarlahn and
Zaldeaan guards patrol the streets of Zaldeaa City and
train together, suspiciously, resentfully, or
competitively. Fights broke out over who had burned the city
gates, and names were named, but Ruarnon wasn't convinced
of the guilt of anyone. They wondered if Governor Derlan had
sent men to cause trouble for their army before he died, but
accepted that they would probably never know.

Companion Armar informed them that Captain Nish had
left to pursue the Zaldeaan army before they arrived. Nish's
son had joined the army with Ruarnon's cousin Coroth, and
Nish sought them at sea. Ruarnon was uneasy about sending
an entire ship of elite soldiers in pursuit of their parents, uncle,
and cousin in the west so early in their occupation of the
Zaldeaan Realm, especially when labour was so scarce. Every
spare set of hands was needed to plant enough crops for the
Realm to feed itself in the year to come.

Ruarnon offered a generous reward to anyone with information about three 'distinguished visitors' to the Zaldeaan palace. They circulated artists' sketches of their parents far and wide. Still, the testimony of their parents being smuggled out in the dead of night remained the only reliable evidence, until they received a letter from Governor Iagl.

To Their Benevolence, Ruarnon of Tarlah and the Zaldeaan Realm,

I have received reports of the comings and goings of a possible westerner from my port city. He arrived in Edesinia eight weeks ago on a small, strange ship, posing as a North Lander. He left on foot and returned with two ill persons, a dark-haired woman and a blonde man. Then he went again and returned two weeks later with another sick man, who was dark-haired, at which point he departed, and the North Landers say he rounded their coast.

I could not trace his comings and goings outside Edesinia nor identify his captives. He was very wealthy, paying for port taxes and provisions with silver, though our harbour records do not mention him conducting any business. He spoke our language but required directions to Zaldeaa City.

We have finished hunting damars here, and my wife and I would like to invite you and your companions to visit at your earliest convenience,

Yours,

Governor Iagl

A week after their coronation, Ruarnon summoned their Royal Council, Lenaris and their four guests to the Zaldeaan Hall of Writing, where a table was set up between writing desks. Their advisors had serious reservations about Ruarnon taking Linh, Michael, Fiona, and Troy on as Companions, but Ruarnon already had older, experienced advisors to discuss policy with, and they needed friends their age. They wanted people who thought as freely and boldly as they did and who challenged their thinking and were good company, and they found all of those things in their Australian guests.

The Council seemed more accepting of Lenaris as official King's Companion. Her upbringing and training as Pamoran's daughter, and Takanis' protégé made her an appropriate candidate for a Companion.

At Ruarnon's request, Michael read Iagl's letter aloud to the Council.

"Your Benevolence trusts Iagl?" Monin asked suspiciously.

"I do. The timing fits for my parents and Companion Pamoran being the people he refers to."

All Ruarnon felt was relief. Part of them had feared there was no trace of their parents because they had been murdered after the siege. But where had Urmillian and Corina sailed to? If their captor was neither North Lander nor Zaldeaan, surely he was from the Far West, like the damarian ships? But what on earth would Narz want with Ruarnon's parents or Pamoran?

Tor ordered servants to bring the letters from the late Spymaster's chamber that Armar had mentioned in Tarlah. Scholars gave a Migryan translation to Ruarnon's scholar, who translated it into Timbalen as he read.

Dear Excellency,

My name is Narz, and I believe we have a common interest in extending the might of the Zaldeaan Realm and subduing Tarlah. I share your regret that it was not done sooner and that the former king's Peace was so popular.

I believe there is a way Tarlah can be taken without violating the peace. Surely, despite its weakness, the outrage of capturing the Tarlahn King and Queen would provoke the Tarlahns to war? And once Tarlah declared war, our king would desire to defend the honour of our Realm and extend his peace by force?

There is risk involved: the deaths of the Tarlahn king and queen at the hands of those too eager for war may provoke Tarlahns into berserker fury. But you are most welcome to send the king and queen to my country estate by the sea. They will be safe here.

Yours in might,

Narz

"There is no such man in the Zaldeaan Realm?" Tor asked.

Armar shook his head. "There is no one by that name, and there are no private estates on the coast. Grand residences are built behind forests to conceal them from pirates."

"What does the second letter say?" Ruarnon demanded.

Dear Excellency,

It was most unfortunate that your efforts did not work, but I am delighted to hear that we are at war anyway. However, with their allies out of contact and possibly unable to help, I think that more Tarlahn leaders being captured ought to keep the Tarlahns angry enough to fight us until we rout them and earn true glory. Any such persons could keep their king and queen company here.

Please accept this modest gift for your troubles in improving the greatness of our realm,

Yours in might,

Narz

Everyone sat in silence. Narz's excuse for taking Pamoran was nonsense. But taking Pamoran served no interest to warmongers. And Narz's interest in Tarlahn leaders was too broad and ill-timed to be warmongering.

"Is that why they attacked us in the chariots during the siege?" asked Troy. "Why they tried to seize me, mistaking me for Ruarnon?"

"It is folly," said Monin. "What was the purpose of taking more of our leaders? Of what interest could our king and queen, Pamoran, or Your Benevolence be to Narz?"

"His Greatness, Emperor Yarath is interested in establishing trade with the lands of the Far West," said Commander Imphin. "Perhaps this Narz, a western sorcerer-king, has ambitions here in the east? Normally hostages are taken for ransom, but people captured alive also offer information, and kings and queens know a lot more than the average man or woman."

"What information could they possibly have that he would go through such trouble to obtain?" Monin asked.

"He didn't go to trouble," Linh objected. "He tricked the Spymaster into capturing Ruarnon's parents and Pamoran. All Narz had to do was send his man here in a ship and have him contact the Spymaster, then reward the Spymaster with the silver Iagl's letter mentioned."

"Your king and queen know about the Elite Guard," said Commander Imphin, "whose abilities are occasionally taken for magic."

"But there's been no contact with the Far West for centuries," Michael objected. "How did Narz know that the Timbalen Empire or its ally Tarlah or the Zaldeaan Realm exist? How did he know enough about any of them to have any interest in them? How did he know enough about the Warrior's Creed to use it in his letters? He must have had contact with the Zaldeaan Realm before he sent his man east or wrote those letters."

"And yet the letters and the man are the only contacts we know of," Tor added.

"That is more than I can explain," said Imphin.

They discussed Narz for some time, assuming he was the sorcerer who created the damars, who convincingly posed as a Zaldeaan warmonger, who held Ruarnon's parents and Pamoran prisoner, possibly to obtain information they couldn't identify, but with so little information, Narz remained more than they could explain.

Governor Kia's and Ruarnon's investigative ships returned after sailing two weeks west of the Zaldeaan Realm, leaving the Zaldeaan fleet sailing west. With thousands of Zaldeaans missing, Ruarnon asked Aunt Telena to encourage Tarlahn farmers' grown children who could be spared, labourers seeking work, and adventurous crafts people to move to the Zaldeaan Realm to address shortages. Tarlahn commoners arrived and began teaching Zaldeaan women farming and crafts and helping them. Fights broke out with Zaldeaans, but General Aza stationed guards so well that they contained fights before they escalated to skirmishes.

Monin returned to Tarlah to continue acting as regent, and Ruarnon ruled both kingdoms from the Zaldeaan Realm. As the Zaldeaans accepted that their army was lost, Ruarnon experienced multiple assassination attempts. They escaped with the aid of their bodyguards, Lenaris, and the well-trained servants Governor Syenne loaned them. Investigations identified and heavily implicated three high officials.

"Have them killed tonight," General Aza advised from across the Council's meeting table.

The idea made the hair on the back of Ruarnon's neck stand up. But General Takanis nodded in agreement. "Kyura hesitated to spill traitors' blood when he suspected his father's murder, and it may have contributed significantly to his fall."

"As a Tarlahn ruler, a midlun ruler, and Kyura's successor," said Tor, "I do not think you can afford to hesitate where Kyura hesitated."

"Tarlahn and Zaldeaan law agrees," said Companion Noma, "their lives are forfeit."

Lenaris inclined her head. She would appreciate Ruarnon's hesitancy and their reasons for it better than anyone, but she to was unwavering in what she thought had to be done.

Ruarnon turned to their Australian friends.

"Australia doesn't have the death penalty, mate," Troy replied. "It's a bit rough if you kill someone, then later find evidence proving they didn't commit the crime you killed them for."

"I don't think any of us doubts their guilt," said Tor.

"Even I do not doubt it," said Ruarnon. "Their expressions as charges were read, the lies they tried to tell were clear to me. But three of them have sons who may hate me for executing them. Sons who may lead rebellions, like my grandfather did."

"Hire them," said Michael. "Give them jobs where they're not close enough to kill you, but close enough to get to know you. Let them see who their fathers tried to have killed and judge who's the villain for themselves."

The idea of having people killed in cold blood made Ruarnon's stomach churn. But executing those men would be doing to them as they tried to do unto Ruarnon. It would show no less respect, no less decency.

"I do not think half the high officials respect you yet," cautioned General Aza. "I suspect many wonder if they can push you as far as the ones Syenne executed pushed Kyura. You must show them where your lines are drawn. What you will and will not tolerate. That may be the only thing some of them respect."

Ruarnon shook their head in disgust. Try to treat Zaldeaans with decency, teach the women how to farm so they could feed the population while many men were abducted, and those stuck-up louts might only respect Ruarnon for killing some of their colleagues in cold blood? Ruarnon was beginning to like ordinary Zaldeaans, but they resented the high officials as much as ever, and working with the men only gave Ruarnon more reasons to dislike them. But they could not afford to let Zaldeaan officials think they would allow anyone to manipulate them as officials had manipulated Kyura.

"Summon the executioner," Ruarnon ordered. "I want the guilty officials executed in private, their bodies washed and returned to their families. Have a herald announce the evidence against them, the sentence, and that it has been carried out when it is done. And double all guards around the city before the announcement is made."

Ruarnon spent the rest of the afternoon feeling tense. One family greeted the corpse of its head with concern, but only until its sons were offered positions in Ruarnon's palace and the family's livelihood was assured.

One widow rejected her husband's body. "A man who hires assassins to kill a youth is no husband of mine. Bury him in a common grave, like the common criminal he is."

When word of her speech reached the second family and the second high official's body was sent back to the criminal burial ground. Soon after, Ruarnon's Spymaster reported to the Royal Council, "We have received reports of widespread gossip claiming that the executed high officials were cowards for trying to have the king killed by assassins. It appears to be women spreading the gossip."

The reaction to the gossip about Zaldeaan men soon became clear when ranking men asked if they could duel Ruarnon, the duels ending at first blood. Ruarnon couldn't rely on brute strength to win, but they had the skill to outlast and disarm. And they began to win reluctant Zaldeaan men over just as they had earned Tarlahn soldiers' respect by training with them before the war.

Ruarnon didn't think they imagined the way Zaldeaan women smiled at their victories in duels. Nor, after the census they ordered, and the first taxes Zaldeaans paid to their Tarlahn ruler based on the harvest or wealth they acquired through barter, based on what they could afford, did Ruarnon think they were imagining the children's faces becoming less pinched and looking better nourished. It seemed the women of the Zaldeaan realm knew who had their children's best interests at heart and were using rumour and Zaldeaan values to goad Zaldeaan men into line. That and the executions worked: there were no more attempts on Ruarnon's life.

On their visits to the provinces, Ruarnon delivered Tarlahn soldiers to make up missing numbers in provincial armies. Growing Season was over by the end of their tour, and Harvest Season had begun. Once the crops were gathered, Zaldeaans turned their energies to shipbuilding, as sea trade began between the Zaldeaan Realm and Timbalen Empire, and Zaldeaan eagerness for a western expedition grew.

Lenaris persuaded Ruarnon to return to Tarlah for their seventeenth birthday, which involved a feast and a ball. Ruarnon surprised Lenaris by asking her to take her oaths as Companion, and to formally begin her new role, to her families, Tor's and Aunt Telena's approval.

Ruarnon had their first dances as an adult, and danced with more confidence than they had at the Festival Life. They didn't think it came from the gold Regent's circlet on their head, which they wore at their aunt's insistence. And it wasn't from the diamond-studded helmet in the care of the High Priestess of Fahria. It was the knowledge that they had led their people successfully through war and now led Tarlah *and* the Zaldeaans in peace, in a way that would make their parents and Uncle Omah proud.

Two days later, Linh rode among trees branching into a high canopy overhead, through ferns and exotic flowers, with Fiona, Michael, and Troy. They left their guards at the north-eastern Tarlahn border, in respect of the Unspoken Agreement between Tarlah and the Urai, and rode alone into the jungle. Linh listened keenly for anything approaching. Ruarnon expected Urai sentries to meet them, but the only sound was the rustling of trees from birds or monkeys around them as they rode on.

"You know what," Troy said with a smile, "Between Linh and Mic persuading Ruarnon to occupy the Zaldeaan Realm pronto, and Linh getting the governors to the negotiating table, I reckon this prophetess might tell us how to get home."

Linh sighed. They had achieved a great deal more than she expected, but while she and her friends rode from Tarlah City to the Urai Jungle, Narz was still out there breeding damars and plotting whatever he'd been planning since they arrived. They all hoped the jungle prophetess the Urai Ambassador had spoken of could give them answers.

Linh tensed, and Troy cried out in surprise. A bare-chested, broadly built man stood between the trees ahead, wearing a kilt of fern leaves. He looked straight at them, his gaze solemn.

"Welcome to the temple of Prophetess Lylah," he said. "Here, you shall find what you seek."

"Thank you," said Fiona.

They rode past the sentry into a clearing of lone columns, cracked stone floors overgrown with jungle creepers and the remnants of a wall rising beyond. The way on their right was clear, a colonnaded, paved path which Troy led the others down. Linh's gaze wandered over ruins partially tangled with vines and plants on her right until Troy cried, "There's an archway on our left!"

Everyone drew in their reins, and Linh gazed over the vine-covered ground at a medium-sized, ancient stone archway with a fluid script with rounded, spiralling glyphs twining it, set in the middle of what may have once been a grand hall.

"But that means..." said Fiona.

"Red Cloak could have sent us directly here if he intended us to go to Tarlah," Michael finished.

"But if he or whoever *didn't* want us to come, why didn't they stop us?" Troy asked. "Why abandon us and let us roam Umarinaris?"

Linh shook her head.

They rode to the end of the columns, tied their reins to the colonnades, then climbed gentle steps of a yellow stone building beyond and stepped up to a corridor lit by burning torches.

"Hello?" Troy called.

There was neither sight nor sound of anyone.

"Do we enter?" Fiona asked uncertainly.

"Depends how literally we take that bloke back there," said Troy. "He did say *we* would find what we seek, not that *it* would find us."

He stepped inside, and Linh and the others followed. The corridor extended a few steps then opened into a small, dark room. Linh's eyes were drawn to daylight shining from a skylight onto a stone altar. She walked closer. An ancient book lay atop the altar.

"Is that an *Umarinaris Book*?" she asked. "I thought only Timbalens had those?"

"That *we* know of," Fiona replied. "But Nuard couldn't tell us how they worked or where they came from. They could be as old as this temple, made by whoever built this place."

"That is not entirely correct," said a woman's voice.

Linh turned in surprise and saw a tall, warm-brown-skinned woman behind them, with long black hair braided with ferns and flowers, and deep almond-shaped eyes, above a flowing dress of dark purple. There was something ancient and otherworldly about her.

"My name is Lylah, and I am she whom the Ambassador intended you to find. The book is what you call an Umarinaris Book and Guardians made it, but not here. The Unmarinaris Books were enchanted during the Sorcery War so that when an entry is written in one, it appears in all books. This was how Guardians communicated during the war."

Linh shivered. The woman spoke as if there truly *had* been a war involving magic and Guardians...

"We wondered if Red Cloak wrote in it," Michael said slowly, "but he didn't, did he?"

Lylah shook her head. "Prophecy does not mean telling the future. It means seeing possible futures, which in my case, is based on people and choices they make."

"*You* wrote in the Umarinaris Book?" Michael asked. "Did you know that if we read what was happening in Tarlah, that might persuade us to set sail?"

Lylah inclined her head. "I also knew that you might help persuade Ruarnon to invade before Syenne defeated her uncle, and united her army and his to aid Kia's against damars, then fought Iagl for the crown."

"You mean we may have helped end the Zaldeaan Succession War?" Troy asked, his eyes wide.

"I believe you did," Lylah replied. "And I think I know why Red Cloak brought you here. He is one of many people in the Far West who are hidden from me. There, magic never stopped, and the knowledge of how to operate the Gateways of the Umarinaris was retained."

Linh's mouth dropped open. Fiona smiled, and tears shone in Troy's eyes. Finally, confirmation of where to go and who could send them home! But Lylah wasn't finished.

"I suspect Red Cloak saw before I did that while Narz helped initiate war, then invaded with damars, you and Ruarnon acting together are catalysts for peace. I think Red Cloak saw the war that is beginning to rage in the Far West, and what I now see: that Narz's war will sweep Umarinaris.

Magic will return, damars will spread, and catalysts for peace like yourselves will become valuable beyond measure."

Acknowledgements

It takes a village to raise a child, and for me, a book baby. I owe thanks to many people. To my mother Susan, her partner Mel, and my best friend Erin for the book's earliest feedback. To countless friends, family, and persons met on my travels for taking an interest, encouraging me to persist around full time study and teaching until I had a finished book.

Beta readers Aisling and Jared's feedback helped me tackle the woes of writing plausible portal fantasy. Iris and Debbie's feedback led to pacing and story tension revisions. While Lindsay's character feedback helped me revise character arcs, and confirmed structural feedback from an editor was needed.

Enter Amelia Wiens, whose manuscript critique guided me in deepening Ruarnon's character, made Ethlin a point of view character and added tension. Then there were technical fixes, where copy editor Laura came in, while proof readers Susan and Lori scanned the 'final product' for lingering errors.
A collaborative process with artist Judah (aka Glint of Mischief) resulted in a vibe appropriate cover, map and chapter headings I love.

I'd also like to thank my #WritingCommunity friends for their constant support and company throughout my editing and publishing journey. Special thanks to Cheryl and Co., from whom I've learnt much about indie publishing and to everyone who gave feedback on my blurb.

And of course, you dear reader! Thanks for taking a chance on the debut novel of a queer, neurodiverse, disabled author. Mine isn't a voice our world often hears, and I appreciate you taking in my words. I hope you enjoyed them! If so...

Please leave a review!

A few sentences of your overall impressions of Manipulator's can indicate to other readers whether or not it's likely their cup of tea. So I'd appreciate you spreading the word by telling fantasy lovers in your life about it and or leaving a review on; Goodreads/ BookBub/ StoryGraph/ and or a bookstore. (Trilogy links via my books page and QR code)

About the Author

Elise Carlson's love of adventure began with a childhood diet of Narnia and teenage years spent playing Final Fantasy. Fascinated with the ancient world, Elise majored in Archaeology and History at University. Then it was time to travel (Europe, Egypt and Turkey).

Their need to earn a living and a desire to work alongside enthusiastic and imaginative counterparts –children— resulted in a teaching career. They taught in Australia, moved to England for exploration of castles, ruins and stately homes and then New Zealand to explore volcanic areas, mountains and to visit Hobbiton. They are now living, teaching and writing in their native Australia.

To stay in touch with Elise and get *Rebellion is Due,* about a turbulent Tarlah night in Ruarnon's father's youth, sign up Elise's newsletter.

You can connect with Elise to discuss life, books or writing on:

Bsky

Mastodon

RUARNON AND LINH'S ADVENTURES CONTINUE IN
BOOK 2: SECRETS OF THE SORCERY WAR

Narz's murderous damars are back, their handlers are more
worrisome and both bar Ruarnon's path to allies needed to
recover their abducted parents.

The handlers are Linh's chance to confirm her gateway home
(to Australia) —and that sorcerers able (and hopefully willing)
to operate it— lie in Umarinaris' dangerous West.

Pursuing allies and answers, Ruarnon and Linh clash with
evolving, ever more dangerous damars. They learn that magic
is still wielded on Umarinaris, the Sorcery War's deadliest
weapons survived and Nartz has plans for those weapons.

And conclude in Book 3;

War in Sorcery's Shadow

Far from being permitted to enter another world on a whim, Linh, Ruarnon and their friends stand at the heart of a struggle. Narz is more complex than anyone guessed, and what ties Ruarnon, Linh and their friends to Narz could stop a sorcery war in its tracks.

Sythe Series

Three thousand years later, Sythe (founded at the end of Ruarnon Trilogy) is a global peace keeping, law enforcement, monster containing, search and rescue and healing providing organisation.

Sythe Series is told in first person by a teenage tough from the wrong side of town. Rarkin trains at Sythe School to qualify for Monster Containment, which will fund his escape from his abusive father.

But it's a dangerous time to work for Sythe. In the centuries following a Nuclear War that destroyed a continent, and drove modern Umarinaris to abandon modern tech and retreat into city-states, another organisation remained global; Organised Crime. They're about to move against Sythe directly and Rarkin and his classmates will soon be on the front line.

Selfless and brave, with a strong sense of right and wrong and a thrill for adventure and recklessness, Rarkin must overcome personal trauma, compounded, but ultimately assisted by his autism, to make friends at Sythe, trust them and let them in.

The days are coming when his own and his team's lives will depend upon it.

You'll find Sythe Series links on my books page.

Out now!

Out April 2026!

www.ingramcontent.com/pod-product-compliance
Lightning Source LLC
Chambersburg PA
CBHW020241120726
47904CB00001B/48